CRY, VOID BRINGER

CRY, VOID BRINGER

ELAINE HO

First published 2025 by Solaris
an imprint of Rebellion Publishing Ltd,
Riverside House, Osney Mead,
Oxford, OX2 0ES, UK

www.solarisbooks.com

ISBN: 978-1-83786-611-3

Copyright © 2025 Elaine Ho

The right of the author to be identified as the author of this work has been asserted in accordance with the Copyright, Designs and Patents Act 1988.

All rights reserved. No part of this publication may be reproduced, stored in a retrieval system, or transmitted, in any form or by any means, electronic, mechanical, photocopying, recording or otherwise, without the prior permission of the copyright owners.

This book is a work of fiction. Names, characters, places and incidents are products of the author's imagination or are used fictitiously.

10 9 8 7 6 5 4 3 2 1

A CIP catalogue record for this book is available from the British Library.

Designed & typeset by Rebellion Publishing
Cover design by Charlotte Strick

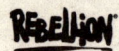

Printed in the UK

to those who love me

1

Hammer

THE MASK ITCHED against Hammer's face.

She tried pushing it around, wrinkling her nose and blinking her eyes, but it only made the spot itch more. She'd spent so long in the damp that her skin had softened, and every rub of the mask against her cheek was a blister waiting to happen.

No, it wasn't the sweat. She'd spent a lifetime fighting in this mask. Perspiration was as natural as breathing. The difference tonight was the rain.

If the Tevurian convoy had arrived on time, her black uniform wouldn't be clinging to her back, her feet numb from the wet and cold. Blisters on her face were fine, but on her heels? That was going to be a week of shitty walking right there, and she wasn't going to spend her remaining scrips on bandages.

It was such drab weather that even the crickets had stopped chirping. On the nonrainy days—and there weren't that many—the insects of the night sang so loud that you could barely hear yourself speak on the road. Not that sound was the problem. The region surrounding Xinquha was so humid that the unfamiliar would've melted in their own sweaty heat first before thinking that crickets were their most pressing issue.

She flicked water off the rattan palm she hid behind, its long slender leaves rustling from the force. Through the mask and branches and darkness, she could just make out the winding path, so slick with mud that it shone under the filtered moonlight. Tall hills flanked this road, a natural protection, their slopes too steep for any yak or horse to climb. Even the ibexes didn't bother.

Her bed-stove in Xinquha would've been perfectly toasty by now. She'd lit a fire under the clay platform before she'd left, hoping to be back before moonrise, but whenever the clouds parted, the full moon flashed its bright round ass, laughing at her for staying out. The bit of charcoal she'd bought with her scrips would've burned out by now, and her bed grew colder every moment she spent here.

Outside, in the rain, no warm bed, and a wet piece of plaster stuck on her face. What a great night. The mask especially irritated her. The eyeholes were too narrow, and whenever she looked up or down, some part of her sight would be blocked by her mask. You'd think whichever lackey had made these uniforms would've given some thought to the fact that fighting required the fighter to, you know, *see*, but this was the nature of the Faceless. When they fought, no one knew their faces or names. To the enemy, they were a singular entity, eternally regenerating and never ceasing.

To her right crouched another Faceless. She didn't know him and she didn't care; any additional body meant more people getting in her way rather than fulfilling the mission at hand. Crescent hadn't moved since they'd taken position behind the copse. He, too, wore a mask like hers, painted black for camouflage, the sculpted grinning mouth and smiling eyes concealing his true mood.

Maybe he was sleeping. Good. She could finish the job on her own.

The lumbering creak of the wagon announced the convoy's approach. The Tevurian Empire's love for steel armor was both their strength and weakness. They lumbered forth in elaborately interlocked plates of mountain-shaped scales sewn on leather vests and skirts, while layered on top of that was mirrored armor—circular discs and rectangular plates linked together with even more chain, strapped to their chests and thighs. It offered a lot of protection, but Hammer could always hear them coming.

And by Ashvalra, they were *loud*. Every single Tevurian soldier was either panting or groaning, and Hammer guessed about forty men guarded this small solitary wagon. If the rain soaking through her clothes made her grumpy, then the Tevurians must've been miserable. Wheels and plated leather boots squelched through the mud, leaving behind a depression more trench than trail. The unfortunate few that were assigned to push the wagon chanted numbers in rhythm, every third count resulting in an elongated groan. Then the whole convoy lurched forward, and they repeated the count again.

Crescent nodded to her. *It's time,* the gesture said. Of course he wasn't asleep. Luck never favored her. Hopefully he wouldn't be as useless as the others.

They crept down towards the road, trailing the soldiers. Hammer reached behind her back, unsheathing a rapier from the hollow handle of her weapon's namesake. It wasn't time to use her hammer yet. They had stealth and surprise on their side, and as much as she hated creeping about in the shadows, it was an advantage she'd rather not squander.

But that didn't mean she couldn't have some fun.

Hammer slid down the mud. She kept her rapier up for balance, pointed straight at the neck of the rearmost guard.

The tip pierced his throat. She grabbed his mouth to stop him crying out, holding him firm until the blood filled his throat and he could cry no more. The creaking iron wheels of the wagon muffled the *thump* of his body on the path.

His fault for being in the way.

Crescent had done the same, without the mud-sliding. His weapon of choice was a pair of handheld blades: two steel crescents overlapping each other, gripped in the middle. He glided them across the guard's throat like a dancer, his weight shifting effortlessly from one leg to another.

Hammer breathed out a laugh. A bit too much fancy footwork for her, but she couldn't deny he looked *good* doing it. Too bad she'd never learned grace. She lumbered to the next unfortunate guard in line, sticking her rapier through his neck. Row by row, they pulled the guards back.

It was after she'd felled her third guard that Hammer thought this had to be a mistake. The rain had made everyone so tired and miserable that no one had bothered to turn around and see the dead bodies that trailed them. Naias wouldn't have tasked Hammer with this mission if she'd known it would be a purely silent one. She'd have gotten another Crescent or Dagger, or even an Axe if she was truly desperate.

Four, five. Crescent kept up beside her. They'd cut through a quarter of the Tevurian guard. There was no way they were getting away with this. She didn't give up her bed to sneak up on tired men who didn't fight back. Someone needed to know the frustration of her chafed thighs.

So she manufactured the battle she wanted. When it came to the sixth man, she let him scream.

One of the wagon pushers turned back and found there weren't as many friends to protect him anymore. He stammered, reaching for what Hammer presumed was his sword, but in his panic he grasped the wrong side of his hip. Hammer sheathed her rapier, grabbed the handle of her maul, swung it over her back, and smashed his face with it. Blood spurted from the back of his head.

Finally.

The caravan ground to a halt. Some shouted for light; others fumbled for their swords. One slipped in the mud, soldiers tripping over him. Hammer swung in a wide arc, smashing three bodies with a single blow.

Weak firelight seeped into the darkness. Some Tevurian had lit the torches attached to the wagon, hoping the fire would reveal Hammer's and Crescent's positions, but all it did was cast moving shadows on the floor and wagon walls. Even better. Hammer kicked a man to the ground, raised her hammer above her head, and shattered his chest. Bones crunched under steel. A most delicious sound.

The cloudlike shapes she'd etched into her hammer shimmered in the torchlight. She wasn't supposed to personalize her weapon like this, but the marks were light, only visible up close, and if anyone was that close, they were the enemy and they were dead. If no one could know her face, they would fucking well know her hammer.

Steel clanked behind her. She unsheathed her rapier, spun, and aimed for his eyes. Heavy armor made for poor back stabbers. Fools, the lot of them, for bothering to try.

She lost count after the thirteenth man or so. Crescent was still doing his elegant dance on the other flank. While Hammer liked to aim for as many people as she could with a single swing, Crescent preferred one-on-one combat. He killed a tad slower than she did, much to her relief. He threaded the soldiers' swords through the hole of his crescent blades, twisted to disarm them, and then cut their throats.

Fine, so he wasn't as good as her, but he was decent. She'd give him that. In previous missions the other Faceless had struggled to keep up with her, but this particular Crescent held his own.

Two left. They'd given up and turned to flee, but they weren't going to get very far in that armor. Hammer paused to wipe the blood off her weapon's handle before giving chase—well, by 'chase,' she meant 'brisk walk'—and an unsatisfying end to a melee that wasn't much of a fight.

So many circumstances swung in their favor tonight, from the rains that muddied the path to Tevu's clanging armor to the wagon's precious loot, which had forced the already-exhausted soldiers to continue their journey at night.

Loot. That's what they were here for. Naias wanted to disrupt the trade routes that linked Tevu to the region surrounding Xinquha, and she'd sent the Faceless out to ambush them.

The rewards were twofold: They stopped goods from flowing back to Tevu and seized much-needed materials for rebuilding their city.

'City.' That's what their queen insisted on calling it. 'Fucked-up village' was a better name, but Hammer wasn't going to risk the lash by mouthing off.

The wagon was no bigger than the span of Hammer's arms. The door itself had three latches, each with its own padlock. If she felt lucky, her hammer could break the locks instead of denting the latches. If she dented the latches, she'd lock them out, and then she'd have to climb onto the roof and spend hours pummeling her way through layers of reinforced iron. *Again*.

Crescent nudged her aside. He pulled out his blades, sticking the sharp point of his weapon into the keyhole, and jiggled. With a *click*, the first padlock fell away.

The dancer was a lockpick as well. She didn't want to be grateful on a mundane mission like tonight, but he was making it very hard. Still, Hammer said nothing. He didn't need to know. Compliments made people cocky and complacent.

Crescent pulled the door open, and the foulest odor assaulted her senses.

Thick chains laced through the hold. Caught in the center of this iron web was a little girl—ten, twelve, maybe—naked, sitting in filth, her hands and feet bound by manacles.

"Shit," Hammer muttered. This was the worst she'd seen yet.

"They're desperate," Crescent said.

Naias wasn't going to be happy. Godchildren sucked up food and fuel Xinquha didn't have, and their powers always amounted to nothing.

But orders were orders, and Hammer wasn't going to let a child die in the cold. She reached for the girl's arm. "You're coming with us," she said, but the girl drew away.

"Don't be difficult." Hammer reached for her arm again, but the girl froze, refusing to move.

Fuck's sake. Rain, cold bed, wet mask, disappointing battle, and now a child who refused to cooperate. She was not in the mood. She grabbed an ankle, forcing her leg straight. The manacles were bound with small padlocks. She'd be able to smash these easily, if the girl stopped drawing away from her.

Crescent entered the wagon with a torch. The hold lit up in a shade of deep orange.

"I don't need the light," Hammer said.

"It's not for you," Crescent said, shoving the torch into her hands. He knelt before the girl.

"Hello," he said, his voice soft and low. "We're special guards from Xinquha. Do you speak Common?"

The girl said nothing.

"A name?"

More silence.

"Mine's Rafaeis," he said. "Don't tell anyone."

"What are you doing?" Hammer hissed. True names were forbidden amongst the Faceless, so in an act of quiet rebellion, they crafted their own in secret. He'd shared his with a child they barely knew. Not a rival, or a famous foe, or a loved one. A nobody. Rafaeis had better hope the child had a mouth made of iron so she wouldn't blab his name to the very next person they met.

Rafaeis ignored her. "We're going to get these chains off you and bring you home," he said. "We need you to stay very still so we don't accidentally hurt you. Is that all right?"

The girl stayed silent, but her legs relaxed. Hammer seized the opportunity, bringing her hammer down, while Rafaeis fiddled with the manacles on her wrists. She had to peel the girl's ankles off the shackles. Her skin had been rubbed raw. Pus and leg hair stuck to the iron, and her seeping wounds stained black.

Hammer wasn't going to complain about her blisters after tonight. "We need to get her to Clement before the infection gets worse," she said.

Rafaeis lifted the girl's bent legs, slowly stretching them out. "It must've hurt a lot."

To Hammer's surprise, the girl gave the briefest of nods. Her mouth stayed twisted in a grimace. She was still in pain, even after being freed. She kept her left arm close to her body, the muscles tensing against no discernible source.

Hammer lifted the girl's matted hair, revealing her bare shoulder. "There," she said, pointing to the bone that jutted out from its socket.

Rafaeis spoke in that kind voice again. "Will you let me fix your shoulder? It'll hurt for a bit, but you'll feel much better afterwards."

The girl nodded, more eagerly this time.

Hammer pressed her hands onto the girl's chest, stabilizing her, while Rafaeis took hold of the dislocated arm. He pulled gently at first, applying increasing force until the girl's joints popped back into place under Hammer's hands. Not so delicious a sound when it came to fixing little children.

The girl tilted her head back, letting out a small moan of relief. Hammer shushed her up.

She had an ordinary face, or at least that's what Hammer thought. Sallow cheeks from starvation, a button nose, golden skin, and black eyes. She wasn't an expert in identifying who belonged to which kingdom, but the girl's wheat-colored hair gave her Maetherian origins away. Not too difficult to hide with some dye. Naias was certainly going to ask for that.

Rafaeis gathered the girl up in his arms. "We'll put you on a yak, and then you can sleep as much as you want," he said. She latched onto him like a baby, her elongated legs dangling astride his back.

Hammer lingered on the battlefield, searching for swords she could take home. Rafaeis headed towards the yaks, but the girl whispered to him. He stopped and chuckled.

"Can I tell her?" he asked, and then he turned to Hammer.

"Viri," he said, the joy flowing behind his voice. "Short for Viridian. That's her name."

Hammer shrugged and returned to looting.

In darkness, blood is black. Black clogged the road, black

stained the mud, black swallowed the hills. When the mud dried out enough to warrant safe passage, perhaps a Tevurian merchant would come across this sight of decomposing bodies in the heat, a reinforced wagon broken open with nothing inside. Tevu would guess it was the Faceless, but they'd have no proof. They'd left no witnesses behind.

Only she'd know she'd slain them, with her rapier and cloud-etched hammer, and that wasn't enough.

Hammer turned to the carnage and pulled her mask off. The slight wind wicked off the rainwater that dampened her face. For the first time that night, she inhaled the cool air. She could see again.

Palm leaves rustled beyond the wagon. A head peeked through the copse, then quickly withdrew again. The boy looked no more than fifteen, perhaps a page to one of the Tevurian knights that traveled along the road.

They'd missed someone.

No one left alive. Naias's orders. Strictly speaking, Hammer should've given chase and killed him, his corpse tossed on top of all the dead masters he'd served.

Strictly speaking.

Fighting against people who matched her blow for blow made her happy. Smashing the skulls of fleeing untrained boys did not.

There was no point in killing the page. Hammer had faced foes greater than him, ones that would've made her the talk of legends, had Naias not stolen it from her. This boy wasn't one of them, and she wasn't going to build her reputation on killing defenseless children.

She wanted to go home, to snuggle under her blankets and sleep. If she hurried, her bed-stove might still have some residual heat to warm her feet over.

The boy's back faded into the forested hills. He'd gotten lucky tonight.

"Remember me," she said, to him and to no one, and whispered her true name into the air.

2

Naias

THE RATTAN ROOF rustled under the rain. Young Faceless initiates and pages put out buckets around the palace to catch the dripping water where the leaves had disintegrated.

This crumbling mudbrick dwelling was meant to be a temporary one. That was the intent when they'd built it two years ago, but they'd run out of resources midway, and so this makeshift structure stayed, propped up by woven attap palms and stripped sugarcane.

Despite it all, Queen Khall still insisted on calling it 'the palace,' and Naias went along with it. If Khall was happy, it made talks easier. She had bigger mountains to climb.

Naias wrapped her horsehair coat around herself, searching for a spot where the water didn't drip. She headed to a corner behind the throne, a spot cloaked in shadow, unceremoniously stepping into a deep puddle.

The room was flooding. If the rains didn't abate soon, this place would become uninhabitable. She'd have to ask someone to stopper the leaks quickly.

At least the most important piece of furniture in the room stayed dry. The throne was elevated by wooden steps and a platform, hastily cobbled together not long after they discovered how rainy it was in Xinquha.

But truthfully, there wasn't much of the throne to save. Its sacredness came from the legend that it'd been carved out of a single angsana tree, but the wood hadn't been treated, and it groaned at the slightest touch. Naias had thrown some expensive-looking furs and silks over it to hide its decay, but she'd only made it look like a disheveled mess.

At least it matched the building.

Khall sat on the wooden steps instead, her knees drawn up to her chest, as she addressed the four men kneeling on the soaked carpet. Half the men's heads stayed down, refusing to meet her eye, but Maka and Jayal sat straight, looking past their queen, past the throne and the furs, directly towards Naias. They didn't bother hiding the sneer on their faces.

Khall held a piece of angsana bark in her hand, scratching her decree on it with a pen carved from a piece of discarded sugarcane. Xinquha's trees had barely grown, and what little palm they could harvest was made into charcoal and shelter, not paper. Earlier in the day, Naias had persuaded Khall that fuel was much more important than this. Khall had pouted, her dainty lips begging to be kissed, and Naias's heart had raced at her queen's displeasure.

"I've marked it with my seal," Khall said, waving the bark in front of the men. "Naias is officially no longer a Faceless, and she will serve as my war adviser. It's only a matter of time before Tevu tries to attack us again, and her expertise is invaluable in keeping them at bay."

When none of the men responded, Khall sighed. "I have greatly appreciated your . . . enthusiastic counsel. But I must make these decisions for myself."

"Respectfully, my queen," Jayal said in the Ashvian dialect, his contempt for Naias evident in his glare, *"it's an unprecedented decree. You must understand our misgivings."*

'Misgivings.' It barely disguised his hate of her origins.

Naias had never liked the way the Ashvian dialect sounded. It was rough and grunting, every syllable heavily emphasized. To the untrained ear, the Ashvians felt like they were constantly shouting. Common was her language of choice, but understanding the dialect was necessary for someone like her to survive.

"If you may consider another decree to be your first," Maka said. *"You need to show you care about the Ashvians. Your succession comes first. Your father chose you the moment he declared himself the Earthly Sovereign, and you need to carry on that legacy."* His gaze flickered to Naias. *"But if you insist on this being your first decree, may I suggest an addendum that she is not released from the Faceless order and she still defers to us in all matters, including war. It's a suitable compromise."*

The Faceless served the Ashvians at large and were considered second-class citizens at best. Jayal and Maka resented having to share power with one they considered beneath them. Naias would've shouted this in their faces if it didn't undermine Khall's authority. She'd chosen to stand in the back corner of the room for a reason. Their relationship was an open secret now that Khallan was dead, and her queen needed to defend Naias on her own.

But Khall said nothing, crouching like a little mouse, staring at the bark in her hands. *Say something, otherwise they're going to start talking over you.*

"This is a position she has no business occupying," Jayal said, right on cue, *"and not just because she's a Faceless. We've never had an Iskanti as an adviser, for good reason. A bunch of mountain barbarians whose allegiances change depending on which way the silver flows."*

Naias bristled. She wouldn't let this insult pass. If Khall wasn't going to back her up, she'd have to defend herself.

"I'm no more Iskanti than you are," she said in Common, mustering her best Ashvian accent. "I have served the kingdom of Ashvi my entire life. I helped our late king take the very spot where you now kneel. Don't question my loyalty."

Jayal's eyes widened in alarm as he realized that Naias could understand them all along, but Maka's face stayed placid.

"But you weren't born here," he said, switching to Common.

"You're not Ashvian. You're Iskanti. The blood tithe bound you to us."

Naias's hand flew to her pistol.

"Please stop," Khall said, her shoulders drooping lower. She'd repeated this argument in multiple council meetings since her coronation, and it ended up nowhere. "If this is the decree that separates you from my service, then so be it."

"Your father hasn't even been dead two months, and already you mar his legacy," Jayal said, pointing an accusatory finger at Naias. "He would've never allowed an Iskanti into our court."

"My father's 'legacy' also included harsh punishments to those who crossed him," Khall said, twisting her arms around herself. Her posture had progressively shrunk since they'd started this meeting, like she wanted to sink into the ground and disappear.

Naias fought the urge to walk over and pull her up. She'd undermined Khall's authority once already, and doing it a second time would be fatal. Jayal would accuse her of manipulating the queen. If they kept this up, a coup would follow, and Naias—already an outsider by Ashvian standards—didn't have any friends to swing the city's support in her favor.

Khall had to do this on her own. They'd rehearsed this, and Naias would have to trust that she'd find her voice. She leaned against the wall, trying to carry an air of disinterest as she peered behind the throne.

"But I'm not my father," Khall continued, muttering into the floor. "I want to be a kinder, merciful ruler. If he were here, he would've flayed the lot of you. Too much blood has been spilled for our freedom from Tevu. I won't shed more from petty infighting."

"An Iskanti infiltrating our court is far from petty—"

"You were loyal to my father, and for that I am grateful. I'll make an announcement that you're retiring from my service. You'll be comfortable in Xinquha, if you wish to continue staying here." Khall drew herself into an upright position. "But your arrangements will go through Naias, not me."

Naias didn't bother hiding her grin. A show of confidence was better late than never. Meekness came naturally to Khall, after decades of being cowed by her father's own assertiveness. Naias never wanted her to lose that quiet sweetness—it was one of the most attractive qualities about her, really—but she needed to mirror her father in moments like this.

Jayal stood up in a huff. "This is unacceptable," he said, marching out of the room, Maka scuttling after him. "I will not answer to *her*."

She'd won. Naias nodded to the initiates, pushing down the surge of glee within. "Escort them home," she said. "Take an Axe or a Hammer with you in case it gets difficult."

When the shuffling ceased and the rhythmic dripping of water was all that remained in the quiet, Khall deflated, like a house collapsing on itself. The confidence she'd spent so much effort on expelled from her body.

Naias hurried over, wrapping her queen in a hug. "You did so well," she said, kissing the top of Khall's head. "I'm so proud of you."

"Is this how it's going to be all the time?" she muttered, leaning into Naias's chest.

"A trial by fire. Leaders need to make difficult decisions and speak them to those who don't want to hear them. You did both tonight."

"It wasn't that difficult a decision," Khall said.

They were finally alone. Naias kissed her fiercely, and Khall's body melted against hers, deliciously soft and warm, reminding her of the days they'd spent together in Quctra. There, the temperate sun shone pure gold, and her thick black hair sparkled in the light. She wanted to lose herself in Khall's gentle hands forever, in those long summer days where the sun never set, and every stroke of her finger made her body shiver.

But someone said "my queen," and the fantasy ended. Naias opened her eyes and returned to the waterlogged palace in Xinquha. An attendant stood by the entrance.

"What is it," Khall snapped, evidently as upset as her.

He'd barely gotten out the words "the Faceless have returned" when Hammer shoved him aside, sauntering into the room, smiling mask and all. Crescent trailed behind, carrying a wet bundle in his arms.

A godchild? Tevu's reconciled with his wife, then. Naias kept her face as neutral as she could. "Nothing else?"

Hammer shrugged. "Bunch of swords, two yaks."

"Are you sure?"

"What do you think?" came the surly response. "Sure, I saw chests overflowing with silver, and I chose to loot the swords instead."

This infuriating woman, always looking to get the last word. Naias dropped the argument. She wasn't going to be goaded into a fight. Let Hammer savor her petty wins; Naias was busy running an actual city.

Crescent placed the godchild on the floor, the carpets squishing under her weight. A Maetherian girl.

"Has she shown her powers yet?" Khall asked.

Crescent shook his head. "Based on what we saw in that wagon, no. Her wounds are infected."

"Send her to Clement," Khall said. "Then I suppose we sit and wait. I want daily reports on her condition. We need to know if she's useful as soon as possible."

"They never are," Naias muttered.

"Which is why I don't want to indulge for long," Khall said. "The Faceless saved Xinquha, not godchildren. My father obsessed too much over finding them, believing there was 'the one' that could turn the tide of our fight against Tevu." She gave a small laugh, gesturing to the leaking roof above them. "We're stretched so thin already. Ashvalra knows we've spent far too much of our silver to keep Clement happy."

Godchildren with undeveloped powers were a costly burden. They ate and drank and slept at their patrons' expense, and then ultimately gave nothing in return. Resources were already scarce, and allocating more to supporting the godchild would make the Ashvians even angrier. She needed Khall's reign to run as smoothly as possible. It was the only way Naias could keep her position.

She needed to keep everyone happy—no, everyone *important* happy.

She gestured to the Faceless. "Make the godchild their responsibility," Naias said. "She can take from their food stores instead of the Ashvians', and she'll stay with them until we know what her powers are."

"What?" Hammer blurted.

"Watch yourself." She'd seen this coming, but it still vexed her that Hammer would openly court disobedience in front of their queen.

"Get Clement to do it," Hammer said, ignoring the command.

"Clement doesn't want to do it anymore."

"Then make him, since you're so powerful now, *Naias*." Hammer spat her true name with contempt. Like all Faceless, Naias had been known by her chosen weapon—Gun—and immediately discarded the name once she became Khall's adviser.

"Thank you for your rescue," Khall said, interrupting them. "But remember that Naias speaks for me. I still expect obedience from the Faceless."

Hammer did not move, but Naias sensed the fury hidden behind her mask. She'd fought with her too many times not to know.

"Take the godchild," Khall said. "She will share your bed and food, and"—she let out a deep sigh—"when we're all inevitably disappointed when her power manifests—"

Naias squeezed Khall's shoulder. A small sign of their bond—her power—and Hammer couldn't do anything about it.

In this small gesture, Khall understood, and the sentence remained unfinished. *The godchild is listening. No need to speak of her future so brazenly.* How lucky that she'd found someone with whom words could pass unspoken and still be understood. She'd never had that with anyone else.

"The godchild is yours," Khall repeated to the Faceless, her hand squeezing back. "Dismissed."

3

Viri

Hammer and Rafaeis led me to another room, nicer than the first. This one had no holes in the roof and the carpets were dry. Chests were stacked on top of other chests, so high they reached the ceiling. Jewelry lay on every table, shiny pendants and rings and necklaces.

But it was smellier. Thicker. A gray haze covered the room, and the candles had a halo around them. I buried my head in Rafaeis's chest.

"Just a bit longer," he said, "and the pain will end." His Common accent sounded so different from mine. If he didn't speak so gently, I would've thought he was barking at me. We weren't in Maetheria anymore.

Everyone seemed so worried about the stuff around my wrists and ankles. I'd stopped feeling the pain weeks ago. The mended shoulder hurt more. It still hurt now, whenever I raised or lowered my arm.

He put me down on a fluffy-looking chair. I sank into its softness. It felt nice, having sat on the hard floor in the wagon for so long.

"We'll come get you when you're healed," Rafaeis said.

"You mean, *you'll* come get her when she's healed," Hammer said behind him.

"*We'll* come get you when you're healed," he repeated, the grin clear in his voice.

But as he rose to leave, I gripped his hand. I didn't want him to go. I didn't want to be left alone again to meet another stranger. He was the only one who'd asked for my name.

no one else did, not when they wrenched her away from the shattered glass, not when the blood shimmered under her feet

"We'll be outside," Rafaeis said, gently releasing my hand. "Clement doesn't like it when the Faceless enter his quarters. Don't worry. You'll feel much better afterwards."

The door closed behind him and another opened across the room.

He was tall and big with dark wavy hair that fell on one side of his face. He wore batik silks and so, so much jewelry. Every finger had a ring. I couldn't count the necklaces. Two rings threaded through the flesh of his nostrils. A long chain of gold connected the nose rings to his ear. It must have hurt.

Underneath all the beautiful clothes and jewelry, a chain dangled from his ankles. He was bound, like when I was in the wagon. He could only walk in small steps. His wispy dress didn't flutter very much.

He bent down to smile at me. "You must be hungry," he said, in an accent I couldn't place. He pronounced his words like Rafaeis did, but also not. He spoke like the queen, but a drawl lingered at the end of the sentence. This man wasn't from here either.

His hand revealed a bowl of deep-fried buns dusted with sugar. Mantou. I could smell the fat they'd been fried in. My mouth watered.

I didn't take the bowl. I stared at him, waiting for the bargain. When I was in the wagon, they'd offered me food where I couldn't reach, and then asked me to show my powers. I didn't know what they meant, so they took the food away and brought out the stick.

"There's no exchange here," he said, placing the bowl next to me. "Ashvians don't beat their godchildren, unlike the

Tevurians." He spoke this flatly, like he'd said this many times before. He pressed a hand to his chest. "My name is Clement, and I'm also a godchild. My powers come from Strixahava. Do you know who she is?"

books of the gods in his glass-paned office. she'd select one, thumbing through the densely written pages, pretending that she was a professor, like he was

I shook my head, still staring at the mantou. The oil that coated them shone in the light. They looked so good, but I still didn't dare touch them.

"Strix is the goddess of healing. Whatever I touch mends itself." He pressed his hand over my wrist. I couldn't see what he was doing, but it was warm where he held me. Warm and light, like Rafaeis.

He moved his hands over to my ankles, my shoulder, and then to all the places where the skin was still wet and itchy. I hadn't realized I'd been in pain all this time, and he lifted that away, bit by bit. I'd numbed myself, or ignored it because there was just too much. Now I didn't have to ignore anything.

I sank even further into the chair, my body turned to mush. I could sleep a thousand years now. So this was what a godchild was. Everyone kept calling me that, but I didn't know what it meant and why it made me different.

"I can do that too?" I asked, daring to speak. The men didn't like it when I asked questions. My voice came out raspy and hoarse.

Clement flexed his ankles. The chains jingled. "Godchildren manifest their powers in different ways," he said. "Different gods choose different people. Strix chose me, although I don't recall having any consent in the matter. Most of the time godchildren have unremarkable powers. A few drops of water from their fingers. Their toenails grow a bit faster. Little miracles like that. I have my limits too. I only heal small wounds. I can't regrow bones, nor can I bring people back from the dead. I can only use my powers once every thirty hours. Why that number? I don't know. My powers are useful, but not enough when we're at war."

"You still save people," I said, and he pushed a mantou into my mouth. The sugar crunched between my teeth, the oil filling my mouth as I bit down. Airy and sweet. My jaw moved on its own. I was so hungry. When the stick didn't come, I grabbed another bun. I couldn't chew fast enough, it was so good.

"War counts lives by numbers, not by names, little godchild," he said.

'Little godchild.' I didn't like the way he used this name for me. I didn't feel like a godchild and didn't have his powers. Calling me 'little' made me sound stupid.

I spoke through a mouthful of fried dough. "My name's—"

"I don't need your name," he said sharply. "I will call you 'godchild,' and that's how you'll be known to me. Am I understood?"

I shrank back, surprised by the fierceness in his voice. What a strange place, where names were given and not given, and nobody wanted to hear them. Hammer didn't like it when Rafaeis named himself to me, while Clement had given me his name but didn't want mine.

"How do I get my powers?" I asked.

He pushed the bowl into my hands. "Not by starving and beating you." His nose chain jingled when he frowned. "Tevu's desperate, since they only have Engale left."

"Engale?"

"Godchild of wind and tornadoes. Tevu had two godchildren that they sent into battle. One's dead now. I suppose that's why Tevu's prophet wife named you. She has visions of godchildren and paints them. She hasn't publicly named anyone in seven years, until you." He flexed his ankles again. The chains clearly annoyed him. "Your powers will come when they come. We can't hurry it along. I'm supposed to guide you, seeing as I'm the only godchild in Xinquha."

If I wasn't sure whether he'd made this speech before, I was sure of it now. "How many have you helped?"

"A few," he said.

"Where are they? Can I see them?"

Clement opened a chest. He drew out a long stick with a little bowl stuck on the side. Lots of flowers were carved on the handle. He packed the bowl with a black tarry thing, and then struck a match to light it. He pressed his lips to the end of the stick and took a long deep breath.

The room filled with the gray haze again. He turned to me and blew smoke into my face.

"It's time for you to go, little godchild," he said.

4

Hammer

THE RAINS HAD abated by the time Viri emerged through the jewel-studded door. Even though a whole courtyard separated them, Hammer could smell the opium that clung to the girl's body. "What a pain," she said, marching out of the stone-built villa. "Clement couldn't go for five seconds without that pipe?"

Viri toddled behind, her eyes half open. Rafaeis pressed his hand on the girl's back, ushering her forward. "She needs a bath," he chirped behind her, "unless you like chunks of mud in your bed."

Hammer spun on her heel, rounding on him. This night was going from bad to worse. "What do you mean *my* bed? You take her."

"She can't stay in my hut," he said.

"Yes, she can."

"You remember the palace? It's like that, but worse."

"What the fuck were you spending your scrips on, then? Lockpicking lessons?"

"You were impressed, admit it," he drawled. "I saw the way you tilted your head."

She turned away and resumed her march home. "You saw nothing. My neck cramped up."

A low stone wall, built by the dead King Khallan, encircled the Faceless quarter. He'd envisioned a great fortress for a kingdom of his own, but as Tevu continued to pummel Xinquha, he'd run out of silver, and only the foundation of the walls stayed. This was where the Faceless lived: a living relic of a dream turned into a corral, so the Ashvians didn't have to see them.

At least they could walk freely with their faces uncovered here. Hammer immediately pulled off her mask, and then kicked the wall for good measure. "Put Viri in the river," she said, trudging through the mud path. The gravel road had ended well before they passed the wall.

"It's still too cold," Rafaeis said. "We need hot water."

"If we need hot water, we need charcoal, and I'm not spending my charcoal on her."

Rafaeis rummaged through his pockets, producing a folded stack of dried leaves, Khall's seal stamped on each one. That was at least a month's worth of rations. "Take my scrips then," he said. "I don't need it."

This fool. If he kept giving away scrips like this, no wonder his quarters were falling apart. He'd barely have enough to eat, much less maintain where he lived. She peeled off a single note and returned the stack to him. Gods knew he needed it, because his common sense had left him, and she wasn't the type to take from someone who didn't have a functioning roof.

Besides, the godchild had suffered enough for one day, and some hot water for herself wasn't a bad idea either. She grumbled under her breath. Rafaeis had tricked her into being nice. If he did it again, she'd break his mask.

Hammer led them to the small ramshackle hut she'd built at the far end of the Faceless quarter, scavenged together with attap wattle, mudbrick, stone, and anything else she could get her hands on. A curtain of dried attap leaves draped over the entrance, the sloped roof thatched with rattan. She lived closer to the horses than to the rest of the Faceless settlement, and despite the musty smell of dung and trampled grass, she liked it. A row of buckets sat outside the hut, overflowing with rainwater.

Rafaeis whistled softly. "This is impressive. You've even built stilts. Stone, I see. You took them from Khallan's wall?"

"No one's going to miss a few rocks. I got tired of the monsoons flooding my place, and no, you're not invited."

Viri struggled to keep up, one foot plodding in front of the other. Her muscles had atrophied from her time in the wagon. The late night and Clement's opium hadn't helped either.

All three of them couldn't fit into Hammer's hut. Her bed-stove took up nearly all the space she had. She picked out a pot, a dry tunic, a handful of charcoal and brought it all outside. Rafaeis took one of the overflowing buckets and tipped some water into the pot.

She made sure not to say thanks. He'd already noticed her admiration, and she wasn't going to embarrass herself further by blurting out her gratitude. She lit a fire, placing the pot on top of the charcoal.

The three of them sat side by side, waiting for the water to boil. Viri rested her head on Rafaeis's shoulder, drifting off to sleep. He hadn't taken his mask off, even though he was well within his rights to. Everything about this man was strange. His chest rose and fell in rhythm. Crickets screamed in the silence. Hammer still didn't know if he was sleeping.

"At the end of the ambush, you took your mask off," he said, making her jump. "Why?"

Her jaw tightened. This was not a conversation she was interested in having with anyone, least of all with a man she barely knew. She'd done it once with Naias, and that was a mistake she'd vowed never to repeat again. "I heard the wind was good for my complexion. I need to look pretty."

"You whispered something afterwards."

"I whispered for you to shut the fuck up."

He chuckled. "Fine, keep your secrets to yourself. But that was a death wish, Hammer. If we hadn't killed everyone, your mark would be plastered on posters across Tevu. Everyone would be looking to kill you."

"You're no better. You told Viri your true name."

"A name can be fabricated, but a face cannot."

"So your name isn't . . . ?"

His head bobbed from side to side, like an impudent little jester. "Tell me your name, and I'll tell you the truth."

She sighed loudly. "Fine, if it means you'll leave me alone."

"Really?" All his cheeky pretenses stopped. He turned towards her.

Viri slid off his shoulder. She jolted awake, a momentary awareness long enough to decide that Hammer was the more comfortable of the two, and promptly dropped her head into her lap.

Hammer leaned forward, careful not to dislodge her, and whispered into Rafaeis's ear. "I've never told anyone before. You'll be the first. Can I trust you?"

"Of course," he said, a little too eagerly.

She mustered the sultriest voice she could.

"It's Hammer."

For a beat, a carved smile stared back at her, deadly silent. She wished she could see his face, if only for his reaction.

But a laugh burst out from behind his mask. Rafaeis raised his hands in surrender. "I admit, I walked into that," he said. "But I have another secret. Two of mine, for your name."

"Ha, no. If anything, I wish I could unhear it. I didn't ask to be responsible for your name. That's like breaking into my house and giving me a cat. Sure, the cat's cute, but *you broke into my fucking house.*"

His steady chuckle bubbled up into outright laughter. It gave her a surprising validation, one she'd never experienced before. Someone liked her roughness.

The water boiled. It was too hot for bathing, so Rafaeis mixed cold rainwater into the pot. He dipped a finger in, testing it. "I'm escaping the Faceless," he said. "Tonight."

Hammer snorted. Oh, *that* secret, the one that every Faceless had. She shook Viri awake. The girl rose to stand immediately without complaint, as if she'd done this countless times. Sleep deprivation. She'd seen it before, in herself and in the other Faceless initiates.

Against her will, she felt a twinge of sympathy for the godchild, but she brushed it off. Sympathy led to attachment, and Viri would be gone soon enough, like all the other godchildren before her.

"I'll see you tomorrow then," she said to Rafaeis, stripping Viri of the wet clothes they'd swaddled her in.

"I mean it."

"Every one of us did." She tipped the water over Viri's head and down her back. "And every one of us came back."

For all their ruthless training, the Faceless had nothing of material value. They couldn't read or write, and they lived, ate, prayed, spoke, even bowed the Faceless way. Everyone on the continent hated them for the decades of war they'd enacted in Khallan's name. Their marks made them easy to identify. They faced death if they left.

Most chose to serve in Xinquha. Better to be a Faceless than dead.

Rafaeis wiped Viri down with a rag. "This time it's different."

"Sure it is." That's what Hammer told herself on every escape attempt, but after twenty years of trying, it became evident that she wasn't going to leave.

Viri didn't fight as Rafaeis pulled the spare tunic over her. The neck opening was too large and the garment dropped to her calves, but it was good enough. Hammer scooped up the embers from the fire and tossed them under the clay platform of her bed-stove. A little warmth was better than none, and she wasn't wasting a single bit of heat, even if it wasn't for herself. She then led Viri inside, where the godchild climbed onto the bed and promptly passed out.

"A third secret," Rafaeis offered, as Hammer drew the curtain over her hut's entrance.

She turned away with a loud sigh, hiding her rising

enjoyment in this odd battle of persistence. "O Ashvalra," she prayed out loud, "all I want is to mind my own business. Is that too much to ask?"

"I know you killed Pravaja."

All jokes and sarcasm vanished, replaced by a shot of exhilaration. Her hand instinctively wrapped into a fist, ready to defend if he attacked. No one knew. Naias had made sure of that.

"How." Not a question. A demand.

Rafaeis nodded towards her hammer. "The carvings. You had less of them back then, but they were still there."

"So all those questions about my true name were for what, surveillance? Your escape tonight was to inform Tevu and collect your reward?"

He chuckled, shaking his head. "I'm no spy. I just wanted to get to know the person who killed Pravaja and survived, that's all. I was the one that kept Engale away from you."

Her fist relaxed a fraction. "That was you?"

She still remembered the viciousness in Engale's roar when Pravaja died. All whirlwind and fury, vibrating the very blood in her body, threatening to tear her insides apart. Someone had stepped between them, cutting her scream short. It'd made her mad then, because the adrenaline had told her she could fight two godchildren and win, but in reality, the godchild of ice and hail proved to be more difficult to overpower than she'd thought.

Not that she'd ever admit it publicly.

"Look at us," Rafaeis said, leaning against the wall of her hut. "A pair of Faceless warriors who fought the two most powerful godchildren this continent has seen in over a thousand years, arguing over the best way to bathe a child."

She wasn't listening. "If you saw my hammer, then Engale might've seen it too." She liked the idea. Engale wasn't searching for just any Faceless. She was searching for *her*.

Hammer grinned at the thought. "Killing one godchild is luck. Two makes me a killer of gods. *Godkiller*." She held the title in her mouth, tasting its recognition. It didn't sound bad at all.

The smile on Rafaeis's mask did not hide the slight sag of his body against the wall, his long arms embracing himself as he looked up at the attap roof. "So, when your boot's on Engale's face, are you going to unmask yourself again?"

"Why not? Pravaja didn't know the face of her killer. Engale will."

"Is that all you want? Glory in battle?"

Hammer balked. A long time ago, if you'd asked her what she wanted, glory wouldn't have been anywhere near the list. She'd tried not to want it, by fighting and running and rebelling and escaping, but it all led back to the Faceless. She'd given up. In this life chosen for her, the ability to kill was the only thing she could control.

"What else *is* there?"

A long silence passed between them.

At last, Rafaeis pushed off the wall, sweeping into a bow. "It was an honor fighting alongside you, Hammer. It was an honor then, and it was no different tonight. I hope we'll meet again."

5

Viri

I DIDN'T WANT to wake up. It was the most comfortable sleep I'd had, because there was no chain to hold me down. There were a few blankets, patchwork scraps of silk and wool, but they pressed on me so heavily that I couldn't move, and not moving reminded me of the wagon. I'd kicked most of them off, keeping only the lightest one.

After Clement healed me, the rest of the night was a blur. I didn't remember coming here. It was a small square room, and half of it was taken up by the bed I lay on. Clement's room overflowed with jewels and gems, but here I saw walls of dried leaves and cane, a hammer laid against the wall, and a very angry woman sitting in the corner, glaring at me.

"Crescent's late," she said, squeezing a seed so hard that the shell crunched in her hands.

I recognized her voice. Hammer. I hadn't seen her unmasked before. A black square encased in a red diamond was tattooed between her eyebrows. Red lines trailed down the bridge of her nose, spreading across her face like a spiderweb. The skin around her eyes was puffy and dark. She hadn't slept well.

My breath hitched in fear. She looked so different from Clement. He'd stepped out of a painting, brushed with every possible color. She was a fresh stone pulled out of the earth.

Hammer groaned as she stood up, strapping her weapon to her back. "Better get used to my face, godchild. All Faceless have the mark. Are you done staring?"

I didn't want to make her angrier. Angry people meant I would get hurt. If I covered myself, then I wouldn't be looking at her at all, so I pulled the blanket over my head. A sourness wafted up my nose.

Hammer smelled it too. "Ashvalra *fuck me*, what have you done to my bed?"

I'd asked for a privy in the wagon, but they hit me whenever I opened my mouth. I learned not to speak, and peed on the spot. None of the men in creaking armor cared. I thought Hammer was going to treat me the same way, but it was clear I'd made a mistake.

"I spent all of last night cleaning you off," she yelled, ripping the blanket off me. "Turns out I shouldn't have bothered."

Everything was different. I didn't want to be hit. I didn't want to be noticed. Even though I knew hiding didn't work, I still raised my arms above my head. Where was Rafaeis? He'd disappeared, like all the others.

Hammer pulled me off the bed. I tumbled to the floor. My body didn't work when I got scared, so I'd stopped trying to run.

"Godchild," she said, "either you're walking to the river on your own or I'm dragging you by your ankles to get there."

I lay on the floor, half curled into a ball. Being quiet would stop her from beating me too hard. They hit me harder when I cried.

With a loud grumble, Hammer scooped me up in her arms and carried me out. I squeezed my eyes shut. The stick was coming, I knew it was coming. I braced for it.

Birds screeched and mud sloshed underfoot. We came to a stop, and I was too tired to keep my eyes scrunched, forcing me to see the palm-filled riverbank that Hammer dropped me on, and the green water that lapped at my feet.

The beating never came.

Hammer pulled the soiled tunic off my body. "You're not a baby anymore. Bathe yourself," she said, pushing me into the water.

Mountains, so many mountains. They surrounded the city, reaching into the clouds. We barely had any mountains in Maetheria. We had fields, endless fields of mulberry trees that ran to the edge of the shore, and the sea was so clean and blue that you could see the bottom. Crystal, like the citadel—

mirrored shards on the ground, twinkling like snow in wintertime. she tried to step around them, but it was either the glass or bits of brain and she chose the glass

My feet itched. Clement had healed everything, right? Then why did it hurt? Why couldn't it stop and leave me alone?

"Move, for gods' sake," Hammer shouted behind me.

she didn't know why. blue robes and blue flags, an ocean of fabric and a tidal roar of steel as they pointed at her and ran, converging above her. when she screamed, their hands twisted around her shoulder, and fighting back didn't make a difference as her ligaments snapped, bit by bit, separating her arm from its socket

The river was quiet. Water rippled around my waist. Attap palms surrounded me, scratching my skin.

Hammer was gone.

I'd been left on the riverbank.

I knew Hammer didn't like me, and I didn't expect her to stay. The men who took me didn't stay either. I had no idea where I was or how to get back to her hut. I didn't see the path she'd taken. I'd been too scared to remember.

A shadow loomed behind me. I turned to look. It was a man I didn't recognize, with no mark on his face and a whip in his hand.

"Stand up, Faceless," he said, in an accent that sounded more like the queen's than Hammer's. "You're late."

I didn't know what a Faceless was, or what I could possibly be late for. But the men in the wagon had also ordered me around, forcing me to show powers I didn't have. It was better to listen. I tried to stand, but the sight of the whip made my legs not work again.

He raised his hand, and it was that day I knew I'd been rescued from one prison only to land in another.

6

Hammer

HAMMER MARCHED AWAY from the river. Sleeping on the floor was her reward for killing forty Tevurian soldiers. Naias had engineered this to spite her. She knew the godchildren amounted to nothing, but until then, she'd put this on Hammer to make her life more difficult. A whole child.

Tired, frayed, and resentful, Hammer lost her patience with the godchild and left. More than two decades of Faceless training didn't prepare her for childcare. Fighting was easy; she simply aimed her weapon and swung. That wasn't an acceptable solution to an uncooperative baby, apparently.

Despite sharing the responsibility for Viri, Rafaeis was nowhere to be seen. He'd actually left, the stupid fuck, leaving her alone with a child she didn't want.

He couldn't have gotten far. He'd come back; they always did. But his departure still rankled her. Being kind to Viri and asking for her name had been a ruse. He'd bought affection from the child to shut her up, dumped her on Hammer, and didn't have to deal with the crying that came after.

What exactly did he come up with that made his escape so special, anyway? She'd tried every way for the last twenty years, and her face was carved up for it. No, this was his first time trying to leave. She'd been overconfident and hopeful on her first try too. Khallan had quickly whipped that out of her.

She reached the dead king's wall, the separation between the Faceless quarter and Xinquha itself. Her mask lay in her hand, and her fingers traced the contours that formed the false smile where her mouth should be.

Fuck the Ashvians and their rules. Hammer pocketed her mask and walked into the city. She couldn't leave like Rafaeis had, but she could do this.

Fields of rice stalks and sugarcane sprang around the charred spiky stumps of the rattan palms, bordering the path she walked on. Two years ago, Tevu began his final push on Xinquha, intent on wiping Khallan and his dream of an Ashvian kingdom out for good. Pravaja died for his troubles (great job, Hammer) and the Faceless won, but at great cost to the city. The huts, the palms, the livestock—all of it—burned to ash. Impending famine meant the Ashvians, rich and poor alike, became farmers, repurposing the fields for food. A fragile stalemate had remained between Tevu and Ashvi ever since.

The temple of Ashvalra loomed ahead, a large hexagonal gate built from red sandstone, housing Xinquha's market square. Statues of Ashvalra dotted the space, sitting, standing, all holding sheaves of rice, while merchants set up their goods below them, hawking their wares on frayed cloth.

It wasn't much. Besides a few bushels of lemongrass and tubers of wild galangal, farmers sat cross-legged as they mixed ground rice with water, steaming the dough in baskets woven from dried sugarcane stalks. Others milled sugarcane into cups of juice.

In the far corner, barely within the confines of the square, lay the Iskanti trade caravan, the heavily sunburned nomads that traveled from the western mountains with their dried horseflesh and urns of yak milk. Some Iskantis stayed on their mounts—giant ibexes the size of horses—while the handful of yaks that pulled the wagons huddled together, their tails swatting flies away in unison. All the Iskantis were adults; they'd wisely chosen to keep their children away from this place.

The nomads displayed the cheaper goods on the ground, ones they knew the Ashvians were able to afford: skewers of dried meat, boxes of orange peel and peppercorns, and giant jars of yak's milk and yogurt laid out atop felt carpets. Burly guards surrounded the more valuable wares, left on the wagon: mechanical prosthetic limbs from Lakhest, Tevurian steel, Maetherian batik and paper. Hawks circled the air while their handler butchered a fox, pulling out bits of flesh for them to feast on. An invisible wall seemed to surround them. No Ashvian approached them unless they truly needed something.

Hammer stood tall, walking towards an Ashvian rice cake peddler. The statue of Ashvalra he sat under was carved with an outstretched hand. He went silent as she approached.

Her scrips meant nothing here. Ashvians bartered with other goods or traded in silver. Hammer rummaged through her pockets, holding out three uncracked attap nuts: large teardrop-shaped shells that concealed a gelatinous sweet fruit inside.

The man only glared at her.

The bustle stopped. All the peddlers had turned to look, their gaze doing the familiar flick to the spot between her eyes. Black square, red diamond. They didn't need her name to report her.

Swinging your weapon wasn't an acceptable solution here either, apparently.

She gritted her teeth. She'd force herself here, whether they liked it or not. She placed two more nuts in her hand. "Surely this is enough," she said to the peddler.

He brusquely grabbed the fruit from her hand and turned towards the steamers. She waited for the rice cake, but he didn't raise the steamer lid, nor did he grab the ones that sat out on the table. He returned to his seat, waving a fan made of dried leaves, batting away the flies that came to rest.

Please, Ashvalra, she prayed, *please let this be a simple mistake.* Maybe he'd misheard her. She wasn't looking to give anything away in exchange for nothing. "My attap," Hammer said in Common. "If you don't want them, give them back."

He ignored her and waved to another Ashvian, urging him to buy.

No. No, no, no.

He'd robbed her. He knew he was going to get away with this. Any complaint she made would be met with the lash, but she simply could not let this theft stand. He would never have done this if she were Ashvian, and before she knew it, her hand closed into a fist, her body twisting as she pulled back to punch—

A force yanked her arm so hard that she nearly fell backwards, dragging her towards the Iskanti caravan.

"Sorry, sorry," the voice said. "She's looking for us."

"Let me go," Hammer said, the rage still speaking through her.

"Stirring up trouble here rarely turns out well, Faceless," came the response.

A skewer of fox meat was shoved into her hands. She came to a stop in front of the Iskantis. Her savior was one of them: an unmarked man with sharp hazel eyes, dark hair pulled into a bun, and a day's scruff on his neck. His warm skin stayed a shade paler than the rest, like he hadn't been in the sun for long. "Eat."

Despite the humidity, the Iskantis kept their furs on, dry skin peeling off their windswept cheeks. The matriarchs openly laughed and pointed at her forehead. *"Idiot traitor,"* they said in the Iskanti tongue, their intonation angry and sharp, every word a dagger. *"Sin'kuua has bred them soft."*

"It wasn't my choice," Hammer shouted, but the nomads did not understand Common. They'd chosen not to.

"Forgive their rudeness," the man said. "They resent the blood tithe and mourn the children taken away from them. We can't win against Tevu or Khall, so they bully the ones with the least power."

He didn't sound Iskanti, his accent devoid of the nasal pronunciation and their tendency to drop the softer letters. If Hammer had closed her eyes and ignored the furs he wore, she would've been certain he was Ashvian.

She bit down on the skewer, seething. She was Iskanti and she'd been taken by the blood tithe too. None of these matriarchs mourned her. One time she'd tried to escape by hiding in one of the Iskanti caravans, and when they found her out, they'd promptly ransomed her back to Khallan. There was a bigger sense of shame here, amongst people with whom she ought to have the closest kinship but who did not accept her as one of their own.

The laughs soured her appetite, even more so because she didn't like eating fox all that much. The meat was too tough for her, but she chewed anyway, the thin stringy pieces catching between her teeth. She picked them out with her fingernail. Maybe the hawks would like them better, but they stayed perched on the wagon, their beady eyes trailing the scraps she flicked to the ground.

"Don't mind them," the same man said. "They only answer to their handler." He took some raw meat from the freshly butchered fox and, with a grin, dropped it on top of his head.

Immediately, a hawk swooped in. He extended his arm, letting the bird land as its beak searched for more food in his hair. Fuzzy tail feathers wriggled from side to side.

"I assume you're him," she said, her anger fading at the sight of the foraging bird. "Thanks for helping me back there."

He shook his head, gesturing to his lanky body. "I'm a mere traveler. They let me play with the hawks."

"You must know them well," she said, "if they're giving you such close access to their birds."

"I've spent a lot of time with them," he said, bringing the hawk closer to her. "When the Iskantis know you're not a threat, they come around. The hawks aren't any different." He handed her a bit of meat. "Confidence is key here. Extend your hand out and don't pull away. They'll sense your fear."

She liked this man. He didn't ask about her mark or being a Faceless, and he didn't inexplicably hate her because she had Iskanti blood and yet had been raised Ashvian. But as the smile crept up on her face, she was determined not to let it show.

"They won't fear anything if they're dead," she said. "Putting a hammer through them solves a lot of problems. You should try it."

His soft chuckle bubbled up into a proper laugh. A pattern that sounded so much like Rafaeis's own, but it was impossible. This man bore no mark on his head, and all Faceless had the mark. Khall personally oversaw the accounting of every child they took with the blood tithe, and the tattooing process witnessed and recorded by a dozen Ashvian advisers.

Great. Rafaeis annoyed her so much that she now heard his laugh everywhere.

"Keep your body forward," he said, pressing a hand against her back. "They look for a stable perch. If you waver, they won't trust you to hold them."

He was close, too close, the strength of his body catching her hesitance. Long fingers brushed over hers, pulling her hand towards the sky. Hammer was never a romantic, but his touch made her shiver.

She pulled her attention back to the hawk. These birds shouldn't exist. They were razors with wings, and they cut you every which way. She extended her hand under his. Without much fanfare, the hawk took the meat from her open palm and flew away. He let go and the illusion ended, leaving her with an odd emptiness inside.

She'd chosen to be alone, but he'd given her a fleeting moment where she didn't have to be. It annoyed her. She didn't miss intimacy *that* much to fall all over a man for a single touch.

"Simple," he said with a smile. "Do this enough times, and you can call yourself a hawk-hunter."

"Wonderful," she said, in a voice that contained no wonder. "Let me saddle one of these ibexes and go live in the mountains with the people that just called me a soft-bred traitor, and I'll be an expert in no time."

"You're welcome to join me," he said. "I could use a friend. I'm heading to Iskantupu."

Hammer was right. This man wasn't Iskanti. He seemed to be someone looking for his way out of the city. Perhaps he wanted a personal bodyguard, and who better than a Faceless? Now instead of protecting the queen, she'd be pressed into this man's service, a man whom she knew nothing about.

Besides, she had that godchild—

Shit. She'd *left* that godchild. Viri was still out on the riverbank, alone, with no idea how to find her way back to her hut. Regret filled the hole of her diminished rage. She shouldn't have left her. Viri had just gotten out of the worst living conditions Hammer had seen in a while, and she'd abandoned her by the river for what, pissing the bed? A problem easily cleaned up with some lye and water?

The man caught the alarm that flashed across her face. "Is everything all right?"

"I left someone. I have to go back." All this worrying was temporary. Once Viri developed her powers, she wouldn't have to care for her anymore.

"My companion left too," he said. "I shouldn't care that they did, but it's hard not to."

Attachment. Yet another complication that made her numerous escape attempts even more difficult. This man suffered the same illness. "You should break up with them," she said. "If you don't feel anything, it's easier to leave."

He smiled ruefully. "If only."

One by one, the hawks landed, digging their talons into the sides of the wagon. The clouds thickened into a large gray mass, blotting out the sun. A heavy wind formed, howling past her ear, kicking up dirt into the air.

The Iskantis shouted at each other, packing their belongings. They tied down the wagon, securing the jugs with rope and sheets of fur.

Over the horizon, a storm of twisting gray clouds sharpened into view, swiftly approaching the city.

Engale. The godchild of the wind was here.

She hovered in midair, in the eye of her tornado, her arms outstretched as she sped along the main road to Xinquha. Hammer had seen her fly once, and it made her furious. The ability to fuck off in an instant. She would've killed any number of Tevurians to have a power like that.

No guards accompanied Engale's flight to Xinquha; she moved too quickly for any horse to pursue. Wrapped around her royal Tevurian blue robes was a long black flag: the right of safe passage. Engale was no enemy, but an envoy.

More importantly, without the force of Tevu behind her, she was defenseless. If Hammer aimed carefully, she could simply throw her weapon and knock Engale out with a single blow. Two godchildren, dead by her hand. Hammer's name would be impossible to ignore.

But the coincidence nagged. Engale arrived here the day after they rescued Viri. She hadn't come with an army. Tevu looked to negotiate, playing politics over lives. If Viri decided to wander beyond the Faceless walls, Engale wouldn't need to negotiate anything. She could snatch Viri up, turn around, and leave. The girl would return to that awful wagon. She'd peeled enough skin off manacles for a while.

Grumbling, Hammer sprinted in the direction of the Faceless quarter. Her day of glory would have to wait.

THE UNNATURAL SILENCE drew Hammer to the fighting pit.

She'd searched the riverbank to no avail, then turned to the common grounds. The fighting pit was located in the heart of the quarter, a wide hole dug out by the Faceless before her, to train the Iskanti children they took through the blood tithe.

The pit spurred the primal bloodthirst that came in all children—they'd cheer as their friends beat each other with wooden swords, shouting for blood to be drawn, not understanding why they wanted it.

But this time the initiates had gone quiet. Their marked heads huddled around the pit. They'd probably cheered once, when the round started, but as the fight progressed, it had become a sight that wasn't entertaining anymore.

Especially when the instructor got involved.

Viri cowered against the wall of the pit, kneeling in the mud. She held her arms up against her face. Her opponent—another girl—had stopped, but the instructor had not: The Ashvian raised his whip. He struck Viri once, twice, three times.

"Get up, you useless shit," he shouted.

Crack.

Crack.

crack went the rod, and all she could do was cry, the pain amplified in the dark damp room

i'm here, naias whispered, her hand firm, fortified. i'm with you, forever

Hammer jumped into the pit, shoving the instructor away. A vein in his forehead visibly throbbed with fury.

"You pushed me," he said.

"You have the wrong child," Hammer said, gesturing to Viri. "This isn't a Faceless. She's a godchild. Our sovereign told me to look after her."

He strode up to her, his face so close she could smell his sickening, sugary breath. "You pushed me," he repeated.

Ah. Mistaken identity wasn't his concern at all; he just wanted to lord his power over others. He'd chosen a fitting career by hitting children. They couldn't hit back.

Her hands itched for a fight. She couldn't hit the thief that had stolen from her, and she couldn't fight Engale. The godchild of wind and tornadoes was probably at the palace by now, and Hammer was here, ankle deep in mud, facing a man who wouldn't stop swinging his cock in her face.

If Naias were here, she would've been able to calm this man down with words.

But she wasn't.

Hammer let him have the first move. He wanted respect, so she gave it to him. The lash hit her arms, and it stung with the fury of Iskandraza's wrath, but she forced a grin. He would not frighten her into submission, like he did to these children.

She gripped the lash, curling it around her forearm, pulling him close.

He clung on, knuckles white with fear, even though he knew what was coming. That was the problem with people in power. She'd given him every chance to let go and flee, but people like him hid behind their weapons, no matter what. Once she took them away, they were nothing.

"Good night," Hammer said, and punched him in the face.

The children gasped. If one of them didn't report her, the instructor would do it himself, whenever he regained consciousness. She was firmly in trouble, and there was nothing to be done about it.

She still tried. "I won't tell if you won't," she said to the initiates above her, putting a finger to her lips. "Go enjoy the rest of the day."

Viri hadn't moved since Hammer jumped into the pit. It irked her that the girl was so passive when she should fight, but now, in the wake of the instructor's lash, she understood. Viri had learned to become helpless—her only solution when faced with a power she couldn't overcome.

Sympathy twinged in her heart again, and this time Hammer chose not to ignore it.

"Come on," she said, more to herself than the godchild. She gathered Viri in her arms. "Let's get you home."

7

Naias

THE THRONE GROANED loudly when Khall put her weight on it. Water had found its way into the wood in spite of it all.

"I don't think you should sit there," Naias said. "It'll be a distraction."

Khall nodded, moving to sit on the steps. They'd taken the carpets out to dry. Shafts of light streamed through the holes in the roof, creating dancing shadows on the naked mud floor.

"Look, a little light show, just for us," Naias whispered to her queen.

Khall twisted her hands around her barkcloth dress. Speaking to her former advisers was one thing, but negotiating with their enemy required more confidence than she had exhibited last night. Despite Naias's lessons, they weren't ready for Engale. Faceless assembled by the sides of the room, standing at attention. Naias had called for more of them than necessary. A show of intimidation would hide the condition of the hut they called a palace.

They had nothing to dazzle Engale with—Khall didn't even have a nice dress for occasions like these. She'd spent all that silver on Clement in the hopes that, if she ever got caught in an assassination attempt, the gifts would be payment enough for his prompt help. He liked batik silks and fancy things, and the greedy little man reveled in stripping Khall of what little possessions she did have. Naias had insisted Clement didn't need it—he was chained here, after all—but since Khallan's passing, his daughter's grief had manifested itself in a great fear of death. No matter. Khall needed time, and then their dead king would become a distant memory.

Naias tried more jokes, attempting to ease Khall's nervousness. "Engale might actually speak in coherent sentences this time."

Khall breathed a polite laugh, but her hands didn't stop fidgeting. The joke wasn't funny, and they both knew it.

"Your father taught you how to rule," Naias said, squeezing her shoulder. "You'll do fine."

"My father taught me Ashvian history and how to beat people into obedience," she muttered back. "Let's not credit him with the work I had to learn for myself."

The wind blew the flimsy door open. A woman strode through. A fuzz of gray hair dusted her head, her petite body wearing tailored cotton, dyed in royal blue. She turned in circles as she unwrapped the black flag around her person, surveying the room from roof to floor.

Naias opened her mouth to introduce Khall, but Engale spoke first.

"Fuck the gods, this place is a mess," she said, throwing the flag aside. "You live in this squalor?" Her Common was Tevurian accented, smoothed over and atonal, the opposite of everything Iskanti.

Put her in her place, quickly. Her darling was still untried, and met Engale in good faith. Naias would not let this insult be her reward.

"Godchild," Naias said, her voice sharp, "you speak to Khall, the Earthly Sovereign of Xinquha and the rightful ruler of the occupied territories of the kingdom of Ashvi. I suggest you show some respect."

Engale stopped shuffling. She laughed, her baritone voice nothing like the breezy power she commanded. "Sorry, are we truly going through with this farce?" She swept into a bow so deep that her head nearly touched the floor. "I'm deeply honored that the Earthly Sovereign has deigned to meet such a humble servant of the Tevurian Empire, and I am a thousand times grateful."

A mocking gesture from one who didn't care for the tradition of diplomacy at all. Naias looked to Khall, hoping for some expression of anger to put Engale on the back foot. The queen said nothing.

Engale sprang back into position, clasping her hands together. "Are we done with the formalities? I would've come sooner, but Tevu insisted on an escort for my 'protection.' From who? They need protection from *me*. One flick of my wrist and they'd be off into the sky. There's still a whole company of the Reborn catching up, Khall, a whole company! Tevu even wanted to pull the garrison at Haksa, but that's, what, five people? More baggage of useless men. Thank Ashvalra they didn't come. Horses move *so* slow. Do you know how long it would take to get here if I waited? Ages and ages—"

Khall was letting her ramble, ceding space that she didn't have. If this carried on, Engale would eventually barrel her way through with words, demanding things from an overwhelmed and confused queen. Naias needed to rebalance the scales of power.

"State the reason for your arrival," she said.

Engale blinked back to attention. "Right." She pulled a letter from her pocket, and her gaze darted about the paper. She scoffed, tossing it into Khall's lap. "Tevu wants the godchild back."

This was a loaded demand, one that already presupposed that Xinquha was behind the convoy ambush. Naias stepped in before Khall could say anything. "We have no godchild here." Unless Engale provided proof, she wasn't going to confirm they'd done it.

Khall's head stayed bowed as she read the letter. Naias shouldn't have talked her out of sitting on the throne. She hunched on the floor like a peasant, while a godchild hovered above, literally speaking down to her.

Engale flexed her hand, only to stare at it in puzzlement, like she'd just become aware of the limbs that made up her body. "Did I lose them? My gloves . . ."

"We don't have the godchild," Naias said, her voice louder.

Engale's head snapped up. "They're certain you took her. Don't ask me how. I don't sit in when the prince convenes his military court. It's boring. I'm just a messenger following orders. Every argument prolongs my stay here, and I'd like to get out of this shithole as soon as possible. I mean no offense." She sank into another mocking bow, her hand still twitching.

I could kill you with a single gesture. If she so wished, Naias could order the surrounding Faceless to run their weapons through her. She'd respected the right of safe passage, and Engale continuously chose to stamp on that hospitality.

Khall gasped, bringing her fingers to her lips. "It says here Tevu will recognize me as the rightful ruler of Xinquha," she said to Naias, unable to disguise the eagerness in her voice. "We won't answer to the empire anymore."

None of this felt right. This was the first time Tevu bothered negotiating for a godchild. His prophet wife had named so many in the last forty years of continental war, and not once did he bargain for one. Save for Engale and Pravaja, the rest of them turned out useless. Did they know something that Naias didn't? Impossible. His wife could only recognize godchildren; she didn't know what exact powers they held.

No, fear was the most likely answer. Pravaja was dead, proof that a well-trained, nonmagical army could defeat a being blessed by the gods themselves. If Khall got her hands on a powerful godchild, victory would tip in their favor. Tevu needed to squash that possibility. Better for them to recognize a small part of her kingdom than risk a godchild that could rival Engale.

"The letter doesn't say anything about the Bay of Haksa and the other territories that belong to you, does it?" Naias said, trying to prompt Khall along. "Just Xinquha."

Engale shrugged. "You get your freedom from Tevurian rule. One city, three cities, what does it matter? You can't even rebuild this one, much less govern three. Have you seen my gloves? I swore I brought them here . . ."

Khall finally put the letter down.

Good. Engage with her, not the letter. Stand up and don't let her tower over you.

"Forget your gloves," Khall snapped. "Your flights of fancy aren't endearing. Tevu burned Xinquha down and left us with scraps. Your brutality is why the empire is fragmenting. Maetheria's making overtures. Lakhest left a decade ago. Give me my kingdom back, and you can have the godchild."

Engale cackled, honed steel screeching against stone. "I'm not going back to Tevu with that offer. They'll laugh me out of the room. We don't even need the godchild all that much."

"Then why do you want her?" Khall asked.

Naias wanted to scream. She'd known the answer the moment Tevu volunteered to give up control of Xinquha. She loved Khall, but the queen could not afford to be so naive. That question laid bare her inexperience, blatantly showing her ignorance that the godchild was far more useful now than her powers would ever be.

Engale knew it too. "Take a guess," she said, a sly smile on her face. "I can walk you through the steps. It'll take a while, but you'll get there."

Khall was out of her depth, and her sweet, mild-mannered nature meant that she'd be bullied into submission at every turn. She needed a protector. Naias answered for her again.

"Because you're the only one left, and they don't think you're powerful enough."

For the first time since Engale entered their court, she stopped fidgeting. Her attention slowly turned to Naias, dramatically flicking to the mark on her forehead: a heavily scarred cerulean sun encased in a yellow circle.

"I wish I was as lucky as you," Engale said. "One word from your queen and"—she snapped her fingers—"you're no longer a Faceless. If only I could do the same for my powers. I'm happy for you, truly, that you've escaped the blood tithe. I've heard the stories. You scour the Iskanti mountains and take their children away, and then teach them to swallow their screams when their arms break. It's worse here than in Tevu. You borrowed our practices and sprinkled on a generous helping of unnecessary cruelty."

Engale was baiting her into responding. Neither of them were paragons of virtue, and fighting over lists of committed atrocities confused the reason why they were here: the godchild, in exchange for Xinquha's freedom.

"At least we treat the Reborn well," Engale continued. "We don't brand them with hideous marks, for one, and we give them names, houses, families. They're full citizens of the Tevurian Empire."

"Don't speak to me about treating people well," Khall said. She rose from the stairs, crumpling the letter in her hand. "You refused the godchild food and beat her."

Engale's impertinent grin returned. Khall had taken the bait, and they both knew it. "Tevu accelerates the process for godchildren," she said, skipping past the queen. "At least we don't murder them when their powers amount to nothing. That's what you do, right?"

She sat on the throne. The chair groaned loudly under her weight, and she barked out a laugh of delight. "Gods, this is a creaky old thing, isn't it? I think if you bounced on it hard enough, it might break."

She'd gone too far.

Naias drew her pistol. The rest of the Faceless unsheathed their weapons. A cascade of steel pointed at Engale's heart, while Naias fixed her gun on her head.

"Get out," she said, reverting to the emotionless demeanor of her Faceless training.

Engale's smile disappeared. Her face went still, like a sheet of ice. "I won't die today, Faceless," she said, her singsong voice fading, "and I'm not dying until I find the one amongst you that killed Pravaja."

"You're speaking to her."

Engale guffawed. "No, I'm not. A Gun didn't kill her."

Naias had the upper hand, *she had it*, and she couldn't let it slip away. "You can't even remember where you put your gloves today. But I'll humor you. What weapon, exactly, did your addled mind conjure?"

Engale leaned forward, pressing her head on the end of the pistol. "So, what, you can get to them before me? No. I know what I saw. No one else can tell me otherwise. Pravaja was there. That day the universe crystallized before me. Icicles reflecting on silver. The visceral reality freezes, and I will not let anyone shatter it, least of all you." She enunciated this so clearly, all disrespect in her voice gone.

"I imagine you weren't even present," Naias said, not letting the sudden turn in the godchild's words unnerve her. "It must've been difficult, watching your lover die. I wouldn't blame you at all if your mind broke at such heartache." If her enemies stubbornly refused to follow the rules of diplomacy, why should she? Her finger slid over the trigger. End Engale, and rid their lands of this problem once and for all.

But the godchild abruptly rose from the throne. "Well, this went badly," she said with a laugh, bleeding out the tension in the room. "I'll let Tevu know you've refused all their terms. You're clearly ready to fight us. Look at how grand your palace is."

She hopped down the steps, like a child at play. When she quit the room, she flicked her wrist, and as the door swung shut, Engale tossed her final insult.

"At least try to dress like royalty. You look awful."

BEHIND THE THRONE room lay the monarch's personal chambers. Naias lifted a heavy curtain, and Khall scurried through, head in her hands. The fresh citrus scent of summerbell flowers wafted through the threshold.

It was better than the flooded lean-to Naias had once called home, but Khall's quarters were still a form of imprisonment. For fear of assassination, the dead King Khallan hadn't built windows here, and when Khall took over, she could no longer wake to the sunrise. Like a spring blossom in the desert heat, she wilted, her protruding veins tinting her warm skin green.

As a poor substitute for the sun, Khall allowed herself one small luxury: dried summerbell flowers, which she bribed Iskanti traders to obtain. She soaked them in water, letting the gentle perfume waft through her room, reminding Naias of the brilliant gold fields in Quctra.

"That horrible woman." Khall grabbed the hem of her barkcloth dress and ripped it apart. Her voice shook. "Laughing at me and my city, my claim, my dress—"

"You made the right decision." Naias grasped the queen's hands, stopping her from shredding her dress entirely. "We spent more time rebuilding Xinquha than worrying about looking the part."

Khall angrily wiped away the tears on her face. "I should have had something. Some jewelry, or gold. A ritual. I should've taken one of Clement's rings. He wouldn't have noticed."

"He *would* have noticed. And if you took from Clement without his knowledge, you'd be further in his debt. He'd demand more things that are impossible for us to get."

Khall had no more answers. She pressed her face into Naias's shoulder and bawled.

"I don't know what to do," she said.

Naias kissed the top of her head, pulling her into a tight embrace. "Engale is difficult to speak with at the best of times," she said. "You did your best."

She meant it too. Given Khall's inexperience, the negotiation had gone as well as it could have. They hadn't given up the godchild, but Tevu hadn't ceded any land back to them. The hurt was personal. Khall always crumbled at the slightest insult. Khallan had thought that yelling at his daughter would teach her strength, but it had only made her learn to yield. Naias foresaw a lot of crying in her future. She didn't mind.

She loved Khall tender like this, a quality so different from the dead king she'd once served.

Someone paced beyond the curtain. "My queen," a shaky voice said, "I seek an audience with you immediately."

"Not now," Naias said.

But the curtain lifted regardless.

The instructor was in a sorry state, his clothes caked in mud while he nursed the rapidly purpling bruise that was developing around his eye. "I want to report a Faceless for insubordination," he seethed, spit flying out with every other word.

Khall barely looked up. She was in no mood to deal with anything beyond her feelings.

Naias sprang into action, sitting Khall down on her bedstove. "I'll take care of this," she said, kissing her again.

The instructor did not look happy. "My sovereign—"

Naias grabbed his arm and pushed him out of her chambers, closing the curtain. The instructor didn't like her. His gaze stayed fixed on her forehead, the only physical mark that separated her from the Ashvians.

"Report, then," she said. "Which Faceless hurt you?"

"Black square, red diamond."

Naias suppressed a sigh. *Not again.* "And how did this happen?"

"I was in the fighting pit preparing the initiates for their morning drill. She jumped in and hit me. They tried to pull her off, but she didn't stop."

From the look of the man, he was hit once, in the eye, but Naias wasn't in the mood to quibble over details. "And why did she hit you?"

"No reason. Unprovoked."

Naias barked out a laugh. This was a lie. "No. That particular Faceless doesn't get into fights unless someone gives her cause. She picks a fight over the most trivial things, yes, but she prefers keeping to herself. So, what did you say, or do, to annoy her?"

He swallowed. "She claimed one of the initiates in the pit was a godchild. She even used our queen to lie about it."

She raised a hand. "That is no lie. Queen Khall did put a godchild in her care."

"Ah, well, you see . . ." He fumbled to recover, but Naias saw the wheels turning, padding out his case with half-true justifications and redirecting blame. She knew this rambling all too well, from a long time ago, when her Ashvian handlers unburdened their mistakes on her.

". . . and the Faceless left the child on the riverbank, alone, while I was doing my job, rounding up the ones that refused to come into the pit—"

"I've heard enough," she said. "I'll see to it personally."

She'd given a statement vague enough that implied punishment, but she would do nothing of the sort. She'd counted on Hammer losing—even better, accidentally killing—the godchild. All godchildren's powers amounted to nothing, and this move would've solved three problems in one blow: Tevu couldn't take her back, they wouldn't have an extra mouth to feed, and it'd make Hammer's life miserable. Hammer had done exactly as Naias expected.

But the situation had changed. Pravaja was dead, and Tevu needed a replacement. Now every godchild had potential, and they were important enough that Tevu had risked sending Engale into their territory to negotiate for her release. Viridian was leverage, and thus she had Naias's attention.

"You're dismissed," she said to him, passing behind the curtain. The satisfaction of turning away from an Ashvian never lost its sweetness.

She returned to Khall stifling her cries into her pillow. "I'm no queen," she said, as if Naias hadn't left the room. "I don't know what I'm doing, I'm trying so hard, I really am."

Her pride was deeply wounded. A little more confidence and fewer questions in court would've served her well, but there was no point in regretting what should have been done.

"Khall, darling," Naias said, "even if you'd laid out a whole feast for Engale, she would've thrown it back in your face. If anything, Tevu probably wanted this talk to fail, if they sent her of all people to negotiate."

Blaming Tevu calmed her down. Her sobs quietened. Naias sat on the bed-stove, running her fingers through Khall's long hair.

"Let's keep focusing on rebuilding Xinquha," Naias said, redirecting her hurt into something productive. "We've only had two years since the fire, and your father passed not two months ago. You'll be a great queen when you rebuild the city, as your father promised—"

"With what?" Khall looked up with reddened eyes. "We're in shambles. Look at the state of my roof, my throne. This place used to be the breadbasket of Tevu's empire, and we've only managed rice and sugar for the past two years. We've no goats or pigs, not even a chicken. No one's come to help us. We have some surplus to trade with, but Maetheria doesn't need our food, we're still at war with Tevu, and the Iskantis will just cheat us out of our silver."

Naias bit back a retort. Khall had been raised with prejudice, and admitted as much to her. It was Khallan's fault, and she was doing her utmost to change it.

"Yes, we need money," Naias said, sitting her queen up and covering her in blankets. "But it'll come with time. We'll reallocate the fields for rattan palms, and we'll get the weavers to make baskets and chairs from that and sell them. Eventually we'll have enough money. We just need patience."

Khall wriggled away. "No. We need money now. We need places that'll take our grain. We need to trade. We need . . ."

She stopped abruptly, eyes widening. "Trade routes," she said, throwing off the blankets and rushing to the map on her table. "The Bay of Haksa will give the seas to us. It was ours by right. My father always talked about how Haksa and Xinquha were two halves of the same whole. We need to take it back."

She'd heard those words from Khallan's mouth one too many times.

'Taking it back' meant battle.

She stayed on the bed-stove, unsettled by her queen's growing excitement. Khall had seen so much of her father's methods in war, surely she didn't want to perpetuate this part of his legacy. "I don't think war is the right decision. As much as I disagree with Jayal and Maka, they're right. You need to select an heir first. We can select one of your Ashvian attendants, or perhaps you'd want to groom one of the Xinquhan pages."

Khall shook her head. "That can wait. Xinquha rots every passing day. When we had a kingdom, this city prospered because of Haksa. This city was never meant to be self-sufficient. Engale said that Haksa couldn't even spare their soldiers to accompany her. That means the city isn't well fortified. Do you think we could take it?"

"I have supreme confidence in the Faceless," Naias said, not committing to an answer. She wouldn't make promises she couldn't keep.

"And they don't have Pravaja anymore," Khall said, getting visibly excited. She paced the room, a large grin on her face. "They're going to want to protect Engale as much as possible. They move like snails. We've always had the element of surprise against them. This can work."

She wasn't listening. Naias needed to be more direct. "Darling, I told you I don't want to fight anymore."

Khall stopped, her brow softening. She knelt before her. "I'm sorry. I promised you no more wars."

But her queen looked so terribly forlorn in the damp and dark. No matter how many summerbell flowers they soaked, it never disguised the musty smell that lingered in the room, a constant reminder of the mold that thrived within these walls.

Naias hated to see her like this. She belonged to the sun, her body glimmering in its rays, a perfect avatar of what the kingdom of Ashvi and a descendant of Ashvalra were supposed to be. Life and the sunrise, as rich as the earth. She didn't belong here.

But dreams and pretty images hadn't gotten her this far. If

Khall wanted war from her, then she'd counter with a bargain of her own.

She started small. Only a fool would turn down her first request. "If I help you with this," she said, "I have two conditions. One: We need allies. Send for the Maetherian envoy to speak with us. They've been pushing against Tevu for a while now. Maybe they'll help us in our fight."

"We have a Maetherian godchild with us," Khall reminded her. "Maetheria will be searching for her, if they haven't started already."

"But they don't know that we intercepted the caravan," Naias said. "Not yet. Disguise her as one of the Faceless initiates until they leave. We can use her as leverage against Tevu. If they're so desperate to get her back, we can negotiate better terms when we have both Haksa and Xinquha."

"Haksa and Xinquha." Khall's lips twitched into a wistful smile. "Maybe Pakaala and Quctra in the future. The dream my father always had. The kingdom of Ashvi, restored to its full glory. We could do it."

She didn't care about Khallan's legacy. What mattered was what she could do now. "We can take Haksa, but it's defending it from Tevu that worries me. That's why we need Maetheria. Their archers and longbows can help with that."

Khall nodded, laying her head in Naias's lap. "And your second condition?"

Naias drew in a breath. "You make me Ashvian. A full citizen of your kingdom."

The intimacy disappeared. Khall drew back, her gaze flicking up to meet Naias's. "That's quite a condition."

That was not the answer she'd wanted. Did she go too far? Perhaps she should've spun her words out, to confuse and obfuscate, like Engale did, to force the queen into saying yes. Maybe she could try a slight twist of the arm. "You said yourself that what Khallan did was cruel. You wanted to be better. This is your chance."

She'd dared to dream it, ever since she'd first lain in Khall's bed all those years ago. The first Faceless to rise out of the blood tithe, to become an equal in the eyes of Ashvian law. She would no longer be sequestered in the back of the throne room, like an ugly blot on a pristine sheet of paper. Ashvians would stop staring at her, she could stop groveling for their approval, and her life would no longer be chained by how useful she was in battle. If they took Haksa, all the better. The bigger Khall's kingdom, the more places she could be free.

With hard work and time, she could even put an end to the blood tithe. She, too, was a victim of this ghastly practice, and the faster they did away with it, the better. But she was no fool. The Faceless were too important to Khall's fight against Tevu for the order to be abolished completely. She needed to secure her freedom first, through Khall, before she had the power to grant freedom to others.

"Call it a symbol of our love," Naias pressed. "I've spent my life in your father's service, and I hope I've shown that I'm worthy. This is all I ask."

Khall stayed still, her breath cooling on Naias's thighs. An agonizing moment passed. Did she need to pressure her more, or was this enough? Khall needed time to think, but what if the silence Naias ceded her only made her remember the kingdom's old traditions, and the fear of change was too much for her?

Khall lifted her head, letting out a sigh. "I do love you," she finally said. "If we win Haksa, I'll see what I can do."

That was as close to an agreement as she'd ever have. "Then we fight."

The queen broke into a small smile, rising to her feet. "I'll send the invitation to Maetheria," she said. "This time I'll be better prepared."

Naias shook her head. She wasn't going to let Khall's inexperience soil this for her. "Their envoys are beneath you. I'll handle it. I'm sending the invitation to Soridian. I've known him for a long time, and we'll have a better chance of success. You can oversee the feast. You liked doing those."

This made Khall much happier. She hopped into the bed, wrapping Naias in a hug. "Just like how we used to do it in Quctra. What a simpler life then, when I didn't have to bother with all this." She laughed, but there was a forcefulness in it that Naias understood.

A simpler life. Naias loved and hated those days, when she'd reported to Khallan soaked in blood, collapsing on his feet while the corpses of her Faceless friends danced behind her eyelids. The old king hadn't deemed her important enough to be healed by Clement, so behind his back, Khall had sent for bandages and water, sneaking into her tent when everyone was asleep, staring at her battle-ridden body for hours.

And when Naias had brushed her fingers on Khall's arm and the future queen flushed red, she'd found her way out.

So close. One more battle. Once they'd won the bay, Naias could be free and end the blood tithe, once and for all.

8

Viri

HAMMER PUT ME in the river for a second time. Her rough hands broke the mud that caked my body. She bathed me without saying anything.

I said nothing too. I was still too scared. When my skin was pink and raw, she took me out and carried me back.

The chirping birds and rippling water took over the silence between us. Hammer didn't ask me questions I didn't know the answer to. She didn't order me around or yell at me. We simply were. The Faceless—I knew them now—passed us, each one with a unique mark on their forehead. Red circle. Orange star. Blue wheel.

I'd thought Hammer hated me, but she'd saved me from the whip. She'd stopped the pain and suffered her own. A long red welt ran down her scarred forearm. I didn't know what to feel about her, but at least she didn't hit me.

We reached her hut. Hammer set me on the corner of her bed-stove, draping a soft fur around me. My bruises were showing. Purple and red dots all over my body. I couldn't bend my fingers, because they'd swollen so much.

Hammer sat next to me. She pressed along the bones of my limbs, saying nothing about my scar-striped arms. We both knew where they'd come from, and she didn't need to ask.

"Remember the pain you had in your shoulder? Tell me if it hurts like that," she said.

The touch surprised me. I'd braced myself for a hard prodding, like what the men in heavy armor used to do when I developed sores, but she stayed gentle.

The red diamond loomed in my face as she took a closer look at my bruises. I must have stared too long again, because Hammer said "the symbol marks you as a Faceless. If we defect or escape, it's easy for the others to tell."

I dared to speak. Naias had a mark too, and so did the Faceless who passed us, "but the others don't have . . ."

"Oh, these?" she said, pointing to the spiderweb of red lines across her face. "They mark you each time they catch you escaping. I got caught too many times, and they gave up making the lines look neat."

It must have hurt a lot, maybe worse than Clement's piercings. He was proud of his jewelry, his nose rings likely his own choice. Hammer's marks weren't. I tried to count the lines, but too many overlapped, and the further the lines carved down her cheek, the less straight they were. I gave up.

The muscles she touched made me feel sore, but I didn't scream. "No broken bones," she finally said. "They won't give up Clement's power for a few bruises. The pain will go away after a couple of days." Hammer rummaged through a sack, pulling out a handful of attap nuts, each as big as my fist. She took a cleaver and split open a shell, revealing an oval-shaped translucent fruit inside. She dug it out and tossed it into my lap. "Eat that," she said, opening one for herself. "You'll heal faster. Would've been better with some coconut milk, but the palms all burned during the fire."

I didn't reach for it. Even though I knew no stick would come after, its ghost still hovered in my mind.

Hammer's lips thinned. "You have to eat, Viri," she said softly. "You aren't going to get better otherwise."

A bolt shot through me when she spoke my name. *Viri, Viri, Viri.* Viridian from Maetheria. That's who I was. Not a godchild, not a Faceless. Me.

I picked up the fruit and chewed. The flesh burst on my tongue, sweet and juicy.

"Sleeping arrangements," Hammer said through a mouthful of attap. "You're going to be here a while. We'll share the bed. I may accidentally crush you." She flexed her arm. More muscles bulged out than I'd ever seen on a person in my life. "If it gets too uncomfortable, we'll take turns sleeping on the floor. Don't touch my weapon."

I nodded.

"And no more pissing the bed," she said. "The privy is outside. It's a big trench with buckets, and stinks as high as Mount Iska. You can't miss it."

I stared at the sheets. She'd cleaned up my mess already. This wasn't the wagon, and Hammer wasn't *them*. I didn't need to hide anymore.

"It was my fault," Hammer said. "I was angry and tired. This used to be Clement's responsibility. He's the one who always handled children like him. This is all new for me."

Hammer blaming herself made me feel a little better. Everything seemed to be my fault here, and for once this wasn't true.

I reached for another piece of fruit. "Why didn't he?"

She shrugged. "Don't know. He took care of the last godchild we rescued. Wasn't very useful. Took after the god of the streams, but it was a weak manifestation. Khallan didn't need a sweaty kid. Before him, a child that controlled butterflies, another produced a few grains of sand. Nothing important."

I knew the three major gods who made the world: Ashvalra, Diavijra, and Iskandraza—

names carved into the crystal prism that floated above the entrance hall of her father's university, striking a brilliant array of light when the sun bounced off the glass

—and a handful of lesser ones, but I'd never heard of a god of butterflies or sand.

"How many gods are there?" I asked.

Hammer shrugged. "Don't know, don't care. Your Maetheria would know, and Tevu's prophet queen too, if she saw you in her visions. But *I* think if there's a child controlling butterflies, there's too many gods."

I didn't laugh. If there were more gods than I knew, then there had to be more godchildren, but I'd only seen Clement here.

I asked her the same question I'd asked him. "Where are the other godchildren now?"

Hammer rubbed the mark on her forehead and looked away. Everyone avoided answering it, like they were protecting me from some horrible truth. But I'd seen this truth many, many times. I wanted someone to give words to it.

"Will I die?" I asked.

"We can talk about that when your powers appear," Hammer said.

"No." I turned to her. My body didn't like it. "Tevu took me from . . . They took me, they hit me. I've seen people die. Tell me."

"I—oh, fine. All the godchildren before you have died. So, yes. Most likely."

"How?"

"Many ways. They're drugged with opium first. Most of the time we take them to the northern mountains and leave them there. Iskanti lands. Usually the cold gets them. Sometimes adders."

"And you didn't help them?" I asked.

Hammer looked me in the eye. "No. It was none of my business."

I wasn't surprised. I'd seen the cruelty of the men in armor. It was cruel here too, with the way they marked Hammer's face and how the instructor treated the younger Faceless.

I played with an unopened attap nut in my hand. I'd been taken from one kingdom to another, hit and whipped, and I didn't get a say in it at all. I'd lost so much control over my life. When my death came, I wanted to face it with my rules. "Don't drug me when the time comes," I said. "If I go, I'll do it on my own."

Hammer shook her head. "If you don't want to get dropped in the mountains, here's my advice: When you develop your powers, don't show it off. Especially if it's a shit one, like the butterfly girl. Don't let Khall or Naias know, even if they bribe you with sweets and gems and toys to play with. Pretend you haven't gotten it yet. That'll buy you a few years."

"A few years? I'll stay with you for that long?"

Hammer grumbled. "I might have to work for some extra furs for the floor."

"What happens when they find out about my powers?"

"You might not instantly die when they leave you in the mountains. Hopefully you'll have learned some ways to survive by then."

It ended all the same, but I'd have a few more years if I did as Hammer said.

survive, he said, squeezing her hand before the bullet splattered his brains on the floor

survive

"Thank you," I said, giving the nut back to her.

Hammer cracked a small smile, the first I'd seen since meeting her. "I'm sorry about this morning," she said. "For pulling you off the bed and shouting at you."

I didn't know how I felt about Hammer when she rescued me from the pit, but it came clear now. I wasn't used to her roughness, but she'd apologized for it, protected me from being hurt, and told me how to hide my eventual powers to survive.

Everyone had left, even Rafaeis, the one who'd first asked for my name. Out of all of them, the person that came back for me was the one who didn't want me in the first place. She'd shown me more kindness than anyone else.

I didn't want to be alone anymore. I couldn't help myself. I dove into her arms, clinging to her tight.

"Don't go." The despair in my voice surprised me.

She didn't hug back. "I'm a Faceless, Viri," she said with a helpless shrug. "My life is not my own. I won't be here all the time."

My chest shrank, like I'd been bound up again. My hands throbbed harder. At least she was honest about it.

Hammer gently laid her hands on mine. "But."

I looked up.

"But I promise I'll come back for you, no matter how long I've been away. That's the best I can give."

I let out a sound between a sob and a laugh. The relief I felt. It was such a small promise, a crumb of what I'd asked from her, and yet it was enough for me.

Hammer patted my head. The rhythm was off, and her touch too soft, like she wasn't used to it. "You're going to be staying here awhile, so if your powers end up being starting fires or something"—she pointed to her curtained door—"burn the other huts down first. I don't give a shit. Leave mine alone."

I understood Hammer's sarcasm better now. "I'll do my best," I said, which made her laugh.

A knock rapped against the hut's woven walls. The curtain lifted, and a lean, masked Faceless appeared, his chest heaving, as if he'd run to get here. Crescent moon blades were strapped to his thigh.

Rafaeis. I couldn't help leaping up and running to him. He hugged me better than Hammer, his long arms engulfing me in warmth.

Even though he'd left, he came back. Hammer promised the same. This would be the way we lived our lives together.

"It's not even sundown and you're already back," Hammer said. "How far did you get? The barricades?"

"That doesn't matter," Rafaeis said, breathing heavily. "I just got Khall's orders."

He held out a mask. The same mask that Hammer and Rafaeis wore, the eerie, smiling faces that brought no joy to those who glimpsed them.

A mask for me.

9

Viri

THE NEXT FEW weeks were a blur of preparation. One day Hammer and Rafaeis took me out of the Faceless quarter. We were getting my hair dyed. I bounced with excitement. I was going to look different, in the same way the batik dresses at home made me look different. A new experience.

Yellow-flowered angsana trees and stumpy palms covered the cliffs. Clouds, gray and heavy with rain, billowed above us. They looked so thick and fluffy that I wanted to fly up and sink into them. I could barely see the blue in the sky.

The city felt busier. Ashvians ground rice into flour. The Iskanti caravans stayed longer, skinning and curing goat carcasses for Khall. They'd slaughtered one to eat for themselves that day, roasting it above an open fire. White smoke swirled in pretty circles, the savory essence of mutton wafting through the air. My mouth watered.

"We'll never get to eat that," Hammer grumbled behind her mask, "so don't bother chasing the smell."

We walked downriver, past the wall and through a small field of dead trees. There was no path here. My feet crunched down on brambles and branches.

The smell of mutton disappeared. White smoke turned black, covering everything in a haze. Something was burning.

A group of Ashvians crowded around a building on fire. A charred stone statue lay scattered on the ground. Laborers with pickaxes chipped away, breaking the stone into smaller pieces. I recognized the hole in the statue's chest and the carved vines that sprouted out of it. This was Iskandraza, the Destroyer.

I didn't know enough about him. In Maetheria, the university had a wing dedicated to studying the gods. I'd tried reading the books, but they were too complicated to understand. I was young, more interested in the reflections on the glass walls than words on paper. Gods weren't part of my life then. They were for adults who wanted answers about the world.

I wish I'd tried reading the books better.

"They finally burned it down," Rafaeis said. He carried a small bucket of black paste. It smelled awful, like raw meat left in the heat for too long.

"Better to feast in the temple of a dead god than in that leaking shithole they call a palace," said Hammer.

The ground rustled. Something ran across my foot. I caught a glimpse of a bushy tail before it disappeared into the smoke. The animals were fleeing the fire.

"Oh, free game," Hammer said. She crouched down, her hands out, and stood completely still. Rafaeis put his bucket down quietly, bringing out his crescent blades. His hands flashed in and out, like a snake striking its prey.

In the end, Rafaeis caught two lizards and a mouse. Hammer caught none.

"I win," Rafaeis said, grabbing a stick from the ground and spearing his catch with it, but Hammer stood still, focusing on the dead tree branches above us. She reached up. Wood snapped and she disappeared into a blur of leaves and dirt. A sharp yelp split my ears.

When the storm settled, Hammer sat on top of a thrashing lizard nearly my size, her hand pushing down on its neck. Rafaeis grabbed its tail, stopping it from throwing her off.

"All right, you win," Rafaeis said with a laugh, "but these are too poisonous to eat."

Hammer shook her head. "We have to kill it. This one's corrupted. See the black spots in its front legs? That's why it didn't flee."

"It's a small infection," he said. "It might get better on its own."

"If we can't save it, we kill it. Better to put it out of its misery than let it suffer half a life."

"Let it go, Hammer." Rafaeis's voice had an edge to it. "It'll recover."

She held her hand out. "Blade."

Rafaeis didn't move.

Hammer's hand curled behind her back, grasping the handle of her weapon. "I will smash its fucking head in if you don't give me your blade. Do you want lizard brains splattering all over you instead?"

pink on the glass, pink rippling in the light

I spoke. "Let it go. Please."

Her mask snapped to face me, a false grin that told me nothing of how she truly felt.

I wish she'd taken off that mask. I wanted to see some form of regret, or distress, or pain that helped me understand that ending a life hurt her too. Maybe I put these feelings on her because *I* felt them, when she'd never experienced anything of the sort. Maybe she was a cold-blooded killer all along.

But Hammer let out a loud sigh.

"Fine," she said.

They stepped back. The lizard darted away, running towards the river. A splash echoed in the distance.

Rafaeis retrieved the bucket of black slime. His arm wrapped around my shoulders. "You did well," he said, squeezing me briefly. "Turns out the hole in Hammer's heart can be filled after all."

Hammer didn't like showing how much she cared, and if I got to her, it was a great accomplishment. I broke into a smile.

Hammer stalked past us. "Next time you won't be so lucky," she muttered.

I didn't know if she meant that for the lizard or me.

* * *

We stopped far downriver, where the clear waters turned brown with mud. Xinquha had erected barricades along the path and on the river, sharp wooden sticks lashed together and pointing towards, as Hammer told me, the only entrance and exit out of the city.

We found a clearing where the palms didn't prick. After making sure no one was close, Hammer took her mask off and kept her back to the city. Sweat had dampened her face, but she looked calm, donning a pair of rawhide gloves like she'd done it a hundred times before. Letting the lizard go didn't seem to have bothered her.

Flies buzzed around us. I shooed them away.

"Sit still," Hammer said, tossing another pair of gloves to Rafaeis. He put the bucket down next to me. I wrinkled my nose.

"Fermented leeches in vinegar," Rafaeis said. "We have an abundance of both. The mixture's very strong, and that's why it stinks, but your hair will stay black once we wash it off."

"I'll smell for ages," I complained.

"It's to hide you from Tevu," said Hammer. "I don't think you want to go back." She scooped up the black slime and spread it on her gloves.

I stopped fidgeting. She was right. I didn't want to go back.

"There are a few things you need to remember," Rafaeis said. He tugged on my clumped-up hair, separating it into locks. "You're pretending to be one of the young Faceless initiates. We have no names, only our marks. Our names are assigned when we choose our weapons."

"Which is why it was a terrible idea to tell her your true name," Hammer said.

Rafaeis winked at me, putting a finger to his masked lips. "You haven't told anyone so far, have you?"

I shook my head. After Clement's insistence on calling me 'little godchild,' I knew better than to utter Rafaeis's true name in public. There was a power to names and knowing them. I didn't know what this power was, but it felt important in Xinquha. The moment we met, Rafaeis had trusted me not to reveal it.

"But why did you tell me?" I asked. "I didn't know you."

"You're a godchild," he said simply. "Everyone wants your power, but no one wants *you*. I know that all too well."

Hammer gave Rafaeis a curious look. "So you weren't lying. That's your actual name."

Rafaeis chuckled, nudging me with his elbow. "Look, Viri, you've cost me," he said. "She was going to give me her true name before you asked."

"I was never going to," Hammer said, rolling her eyes. "What I don't get is you wearing that mask all the time, even in the quarter. That thing must stink on you."

He shrugged. "I like it."

Her lip curled in disgust. "Fine, enjoy your acne." She squatted behind me and combed the dye through my hair.

Hammer's hands were all force and speed, like a raging wave, intent on working the dye into as much of my hair as possible. My head tilted in the direction she tugged, but as rough as she was, she never yanked hard enough to cause me pain. It felt like being firmly scrubbed down with a prickly sponge.

Rafaeis was more deliberate, like the flowing river we sat on. He picked out the parts Hammer missed, thoroughly fingering my locks, making sure every single strand was coated. My scalp tingled with his touch, like the satisfaction of an itch being scratched.

I seared this feeling into my mind. If I couldn't identify them by their faces or calling out their names, then I would identify them by their hands.

"Remember, you have no name," Rafaeis said. "If you're summoned, refer to yourself as 'Faceless' or 'initiate.'"

"If anyone asks, you're Iskanti," Hammer said. "You were taken because of the blood tithe. Nobody on the continent cares if we go missing."

Rafaeis tapped his chin. "You came from, ah, Lhantujin. It's so deep in Iskantupu that people won't ask too many questions about it."

I nodded. Initiate. Iskanti. Blood tithe. Lhantujin.

"And your Common accent sounds too Maetherian," Rafaeis continued. "You round your words and slur your sentences together. It's too soft."

"The Ashvian accent is rougher," Hammer said. "Everything comes from the throat. Imagine that you're constantly shouting at someone."

I repeated Hammer's words, mimicking her accent. Spit accidentally flew out of my mouth.

She winced.

"A good start," Rafaeis said cheerfully.

With their help, I repeated sentences and words that I'd have to say. The Ashvian tongue felt angry, like a dog yipping at a tiger. I hadn't realized how much of my voice came from pressing my lips together. Now I had to open my mouth wide to project the words.

Together, they covered my hair in paste, while I continued to sputter phrases into the air. Rafaeis twisted my locks into a bun, pinning it to the top of my head. "We'll let this dry for three days and then wash it out," he said. "By the end of it, you should have completely black hair."

"Let's work on your Faceless bow," Hammer said, taking her gloves off and getting to her feet. "Stand straight and cover your face with your right hand. Bend forward a little."

I followed Hammer. It wasn't too hard, bending up and down. "It's different in Maetheria," I said. "We had a curtsy."

"What else do you remember?" Hammer asked. "Before you were taken?"

"The food," I said immediately, because I didn't want to remember anything more than that. "I miss the food there. Radish chili kueh and spicy rice noodles."

Rafaeis audibly swallowed. "West Maetheria," he said. "Near the university?"

I looked down, picking at a bugbite on my leg. "Yes."

"And your parents?"

This was getting too uncomfortable. I didn't want to remember, but the words came anyway.

"Papa was a scholar," I said. "He was a professor at the university. I was with him most of the time. Dada was always traveling. I don't know what he did. He never came home."

he wept by his books, stacked to the ceiling in their little wooden cottage, writing letter after letter begging him to return, for their daughter's sake

Hammer suddenly knelt before me, gripping my shoulder tight. Her irises glowed golden brown, reflecting the setting sun.

"It's a bittersweet memory," she said, "but hold on to it. Remember what your parents looked like, the place you lived, the books you read, the food you ate. Sear it into your head. These coming days will force you to forget, because your past is dangerous to them. You are Viri. No mask, no dye, no change of name will ever strip everything that made you. Remember that."

I hadn't heard Hammer speak with that kind of sincerity before. She didn't cover it up with jokes or deflect with sarcasm. This was new.

Rafaeis looked on, nodding.

"I promise," I said.

Hammer handed me the mask. It was tough, made from pieces of dried leather and painted in black. I ran a finger over the openings.

"Will I get a mark on my head, like you?" I asked.

"You're only pretending, Viri."

"She can pretend to have one," Rafaeis said, dipping his little finger into the dye. He drew a *V* on my forehead. "See? V for Viridian. Now you won't forget your name."

I laughed, but Hammer tutted, using her sleeve to wipe the dye off my face. "This stuff burns through skin. Don't do that."

Let us stay this way. If I could stop time, I would've frozen that moment and relived it forever.

When I look back on the peaks and valleys of my life, I separate it into two phases: Maetheria, and not. In those days after my abduction to my eventual death, that moment by the river was the happiest I'd ever been.

10

Naias

THE PALACE WAS no place to feast the Maetherian envoy, so Naias had had the temple of Iskandraza burned instead. She directed the ruins of Iskandraza's statue to be mounted behind Khall, his gaping chest scorched black. A symbolic gesture to show Ashvalra's triumph over him, and whose descendant ruled here.

The cloudless sky was a good omen. No monsoon tonight. They would feast under the stars. Faceless initiates and Ashvian attendants stood behind the carefully arranged tables and cushions, giant thatched fans in their hands. The dazzling bonfire in the center of the ruins would hide most of the city's squalor.

Khall, on her part, had given up her summerbell allowance. She'd traded her silver with the Iskantis for a handful of Maetherian purple peppers, renowned for their spiciness and numbing qualities. They'd worked them into the mutton and galangal soup they'd let simmer for days.

Naias would have to eat tactfully if she wanted to retain control of her mouth at the end of the dinner. She rocked on her heels, sensing the slight rumble that indicated Soridian's approach.

Khall stood beside her, smoothing down her barkcloth dress.

"With what we had left after the mutton and peppers, I wasn't able to trade for radishes," she said, rambling through her anxiety. "I told them to make sweetened rice cakes instead. I hope that's enough."

As much as Naias wanted Khall to not attend the feast altogether, the rules of decorum meant she had to attend these events, even if she contributed nothing at all. Her absence would be an insult to the envoy, an implicit gesture that their queen had better things to do with her time.

"It is," Naias said, planting a quick kiss on her head. "Remember, I'll take the lead in these talks. You can relax and enjoy the fruits of your hard work."

Two horses yoked to a roofed carriage trod towards them. A small Maetherian and Faceless escort flanked it, all on horseback. Naias had insisted on sending the invitation on horses instead of yaks. Their window of opportunity to attack Haksa was getting smaller each passing day, and they needed to secure Maetheria's alliance quickly.

The carriage door opened. Soridian stepped out, silks of green and pale yellow fluttering around him, motifs of mulberry trees and butterflies drawn with batik. Simple and dignified, unlike that eyesore on Clement, who hoarded every conceivable color under the sun.

Soridian floated to a stop before Khall. He extended his foot back and sank into a deep curtsy. "Earthly Sovereign Khall," he said, "it's an honor to meet you, and I thank you for this invitation."

A formal, predictable, and respectful greeting. Naias quietly breathed a sigh of relief.

"It's my great pleasure to receive you too," Khall said, just as they'd rehearsed. "Thank you for coming on such short notice. Naias has spoken very highly of you."

Soridian rose, his eyeglasses twinkling in the firelight. "By the gods, Naias, you look even more beautiful than before."

If she put him in a good mood, he'd be more amicable when the small talk led to the actual reason for the invitation. She humored him, matching his flattery with her own. "And I can see the gray in your beard now. A man of dignity, like you always wanted."

He scratched his chin, grinning. "Dreams do come true."

"You've had a long journey," Khall said, gesturing to the feast. "Please, sit."

Naias had arranged the tables in a large square around the bonfire. At the head sat Khall, her table and seat cushion elevated on the pedestal that used to house the statue of Iskandraza. Soridian's table, and hers, lay to Khall's right, down the steps, angled so the bonfire blocked them from her view. They were close enough to Khall to not give offense to the envoy, but far enough that the queen couldn't meddle when Naias started talks. The Maetherian escort filled the remaining seats.

An Ashvian attendant approached Khall, setting a porcelain tray of food on her table first. He then picked up a chunk of mutton from her tray and ate it. Khall nodded and waved him away.

"The girl fears poison, I see," Soridian said.

"Who can blame her, after what happened to Khallan?" Naias forced a smile. "I've told her time and again it was simply a combination of old age and bad luck, but she's still paranoid. It's only been a few months. Give her time and she'll stop worrying."

Soridian was served second. Roasted loins of lamb sat on green-glazed porcelain, while steam rose from a large bowl of rice noodle soup. A sprig of Maetherian pepper garnished the noodles, its tiny dark purple berries a hint to the mutton broth infused with its spiciness. A plate of sweetened rice cakes rounded out the meal, while a cup and flask of wine finished the arrangement off.

Naias glanced at her tray. She'd gotten the lamb's neck, and no peppers decorated her bowl of noodles. It didn't matter; the feast wasn't for eating. "Forgive the sparse fare," she said, attempting some false modesty, "but the Tevurian embargo has made things quite difficult for us."

Soridian shook his head through a mouthful of soup. "Oh, no, Naias, this is perfect. You even sourced our peppers. You know how to keep a Maetherian happy."

Naias chuckled, quiet enough to sound polite, but loud enough to compliment his sense of humor. Every word had been practiced, every gesture rehearsed. "You get an upset stomach when you even *look* at anything plain. I wanted to make sure you were comfortable."

He smiled, raising his cup of wine. "To the Earthly Sovereign," he shouted above the crackle of the bonfire. "We wish her eternal strength and excellence."

"Eternal strength and excellence," echoed the rest. Bloviating phrases that meant nothing except to inflate Khall's sense of self-worth. Naias quickly raised her cup too, but under the tablecloth, her leg jiggled impatiently.

When the toasts were done, Naias gnawed at her bit of lamb. It was still too early to discuss alliances. She'd start with an informal conversation first. "I wonder if you have any tomes in your university about ridding tattoos done on the human body," she said. "Without leaving those terrible scars."

Soridian blotted his mouth on a rag. "Ah, for that sun on your forehead? I can inquire, but truthfully, if we had such knowledge, we'd have capitalized on that decades ago."

She sensed the implication in his words. When Khallan's hold over the Faceless was still new, the dissatisfied had fled his lands. Maetheria had always viewed the blood tithe with distaste, claiming it to be unnecessarily cruel, but that didn't stop them from returning the deserters and getting a hefty sack of silver in exchange. Soridian had opened the talks with fire, and she had to meet it.

"A blessing in disguise," she said. "Those recaptured Faceless freed us from Tevurian rule. We took and defended Xinquha, and even killed Pravaja."

"Funny you say 'we,' Naias. You aren't Ashvian. Khallan's fight was never your fight."

Not this again. She could match Jayal's and Maka's hostility with threats of her own, but Soridian's benevolent prejudice stung more. There was no verbal pistol to draw on him. She was so nearly a citizen of Khall's kingdom, and she would get there a lot quicker if people stopped telling her she wasn't.

She shrugged, pretending the remark didn't bother her. "The Ashvians have treated me as one of their own. I speak the same language, defend the same land, eat the same food, and pray to the same god. All the things an Ashvian does."

"And yet you search for a miracle cure to rid yourself of that mark on your head," he said, slurping down another mouthful of noodles.

"A cosmetic procedure. Its existence doesn't affect me anymore, now that I'm Khall's adviser. I admit that it's an upsetting practice if you've only heard about it, but we are free of the empire. You still answer to Tevu and pay your tithes to them. Haven't you had enough?"

He shrugged in the same nonchalant way that Naias had. "Tevu lets us keep our senate. They give our university complete freedom. In return, we send them paper, spices, and batik silk. It's an agreeable arrangement. Ashvi, on the other hand, enacts the blood tithe on lands they do not own."

She found her opening. "We've created a military force that crushed a century of Tevurian dominance. Despite our methods, you cannot question the outcome." She gestured to Iskandraza's ruined stone body. "A group of five hundred took this place. I guarantee you more than five hundred Maetherians will die when you inevitably break from Tevu."

She pushed her food aside, scooting her cushion towards him. "Despite all you said about 'agreeable arrangements,' I know it's not all pleasant there. Tevu's constant expansion has taxed your production. They demand more paper to write on, more batik to trade with. Then they take your scholars to advise their campaigns on acquiring more godchildren and land, leaving you with scraps. How is your university holding up with this shortage? I imagine it cannot flourish as much as they would like. You return escaped Faceless to us for silver because you don't have enough batik and paper to trade with anymore. But I suppose these multiple grievances balance out the blood tithe, a practice that doesn't involve Maetheria, or Lakhest, or Tevu."

Did she want to throw in Tevu kidnapping the godchild? She'd come too close to admitting their involvement if she did. That morsel of information could be saved for another time. She'd given him enough to doubt Tevu's integrity.

Soridian's wrinkled brow etched with pity. "I don't understand how you can speak of the blood tithe so candidly, when you were wrenched from your own family."

He would not sway her with sentiment. If Naias needed to obfuscate her past to gain his trust, then so be it. "My parents gave me up because we were on the brink of starvation. I would have died otherwise. Being in the Faceless saved all of us."

He ran a finger along the rim of his wine cup, unconvinced. "But you're now raised into a life where you have no choice but to fight. Is that 'saving' you?"

She had to refocus. If she let him take control, the conversation would only end in debate about what constituted saving and not, and if the Faceless knew more beyond the life they led. As befitted his background, Soridian enjoyed talking about abstracts much more than delivering material promises. She would not walk into his philosophical traps tonight.

"The way you speak of the blood tithe makes it sound like we keep the Faceless in dungeons and torture them into obedience," she said, rising to her feet. "Let me take you to the training grounds. See for yourself what we actually do."

IT WAS ALL prepared, of course. Naias never left anything up to chance. Two masked bodies circled each other in the fighting pit, while the unmasked Faceless crowded above, cheering for their chosen winner. Cups of wine sloshed in their hands. If Soridian didn't like the rougher atmosphere, rows of Faceless practiced moving drills in another part of the grounds, scaling up the mountains that abutted the quarter with nothing but their hands and rope.

"No torture here," Naias said, escorting him down the path. "Only camaraderie and discipline."

"And that?" Soridian pointed to where they'd come from: the ruins of Iskandraza's temple. "Was burning that down an act of discipline too?"

Naias tried not to let her confusion show. Of all things to be concerned with, religion should've been the last issue on Soridian's mind. "We worship Ashvalra. Iskandraza murdered her. He has no place here."

"Ashvalra, Iskandraza, Diavijra. They're all our common gods. What I see is intolerance."

"Those three have been dead for millennia, and their children are going with them. Dead gods don't care about our prayers. The living ones certainly don't." Why was he so preoccupied by this? Soridian was an intellectual, not a priest. "Most of Maetheria doesn't worship anymore," she said. "You study them and why this waning is happening. This shouldn't bother you."

Soridian pursed his lips. The facade of amiable politicking vanished.

Shit. She'd misspoken.

"Faith and logic have been intertwined since their birth," he said. "Faith drives us to make sense of the world. The reason why seasons change, why the seas have risen, why the mountains are formed. We honor the ones that made our world, even if they're no longer there to hear us. Maetheria gives thanks through logic, finding a system and structure to understand the gods' decay. This is the nature of respect. It's an understanding and allowing the beliefs of others to coexist. Tevu does this. Khall does not."

She let him condescend. Feasting in the temple was a badly judged decision. Soridian had interpreted Khall's expression of power as an insult.

"Tevu takes advantage of your respect," she said, passing the fighting pit. "How many times have you pushed against them using their sanctioned methods only for it to result in nothing? You bring your grievances to the emperor, whose decisions override your senate—it hasn't stopped them from robbing your lands and kidnapping your people. Their system protects them. Not you."

This was as close as she dared to tread about the godchild. Soridian was smart enough to know that she didn't use the word 'kidnap' lightly.

She pressed on. "Yes, we have some distasteful practices. But none of us are perfect, and I'd be bold enough to count Maetheria in that. And this is why we ask for your help. We march on Haksa in a month. It's a fortnight's hard ride from here. We need help fortifying the city when we take it."

"This 'we' thing again, Naias." Soridian pinched the bridge of his nose in frustration. "We've known each other a long time. It would be remiss of me not to say that the Ashvians will never accept you." He pointed to her forehead. "You have *that*, and it'll mark you forever."

What hurt the most was that Soridian cared. He spoke like he truly thought she'd made the wrong decision, pledging loyalty to a kingdom that had little respect for her. He deserved to know why.

She lowered her voice. "If we win Haksa, Khall gains a foothold in reestablishing the kingdom of Ashvi. I'm her adviser now, and soon I'll be a citizen, the first of many. I'll be able to make change. It'll take time, but I can stop the blood tithe."

Soridian came to a stop at the edge of the quarter. The horses grazed on the pastures beyond. "That is the most honest thing you've said to me all evening," he said. "Now tell me about this godchild."

He pointed in the distance. A masked initiate fed attap fruit to a horse.

Her heart leapt. He'd distracted her with all this philosophical talk, causing them to walk past the fighting pit. She'd planned to impress him with the Faceless, perhaps stop and watch the fight, and return to the feast when the raucousness died down. She didn't even know this was Viridian. She'd ordered Hammer to hide her. Why was she out here feeding horses in the open?

"A stable hand," she lied, "but let us get back to—"

"Please. That child is playing, not working. No instructor and no whip. Separated from the others and relegated to the edges of the quarter, so your invited guests wouldn't see them. Has Tevu's prophet queen named another godchild?"

Naias couldn't bluff her way through this. Soridian had a keen eye, and she'd have to find her lies in places that he hadn't observed himself. "No, Mohyri painted this one when she was with us. We kept the portrait and found the girl a year ago, in the mountains. She was quite ill. The Iskantis were all too happy to turn her over for some silver."

He narrowed his eyes. "Iskanti, is she?" He turned to the child, beckoning her over.

Naias raced to interrupt. This was all going horribly wrong. "Perhaps it's best you not disturb her—"

"You must have heard the news that Tevu took a child from us," he said, menacingly slow. "I would hate to think this rescue was linked to that." He broke into a wide smile as the godchild approached, as if he'd just shared an amusing joke. "Hello," he said.

Viridian butchered the Faceless bow. Instead of leaning forward, she stumbled, thrusting a leg backwards before she caught herself.

Naias held back a grimace. This was a disaster. If she stopped Soridian now, he'd become suspicious, but if she didn't, the godchild might reveal she was the one they'd taken from Tevu, who in turn had taken her from Maetheria.

She was trapped. Hammer had deliberately left her here, to make things harder.

I will kill her for this.

"What is your name?" Soridian asked.

"I have no name, Eminence," said Viridian, in a perfect Ashvian accent.

The envoy shook his head impatiently. "Let's not play games. I know you're a godchild, and you aren't part of the Faceless order. What is your name?"

Was Viridian panicking, as Naias was? Short breaths and a racing heart? The godchild's masked face told her nothing.

"I never had one, Eminence," Viridian said, her voice even. "I was a sick child, so the Iskantis never bothered. You can call me 'initiate,' if it pleases you."

"And which part of Iskantupu did you come from?" Soridian asked.

"Lhantujin."

"Ah, Nasuporena's people. And what is the color of Lhantujin's banners?"

The godchild fell silent. Naias didn't know the answer either. All the Iskanti clans blended into one; tradesmen were tradesmen, and their clan politics weren't her concern. Soridian, however, with his knowledge of traveling the continent as a Maetherian envoy, would certainly know. She had nothing to save this talk that was spiraling out of her control.

But Viridian spoke again.

"Purple and black, Eminence," she said evenly.

Soridian peered atop his glasses. "Well remembered. From a book you read somewhere, I suppose, since you also know a bow that's neither Ashvian nor Iskanti. The right foot back, that curtsy, that's a Maetherian bow."

Naias clenched her hands, trying to stop them from trembling. *Say it was a mistake. Say you learned it somewhere else. Say you stumbled. Say anything but Maetheria.*

The godchild spoke quickly. "I'm sorry if it looked like a bow, Eminence. I lost my balance midway. I was surprised to be called."

From the frown on Soridian's face, he didn't seem convinced. Naias had to salvage this. She ground her foot in the mud, preparing herself to slip and blame it on the drink. Soridian, ever the respectful diplomat, would have to escort her back to the feast, and they'd leave this cursed place forever. A crude exit, but her desperation didn't care for finesse.

But he suddenly burst into laughter. "Of course," he said. "Forgive an old man. Our bows get confused with falls far too often, yes."

Naias pressed her lips together, plastering the falsest smile on her face. If they ever made it back to the feast, she'd need more than a flask of wine.

But Soridian wasn't done. He spoke again. "If you'd be so kind, please take your mask off for me."

Viridian hesitated, her head turned towards her commander for approval.

Naias hooked her arm around his shoulders—casual, but firm—and steered him away from the pasture. "You've demanded enough for one night, Soridian. Listen to her voice. She's not Maetherian, nor the child you're looking for."

He shrugged her off. "Please indulge an old friend."

What else could she do? He'd honed their friendship into a weapon, backing her into a corner. Refusing would only make him suspicious. He was no friend at all.

She had no choice. Her arms dropped uselessly to her sides. She gave a curt nod, her heart sharpening with fear.

The godchild pulled off her mask. Coal-black curls covered her head. With her dark eyes and golden skin, she looked just like any Iskanti. She could pass, and if Naias couldn't see it, surely Soridian couldn't either.

The Maetherian envoy studied her face for a long time. Nothing. Not a quirk of an eyebrow, nor a gasp of realization. He didn't recognize her.

"I told you she wasn't Maetherian," Naias said with a smug smile.

He took his glasses off, carefully cleaning them with his sleeve. "One last question, godchild. This stifling, rainy weather in Xinquha agrees with you?"

Viridian looked down in silence, deliberating much longer than she had with the other questions. "I like it," she finally said. "When the sun sets on the river, everything shimmers in a prism of light."

He put his glasses back on, his steel gaze reflecting the fire blazing behind them. "Thank you for your time, little one. I hope the Ashvians treat you well."

Naias pushed him away, forcefully this time, towards the controlled table arrangements of the feast.

Soridian kept his hands behind his back, his head hanging in deep thought. "You said you intend to march on Haksa in a month," he finally said. "Maetheria doesn't have your speed. I have to convince the senate first, and who knows how long that'll take. Even then, our army walks most of the way. We've neither cavalry nor shock troops to meet yours."

"I'm not asking for that. Only your regular troop of longbows and archers, to assist in fortifying the fortress when we take it. As a deterrent to Tevu."

"And when our reinforcements inevitably leave, how will you keep control of the bay?"

"The same way we do at Xinquha," she said, waving a hand to the retreating shadow of Khallan's wall behind her. "The roads out of Haksa lead to Maetheria and the port of Pakaala, Tevu's territory. If you're our ally, we only need to defend ourselves from one direction."

"And what about the Iskanti clans to the west?"

"Tradesmen and raiders. The tradesmen leave us alone, and the raiders aren't a threat. We've all had skirmishes with them, your people included."

"So we'll meet you at Haksa, then?"

Naias blinked. The talks had nearly resulted in disaster, no thanks to Hammer's laziness, and yet here Soridian was, giving her what she wanted. "You're agreeing to the alliance?"

He ambled to a stop just before the ruined temple, looking up at Iskandraza's empty chest. Khall sat alone, while the remaining Maetherian escort danced for her entertainment.

It was a silly, florid jaunt with too many steps and too little passion, but that didn't bother the queen. She laughed and clapped her hands.

"We've known each other a few years now," Soridian said. "All alliances are based on some modicum of trust. I helped you get your power. In return, I hoped I could trust you."

"And you can," Naias said. "Of course I remember how you got us here. I owe you. I've told you about getting rid of the blood tithe. Khall herself doesn't know about this."

"She should, because the Ashvians aren't going to be happy when they hear that from you."

His persistent lack of confidence in her was aggravating. Naias flashed him a polite smile. "Don't worry, they will. Once I'm a citizen in the kingdom of Ashvi, I'll hold more power than them. I'm an adviser to their queen. They'll have to listen to me."

But Soridian's face fell, his downturned mouth mourning her bright future. "Perhaps I was wrong about you," he said softly. "You're much more Ashvian than I realized. You play with people to bend the world to your will, no different from how Khallan rationalized keeping the blood tithe because it might one day take down an empire. Do you think the end justifies the means?"

She bristled. He'd built her into some sort of emotionless manipulator. That was absolutely false. She was a *leader*, inspiring her queen to do the right thing, and leaders had to make difficult decisions. If she sobbed at every sick child and dead dog, nothing would get done.

Defending herself wasn't the right move. It'd make her look weak, sensitive. She had to respond with an attack of her own. "Soridian, all this philosophizing is precisely the reason why you haven't won your freedom from Tevu. You think it wise to consider everything before acting—strategically, logistically, morally—but it only makes you indecisive. Do what needs to be done."

He observed her for a long while, searching for something in her face. "Then I promise you this: I'll meet you at Haksa with our army. I must leave immediately and inform our senate, if we're to time this right."

Naias grinned so widely that she thought her lips might crack. Her little speech had spurred him into action. "Thank you. I owe you twice over."

But Soridian did not mirror that joy. "Take care of the company you keep, Naias. Khall and her father desecrate our common gods and have taken children from a defenseless people, molding them into tools for a battle they have no stake in. You are one of those people. You say you have the power to change it, but based on what I've seen tonight, I don't know if it'll change at all."

He nodded to Khall and sank into a curtsy. As he climbed back into his carriage, the look he gave Naias was one of immense sadness.

"I genuinely wish for your success," he said. "For the sake of our friendship, I hope your games were worth it."

11

Hammer

AFTER THE FESTIVITIES were done, Hammer, drowsy with ricewine, went to sleep. She lay straight on the bed-stove, like a dead person, while Viri curled in the corner. After a few weeks of jostling, they'd managed to find a comfortable enough position to share the bed. It wasn't perfect—Hammer still woke with the occasional stiff shoulder—but it was a better arrangement than sit-sleeping and making her whole body sore.

The curtain to her hut abruptly flung open.

An intruder.

Hammer jolted awake, her fist raised to strike. Viri stirred from the bed.

An angry voice pierced the darkness. "You sabotaged me."

Oh, it was her. The squawking parrot, the whiny mosquito, whatever you liked to call a nuisance that refused to leave. The leech that stuck to your ass. *Her.*

Hammer groaned and sank into the mattress, pushing Viri's head back into the pillow. "Go away."

Naias grabbed her shoulders, yanking her out of the bed, taking the furs along with them. Alcohol wafted from her every breath. Hammer wrestled against her grip, her elbow knocking against her weapon, sending it to the floor with a loud metallic *thunk*. Viri startled into wakefulness. As the commotion unfolded, she shrank against the wall, as if she wished to melt into it.

Naias could hurt her. Hammer's hut was so small, one swing of her arm could end up hitting Viri instead.

This wasn't the place to fight. Naias was going to get what she wanted, and Hammer needed to get this half-drunk parasite away from Viri as quickly as possible. She stopped struggling and climbed to her feet. Naias shoved her out of the hut.

Hammer flashed a smile at the godchild, more anger than glee. "I'll be fine," she said. "Go back to bed. I'll join you later."

Naias's grip stayed tight around her shoulders, pushing her to the heart of the quarter. The braziers had all burned out, the night closer to sunrise than not. Smokeless, dewy air filled her lungs, while crickets played their songs in the forested mountains around them. If she closed her eyes, she could forget she was ever here.

A big black hole loomed before her. The fighting pit, where she'd rescued Viri not so long ago. Naias wanted her in it, alone, so she could shout and scream and pelt shit on her without retaliation, but Hammer wasn't going to obey. She turned her leg, redirecting the force away, letting herself circle the pit instead.

Naias clenched her fists, stalking after her. "I have done *so much* to protect you, and all I ask is one small thing. One tiny, minuscule thing. Follow my orders. You can't even do that."

Hammer made a show of yawning. "I've had such a busy day, you might want to be more specific. Has the instructor complained about me punching his face in yet? That wasn't my fault, by the way, it was his. What else . . . Oh, right, I admit it, I stole some of the mutton." She hadn't. "Sorry if that ruined your plans for the envoy's dinner, or whatever it is you do."

Naias shoved her, much harder this time. She tumbled to the ground. Clouds of dust swirled in the air.

"Don't be obstinate," Naias said. "You knew to keep her away from Soridian. What do you think the disguise was for? What was she doing by herself, feeding our horses?"

Hammer picked herself up from the ground, taking extraordinary care to brush away each grain of sand that stuck to her arm. Truthfully, she had gone to get some ricewine. They'd rationed it out to the Faceless during the feast, presumably to show how generous Khall was to her enslaved soldiers, and she'd gone to collect her share. Rafaeis said his goodbyes after sunset and always came back the next morning. What he did in between was none of her business.

Besides, she'd sequestered Viri where she lived, at the very edge of the quarter. How was she supposed to know Naias would give a complete tour of the grounds? Who brought an envoy to marvel at a grazing pasture? *In the dark?*

If Naias wanted to accuse her of crimes she didn't commit, she was going to string out her frustration. She shrugged, pretending to be every bit as obtuse as the accusation laid against her. "I don't know," she said. "You told me to ambush the caravan, I ambushed it. You told me to take care of her. I took care of her. You told me to dye her hair and plant an Iskanti origin story. I did that. Now it turns out you wanted me to hide her. I can't keep up with all the shit you tell me."

"We got the alliance, and no thanks to you," she said. "I had to convince him she wasn't Maetherian."

"Is this what you woke me up for? Applause?" Hammer clapped her hands together, every beat as slow as possible, the sarcasm amplified in the silence of the night. "Congratulations, what a great achievement. Now let me go back to bed."

The scarred cerulean sun loomed in her face. "My friendship with Soridian has been damaged because of you," Naias said. "He saw through the godchild's disguise and accused me of manipulating people."

"He's not wrong," Hammer said, pushing past her.

Quick as a dart, Naias pressed her thumb in the hollow of Hammer's throat. "I'm trapped in the system as much as you are," she hissed. "At least between the both of us, I'm trying to make change. All you do is sit there and fuck things up for me."

Hammer coughed out a laugh. "All *you're* doing is making yourself look like a groveling fool in front of those that keep us here. You want change? Burn this place down. Kill everyone. Your lover queen too. Tevu had the right idea."

Naias bared her teeth. "Keep digging that hole of yours. Stay out of my way. Or I'll kill you."

There was a sadistic glee in seeing her like this, unable to bully Hammer into doing what she wanted. Hammer smirked. "I'd like to see you try, whore."

She'd gotten to her. Rage flooded Naias's face, and she pulled a dagger from her belt, drawing it across Hammer's neck. She was slow, too slow, made complacent from all the dining and chatter. Hammer took a step back, letting Naias swipe at air, and then turned towards the weapon racks, picking out the rapier from the lineup.

The noisy patter of footsteps approached behind her. She shook her head. For a person whose chosen weapon was a gun, Naias moved like a Tevurian soldier.

Hammer took a lazy swing in her direction. Naias hopped back, sheathing her dagger with one hand and pulling out her pistol with the other.

Oh, she was being serious.

Hammer dove to the side, the gunshot ringing in her ears. Naias never missed, but the drink made her sloppy.

Time to bring this fight to an end. She scrambled to her feet, closing the distance between them. Naias reached for her dagger, but Hammer slammed her shoulder into her stomach, hurling them both into the fighting pit.

They landed with a dull *splat*, the mud cushioning their fall. Hammer wrestled to thread her thighs around Naias's writhing body, locking her left arm in place.

"I think there's been a bit of a miscommunication," she said casually, picking the mud out of her fingernails, despite being covered in filth. If this woman was going to make her life difficult, she'd make her assault on Haksa as painful as possible in return. "You put Viri in my charge, so let's fully commit to that. I don't want you waking me up in the middle of the night complaining that I don't follow instructions. From now on, wherever I go, Viri will follow. Fair? When you send me off to Haksa, she'll be there with me."

Naias squirmed beneath her. "No," she said with a mouthful of mud. "Xinquha is safer, and the godchild will only slow us down—"

"No more than Clement will, and I assure you Khall's bringing him along."

"Clement is useful. She isn't—"

"Should've said yes." Little by little, Hammer pressed down, letting her weight rest on the back of Naias's extended elbow. Ligaments snapped beneath flesh.

Naias screamed. "Fine, fine! Let me go."

Hammer released her grip. "You chose the gun as your weapon because you've never won a brawl with me. Maybe you should stop drinking so much. It makes you really fucking stupid." She climbed out of the pit, scraping off as much mud as she could.

The whites of Naias's eyes glared at her from below.

12

Viri

I WAITED OUTSIDE Hammer's hut, my heart racing. Terror swallowed me and I couldn't think of anything else.

So much had happened at once. Dada had come to Xinquha and called to me in the pastures. I was startled to see him there and forgot I was supposed to bow the Faceless way. I didn't know why he was there or what he was doing. Did he come to find me, or was it an accident? All I knew was that he was alone, surrounded by the Faceless. I was a godchild. They'd dyed my hair and changed my accent because they'd wanted to hide me. Names had power here. If I'd named Dada, he would've been taken too.

So I played along. I said the things that they taught me to say. Except one. Dada didn't notice. He didn't even recognize me. I wasn't surprised, but it was all right. I had Hammer and Rafaeis. They'd stayed around longer than he had.

Until now.

Hammer was gone.

She'd left me, just like Dada had all those years ago. I'd never seen Papa cry as much as that day.

If someone took me away now, no one would notice. I wanted to stay inside and hide, but her hut was too small and I would be found instantly if they entered, yet the open darkness was too unknowable for me to run into. And so I hovered here, between the hut and the grazing pastures, clutching the curtain so hard that the leaves crumpled in my hands.

I heard Hammer before I saw her. Her bare feet squelched on the ground. She wasn't limping, and I didn't hear panting or groaning. But that didn't mean anything.

She came back.

I ran to her. My legs wobbled because they didn't want to work, but I forced them to move. She looked filthy, like she'd fallen into the mud. I grabbed one of her arms and wiped the muck off. She'd poked and prodded me when she rescued me from the whip, so I mimicked what I'd learned, even though I didn't know what I was looking for, except blood.

"Are you all right?" I asked. "Do you need bandages? Water?" I let go and hurried towards the line of buckets Hammer kept outside to collect the rain. I could barely lift one, water splashing onto my tunic as I hoisted it with my entire body.

Hammer chuckled behind me and took the bucket with a single hand. "Only to clean myself with," she said, and stripped off her dirty clothes. She picked up a pail woven from sugarcane, dipped it into the bucket, and poured water over her shoulders.

"I wish my body worked," I burst out angrily. "I could've done something."

Hammer stopped mid-bath, holding the empty pail over her head. "And what did you expect to do if your body did work?"

"I don't know, I could've fought—"

Hammer laughed. "Naias used to be a Faceless. She received the same training I did, while you've had none. Nothing would've changed if you fought her."

I didn't like that she laughed at me. "Or I could've screamed, or, or—"

"And you would've just scared the horses. Viri, I left the hut because she put you in danger. This was the best outcome. You and I aren't injured, and Naias . . . Well, let's just say she won't be waking us up in the middle of the night anymore."

Just because Hammer wasn't hurt didn't make it any better. "I hate it," I said through gritted teeth. "I couldn't do anything when Papa . . . when they took me from the university. I'm so useless. I should've fought. I should've stopped her from taking you away."

Hammer frowned and went quiet. She continued to clean herself, water trickling to the ground. I thought she agreed with me and was too polite to say it out loud.

I curled up by the hut, where I'd shredded Hammer's curtain. My hands and legs still shook. Naias had taken Hammer away, she had a gun strapped to her hip, she was going to take it out and shoot me and her and *she relived the bullets again, flashes of blue light instead of yellow flame, mechanical thunder cracking in succession, bang, bang, bang*

A gentle hand rested on my head, tilting my gaze up. A dried and dressed Hammer gave me something between a smile and a scowl, but she looked at me like Papa did before he said he loved me. I must've been imagining it. Hammer didn't even like me, much less love.

"Some people freeze, and some people fight," she said. "You freeze, I fight. Honestly, I fight too much for my own good. It gets me in trouble. Like tonight. You aren't a Faceless, don't ever wish to be like me. This life isn't for anyone. I was annoyed when I rescued you from that wagon, but I understand why you do it now. Your body doesn't work, because you're scared. I know, because I'm scared too. All the time."

I blinked. "All the time?"

"All the fucking time."

It was hard to imagine that Hammer could be scared, because she only had two moods to me: irritated and angry.

She carried me back into the hut and put me on the bedstove. "Fear is normal, Viri, don't get mad at yourself for reacting the way you do. It's who we are. Fighting because you're scared is a goatshit response anyway, and besides"—she pushed my head into the pillow we shared—"you're coming with me to Haksa, so don't worry. I'll protect you."

She settled into the bed, face to face with me, and hooked an arm around my back. "I don't trust you alone in my hut either," she muttered, drawing me close. "You're going to set fire to it while I'm away. I'll come back to a pile of ash."

"No, I won't," I said, an inkling of a smile returning to my face.

"Yes, you will. I feel it in my bones. Now shut up and go to sleep."

I took in four, maybe five breaths before her arm grew heavy. Her snoring overtook the crickets singing outside.

It didn't seem like she was scared. She fell asleep before I did, like this happened to her every day. But she'd admitted a weakness to me, that small crack in her stone armor. It's why she fought so much, and why she never stopped fighting. And then when she so casually said that I was going to go to Haksa with her . . .

A strange feeling stirred within me. It felt like my chest had grown three times its size, creating this space that I didn't know I had. A kind of warmth, a happiness. Hammer didn't need to do this, or say anything to calm me, but she did.

She didn't even pull the blankets up. She was that tired.

I wriggled a little out of her grasp, just far enough to pull the scraps of silk and felt over her body. After making sure her feet were properly tucked in, I gazed at her webbed face.

Black square, red diamond.

She'd kept her promise.

This feeling kept growing bigger and bigger. I didn't want to wake her and tell her this. She'd get grumpy. But it couldn't fit inside me. I wanted to give it to her, just as her words had given it to me.

With the lightest of touches, I softly pressed my lips on her mark, and kissed her.

13

Hammer

She pushed her rake across the grass, scooping up horse shit. The Faceless took it in turns to maintain the grazing pastures near Khallan's wall, but Hammer always liked this work, simply because she didn't have to talk to anyone. There was too much shit here, almost five hundred horses divided into herds, and the pastures ranged from Hammer's hut to the uncultivated steppes, ending at the steep mountains that blocked off Xinquha from the rest of the continent. If they left the manure alone, the grass would sour. The Ashvian rice farmers required fertilizer for their crops, and so it fell to the Faceless to provide it for them.

Thankfully no rain had come for the last two days, which meant no mud for her to sink into, no blisters on her heels, and no stink and rot that came with the humidity. If Rafaeis were here, he would've made some trite comment about "wonderful weather" and other sun-related nonsense. The man never stopped yabbering, and for some reason she laughed more whenever he was around. She was glad for his absence.

Viri had volunteered to help, but Hammer told her to go play with the horses. She pointed to her mare, the biggest horse in the corral, black and stout, grazing on her own. The other horses gathered in groups of twos and threes, and they gave this mare a wide berth.

"She reminds me of you," Viri teased.

Hammer tossed shit into a wide-brimmed pail. "I'll take that as a compliment."

"Can I ride her? I've ridden before. They taught me at home."

"Maetherians have ponies, not horses. You might as well ride a dog."

"Please?"

Her voice was quiet and sincere, like she'd never been given anything in her life and had no expectation of receiving it, but she still wanted to try. It got to her. Hammer couldn't turn her down.

Besides, they were marching on Haksa soon. That meant Viri was going to be trapped in another wagon for at least a fortnight, and Hammer didn't know if she'd be allowed out. Viri needed to enjoy the sun and stretch her legs one last time.

"Fine," Hammer grumbled, clicking her tongue to summon her mare. She tied the lead rope around the horse's mouth, fashioning some quick reins. Then Hammer crouched down, lifting Viri up by the waist, and mounted her on the horse bareback.

She handed Viri the reins. "No galloping, no running, don't agitate her. Stay where I can see you."

Viri smiled, blowing a lock of her dark hair out of her face. "Yes, Hammer."

Hammer returned to shit-scooping duty, but she could no longer enjoy herself. Instead of the calmness of quiet, repetitive work, she now had to track Viri out of the corner of her eye and make sure she didn't get hurt.

Your wounded bird.

She couldn't date this memory, except she'd already been a Faceless. A hawk had gotten tangled in one of the fishing nets. Somewhere, maybe Quctra, maybe here, she couldn't remember.

What she did remember was how another Faceless (Sword? Dagger? Didn't Khallan experiment with Krises once?) dove into the water, uniform and all, and pulled the net to shore. The bird beat against his protective embrace, beak snapping through the net, talons scratching his arms to bleeding, but he persisted, using his dagger (ah, yes, it was a Dagger) to cut the twine that twisted around its broken wings, strand by strand.

The fisherman whom the net belonged to didn't like it.

He hit Dagger repeatedly, until blood matted his hair, but still Dagger worked on dismantling that net. When violence didn't dissuade him, the fisherman ran to Khallan, complaining that his livelihood was ruined; he wanted compensation; he wanted retribution. Dagger was disciplined that day. Whipped a hundred times and all his scrips confiscated. He had to rely on the other initiates' generosity in sharing their rations with him.

Hammer didn't know why he went through all this trouble to rescue an animal who didn't give a fuck. This one good deed punished him thrice: by the bird, by the fisherman, by Khallan. She said as much by his bedside, as he lay on his stomach, his back more blood than skin.

"You're an idiot," she said.

He grinned, despite his pain. "When you find your wounded bird, you'll see."

She still thought he was an idiot. People formed stupid attachments with rescued things because they were small and vulnerable, but in the end, they were more trouble than they were worth. That was the most irritating thing about Viridian. Against all reason, she was Hammer's wounded bird—and she fucking hated birds—scooped up in the middle of the night from an iron wagon.

When Naias barged into her hut last night, her first thought had been to protect Viri. Not herself. This was what Dagger had meant when he said "you'll see." The bird was a stranger to him, yet he loved it so much that he did anything to save it, even if it hurt him.

She was glad that Viri was safe, but it exhausted her to keep an eye on her all the time. How on earth did mothers handle unruly children? Viri was far from that; she'd been quiet and curious, obeyed instruction—Hammer had lucked out with her, really—and yet danger happened at the least predictable of times.

She grumbled, flinging her collected shit into the pail with more force than usual, knocking the whole thing over. If the godchild hadn't been there, she would've kicked Naias straight in the stomach and laughed, and the ensuing fight would've ruined her hut. Worth it. She'd destroy her own hard work for a moment of spite.

But not now. Not with this child.

Viri played with the mare's black mane. She met Hammer's gaze and waved, seated against the whitest of cliffs, beaming on a rainless day.

she had a horse too, and iskandraza's sky loomed like a giant dome above her head

She saw herself in Viri.

When Khallan enslaved her into the Faceless, no one saved her. More than two decades had passed since then. She was beyond salvation, but here, she had the chance to stop that happening to another.

Besides, Viri's powers would amount to nothing. When the time came, Khall wouldn't notice if Hammer stole this child back from the wasteland.

All these unexpected feelings wedged themselves in her head and chest, a mixture of love and frustration, annoyance and warmth.

She was Hammer's wounded bird, and now Hammer was the idiot.

14
Viri

THE FACELESS BROUGHT only one supply wagon when we marched on Haksa. If Naias had had her way, we wouldn't have had one at all. Faceless didn't need supplies following them when they traveled. Hammer and Rafaeis had let me watch when they saddled their horses, three to a man, loading skins of ricewine and mare's cheese. Strings of dried lizards and mice hung across their saddlebags. When the Faceless rode, they swapped to a fresh horse every few hours, letting their other mounts gallop freely alongside them. We moved quickly along the road.

Well, they moved quickly. I was stuck behind in the supply wagon filled with Clement's and Khall's belongings, flanked by a handful of Faceless initiates.

I'd carved out a spot amongst the sacks of rice, sugar, furs of the softest wool, and a chest that smelled like the smoke in Clement's house. The wagon resembled more open cart than caravan. Goods and wooden poles were stacked atop one another, a mountain lashed together with thick felt, creating a makeshift cover for me. But whenever we stopped to rest for the night, they took the poles and felt, using them to pitch Clement's and Khall's tents. Only they got to have shelter. I didn't like sleeping outside. Flies buzzed in my ear and the mosquitoes stung me, making me itch all day.

Every bump in the road made a new part of my body sore. At least I wasn't bound. I could peek through the felt to see the night sky above.

But the dark and the quiet didn't change. The creaking wheels of the wagon sounded exactly the same. The horses huffed, pulling the wagon along the mud to Haksa. No one was here to distract me tonight. Hammer and Rafaeis were with the rest of the Faceless, and my thoughts inevitably wandered to—

books lay atop books in every corner of his office, but she liked the glass walls better, a kaleidoscope of people walking in a million different directions, left, right, upside down, until she realized she was alone, again, and threw a fit on the floor

My throat ached. I'd avoided thinking about him for so long. Of all the things to miss about him, it was this one. I'd tried to forget this memory, to think about the times when we weren't in the university, but it clung to me like a stain I couldn't wash away.

But weren't all memories, good and bad, part of me? Hammer told me to remember the bad ones too, but it hurt my chest to think about it. I curled up, burying my face in my knees.

The wagon floor shook. A Faceless peeked through the supplies. The mask's smiling lips cast a sharp shadow in the moonlight. If this were another time, maybe I would've been frightened to see it.

The face spoke in that same calming voice as when he rescued me from Tevu. "Remember me?"

I smiled. Papa disappeared from my mind. "Crescent." Rafaeis was a name only meant for us. It had no place here, on the overgrown road between Xinquha and Haksa.

"Clever girl," he said, slipping under the felt with me.

I leaped into his arms and gripped him tight. He smelled of stale sweat and shards of horsehair clung to his black uniform, but I didn't care.

He pulled me close, returning my hug. "I missed you too. We have to be quiet. I'm not supposed to be here. This journey hasn't scared you too much, I hope."

No, it hasn't, but the words didn't come out. It wasn't true.

I didn't cry. Crying was something a younger Viri would've done. She cried when Papa wouldn't let her play in the water. She cried when Papa told her to stay put in his office. She cried when his *bones cracked under flesh, the clear liquid that spurted out of his skull, she was crying, always crying, the tears blurring the last memory she had of him*

Crescent rubbed a gloved hand on my cheek. "It's been hard for you. I'm sorry I haven't seen you enough."

I wanted help. Every time I tried to run away from it, the memory always came back. Clement had shut me out, and from then on, I knew my struggle in finding my powers was going to be a lonely one, but Crescent and Hammer being here made it bearable. They'd made a promise to come back. I wanted him to know.

"Papa died protecting me," I blurted, giving words to the memory. "When they took me from the university, he fought until Tevu killed him."

He stroked my head. "It's our nature to remember difficult times more than the happier ones," he said. "He fought for you. That means he loved you."

I couldn't merge Papa's death with the warmth of his love. Everything changed when Tevu murdered him. A woman I didn't know had named me as a godchild and wrenched me from my home. It was impossible to think that anything good came of it.

"The Faceless aren't allowed to love," he said, sifting my hair through his fingers. "When we get captured, there isn't anyone who's willing to protect us. We die or get ransomed. And that loneliness turns people. They drown it in drink and blood. I see that they're doing it to you." His voice turned thick. "They're making you forget who you were."

"They won't," I said angrily. It was impossible to forget Papa, and Hammer, and him. Even Dada. "They won't make me forget."

"They'll try," he said. "You are young and pliant, as I was, when they pressed me into the Faceless. They've taken your name and dyed your hair, and when they stuff you with food and lash you enough, one day you'll prefer to sit instead of stand, to bend instead of fight. They'll give you the gifts they gave Clement, furs and jewels and everything you'd ever want, and then you'll sink into the sweet oblivion of sleep, forgetting all that made you. But it's *love*, Viri, love from those who fought for you, those who saved you, and the people who you'll save, no matter what your eventual powers are."

He had the same story as every Faceless: taken as a child, and shaped into a killer. He'd always been breezy and cheerful about his circumstances, which made me think he'd escaped punishment more times than Hammer, or he'd joined the order out of his own volition, but I was wrong.

Hammer had beaten love out of herself. He'd kept it.

My jaw tightened with determination. "I won't bend," I said. "I'll save you, and everyone else."

He shook his head. "I don't need saving. I know where I am. I help those who've been destroyed from within. Ones who feel nothing. I help them remember."

"Hammer," I said. I'd sensed it when they dyed my hair by the river, when he begged for her name and she didn't give it. The sarcasm that resurfaced when we got too serious, like she was afraid that showing how she truly felt would hurt her.

Crescent didn't nod or say I was right. His mask stared at me, plastered into an eternal smile. "Focus on yourself first, Viri," he said instead. "You're a godchild. You have a harder road than any of us. Prepare for the day when your powers amount to nothing in Khall's eyes. They'll separate us and take you away when we're distracted. We won't know what will become of you until it's too late."

The wagon lurched to a stop. Outside, people shouted from afar in a language I didn't recognize. Horses screamed. Steel clanged against steel. A force slammed against the wagon, throwing us into the chests of batik.

"A raid?" he muttered to himself. "I have to go. Hide yourself."

I held him close, longer than I should have. His ribs bumped against my cheek. "Don't die," I said.

"I won't."

He hopped out of the wagon, unsheathing his half-moon blades. I shrank behind the supplies, pulling the felt above me, and covered myself in darkness.

15

Hammer

BEHIND HER MASK, Hammer saw her own people, and in them, herself.

Iskantis on ibexes rode down the hills that flanked the road. The sheer cliffs were no obstacle for them, steering their mounts with only their legs, both hands drawing their bows. They loosed as one.

Faceless fell around her. Horses reared and bolted, trampling over their riders.

The Iskanti were mostly a loose network of matriarchal clans who preferred to trade than fight, but raids had become more common in the last few years. She'd had skirmishes with these raiders multiple times along the road to Xinquha, particularly when ambushing Tevu's trade caravans, but the last time she'd met a group as large as this was almost a decade ago. Tevu had tried to initiate them as mercenary units during Khallan's war.

'Tried.' They were undisciplined, slow to follow instruction, and fled when it pleased them. Tevu's strategy of fielding Iskanti fighters had ended in colossal failure. The line had broken almost immediately.

Perhaps their supply of Tevurian caravans had run dry, and they'd set their sights on a bigger target. Whoever had sold out this march to the Iskantis was not her problem. That was for

Naias and her precious queen to figure out. Hammer needed to defend the retinue.

Giant balls of fire—kindling smothered in tar—rolled down the hill, exploding as they crashed into the Faceless. Singed flesh tainted the night air. The balls left flaming trails in their wake, trampled over by the endless waves of Iskanti ibexmen that followed.

At the front of the line, the Iskantis had pulled Khall down from her horse. In contrast to the Faceless, who wore nothing but leather and black cloth, Khall had encased herself in her father's stolen Tevurian armor, interlocking links of mountain-shaped steel strapped to every part of her body. Her helmet—a carved figure of Ashvalra pulling up the earth—shielded all of her face.

None of this protected her. The Iskantis pulled her helmet off and pinned her down. One straddled her and raised his sword above her head. Khall shrieked in terror, her body fruitlessly struggling under the weight of man and armor both.

A pistol shot rang through the din of battle. Khall's executioner fell, slumping atop his victim.

Naias marched forward, nimble hands already reloading her smoking gun. In the distance between herself and the approaching Iskantis, she felled another two men. Her commander wasn't as agile or quiet anymore, but her aim was still excellent when she wasn't drunk.

The Faceless swarmed Khall, dragging her behind a crag. Clement had been hiding there too, and she scrambled behind him, armored gloves clamping down on his shoulders.

Naias barked her orders. "Scatter, scatter. Lure them into the mountains. Let them chase you."

"What are you doing?" Khall screamed. "Don't leave. Form a shield wall. Come back and protect me."

Naias ignored her. "Scatter." She cocked her pistol and fired, knocking an Iskanti off his mount.

"I nearly died," Khall continued to scream, *"I nearly died—"*

Hammer didn't stay to listen to the end of their bickering.

Naias was right. The only way to stop the Iskantis from harassing them was to spread out, so their volley of arrows and balls of fire didn't hit everyone at once. No matter how skilled the Faceless were, nothing could survive a barrage of arrows aimed in their direction.

She kicked her horse, galloping away from the bulk of their army. The remaining Faceless spread out into the forest for cover.

The Iskantis gave chase. A dozen men on ibexes galloped after her, their arrows nocked. Naias knew what she was doing when she ordered them to flee. She'd counted on the Iskantis' lack of experience and discipline, letting them believe that the Faceless' retreat meant their victory.

Hammer dismounted, weaving through the trees. Iskanti arrows whistled past her, hitting trunks and branches. She found a large tree and dove behind it. The darkness and her black uniform would conceal her.

The whistling stopped. Their supply of arrows had run out.

Her time to shine.

She jumped out of her hiding spot and sprinted back down the mountain. An Iskanti fumbled with his quiver, and she seized the opportunity, leaping up as high as she could and unleashing her weapon on his face.

Once the Iskanti raiders lost the advantage of distance, their melee skills were pitiful. That was how it'd gone during Khallan's war, and despite having had a whole decade to regroup, they'd learned nothing.

It was an easy slaughter. The fight turned. Gunshots rang through the air, thinning the worst of the arrow volleys. Axes and Swords dove towards the Iskantis who foolishly gave chase, slashing their knees to fell them.

A ball of fire blazed on the main road. The supply wagon had stalled, the horses that pulled it slaughtered. The Iskantis who hadn't given chase circled it, hoping to gain some quick loot before fleeing. A hundred men, maybe more. Hammer was good, but not that good. She couldn't kill them all by herself.

She should've continued to lure the Iskantis into the mountains.

That was the best way of defeating them. But if they lifted the covers and saw a girl hidden there, they'd take her, even if they didn't know who or what she was. Viri would be abducted, again, and fuck the gods if she'd allow it to happen on her watch.

She yanked an Iskanti off his ibex, stabbing him with her rapier, then grabbed his bow and loosed arrows at a dozen others whose backs had been turned to her. She mounted the beast, charging its enormous horns into the horde that swarmed the wagon.

A Faceless man stood before it, his hands holding bloodied crescent moon blades. Rafaeis. It had to be him. Corpses surrounded him, disappearing under the feet of the Iskanti men who rushed to take their places.

Her ibex stumbled, from being hit or tripped, she didn't know. She leaped off the mount, hammer in hand, smashing those under her. Iskantis in iron lamellar and furs blocked her way, each one wearing an armband of red and yellow.

Fear was a shit emotion, useless in its raw form. But when reshaped into anger, it infused a strength that all the physical training in the world couldn't give her.

Hammer swung wildly, her namesake in one hand and her unlatched rapier in another, cutting a path through to him. But whenever one fell, two more appeared.

She could hear him panting, every breath a gasp. He'd been here a while, single-handedly stemming the overwhelming tide of the Iskanti horde. He dodged to the side as an Iskanti swung at him.

Something screeched above. A hawk dove towards her face. She couldn't duck in time. Its talons scraped her mask, searching for purchase. Wings beat against her ears while a beak dug into her mask's eyeholes, lacerating her eyelids. It was trying to pluck out her eyes.

She dropped her rapier, grabbed the hawk, and tore it in two, flinging its carcass back into the Iskantis' faces. Rafaeis locked blades with another, but the tide of men surged forward.

One Faceless could not win against a hundred others.

A blade pierced his stomach. And another, and another.

Somewhere, a child screamed. Viri emerged from the shadows of the wagon, her hands scrabbling at Rafaeis's clothes, trying to drag him back in. His blood spilled readily, red staining the ground.

"*No,*" she and Viri screamed together—

—and the world stood still.

Her vision darkened. Her lungs went empty. She gagged, trying to gulp in air, but her throat wouldn't open. Her fingers and feet swelled up, tearing her skin open. Blisters bubbled on her tongue.

What is this?

Her muscles soured, withering under her own weight. She collapsed. Her swollen hands fumbled in the darkness for something to grab, and her fingers met dirt and stone.

I am going to die.

She was drowning and being dried out, her organs shrinking, body expanding. Her heart raced faster than she'd ever experienced. It would explode if she didn't get air, she needed to breathe, *she needed it right now*—

And then it stopped.

All at once, life returned.

Her throat made a wheezing, unfettered noise. She sucked in the cool air, desperate to fill her lungs again. The heat behind her mask was too much. She yanked it off. Hammer stumbled to her feet, retching up bile.

As the dark spots in her vision receded, the night sky faded into view, the mountains, the forest.

The black field of corpses.

The entire Iskanti horde that surrounded them had died. Bloodshot eyes bulged out of their sockets, their mouths foaming blood, their arms curled up into their bodies. The godchild stood alone amidst the massacre, her tiny body trembling in shock.

"Viri." In her name lay Hammer's question, but she wasn't sure she wanted to know the answer.

"I . . . I did this," Viri stammered. "This is my power."

16

Viri

THE SHADOWS MOVED again. Another wave of Iskanti raiders approached.

Even though she'd just thrown up and blood seeped out of her eyes, Hammer moved so quickly in those few moments. She gripped her hammer in one hand and her rapier in the other.

I stood frozen, staring at my hands. What did I do? It'd come so suddenly, and I'd nearly taken Hammer with it. She was clearly weakened, her back hunched, panting heavily, but still put herself between them and me.

She lunged with her sword, stabbing one through the throat, and then brought her hammer down, caving in the skull of another. Even in her state, she moved boldly, like a well-rehearsed dance. Her face betrayed nothing. No pain, no anger, no exhaustion.

Behind me, Rafaeis lay unconscious, blood seeping from his dozen wounds. His chest barely moved, his breaths so slight that he could pass for dead.

He couldn't die. Hammer couldn't die.

survive

Something cracked behind me. Hammer stepped around, swinging her weapon into the Iskanti's chest. Blood spurted in my face, but I didn't care. The wave approached. In front of me, behind me, everywhere. Hammer's back stayed pressed against mine, shielding me as best she could.

I couldn't do anything when Papa died. I could now.

I raised my hand. It was easy to summon this power, like throwing a rock tied to a string. I could fling it out a short distance, and when I wanted it to stop, I pulled the string and the rock came back.

The Iskantis before me collapsed all at once. Their ibexes fell too, their horns goring those who ran ahead of them. Everyone choked. Each eye looked in a different direction. Red foam bubbled from their mouths.

I couldn't pull the string back too quickly. If I did, they'd live.

One by one, they stopped twitching. A dead body didn't look any different than a sleeping one. They littered the road.

I didn't get all of them. It became clear that my power only affected those that I could see. I turned to my left, making sure Hammer was still pressed against my back. I raised my hand and threw the rock again. More men fell.

I didn't want to think about it. Rafaeis lay in a pool of blood. These men had run their swords through him. They were bad people. Without my help, Hammer would die too.

In the distance, the Iskantis shouted. The hawks circling the air returned to their outstretched arms. The wave coasted to a stop, right at the edge where the corpses lay. Where the darkness protected them from my sight. The limit of my power.

They turned their mounts, disappearing into the forest. Hammer didn't give chase. She hooked her leg across mine, still putting herself between me and the retreating men.

The galloping faded away. Smoke wafted from the extinguished fireballs. I could hear fighting in the distance. The main force ahead killed the remaining stragglers.

We'd won, and yet I wasn't smiling.

I couldn't look away. Hammer had already reacted, pressing

her hammer into my hands. My body dropped with the weight.

She rummaged through the partially burned wagon. She pulled out a batik robe, tore it into strips, and wrapped it around Rafaeis's body.

"We need to stop him from bleeding out," she said thickly. Her face and fingers were still swollen. "This'll buy him some time until we find Clement."

With a loud groan, she hoisted him in her arms, tilting his head to rest on her shoulder. I followed, dragging the hammer behind me.

"Don't tell anyone what just happened," she said. "Pretend you didn't use your power. This is a weapon of war, Viri. If Khall knows, you'll be hers for the rest of your life. Do you understand?"

I was still in a daze. So much had happened at once: the fight, the fires, my power showing, Rafaeis protecting me, nearly killing Hammer. Words were wind in that moment, and I didn't know what Hammer truly meant when she said I was a weapon of war.

I thought I'd seen war, in the twitching bodies of those that had died before me, in the corpses that trailed the road from Tevu to Xinquha, in the leaking brain of Papa as he bled out on the university floors. I thought I understood.

The words spilled out of me. "Yes, I do."

Gods, how I wish I'd listened.

17

Hammer

She ran up the road, searching for the crag where she'd last seen Naias and Khall. They couldn't have gotten far.

His body kept slipping. The blood drenching her arms made it difficult to carry him. She passed Faceless looting the remains of the Iskantis, while others coaxed their horses and fleeing mounts back from the forest. Hammer pushed past them.

At the head of the company sat Khall, sweating in her heavy armor. A small campfire had been lit before her as she rested, a skin of wine in her hand. She'd been crying, her eyelashes wet and cheeks flushed red. Clement stood beside her, his hands folded into his robes. He looked none the worse for wear, save for a glossy sheen that coated his face.

An Iskanti man knelt before Khall, his arms bound behind his back, but Hammer didn't care whom they'd captured or why. She crossed the threshold, heading straight for Clement.

Yet again, a cerulean sun blocked her way.

"What are you doing," Naias hissed. "You look like shit. Put your mask back on."

Rules, rules, rules. Every other complaint was about her mask or disobeying instructions. Yelling at her about the little unimportant things while Rafaeis was right there, bleeding out in her arms.

Hammer shoved past her and met Clement's alarmed gaze.

"Help him," she said, in a voice more desperate than she expected.

Clement smiled feebly, but he didn't move. They both knew who held the ultimate decision to heal Rafaeis, and it wasn't him.

Khall's rasping breaths filled the silence between them. She wiped her damp hair away with a shaky hand.

"He can wait," she said, every word trembling. "Don't ever interrupt my court again."

What court? There was no court. Just a terrified queen untrained in combat, sitting on a pitiful excuse for a throne, holding up the march so that she could calm her nerves. Fuck Khall, fuck Naias, fuck the Faceless and all their rules.

"He will die in the next hour," Hammer shouted. "Let Clement help him, please."

"*I* nearly died," Khall screamed. "Leave me!"

Rage flashed through her. She wasn't going to be callously dismissed like this, not when she had someone to save.

Naias approached, her bloodied dagger sheathed in her belt, her spent pistol holstered.

Hammer knelt, carefully setting Rafaeis's body down. They gave her no choice. If they refused her, then she'd take Naias hostage with her own dagger. She'd bargain for Rafaeis's life, and if Khall wanted her lover alive, she'd be forced to agree.

She pretended to scrape the blood off her arms. Out of the corner of her eye, the dagger flashed in the firelight. An easy reach. Hammer always won in close combat. Naias wouldn't have time to reload her gun. A little closer, and she'd be in range. Rafaeis couldn't die, not here, in the middle of nowhere—

Viri stepped between them.

No.

"Save him," Viri begged. "He risked his life to protect me when they attacked the wagon. I got my power. I killed everyone there."

The world slowed. No one moved, all stunned to silence.

Naias frowned, squatting down to meet Viri's gaze. "Godchild, you said you killed everyone?"

Instinctively, Hammer gripped Viri's arm, but keeping her close protected against nothing.

"Yes," Viri said. "Save him first, and I'll tell you everything."

Naias looked to their sovereign. "You need to allow this."

Khall trembled so much that Hammer couldn't tell if she was shaking or nodding. Naias forced this ambiguity into an agreement, beckoning Clement to come forward. "She has granted you permission—"

Clement didn't wait for her to finish. His leg-irons strained as he hurried to Rafaeis's unmoving body. He threw his rings on the ground and pressed his hands over the wet silk that bound his torso.

"I have to get the arteries first," he murmured. "He doesn't have long."

Hammer held her breath as red foam bubbled out of Rafaeis's chest. Clement's hands glided across his body like a musician plucking a zither, searching for every wound, from vein to muscle.

"Help me sit him up," he said. "He's bleeding inside. We need to drain the blood out of him before I can close him up."

It seemed like such a backwards notion to drain him out when he'd lost so much already, but Hammer wasn't going to pick a fight with the godchild of healing. She seized Rafaeis's arms, pulling him up. His back pressed against her body. Thick red liquid pooled under them.

"Let's just hope he has enough to survive," Clement said, running his hands over Rafaeis again. Beneath the ruined uniform, his skin knit back together, leaving behind a faint shade of pink.

With a sigh, Clement let go. "It's done."

After what seemed like an eternity, Rafaeis eased back to life, coughing up blood. Red sprayed out of the mouthpiece in his mask. Clement reached to remove it, but Rafaeis gripped his hands.

"Don't take my mask off," he rasped.

Clement frowned, but didn't press the matter. "Fine. But you need to rest."

She stared at his body. Bringing a man back from the brink of death should've been more theatrical, where the magically healed sprang to their feet and danced away. Clement's work resulted in a semi-naked man lying in a pool of blood, propped against a human chair, his clothes shredded to pieces and his mask still bafflingly intact. His chest heaved with every breath.

Hammer closed her eyes, her head falling back in relief. *Thank you, Strixahava, for clawing him back from the Destroyer's waiting hands.*

Naias tapped her foot. "Are we done? We have to move. The Iskantis know where we are. Take the prisoner, we'll find a place to make camp, and then we can figure out what to do with him." She pointedly looked to Viri. "Remember we fulfilled our promise to you. If you escape, I guarantee you Crescent will not see the light of day."

Viri nodded, a startled doe cowering before a hunter.

Hammer growled. Any threat against Viri was a threat against her. If she hadn't been supporting Rafaeis's body, she would've walked over to punch Naias in the face. How lucky that Viri had chosen to step between them. Hammer wouldn't have hesitated to take Naias's life in exchange for Rafaeis's. She knew in the deepest recesses of her heart, she genuinely would've killed her.

She frowned at the ferocity of her own thoughts. She didn't like Rafaeis that much.

Did she?

No, she was bitter. Bitter at Naias, at Khall, at the arbitrary rules that bound Clement and the Faceless. Bitter was manageable. Love wasn't.

Hammer scooped Rafaeis into her arms once again, nodding for Viri to follow. "I'm taking him to the wagon." She didn't bother waiting for Naias to say no.

Some of the supplies had burned in the fire, but the wheels

turned well enough. A pair of captured ibexes were yoked to the wagon, in place of the horses that died during the fight. Hammer laid him on the furs. His blood stained every surface he touched. She'd have to make it up to Clement later.

Viri hoisted herself into the wagon. "I'll take care of him," she said, but before the shadows claimed her, Hammer gripped her wrist.

She wasn't angry at Viri for revealing her power. How could she be? Hammer had spent her life doing the opposite of what Naias told her to do. But she saw the talons closing in, and she couldn't stop it.

Fuck it, she still tried.

"Don't tell them everything," she said. "Lie about what happened. Make your powers sound weaker than they are."

Viri patted her hand, gently twisting away. "It's all right. I promised them. His life for my help. They want Haksa, right? I'll help them take it."

A promise.

four horses fled and four people knelt, their necks on a wooden block, while a scarred man raised a greatsword above his head. a young hammer offered her frozen hands, standing in the cold iskantupu wasteland. take me instead, *she begged,* promise you'll let them go, *and he said yes and killed them anyway*

Her charge stood over that same cliff. Hammer wanted to claw her back, to shield and hide her, but Viri didn't want it. All Hammer could do was speak.

"Promises mean nothing when you aren't given a choice."

Viri took a long look at her and broke into a weak smile. "I want to try."

18

Naias

SHE ORDERED HER men off the road, making camp on top of a rocky hill. If the Iskantis were going to attack again, she'd see them coming. The Faceless fed on their reserves of ricewine and cheese, resting alongside their horses. The initiates unloaded the wagon, mounting the wooden poles that formed the foundations of Clement's and Khall's tents.

Naias hadn't planned on making camp tonight. She'd hoped to cover more distance than this, so Haksa had less time to prepare in the wake of their advance.

To make things worse, their numbers had shrunk. Out of the two hundred Faceless they'd brought with them, a handful were dead and another thirty injured. She'd sent them back to Xinquha. With careful planning, she could still take Haksa with a hundred and sixty-odd men and an untested godchild, but they had to move quicker than this.

She had no chance tonight. Khall had suffered her first exposure to battle, and the encounter had shaken her deeply. Naias hadn't helped by overriding her orders. Her queen was understandably upset and needed to recover, so making camp was the compromise.

But a leader couldn't rest, at least not fully. They still had to deal with the Iskanti prisoner and the godchild.

She had everything prepared. Once the tent was erected, she lit some candles and padded a stool with a thin blanket. The prisoner waited outside, bound and gagged, waiting to be summoned.

Khall sat in the corner, her entire body still trembling in the aftershock of the attack. Damp hair plastered across her face. Despite the fact that she was boiling in that case of steel and iron, she refused to take it off.

Naias forced a smile, tentatively placing her hand on Khall's. "Everything's fine. You're safe now."

Khall drew away. "You disobeyed me," she said. "I am the Earthly Sovereign. You follow my orders."

Perhaps she could try pushing back gently. Khall needed to understand that Naias had a lot more experience in battle, and she was her adviser for a reason. "I know, and I'm sorry. Forming a shield wall was a viable strategy too, but the arrow volleys would've killed more of us if we stayed together."

"I don't care. You're a Faceless. I am queen. You follow what I say."

"I'm not a Faceless anymore, I'm your adviser—"

"I NEARLY DIED," she screamed, "AND YOU DIDN'T CARE. I AM YOUR QUEEN!" She tried to get up in her armor, but she ended up collapsing on the floor, rocking back and forth like a petulant child.

Naias couldn't summon up the sympathy. She'd spent her whole life in battle and encountered many a close death, and she'd never lost her mind like this. She'd saved her only to be yelled at. It'd been a long, exhausting night, and she wanted nothing more than to sleep.

But she had to pretend, if she wanted to keep Khall's love.

Naias hoisted her to her feet. "This is your first time being attacked," she said, stripping her of her armor. "I know you're terrified. I was too when I fought my first battle. It's a harrowing experience, but you mustn't let it overwhelm you. Take a deep breath."

She pulled the breastplate off. Sweat soaked the tunic Khall wore underneath, a singular dark stain that spread across her armpits to her chest.

"There's no one here to kill you," Naias said. "The Iskantis aren't here anymore. Only we are. You're not injured, see? You're well, aren't you?"

Khall nodded, breathing heavily. The anger gave way. Tears filled her eyes for the second time that night.

She let her cry. Khall needed release, and the faster she calmed down, the easier Naias's job would become. She couldn't fight Tevu and her own queen at the same time.

"Being scared is normal," Naias said, taking a seat beside her. "But it's something you need to get used to. You decided to take Haksa. There will be many more battles to come. The Faceless may be a great fighting force, but we'll all be useless if you lose your nerve. We're together in this, darling."

Khall grabbed her close and crushed her lips against hers.

Naias stiffened. Both of them smelled foul, soaked in their own sweat. There was little trace of the summerbell perfume Khall had put on this morning, while Naias was caked in gunpowder and dried blood. She desperately needed a bath, but the Iskanti prisoner waited outside. Precious seconds ticked by, time that could be used for anything better than watching someone cry.

But she needed to mollify Khall, and if this kiss meant the queen would do what was asked of her, then Naias would do it. She gently pushed her tongue into Khall's parched mouth, pretending she wanted it all along.

"I love you," Khall said, her hand fumbling for her breast.

A normal reaction. The thrill and fear of battle needed a release. Naias found it in Hammer a long time ago, until she didn't. This was not the place for it. They'd survived a skirmish, not a battle, and there was still so much to do.

Naias gently plucked her hand away. "I promise we'll have time for that," she murmured, "but I need you to be queen for a moment. There's an Iskanti prisoner outside."

"I don't want to," she said, but she let Naias take her by the hand, leading her to the cushioned stool.

The Iskanti looked indifferent to being captured. He wore a yellow-and-red armband, his lamellar armor stripped from him. Blood dripped from a slash in his cheek.

"Your name," Naias said.

The prisoner said nothing. As befitting an Iskanti, he didn't understand Common.

This questioning was going to be hard. Naias hadn't spoken Iskanti since she was a child, and her vocabulary was limited to a handful of basic words. King Khallan had spoken some degree of the language; he'd had to if he wanted to enact the blood tithe as he scoured Iskantupu. He fed the nomads with lies, promising a better life for their children. They stupidly believed him, giving them up to the elite order he later called the Faceless.

He hadn't taught Iskanti to his daughter. Why learn the language of barbarians?

Naias tried. She needed information. *"Who sent you?"* she asked in Iskanti. The words came out all wrong in her Ashvian accent, losing all the intonations of their speech.

He scoffed at her attempt.

Khall shifted on her stool, biting her lip. She kept looking to Naias, waiting for comfort, the kiss, the reassurance that she knew what she was doing.

But this was no time to be gentle. If Khall wanted Haksa, she needed to be quick and decisive, especially when they were camped out in the open like this. Naias had to do all the work, and she wasn't even a full citizen of her kingdom. She marched up to the Iskanti, holding a dagger to his neck.

"Who sent you?" she hissed.

The man matched her gaze and grinned. "You."

THE PRISONER MUST have misheard.

"Liar," she said in Iskanti.

He shook his head. *"Blue sun, yellow circle. I remember."*

"What is he saying?" Khall asked.

Naias ignored her. *"Liar,"* she repeated again.

"You said to kill queen. On road to Haksa, on this day. *You wanted her dead. You promised she had fewer Faceless guarding her.*"

Khall paled, understanding the limited Common that they spoke. "You wanted me dead?"

Naias couldn't fight against two fronts. Khall was already deathly afraid of assassination; this would only heighten her paranoia. He would not manipulate her queen against her. "Khall, this man is our enemy. I'm being set up."

"By who?"

"Think." Naias's voice raised a fraction higher. This girl and her stupid questions. "If someone set me up, would they reveal their identity to me?" She marched up to the prisoner, tearing off his armband. She'd need someone to find out which clan he belonged to.

She groped through his clothing, searching for anything that might incriminate him. A necklace with a locket. A carved figurine of Iskandraza, presumably for luck. She tossed them away.

In the sole of his shoe lay a hard round object.

Aha.

The ghost of King Khallan's face stared back.

Dirt and time had dulled the silver coin, but Khallan's profile was clearly imprinted on its face. She'd looked up at those flared nostrils one too many times. These coins were a rare sight these days. When Khallan rebuilt Xinquha, he exhausted his reserves of silver to import food, fabrics, and wood from Maetheria and villages sympathetic to his cause. Fearing Tevurian retribution in doing business with a traitor, these places melted and reminted the silver in their image.

Naias waved the coin in his face. "Who gave this to you?"

"You," he said.

He wasn't going to give her any answers. Naias rolled the coin between her fingers. Someone had hoarded this silver for at least a decade. Evidently its material value meant nothing to its owner if they'd chosen not to melt and trade for it. A wealthy person, perhaps, but keeping it would only incriminate their sympathy to Khallan's struggle for liberation.

Only the most loyal would keep a coin like this. It was a reminder of Khallan's reign, and they were willing to part with it in an assassination deal. More importantly, they wanted to frame Naias in the process.

She knew just the men who would do such a thing.

"Jayal or Maka?" Naias asked the prisoner. "Which one told you to blame me for it?"

Nothing in his face showed any recognition of their names.

Khall broke in. "Jayal and Maka? What about them?"

"They did this," Naias said. "This coin belonged to them, I'm sure of it."

"What proof do you have?"

"The proof's right here," Naias snarled, her patience wearing thin. "No one carries these coins anymore. They're too dangerous to keep. They never stopped moaning about how their lives were better when your father was around. They hated me, remember? They plotted your assassination and framed me for it."

The Iskanti laughed. "No men. Only you. Naias. Gave silver for queen's head."

He knew her true name. Jayal or Maka must have given it to him, but this information sent Khall spiraling. Her breath hitched. "You said the Iskantis weren't going to attack, but they did. They nearly killed me, and then you told the Faceless to scatter, and you left me defenseless, telling them to ignore my orders, you lied to me, you planted this, you set *them* up because you wanted me dead, like how you killed my father and poisoned him—"

Naias snapped.

She gripped Khall and shook her. "Khallan died because the food was bad. We were all ill. He was unlucky and suffered worse than the rest of us. Why would I kill him? Think. I won Xinquha for him. I am here because of him. Why would I kill the very man who saved me?"

"I don't know," Khall said, instinctively shielding her face.

Naias's fingers dug deep into her shoulders. The anger she'd suppressed to placate this soft queen burst out of her. "I spend every night with you. Why would I go through the trouble of paying an Iskanti to assassinate you when I had the opportunity to do it myself, multiple times? Why did I accompany you on the road if I'd planned an ambush? Why didn't I leave before the attack, so I'd be out of danger?"

"I don't know, I don't know," Khall cried.

Naias shoved her off the stool, fury flooding her head. Now she understood why Khallan was so angry with his daughter all the time. "No, you don't know," she shouted. "You don't know anything besides crying. You're being hysterical, and you need to stop that *right now*."

Khall crouched into a ball and sobbed.

Naias pointed at the prisoner. "Order his execution. Kill him."

"Naias, why are you doing this—"

"Jayal and Maka rely on your mercy," she said. "If you let this man go, he'll ride back to his masters unharmed, and he'll inform them of our position."

"No," she said. "I don't want to."

"What you want has nothing to do with being a ruler. If you don't kill him, we're exposing ourselves to attack again. We'll never take Haksa at this rate." *I want my freedom and this Iskanti has to die for me to get it*.

Khall's reddened eyes peeked out from her disheveled hair.

"Do it," Naias shouted. "Be a queen."

She gave the smallest of nods, but that was enough. Naias drew her dagger and stalked towards the prisoner.

The Iskanti spat at her feet. *"Traitor scum. The blood tithe has blinded you. That dagger should be aimed for her."*

"Shut up," Naias said, and palmed the dagger between his ribs.

Khall, to her credit, did not scream. She might have been soft, but she'd seen Khallan do worse.

He fell face-first. She pushed his body out of the tent. A trail of blood followed. A good thing they hadn't brought any carpets with them. She swept the stains over with her boot.

She beckoned to the Faceless guarding the tent. "Bury him in the woods," she said. "Make sure the Iskantis can't find him. I also want an initiate sent back to Xinquha. Have the garrison put Jayal and Maka under house arrest. Bar them from having visitors, letters, or communication with anyone. Not a single hair will leave their homes, understand?"

When they left, dragging the corpse with them, Naias breathed a sigh. They were alone again. It was over, but there was nothing good about the work at all. She'd run herself hoarse from all the shouting, and the past few hours had sapped her of all her energy, emotionally and physically. She didn't want to share Khall's bed. The stars would be her companion tonight.

As she made to leave, Khall spoke from inside the tent.

"We still need to deal with the insubordinate Faceless."

Dread churned in her belly. Not this again. She'd hoped Khall had forgotten about the slight.

"Which one?" she asked, pretending ignorance.

"Black square, red diamond." Khall walked out. Her cheeks were wet and her body shook, but her stare remained hard. "A hundred lashes for her, tonight. See to it that she learns never to interrupt my court again."

Torture was a relic of Khallan's reign, and she didn't want Khall to walk down the same path. "You said you wanted to be a merciful ruler," she said.

"I did. I promised not to be my father. But someone died. I have blood on my hands now."

"That was different. The Iskanti needed to die so that we could be safe. This Faceless only interrupted you once, and she had someone to save. That's not worth your cruelty."

Khall burst into an incredulous laugh. "This isn't cruelty. This is discipline. The Faceless isn't going to die. What *you* forced me to do was cruel."

A hundred was too much. Naias still had the scars on her back to prove it, and so did the dozen Faceless whom she'd had to whip. She hated it, torturing her own.

"Thirty," she said, bargaining down the number. "Another of her order was dying. She was desperate."

"The Faceless will not interrupt me for anything. They attend me, not the other way around."

"Fifty. They are still my people."

"You're not a Faceless anymore, as you've constantly reminded me." Khall wiped her tears away. "A hundred lashes, and then get her to prepare testing the godchild. When we next make camp, I want to know everything about her powers."

Naias swallowed, the quick chain of orders snapping her into obedience. She'd upset her. She'd taken control and pushed too far, her influence too obvious. Khall was going to mend her fear by throwing her power around for a while, and when she calmed down, she'd realize Naias was protecting her all along.

But the unanswered question still burned. "Darling, you believe me, right? I didn't send the Iskantis to assassinate you."

Khall looked down at her own shuffling feet. "I believe you," she said, in a voice all too casual and friendly. The same voice that Naias used on Soridian, lying about her past.

Paranoia knew no logic. Khall was convinced her father had been killed, and it didn't help that she'd nearly died this night from an assassination attempt. Naias had to prove her innocence. She had to find Jayal or Maka and force a confession out of them. If she didn't, her freedom might as well have been a passing dream. In the meantime, she had to placate her queen and regain her trust until she found the true culprits.

She bowed. "I'll have the Faceless prepare the lashing for your viewing tomorrow morning."

Khall shook her head. "I didn't say another Faceless, and I didn't say tomorrow. I may not know a lot of things, as you say, Commander, but at least I know the importance of wording my orders. My father knew all too well the perils of vague bargains. You won't get that from me. You will deliver a hundred lashes to the Faceless with the black square and red diamond, tonight. Dismissed."

19

Hammer

A NEW GROUP of Faceless encircled the unloaded wagon, ostensibly to protect Viri. Naias's orders. Hammer refused to move from her position. The godchild was her charge and she would see her safe.

Well, she'd vowed to, at least. Now that Viri had turned out to be useful, her days as guardian were numbered. Khall and Naias would want full control over Viri's life, avoiding the pitfalls they'd had with Clement. They'd let him go too far with his requests. Viri would not be so lucky.

Viri's messy hair peeked out behind the sacks of rice. "Is Clement's tent up?" she asked, her voice weary. She hadn't slept since the attack.

"Yes," she said, pointing to the larger one of the two.

Viri turned to Rafaeis, whose body slumped across the wagon floor. She hoisted him by the waist, grunting under his weight, attempting to drag him out.

"Oh, Viri, what are you doing?" Hammer rushed to help. His masked head lolled onto her shoulder.

"Please put him inside," Viri said. "He can't sleep out here."

Hammer raised an eyebrow in Clement's direction. Through the raised flap of his tent, he sat on his chest of silks, quietly watching all that unfolded outside.

Clement tolerated no one—Ashvian, Faceless, or even Khall—in his quarters. Being the sole godchild in Xinquha, Clement had bargained his way into living alone. Viri didn't know that. Her tiny body continued to tug against Rafaeis's heavy and sweaty one, grunting against a weight that she couldn't carry on her own.

Clement's face scrunched in irritation, as if sympathy had accidentally leaked out in that shriveled heart of his.

"One night," he muttered.

Hammer pushed her luck. "And what about Viri? You can't possibly let a child sleep out in the cold too, after all that's happened."

His expression soured even further. "Fine."

She grinned. Guilt was a good look on him. Hammer gathered Rafaeis up in her arms and waltzed into his tent. She'd always wanted to take a closer look at his things.

The space was much smaller than Clement's regular dwellings, uncluttered by resplendent furniture and shiny trinkets. Nevertheless, he'd brought his pipe and a chest of opium with him. He'd been in the tent for barely a few minutes and it already reeked of smoke.

"Your poor lungs must be begging you to heal them, after sucking all that shit into your body." She laid Rafaeis on the rugs she'd bloodied earlier.

Clement chuckled. "You confuse me for Chatrasaya. She cleanses. Strixahava merely knits what is torn, and my lungs, unfortunately, are not torn."

She ripped off the makeshift silk tourniquet around Rafaeis. Blood had stained it so black that she couldn't tell its original color anymore. "Sorry about ruining your clothes," she said, wadding up the scraps. "And your carpet. My scrips for the next two months are yours."

He shook his head. "You owe me nothing. When people are dying, you do everything to keep them alive."

This was the first time Hammer had seen Clement sentimental. In Xinquha, he hid in his villa, only emerging when Khall needed him to heal someone. He didn't bother talking to the rest of the Faceless, only the godchildren they'd rescued. Eventually he'd pushed even them away. Hammer chalked it up to selfishness. That, or he was just a grumpy old fuck.

Apparently she was wrong. "You do care after all."

Clement studied Viri, whose hand stayed gentle on Rafaeis's chest. Her hand rose and fell with every breath.

"It's hard not to," he said softly, "if you're the only person who can help."

But he blinked, and the vulnerability ended. He waved his arms, driving Hammer out of the tent. "Out, out. When he wakes, you'll know."

"Wait." Viri chased after her.

Hammer made her way to the wagon, where she'd carved out her spot to rest. She'd recovered her horses, and her saddlebags lay with her hammer. She fished out a chunk of mare's cheese. "Get some sleep, Viri."

"I'm sorry." Her body sagged as she approached. "I'm sorry I hurt you. I didn't mean to."

Guilt only looked good on people she didn't like. Viri had never looked more fragile. Her distant gaze—all too familiar to Hammer—meant that she was not here; she was still in the skirmish, repeating the moment she'd used her power and brought Hammer down, along with the hundreds of other men that she'd choked to death. The night had taken a heavy toll on her. She'd killed for the first time. Hammer wanted to hug her, to take her pain and burn it, stamp on the ashes and burn it again.

She knelt down, placing a gentle hand on Viri's weary face, bringing her back. "You had reason," she said. "It was us or them. You chose us. We'd all be dead without you." She sat on her haunches, broke the cheese into two, and handed the larger half to Viri.

"My first kill was an accident," Hammer said. "Khallan was in Quctra, testing us in small fights against Tevu. I'd just gotten my mark. I was ten, a little younger than you. I didn't even know how to ride a horse, but they thrust me into battle anyway. I'd been waiting for hours, hidden in the wheat fields. Out of nowhere, a Faceless boy my age appeared in front of me. He scared me so badly that I swung my hammer at him." She threw up her hands. "And that was that. It was such a stupid kill.

"I thought that was the end of everything. When you first feel it, you think you can't come back from this. But tomorrow comes and you're still alive. It isn't the end. Time moves on. The sun rises for another day, and every day after that. Sometimes the mornings even look beautiful. It's a hilariously cruel joke, like the world's telling you what happened yesterday was all in your head."

Hammer wasn't sure if her words were meant to comfort. She simply spoke them, unfettered by sarcasm or mockery, exposing her own weakness. It felt like the right thing to do, after seeing Viri hurt so much.

What had this child done to her? She didn't like it, her rough edges sanded down by sentimentality. She was barbed for a reason.

Viri said nothing. She didn't expect her to, not this quickly.

She gently pushed her in the direction of the tent. "Get some rest. You've had a long day." *And longer still*. Viri had the power of gods now. She didn't know how to prepare her for that. All she did was hit things until they died, and this problem couldn't be solved by sheer force alone.

When Viri disappeared behind the felt, Hammer forced herself to sleep, leaning her head against the saddlebags.

"It's time," an annoying voice said.

Not this fucking mosquito again. She cracked open an eyelid.

Naias held a whip in her hands.

Hammer groaned. "This is the second time you've woken me. You really need to find some other form of entertainment when Khall can't give you what you want."

"I tried to get the number down."

"If the number isn't zero, you didn't try hard enough."

Naias picked at her mark in frustration. "For all your martial prowess, you are such a fool. Shouting at Khall and interrupting her? What did you expect was going to happen?"

"Oh, shut up, it could've been worse. I could've killed you. Or her. Queenkiller's a nice title, don't you think?"

"If you're not going to be serious with me, then I can't help you."

Hammer let out a bitter laugh. "I don't need help, least of all you." Naias never thought about aiding anyone, and if she did, it was so she could get ahead of everyone else.

"The godchild was more effective in bargaining for Crescent's life. You should do that, instead of"—Naias waved a dismissive hand—"whatever it is you're doing now. If you constantly push against this tide, we all drown."

"There is no 'we.' You want pawns that will get you your freedom, and Viri foolishly volunteered." Hammer turned to her side, the sight of Naias too irritating for her to tolerate. "How lucky that she made it easy for you. Now she'll be taken by Khall, prodded and pried to see which god her powers belong to, and have the rest of her life mapped out through the games kingdoms play. I hope destroying her life was worth it. Just because your mother fucked you over doesn't mean you need to do the same to others."

"I will not hear my family pass your lips again." Naias's voice was chilled, cold. "You fight against the Faceless, against me, thinking it'll change things. You're not. You're burning it all from within."

"Burning the Faceless down sounds better than kissing Khall's feet and praying she sees you as an equal."

Naias shoved Hammer onto her back, scowling. Her breath reeked of alcohol again, pungent and sick. "If we turn against Khall, Tevu retakes Xinquha. We're leaderless with marks on our heads. Where do we go? The Iskantis, who hate Tevurians and Ashvians alike and call us blood traitors? Or do we beg

Tevu for forgiveness and hope they cut off our tongues instead of our heads? Or Maetheria, who are such cowards in their own fight that they'd sell us out the moment we enter their lands? We don't belong anywhere. Only here. Khall's victory ensures our survival, and you're stupid if you can't see that."

Hammer forced a grin, pretending all she said didn't bother her. She was deeply aware of their entrapment—her tattooed face was proof of it—but Naias practically begged to be goaded into a fight. If the lash came regardless, she'd make this parasite suffer too.

But Naias stepped back, sucking in air. She buried her head in her hands. "Why are we always like this?"

Hammer wanted to shout in her face. *Don't you see? I loved you, I loved you so much it hurt to breathe, and you left me because Khall was your way out, and you told everyone you killed Pravaja, not me.*

"You wanted to survive," Hammer said instead. This was the kindest observation she'd ever grant her. "It was all about you. You take people and leave them behind when they're no longer useful. I, on the other hand, rescued one of my own and saved Viri. Helping others is a useful skill. You should try it sometime."

The regret vanished. Naias slapped the crop against her palm. "I tried to help you, and this is my thanks."

Hammer pointedly looked at the whip. "Thanks."

With gritted teeth, Naias grabbed her arm, hoisting her to her feet. "A hundred lashes. I'll be counting. When we're done, you'll need a fresh set of clothes."

20

Hammer

When Clement left his tent for morning prayer, she sneaked in. Viri was already gone, summoned into the care of Naias. Hammer kept her mask on. If anyone spotted her entering, at least she'd keep her anonymity. Rafaeis had to be awake by now.

Some part of her laughed for being worried about him, as if she actually did care about the fate of anyone besides herself. He was infuriating and stubborn, his temperament too cheerful for the life they led, but she liked him being around, despite all reason. She had to sand herself down for Viri, but Rafaeis . . . He fit around her, rough edges and all, never expecting her to be more than she was.

Naias, on the other hand, always resorted to power when she couldn't win, inflicting punishments Hammer couldn't escape from. Last night's lashing was yet another one of those episodes. Her commander left her back in tatters, whipping her until the pain sucked away all her strength to stay upright. Then she propped her back up, gagged her mouth to muffle her screaming, and the lashing continued.

Her back hurt a thousand different ways, and she'd managed to bandage herself with some clean barkcloth (trading half her monthly scrips for it annoyed her most about the whole affair), but she'd done a poor job of it. She could feel the exposed spots where she couldn't reach, watery fluids from her wounds seeping into her new clothes.

Rafaeis still lay on the rugs, but his uniform was fresh, the blood from his mask cleaned off, all a smooth shade of black. He was still asleep. His breaths came deep and long. Compared to the horrible wheezing he'd made last night, the quiet was a blessing.

Even though they had made camp for a few short hours, Clement had decorated his tent nevertheless. Little keepsakes peppered the room—an hourglass filled with sand, a glass pendant with a drop of liquid in it, an aquamarine stone encasing a tiny yellow butterfly.

"I'm fine," Rafaeis said behind her.

She jumped, knocking over the keepsakes. The sun had barely risen; he shouldn't have been up. She gave a curt nod and gathered up the trinkets, as if she were in the midst of packing up Clement's things.

"Not even a word from my savior, who crossed our queen to save my life?" he asked, mockingly hurt.

He was so quick, there was no point in pretending. She grumbled loudly, unmasking herself. "How did you know?"

"Not many people would risk entering Clement's tent to see how a mere Faceless was doing. And I remember who brought me here. Strixahava healed me of my wounds, not wiped my memory."

He sat up, pushing over a small bowl of hard sweets, colored a rich amber and dusted in sugar. Ginseng candy, a luxury in these times when every little bit of weight slowed them down, and even rarer here, given that the root only grew in the sunnier regions of Tevu.

"Clement's," he said. "He gave some to Viri and she shared them with me. Ginseng helps calm the body down, or activates it, depending on which story you hear. I suppose it does whatever you need it to do. I've had one, it's excellent. It's like an orgasm in your mouth."

Her expression soured. "I think that's called something else."

"Try it."

She picked out the smallest one, putting it on her tongue. The sugar dissolved almost instantly, a brief appetizer before the earthiness of the honeyed ginseng took over.

It didn't taste like an orgasm in her mouth.

"I'm surprised you remembered me," she said. "I thought you were unconscious for most of last night. Viri wanted to drag you into the tent on her own. She was so worried for you."

His shoulders slumped. "Where is she?"

"Taken by Naias. She's trying to figure out which god she belongs to. I have to go hunt foxes in the mountains for her test. Part of my punishment for interrupting the queen."

He heaved a deep sigh, all too aware of the burden of the godchild's power. "She told me about it. She said she nearly killed you."

"It left as quickly as it came. None of us expected it to happen. But that way of dying . . ." Hammer shivered. "It's like wringing out a wet rag. Everything inside you shrinks and squeezes. You can't breathe. You boil alive inside. It's a terrible feeling. We're warriors, you and I. When we hurt, we bruise and bleed. Our bones crack. Viri kills without bloodshed, but in that moment, I experienced more pain than any flesh wound."

Rafaeis's fingers brushed over hers, and she blinked back to attention. A gentle touch, the same way she used to bring Viri back.

"I'm sorry," she said. "You're the one who nearly died, not me."

His laugh was oddly joyous. "Ah, to soothe my frayed soul, I seek a piece of remedy."

"Which is?"

"You could tell me your name."

She swallowed her smile, reaching for another piece of

candy. She liked this, this odd poetry that they composed in tandem with each other. Unlike her constant fights with Naias, Rafaeis sparked a different kind of verbal sparring, one that she could match with words and wit and left her wanting more at the end. "It's good that you've recovered, so I can hit you again."

He feigned a flinch. "I didn't think hitting a little wounded rabbit was in your character."

"If you liken yourself to a rabbit, you are far more injured than I realized. Should I get Clement to heal you one more time?"

"And spoil our first date? I absolutely refuse."

She flicked the sweet at him. It bounced off his mask with a dull *thunk*. She'd let him flirt, but this was too close to the mark. She hadn't admitted anything to him, and she didn't plan to. "We are not on a date."

"Are we not?" he asked, leaning closer. "We're alone, under a tent that's bigger than the queen's, sharing a sweet whose worth is more than the entire wagon combined. It's an expensive meal, and yet all I ask is that my date reveal her name to me."

She veered to avoid him, but her back cracked open. A yelp escaped her lips. She'd reopened a wound, somewhere.

He grabbed her arm, pulling her back into a sitting position. "I heard you outside last night," he said, the playful lilt in his voice gone. "I'm sorry."

She shrugged. "It doesn't matter. Naias was going to hit me one way or another. She finds her excuses."

"Let me help. It's difficult to dress wounds on the back by yourself."

Hammer wanted to say no, but she saw the gratitude inherent in his sunken shoulders and upturned hands. The sarcasm died in her mouth. "You don't have to feel guilty," she said, pulling her uniform off. Crusted fluid tore against her skin. She pressed her lips together, holding in her pain. "A lashing in exchange for a life. I'd do it again."

"You're too rough," he said. "Let me."

With his long fingers and delicate touch, he peeled off her dressings. She gave him what was left of her barkcloth, and he wet the end of it with a wineskin, cleaning her wounds.

"I expected her to be kinder," Rafaeis murmured, pressing into a deep cut.

She allowed herself to hiss for this one. "I may have made her mad before we started."

"A thousand little rebellions and nothing to show for it." Rafaeis unfolded the rest of the bandage, pulling it around her back.

"I saved Viri's life and yours," she said, turning to him. "That's something, right?"

He'd taken his mask off.

She'd expected something jovial and round, perhaps an open mouth in constant laughter. But his long, chiseled face looked solemnly at her, all sharpened hazel eyes and black hair, with a day-old stubble that covered his chin.

Her breath caught. She recognized him.

"You're the Iskanti hawk-hunter," she said, her jaw agape. "The one who took me away from the market."

He had the gall to blush. "You do remember."

Heat rose in her own cheeks. She remembered how close he'd stood, his body a pillar of silent strength as he taught her confidence. How her hand nestled firmly in his and time froze, crystallizing a future where she didn't have to be alone.

This was all of Rafaeis. A flirter, a teacher, a Faceless.

An unmarked Faceless.

She gawked at his forehead. This was why she couldn't identify him at the market. All Faceless had the mark. "How—"

"A godchild that I met long ago, in an Iskanti caravan. I've hidden my face since. Blue lotus, green circle, if you were curious. It's still in the Faceless record books somewhere."

"Where's this godchild now?"

"I don't know. I was hoping to find them."

"You didn't go with them once your mark was erased?"

He shook his head. "Khallan's war made it impossible. Everything was chaotic then. I lost contact, and . . . Well, every Faceless that ventures out alone either comes back or dies."

Even without the mark, surviving alone on the continent was brutal. Anyone escaping left empty handed and penniless, resorting to robbing others, brawling, or begging in the streets for the rest of their life. At least the Faceless gave them rations and a roof above their heads.

"Still, I thought the Iskantis were my way out," he said, running a hand through his hair. "I sought the clans whenever I could, but because they hate and fear the blood tithe, the trade caravans rarely came, and when they did come, it was always a different clan. It took me years to gain their trust. I learned Iskanti, though I'm still not fluent in it. I studied how they played with their hawks, learned to greet them properly, to match their way of conversation, remembering their banners and their matriarchs. Then the time came. One of the trade caravans agreed to take me with them, for a distance. I'd hoped to continue my search for the godchild in Iskantupu. When you met me, I was about to leave."

His claim that night was true. He *was* preparing to escape. But he'd appeared in her hut the next evening, out of breath, and stayed.

She frowned. "Then all that talk about how you left someone behind and she didn't want to come . . ."

"That was you."

Oh.

He kissed her, taking quiet control, his body gently supportive as they explored each other, in rhythm and in breath. He still tasted of the candy they'd shared, the warmth and sweet mingling with her own.

His fingers glided down her back, achingly soft. The wounds stopped him from embracing her completely. Hammer rarely found time for regret, but in that moment she wished she hadn't taunted Naias last night.

Footsteps approached beyond the tent.

Rafaeis broke off the kiss. "There's not much time left," he murmured, reaching for his mask. "I can't let them see."

"Wait." She raised a hand to touch every corner of his face, to feel every wrinkle and bump under her fingertips, searing his features into her memory. *So little time to remember so many things.*

She was prepared for wounded birds, but not *love*.

"Elera," she blurted. "Elera's my name."

He smiled, his skin crimping under her hand. "Eh-leh-ra," he said, tasting the syllables. "A name to a face, finally I can die in peace."

In the flare of young love, she still managed to keep her head. "After all this effort to get you back? Your dying again is just offensive."

He breathed a laugh, touching her cheek in return. In parallel, they bared themselves to each other, in face and in name.

"Thank you, Elera," he said, "for saving my life."

21

Naias

By midmorning, they'd broken down the tents and continued their march. On Khall's orders, the Faceless surrounded her and Clement, forming a circular perimeter as she trotted down the road.

There was no room for Naias. She trailed behind the formation, her horse closer to the wagon than to Khall herself. The ghost of Khallan had manifested in more than a silver coin last night. Whenever an adviser had fallen from favor, he'd ordered them to sit in the furthest corner of his court. He'd kept them there for a week, and the adviser had had to crawl their way back, loudly begging forgiveness in front of the entire court. A petty show of power, a lesson that Khall absorbed.

Hooves struck muddy earth as an Ashvian page approached Naias. He skidded to a stop and saluted.

"A skeleton crew mans Haksa," he said. "What's left of their forces are housed inside the fortress. They come out and rough up the civilians when they get drunk, and then ignore the Haksanis' requests for justice. The Haksanis were very . . . spirited in their complaints."

While her queen licked her wounds from perceived slights, Naias had an invasion to plan. "What about the city gates surrounding Haksa?"

"The southern city wall is the most fortified, given that it faces Xinquha. A few Reborn are stationed on the western gatehouse, to wave in traders from Tevu, but the eastern wall—the one that lines the shore—is completely unguarded."

"And the fortress itself? There was a postern by the sea when we last took this place. Is it still there?"

"Yes. According to the fishermen, sampans still dock by the gate, but they haven't seen any guards."

Naias had suspected as much. The city surrounded the fortress, and the sea covered the rest. Tevu didn't care about a naval attack; they controlled the strait with their caravels, and the Faceless was purely a land army. If Naias intended to take Haksa, they'd have to scale the southern city walls, kill the Tevurians stationed there, cross the city itself, and then siege the fortress. A frontal attack would be suicide. They could sneak in via the postern, but it was an extremely small gate and designed for escape. It was no way to pass an army through.

The lack of options didn't daunt her. She had other plans.

"Thank you," she said, dismissing him. She'd have to tell Khall about this, as soon as she calmed down. The queen's steel armor glinted through a tiny opening in the mass of black uniforms.

I'm being left behind. It hurt that they'd argued like this. As time discarded her anger, the underpinnings of her love for Khall took over. She could've handled it better. In the heat of battle, when she was busy trying to control all the pieces on the board to survive, she'd lost her temper. The Faceless required an unsentimental, emotionless mask to survive, where anyone was expendable in the pursuit of victory.

But she wasn't a Faceless anymore. Khall had gotten caught in her frustration, a newly crowned queen who hadn't experienced any fighting, who was terrified she was going to die on a muddied road, hacked to death by some Iskanti raider. It didn't help that Naias had been implicated in the attempted assassination. Of course Khall was shaken. Other than yelling rhetorical questions at her, Naias hadn't done anything to make her believe otherwise.

"Naias?"

This was her fault. She'd made Khall upset. Never mind that it had hurt her chances of being granted her freedom, it'd hurt the person she cared for the most. She should've given herself over when Khall reached for her breast. If she'd placated her queen, Hammer's infraction would've been forgotten, and she wouldn't have had to lash anyone.

"Naias."

She groped for the coin in her pouch. If Jayal and Maka weren't in Xinquha, then the identity of the instigators was all but settled. Once they reached Haksa, she'd have to deal with them and win back Khall's trust again.

Something tugged on her leg. Naias blinked back to attention. She hadn't noticed they'd stopped. A girl clad in steel stood by her leg, dark eyes peeking through her helmet.

"Khall?" Naias asked.

The queen had dismounted at some point and bridged the distance between them on foot. She pulled off her helmet, her face contrite. "I'm sorry," she said. "I'm sorry for what I said last night. I didn't know how difficult it was for you. That fear I felt . . . You went through that every day when you fought for my father. It changes you. It changed me. I'm sorry I never knew."

Khall hadn't come as a queen—she could've simply summoned Naias—but had chosen to come to *her*, tugging on her leg like a page seeking her master's attention.

This wonderful, beautiful girl. Ignorance was her only crime, and she'd spent the night trying to empathize with Naias's life. She was learning, and wasn't that what Naias wanted?

"Oh, darling." She slid off her horse and cupped Khall's face, the only exposed bit of skin that she could find in her metal armor, savoring the brief warmth that emanated from her cheeks. She kissed her, genuinely this time, Khall's soft, plump lips pressed against hers.

"This is why I don't want to fight anymore," Naias said, burying her face in Khall's hair. "Battle turns me into someone I don't like, and I took it out on you. I'm sorry."

"I forgive you," Khall said.

Thank Ashvalra. The queen still loved her, and the Faceless remained a distant memory.

Naias bent to one knee, picking up the helmet. She kept her head down, presenting it to Khall with both hands. "My sovereign, I want you to know I never intend to disobey you. Every decision I make has you in it. I can't imagine a future without you."

She truly couldn't. If not for Khall choosing her to be her adviser and openly disregarding Khallan's old guard, Naias would've languished in the Faceless, as Hammer did, forced to cover her face and discard her name. Her position depended on Khall's survival, and she wasn't going to let that go.

Khall grasped her hands, holding the helmet with her. "You came from this," she said. "This life . . . this fear, it can't continue. I would've died if I lived like this every day."

"My father created the Faceless so he could retake his lands from Tevu." Her laugh came bitter and hard. "I didn't want to be like him, and yet here I am. There's so much work to do. You're right; I need to secure an heir. This attack has only brought to the fore how fleeting life is. But when that's done, my kingdom ends at Haksa. There won't be any need for the Faceless to live the way they do. I promise you I'll stop using the blood tithe. It took my father a lifetime to grow the Faceless, and it'll take another lifetime to dismantle it. But I'll try, for you."

Yes, that was who she wanted Khall to be. A queen who sought to do good, despite all the horrors she'd seen. It was a mistake forcing Khall to order the Iskanti raider's execution. Naias should've done it herself, surreptitiously, without having to stain the innocence of the woman she loved.

Naias brimmed with tears, her gratitude leaving kisses on Khall's hands. "You don't know how much that means to me."

Khall smiled, a beacon of light in the misty morning. "Haksa first, and then the future."

22

Elera

RAFAEIS RODE UP to her, crescent blades strapped to his thigh. "I'm ready," he said.

Summer touched not the mountains of Iskantupu. She flicked her mare's reins, riding off the main road, up into the undulating, snow-covered hills. Guarding against future plots, the Faceless had fanned out, scouting in all directions. They passed the basin that enveloped Xinquha, and climbed up north. The air turned cool and dry, a relief from the humid, rainy weather they'd suffered.

The snow lay a pristine white, untouched by man or animal. It was easier to hunt the foxes and hares here; their footprints gave them away. Wild hawks flew overhead, shadows in the sky, searching for prey.

She followed the birds, guiding her horse up a ridge. The midmorning sun reflected off the snow, glaring like the heart of a fire. She squinted into the distance. Far too bright, which made it even harder to see.

Rafaeis didn't harbor any difficulty in the light. He took out some dried meat from his saddlebags and clicked his tongue, signaling to a hawk that flew above them. After a few moments, the hawk dove, but as it approached Rafaeis's outstretched hand, it spread its wings to control its descent and elegantly pecked the meat out of his fingers.

"Do you know these birds?" Elera asked, utterly confused how a wild bird could react so sweetly.

"No," he said, letting the hawk perch on his arm. "But this one's old. See the brown tail? Juveniles have white patches on them. This bird probably belonged to an Iskanti once, so it's familiar with human company."

"Iskanti trained," she said, reaching for her hammer. "They taught these birds to peck the eyes out of their enemies."

Rafaeis shook his head. "You have quite a bit to learn about your own people." He fed the hawk again, humming a tune in Iskanti. The bird flicked its tail, twitching from side to side, as if it, too, were listening.

> *Sleep, child, and dull your mind*
> *Let bright-eyed time thicken to mud*
> *Sludge-slow, hail-frozen,*
> *Yet blue-fletched arrows draw warm blood*
> *Sleep, child, and strike your eyes*
> *From the crawling maggots in blackened guts*
> *The open corpses, icy hands bent*
> *The faceless king from the battlefield struts*
> *Sleep, child, and still your throat*
> *Before your mislaid zeal cries "war!"*
> *But should you dream of stubborn glory*
> *Gurgling death dimmed from the fore,*
> *Know a thousand before you swore the same*
> *And all forgot the truth of yore:*
> *On Mount Iska the Destroyer lies dead*
> *Our eternal vengeance is no more.*

Elera faintly recognized the song, forgotten notes from an old Iskanti lullaby, sung to her when her parents were still alive. The lyrics struck her differently now that she was older. Like all Iskantis, her family were nomadic shepherds. They didn't know how to fight when Khallan arrived. Passivity was her betrayer.

Until now. The Iskanti ambush had taken all by surprise. Their melee skills were still piss-poor, but they'd learned to arm themselves in the last decade of Khallan's war.

"Not spies, then," she said, trying to pull an answer out of him.

"Not everything's coming to kill you," he said with a laugh. He tossed her a bit of meat. "Try it."

She barely caught the meat with the tips of her fingers. "I can't feed a bird *and* ride."

"Remember what I taught you. Your arm is their perch. If you waver because you're afraid, they won't trust you either."

She held out her hand, keeping one eye shut. Hopefully the hawk preferred the meat in her hand to the eyeball in her skull.

Another brown-tailed hawk dove from above, an enormous flapping silhouette in the bright sunlight. Elera could barely see. She flinched, the twitch of her arms accidentally pulling her horse to a stop.

The hawk quickly pecked the meat out of her fingers and flew away.

"I've never seen such timidity from you in battle," Rafaeis teased.

"That's different," she said, checking her fingers for scratches. "Battle's about putting all your force into a swing and letting it connect with as many people as possible. I'm not beating hawks to death here, am I?"

"Is this why you have such trouble with Viri? It's either 'fuck off' or 'you're dead'?"

"Fuck off, and she's not dead."

They galloped along the ridge, the hawk holding steady on Rafaeis's extended arm. It stretched its wings, catching the wind as they rode, a perfect picture of the Iskanti nomad. She felt the tiniest twinge of jealousy. Birds were adorable when they weren't slicing you up. Rafaeis had the ability to coax that side out of them, while she attracted claws and beaks by merely existing.

"You handle the hawks like you've known them your entire

life," she said, "but you told me you only played with them when the Iskanti caravans came."

He laughed. "I'll take that as a compliment, but you've never seen an Iskanti hawk-hunter up close, have you?"

"Sure I have. When they're busy commanding their hawks to fucking kill me."

"Ah, but you've not seen the way the Iskantis care for and bond with them. You stayed by the trade caravan in Xinquha for a reason, and I suspect it's not that different from mine. We're not Ashvian, but we're not Iskanti either. I even less so. I don't know where I came from." He pointed to his hazel eyes, the only physical indication that he was not fully Iskanti. "The furthest I can remember was being an orphan in Quctra. I picked pockets and burgled homes to survive."

"So that's how you knew how to break the locks on Viri's wagon. Fucking thief."

"One unlucky day I picked the pocket of Khallan. He caught me, and that sealed my fate."

She shut her mouth, mortified. "I'm sorry."

He shrugged. "Old wounds. They hurt less as the years pass."

A ball of yellow fur wriggled in the snow. A steppe fox: their prey. Rafaeis flicked his arm, launching the bird into the air. The hawk tucked its wings and swooped down. A yelp, and both animals disappeared in a cloud of white. As the frenzy settled, the fox lay trapped, struggling under the hawk's talons. Rafaeis pried the fox out of the bird's grip, placing it in a cage.

They needed these animals alive for Viri to test her powers on. Using animals and insects was the way they tested the abilities of all the godchildren, but this time the fox would not be so lucky.

The wide blue sky touched the horizon's mountain peaks. No one followed them. They could easily slip away . . . and meet a quick death in the cold wilderness. Only the Iskantis knew this land, and she wasn't one.

The thought passed Rafaeis's head too. "If we found the

godchild that removed my mark and they removed yours, would you leave the Faceless with me?"

"My mark?" Elera laughed, unmasking herself, revealing the spiderweb of red lines on her face. "This mess here? How long did it take to get rid of yours?"

"Eighteen months."

"Two years?"

"No, I said eighteen—"

"Two fucking years. At that rate, mine will take a lifetime, if their power's limited like Clement's."

"That's not my question. Would you leave?"

She checked the cage, ensuring the fox was still alive. The idea seemed so far out of reach, and daring to think of it made her stomach churn. "I still have unfinished business with Engale. And Viri's here too."

"And if we could take Viri with us?"

She rose with a heavy sigh. If he insisted on wasting his energy dreaming of this path, then she'd fight him every step of the way. "Crescent, what you're asking for is impossible. Fine, let's assume that your godchild is still alive, let's assume they haven't been taken by Tevu or Maetheria or Lakhest and they still have their freedom. Can we possibly stay in contact for the five years or however long it takes to rid me of my mark? We're on our way to Haksa. Will Tevu retaliate? Will Khall expand her control to Quctra? Khallan did it, why wouldn't she? Who knows where we'll be in another fortnight.

"Breaking Viri out is the easy part. But where would we go? We can't survive in Iskantupu with just the three of us. And what if she wants to stay and fight for Khall? She's already promised to take Haksa for her. Are we going to kidnap her against her will, just like Tevu did to her?"

She paused, catching her breath, misty exhalations dissolving into the morning sky. The air was thinner up here. It had nothing to do with the encroaching dread of returning to the Faceless, their enslaved lives thrown away in pursuit of a queen fighting for her own freedom. A struggle that meant nothing to her.

Rafaeis approached her, snow crunching under his boots. The hawk moved to perch on his shoulder.

She edged away. He would only whisper dreams that would never come true. "You should've left," she burst out. "You were right. I can't leave. That opportunity passed me by years ago. I can't read or speak Iskanti. I only understand a smattering of it. Look at how terrible I am with birds. I'll never belong. I'll be in the Faceless forever, and the only thing that interests me now is killing Engale. Eventually we all break under the wheel."

"We don't have to," he said quietly, taking her hand.

His touch shouldn't have had such a deep effect on her, but she couldn't pull away. Elera looked down.

"I have," she said.

He brushed his thumb over her fingers. "I don't think so. If you had, you wouldn't be here, riding with me, humoring my amateur attempts at hawk-hunting. You'd be at the head of the company, smashing your way into Haksa. You have some humanity left, Elera, despite your attempt to be seen as some tough, cold-blooded soldier."

It'd been years since she'd heard anyone speak her name. Like a seed nourished by sunlight, a frisson of pleasure bloomed in her withered heart.

Fuck. She'd spent a lifetime chiseling herself into a statue of who she wanted to be, and he'd smashed it all to pieces with the mere mention of her name. "You think too idealistically," she said, salvaging whatever was left of her stoicism.

He laughed and gestured to the snow plains. "What do you see here?"

"What? Is this a trick question?"

"It's not a trick question."

It sounded like a trick question. She raised a hand, shielding her face from the sun. "I see a mountain range of snow. It's untouched, no footprints or campfires, so there aren't any Iskantis nearby. The morning and late afternoons give us an advantage, because the sun casts long shadows, and we can detect them before they come too close—"

"That's your problem," he said. "You're too cynical. You look at this place and see it as a battlefield."

"If you've forgotten, we just survived an Iskanti ambush, and we'll be fighting the Reborn in Haksa."

"I see white snow reflecting the light," he said, ignoring her, "and it makes this place glow brighter than the sun ever could on its own. It's beautiful, and there's no other place like it."

He fed another scrap of meat to the Iskanti hawk, letting it perch on his arm. He stroked its head, and the bird slowly, drowsily, closed its eyes, savoring his touch.

The jealousy flickered again. *Gods, I want joy like that.*

"The reason why these old hawks aren't Iskanti spies is because they let them go," he said. "After a decade of hunting with them, they feast on mutton as thanks, and then release them to the wild. It's a heartbreaking moment, I've heard, since they're given their hawk as a child, and letting it go is like losing a loved one forever. But there are some who cannot bear the thought of that loss, and keep their hawks with them. They become so afraid that they never let the hawk from their sight, chained to their arm with a leash. In time, their beloved birds wilt, until they no longer remember how to fly."

He flicked his arm and let the hawk go.

"You told Viri to remember," he said, "and I told her to love. She holds on to her past and to those who care for her, so that everything she does will be made with that memory. The Faceless might have chained you down, but you still remember what it's like to be free. You may call it idealism, but I call it hope. It makes this, all this, beautiful."

The cynic in her wanted to respond with a quip, to dismiss the blabber that there was a life beyond death and slaughter. But his words filled her with a longing that was deeply, deeply annoying.

Despite all her efforts, she, too, saw the snow that glowed, and the world shone a little brighter for her that day.

23

Viri

WE WERE CLOSE. As the sun set, the lighthouse of Haksa sputtered to life, a distant star in a sea of darkness.

Hammer and Rafaeis had left again. I didn't like being alone with my thoughts. The silence made me relive all that happened, Papa dying in the university, the beatings in the wagon, Crescent's gaping wounds.

Khall wanted to know more about my powers, and I wanted a distraction. I think that's why I forced myself to find companionship in her. I mistook her curiosity for affection.

She summoned me that night, coastal winds sweeping her hair off her bare shoulders, her skin glowing a bright red by the fire. An open book sat in her hand. Without the armor to hide her, she looked pretty.

"Godchild," she said.

"Viridian," I corrected her. I still didn't like being called 'godchild.' I was more than just my power. At the same time, calling me Viri was a kind of closeness she didn't yet deserve. Only Hammer and Rafaeis could call me that.

She smiled softly. "Viridian."

There was nothing menacing in her expression. Only warmth. She held my hand—gentle and snug—and led the way. If I could've forgotten everything that made Khall and seen her simply as she was in that moment, I would've liked her. In a different life, she could've been my older sister.

We walked into a small opening in the forest. Before me, a fox was leashed to a tree.

Khall stood beside me, skimming her book. "I would've much preferred to do this during the day, but—*ah!*"

The shadows flickered. I jumped when Naias stalked out, holding a torch.

She scared Khall too. Her hand tightened around mine. "Gods, Naias, don't frighten me like that."

Naias ignored her. "Testing her during the day is pointless. We'll be attacking Haksa at night, and I need to see the limits of her abilities."

I wasn't naive enough to think that my power stopped at a few raiders. More would die by my hands. Killing the Iskantis didn't feel like the slaughter in the university. It wasn't as stark. At night, blood didn't look like blood.

Would it have been different if I'd killed them in daylight? Would I remember their faces as they died? I remembered Papa's, and his scholar friends', as they lay dead on the floor. But the dozen or so Tevurians that they killed, while trying to protect me? I couldn't describe their faces to you. A red blur.

They were bad people. The Tevurians hurt me and Papa, and the Iskantis nearly killed Rafaeis and Hammer. These people were not worth remembering.

There would be more. I'd promised myself to Khall so that Rafaeis could live. I'd chosen this.

Khall rifled through her book, narrow Common letters squeezed into its pages. "You said that your power only affects what you see, godchild, is that correct?"

Viridian. I wasn't going to keep correcting the queen. If she insisted on calling me 'godchild' like Clement did, I couldn't change it. I nodded.

Naias planted the torch in the ground, foraging around the forest for palms, logs, and stones. She laid them in front of the fox, shielding it from my sight.

"Kill it," Naias said, pointing to the fox hidden behind the obstacle she'd created.

I looked at the palms and summoned my power. The rock and the string. I tossed it out.

When I'd killed the raiders, I hadn't noticed what the power did to my body. Too much was happening. But here, a gust of air filled my lungs, traveling to my head. I felt lightheaded, but I ignored it. If I dallied, I'd prolong the fox's suffering. I sucked in more air, and the light came with it. I glowed inside, like a little candle. It felt good. I hadn't known I held such emptiness within me.

The palms withered and the logs shrank. I'd killed the galangal sprouts in front of me as well, leaving behind a cone-like imprint of the reach of my power.

Through the receding leaves and branches, the fox appeared. The tree that the fox was leashed to shrank to half its original size. I sucked it all in, tasting musky rain and rosewood.

Red spots flooded my vision. I felt like I'd held in my breath for too long. I couldn't get the fox in time. Suddenly, my bottom hurt. In my dizziness, I'd fallen over.

Khall caught me, resting my head on her shoulder. "Do you hear voices?" she asked, flipping through the book with her other hand. "Someone that speaks to you, telling you to kill or do things?"

"No," I said.

She bobbed with excitement. "The power you wield is Diavijra's, the god of the void. Do you know her?"

she never wanted this, but it spilled out of her, every sorrow-infected neuron, every despair electrified

I knew of her, but not enough. I'd never bothered to read any of Papa's books. "I only know she and Ashvalra and Iskandraza made the world," I said.

"Yes, they're our three major gods. They created our world and all the lesser gods that came after them. Iskandraza is the Destroyer. He ended this world once. Diavijra, the Voidbringer, kept it empty for ten thousand years after that.

Ashvalra eventually retook the land from them, which resulted in the life you see today. She is rebirth. Iskandraza didn't like that, so he killed her."

The still-living fox whimpered and tugged against its leash. I wanted to let it go. "It doesn't feel very powerful if it can be blocked by leaves and stones."

"The godspower has been dying for centuries, and we don't know why," Khall said. "If anything, Maetheria should be giving us these answers. Engale and Pravaja are the only powerful ones we've seen in over a thousand years. Before them, the stories of the last godchild are more myth than truth. The books say she summoned a meteor to crash to earth, creating the basin that surrounds Xinquha. That sounds like Iskandraza, but in the same story, she made the ground fertile in the basin for all eternity. She couldn't be both Iskandraza and Ashvalra at the same time. I don't think she existed at all."

Naias skulked behind us, the torch barely illuminating the scratched-up mark on her forehead. She'd scared me twice—once when she pulled Hammer out of bed, and now this. I wanted to stay as far away from her as possible. I gripped Khall's hand. Between the two of them, she was prettier. Softer. Safer.

Khall smiled again, the same one, filled with kindness. "Find her some proper clothes," she said to Naias, gesturing to my black tunic and pants. "I don't want her looking like an Iskanti. And take that black dye off her hair. Bleach it and turn it white, like Diavijra's. I want everyone to know we have a powerful godchild of our own."

Naias's face went strangely still. "As you wish."

I didn't know why it bothered her, because I was the one getting the horrible-smelling paste in my hair again. But she'd frightened me badly, and if this made her upset, then I was all too glad to be the cause.

Khall helped me to my feet. "So you've seen her gift," she said. "What's the plan of attack?"

"If we take the fortress, the rest will fall," Naias said. "The Faceless will swim to the eastern city wall and scale it. We'll create a distraction in front of the fortress gates."

"And then?"

Naias turned to me. "And then it's up to you."

We walked back to camp. I expected some formal ceremony, some ritual that made me Khall's godchild. But Naias only cuffed my ankles in chains. The same binds that I'd seen on Clement.

Khall never stopped smiling.

24
Elera

NOT ANOTHER FUCKING infiltration mission.

Elera gripped the pole with both hands and plunged it into the water, propelling the sampan along the shore. Viri sat by her feet, dressed in black. Her chained ankles peeked out under her robe. Elera wanted to rip them off. She channeled that into rowing faster.

At least this wasn't completely Naias's fault. When she'd assigned the Faceless for Viri's escort, Elera had demanded that she be put on the team. If her charge was headed for danger, then she'd be the first to smash its face in.

Still, it was Naias's fault for coming up with the plan in the first place. Whatever happened to simply walking up and storming the building? With skill (and a Hammer) on their side, it was a straightforward and effective strategy. Naias complicated things too much.

Rafaeis sat on the other end of the boat, a small sack strapped to his back. He was in no shape to fight, but like her, he'd forced his way in. She didn't argue. In a game of persistence, he always won. Besides, he cared for Viri as much as she did.

Haksa's lighthouse loomed above them, its stone walls pockmarked from decades of salt erosion. Its weakened fires barely illuminated Elera's boat, but it still made her restless. She rowed harder. The quicker they returned to the shadows, the safer Viri would be.

"There," Rafaeis said, pointing to a small, dark opening in the cliff face, partially obscured by moss and algae. Empty sampans docked nearby. The postern, Haksa's exit, designed for a quick escape if the fortress fell.

The beating wave of the high tide muffled their approach. Rafaeis hopped off the boat first, padding up the algae-smothered stairs. Elera took her cloak off, soaked it in seawater, and pressed it into Viri's open hands. Naias hadn't bothered briefing Elera for this step, but then again, Naias wished she'd turn up dead most days.

An old gate blocked their passage at the top of the stairs, brittle and rusted. One good swing could bring it all down, but Rafaeis picked the lock with swift ease and ushered them through.

A pair of guards flanked the passageway. She unsheathed her rapier. Her hammer was too loud for the work.

They took them down in unison, then hugged the walls, heading down the corridor towards the lighthouse. Four guards stood watch in front of the tower.

Had this been a regular mission, Elera would've played with her food, finding ways to be cheeky with her kills, but Viri was with them, and her safety was paramount. Everything hinged on getting the godchild to the lighthouse.

She sped up, gripping a guard's mouth before he had a chance to shout for help. The rapier slid into his throat. The two guards behind them didn't have time to draw their weapons before her hammer connected with their faces. Rafaeis drew his blade, and all four guards slumped to the floor.

They worked well together. There was no planning the intricacies of battle and yet they moved in tandem, waltzing to music that only they could hear.

A long spiral staircase led straight to the top of the lighthouse. They could scale the walls or climb the stairs, but there was really only one option available to her. She climbed walls like a cow stuck on a cliff, and that skill was useful to no one.

Rafaeis removed the steel claw and length of rope that slung across his torso. "I think I'll take in the fresh air tonight," he said cheerfully.

What she heard was *I like you a lot, but not enough to climb those stairs with you.*

It drained her to even look at how much she had to climb. Elera groaned, hoisting Viri onto her back. She sheathed her rapier back into the hollow handle of her hammer and strapped it to her front. Water from the wet cloak seeped down her clothes. Great. More chafing. Even when it wasn't raining, she seemed perpetually doomed to erupt in blisters.

"You don't happen to have flying as one of your powers, do you?" she asked in desperation.

The godchild muffled a laugh. "Sorry."

She gripped the walls, taking the stairs three at a time, propelling herself up the tower. The occasional breeze from the tower windows provided some relief, and the air grew cooler as she ascended. Thankfully the roughened stone provided good purchase. Her muscles soured halfway, and every breath turned into a groan.

Rafaeis's masked smile greeted her when she opened the trapdoor, emerging at the top of the lighthouse. He looked none the worse for wear. "Had fun?"

"Fuck you," she wheezed.

The weakened lighthouse flame burned on a large pan, the bottom filled with ash and charcoal. Six pillars surrounded them, long mirrors mounted on each plane. Elera put Viri down, hiding her behind the southernmost pillar. Naias wanted them facing the fortress gates. Besides the small pinpricks of torchlight, the courtyard before the fortress was swathed in darkness.

"And now we wait," Rafaeis said, placing his carried sack beside him.

Elera sat atop the trapdoor. They were exposed, and their only exit was the path they'd taken to get up here. If the Tevurians were alerted, the three of them would have to jump into the sea. She peeked out. It was a far way down. She might as well fall onto stone from this height.

No room for failure. She closed her eyes and let the ocean breeze brush her face, sensing for the smallest change that signaled Engale's presence. It would be spectacular if she came to fight, and yet Elera couldn't rid herself of the worry that she had two people to protect tonight.

Two whole people. It wasn't so long ago that she'd insisted on being alone, and now she was minding the business of Diavijra-in-child-form and a Faceless without a mark on his head.

The thought didn't annoy her.

A swath of black shadows spread up the eastern wall. Every time the tide beat against the shore, the Faceless moved, the roaring waves muffling the sound of their approach. They hopped over the wall and disappeared into the darkness. They'd crossed the city gates without a fight, and now they needed to breach the fortress itself.

Bang.

It began.

Bang.

Elera saw nothing from her position. According to Naias's brief, the bulk of the Faceless company were to batter the fortress gates, Axes and Hammers leading the charge. She heard wood crunching under brute force. She hoped all was going according to plan.

Bells rang. The garrison sputtered to life. The weak lighthouse flame illuminated Tevurians in nightshirts and half-worn plates, stumbling out of their beds. Archers scurried along the ramparts with empty bows, screaming for arrows. Faceless Guns fired from behind the gate, blue sparks igniting the air.

No one noticed the three of them in the lighthouse.

Viri drew back her hood, her jaw tightening. "Tell me when to do it."

More Reborn flooded into the courtyard, nearly dissolving into shadow. The lighthouse flame didn't reach that far.

The archers found their arrows, loosing a volley. The Guns fired again, killing those on the ramparts.

Bang. The gate's hinges groaned under the weight. The Reborn pressed against each other, their weapons out in readiness. No more guards streamed from the corridors. The bulk of the garrison was here.

This was their moment. Elera unfolded the wet cloak and drew it over herself. She planted her hands on opposite pillars, shielding Viri from the lighthouse fire with her body.

"Crescent."

Rafaeis threw the sack into the blaze and ducked under the pan.

The fire exploded with an enormous bang, lighting the night in a cerulean blue. Coppersalt and gunpowder, elements the Guns used for their weapons, stuffed into a bag. Heat surged against Elera's back.

Bright blue flames shot out of the lighthouse, illuminating the furthest reaches of the city. Everything was exposed—including the Tevurians.

The Faceless immediately drew back, dropping behind the fortress walls.

"Now, Viri."

The godchild raised her hand, and an unholy sound screeched from the courtyard.

For all her experience in killing people, Elera still winced. She'd been within the reach of Viri's abilities before. Memories of the agony resurfaced, pricking her with gooseflesh. She pitied them. This was no way for a soldier to die.

The blue fire receded, flicking back into yellow flame. The screams faded away. Bodies covered the courtyard, armor glimmering in the dim light.

Her heart swam with unease. It was all but certain that

Khall would not let Viri go. The godchild held untold power, arguably stronger than Engale's one hurricane. Even Pravaja had had limits to bringing hail; all Elera had to do was run out of the area. Those two were thrown into battle the moment their powers manifested—aged nine, if she remembered correctly—and now Viri followed the same path.

She was going to be a killer for the rest of her life.

Child soldiers, all of them. Khallan had taken Elera from Iskantupu, executed her family, and pushed on her a life of bloodshed. One death became ten, ten became a hundred, a hundred became a thousand. Lives reduced to numbers. Viri deserved better.

Elera gritted her teeth. The responsibility for all these deaths should have fallen on her, a jaded, battle-worn warrior, rather than a twelve-year-old who'd never held a dagger. The gods had no reason to pick them young, but they didn't care about children, or death, or children causing death. They'd made this cruel and indifferent world, and created cruel and indifferent people to lead it.

In the silence, a small group of Faceless scaled the empty fortress walls and opened the gates from within. The rest of their company walked through.

They'd taken Haksa.

Elera grumbled. Fine. Naias was commander for a reason. The Faceless had hidden behind the stone walls, preventing them from being hit by Viri's power. Naias had limited Faceless casualties and created untold devastation to the Tevurians all in one blow. Elera was bitter, not blind.

All that was left was to kill the stragglers or take them prisoner. She wanted to fight. The bloodlust could make her forget her own helplessness. Maybe Engale was amongst their number, sleeping in a bed somewhere.

"Do you have her?" Elera asked Rafaeis.

"Yes, but Hammer, you shouldn't—"

Elera ran down the stairs and into the fortress corridors, killing the ones that stood their ground. These were Tevurian loyalists or stupidly brave, and they had no use for either. These men would fight until they died, and keeping them prisoner was a waste of resources. Years of desolation in Xinquha meant Khallan had learned how to shed dead weight, and he'd learned it quickly. This lesson had permeated into his daughter and the Faceless' code, down to the meager rations they carried with them.

Deserting was the wiser decision, but Elera didn't like capturing them either. Fleeing meant they had little loyalty to Tevu; they could've been forcibly pressed from any part of the empire. Naias saw them as a useful bargaining tool, drawing favors and coin for returning children back to their homelands.

Tools. That was all Naias cared about. She used people to play games with empires and kingdoms. The life of the person was less important than their value. To her, Viri didn't matter. Diavijra did.

Elera killed those that fled anyway. Better to die than be a tool of another kingdom.

As the Tevurians fell around her, she kept her gaze up, bracing for Engale's appearance. She had to come. Pravaja's killer was here, waiting for her lover to exact her revenge.

The night sky stayed clear.

25
Naias

THE BAY HAD seen better days.

Once the misty sun hit Haksa, its true state became clear to her. Four years had passed since Khallan's last stand here, with some of the bloodiest fighting Naias had ever experienced in her time as a Faceless.

Haksa was a key city for Khallan back when he'd fought to overthrow Tevurian might. He'd taken and retaken it from Tevu, but ten years ago he'd finally won it for good, conquering Quctra, Pakaala, Haksa, and Xinquha, restoring a fraction of his ancient kingdom of Ashvi.

But Tevu's prophet queen, Mohyri, had defected to Khallan. Tevu claimed she was abducted, but Naias wasn't sure. Either Khallan fell in love with her, or she seduced him, but their affection seemed real; their lovemaking was so loud they kept her up at night.

Mohyri's arrival signaled the beginning of the end. Perhaps Khallan grew complacent, or he underestimated how much Tevu wanted her, but Tevu crushed his kingdom, took Mohyri back, and forced him to retreat south to Haksa and Xinquha.

Naias had barely seen the city when she'd last fought here. She'd spent all her time on the parapets of the fortress, shooting dead hundreds of Tevurians. The Haksanis and their stone houses were specks, pawns on a map, and the Tevurians little steel dolls, knocked down with a squeeze of her finger. She reloaded her guns so much that the coppersalt stained her hands a bright blue.

In the end, they lost. Khallan retreated to Xinquha, directing his shame and anger towards his daughter. Tevu's bitter victory cost him hundreds of thousands of Reborn, but buoyed by the presence of Pravaja and Engale, he made one final, fatal advance on Xinquha. Naias never heard from Mohyri again, until now, when she'd decided to name Viridian.

Haksa hadn't fared well in the last four years either. Its city walls had been destroyed from multiple battles between the two warring kings, and in the ensuing years of fragile peace, Tevu hadn't sent enough money or men to properly rebuild it. A perpetual half-finished work, the gaps in the stone had been hastily filled with mud and straw to shore up the bay's defenses.

If the past was any indication, the Iskantis that settled in Haksa would've been charged with this backbreaking labor. They occupied the bottom rung of the social hierarchy here—even after Khall's attack, they still came out to work, transporting carts of fish, salt, and seaweed along the docks. Their wheelbarrows skirted around piles of Tevurian corpses.

Despite that, all the signs here were written in Iskanti script, including the directions within the fortress itself. Naias didn't read Iskanti and didn't remember the path to the throne room. The fortress was an asymmetrical structure; endless corridors decorated with stone seashells and strings of pearls. Wings didn't exist, and courtyards did not imply they'd wandered into a central area.

"The last time we came here, we got lost looking for it too," Khall muttered, resting on the base of an encrusted pillar. "What a terribly built place."

Faceless passed them, dragging stripped bodies. Naias didn't complain. Solid stone houses and paved roads lined the city, and the fortress itself stood intact. Compared to the leaking attap roofs in Xinquha, Haksa was a luxury.

She doggedly forged ahead. "Your ancestors built it. They must have had their reasons."

After a long search, she did find it—a room sequestered in the winding corridors on the second level of the fortress. Ocean motifs decorated the walls; pillars had been carved in the shapes of anchors and ropes, seaweed and netting. The throne itself was made of stone fished from the sea, pockmarked and rough.

A dozen Haksanis stood in the room, waiting for their arrival. They wore tailored robes dyed red, the color of Ashvi's banners. Obsidian jewelry clinked around their necks, wrists, and ears.

It begins. Naias suppressed a sigh. Now that the Ashvians were in charge, all the rich and powerful Haksanis would come to flatter and pay tribute, hoping to gain favor or forgiveness. This was a ritual as old as war itself, and she had to tolerate it until it was over.

A man and woman stepped forward. A Lakhesterian prosthetic foot peeked out from the man's robes. He bowed in the Ashvian way—a hand over the heart—while the woman clasped her hands together and bent slightly. The Haksani greeting. They'd come prepared not to offend.

"Our Earthly Sovereign," the man said, "I am Basaa, and my wife, Ayashara. Our group represents the merchants' association in Haksa." He gestured to his steel foot. "You don't know me, but my wife and I fought in Khallan's war."

For him or against him? A useless question to ask. Basaa could only answer one way, and they'd be no better informed for it.

"The kingdom of Ashvi thanks you for your service," Naias said instead.

Khall was still adjusting herself on the throne, her lip twisting as she sought to avoid the spots of coral and seashells that protruded from its corners.

Basaa's gaze flickered briefly to the queen. In his demeanor he understood who held the power here. "We oversee every ship that comes and goes from the port," he said to Naias. "We also employ the fishermen, the haulers, the dockworkers; we pay their wages, which allow them to heat their homes and feed their families. We hope their lives won't be affected by this . . . ah, incident."

Opportunists, all of them. If by some preposterous notion Maetheria invaded Haksa, these merchants would've said the same thing. Wealth was all they cared for.

"Rest assured that we don't intend on disrupting any of Haksa's business," Naias said, politeness bleeding through her teeth. "We're intent on keeping the city functioning as it was before. Nothing will change."

"That is a comfort to hear," Ayashara cut in without a smile. "Haksa tires of war. As a gesture of our goodwill, we ought to let you know that a Tevurian caravel has dropped anchor out at sea. They seek to come ashore." Her voice was clipped and sharp, a hint of the musical Iskanti intonation sliding through her careful Ashvian accent.

Khall's voice rose in panic. "What? Why? Are they trying to kill me?"

"They hold the black flag of safe passage," Basaa said.

"No, I don't want them here at all. Tell them to leave."

Since the Iskanti attack, Khall perceived everything as an assassination plot. Naias forced a smile at the couple. "Thank you for the information. Please leave us a moment."

Basaa bowed. "Of course. I look forward to serving you."

As the merchants shuffled from the room, Naias murmured in Khall's ear. "Tevu has never violated the flag of safe passage before, and they won't start now. You should grant them an audience. Don't you want to know what they have to say?"

Khall gripped Naias's arm. "Could you stay out here and make sure I'm safe? Don't lurk in the shadows like you did with Engale."

The girl was still scared and she needed comfort. Naias held in her annoyance and kissed the top of her head. "I wouldn't leave your side for anything," she said, and she meant it.

"If we're seeing them"—Khall pulled at her dirtied barkcloth tunic—"can you get my jewelry box from the wagon? I need to look presentable."

Naias thinned her lips at the order. She wasn't a page boy.

Khall didn't notice. "And get the Faceless to stand outside the throne room," she said. "I want Tevu to see how disciplined they are. Get a feast ready."

Feasting their enemies? No, this went too far. "They'll be here in a few moments," Naias said, "and we don't know what they want. This isn't a good idea."

"I want to show them we're doing well. Roast something."

Naias clenched her fists in frustration. "Khall, we've just taken Haksa. We've been surviving on mare's milk and dried meat. We don't have food to feast with. It's going to take a few hours to hunt for game, not to mention skinning and cleaning it—"

"Then it should've been done a few hours ago," Khall said, an impatient edge lining her voice. "I don't want to be laughed at again. I need to look and behave like a queen. Isn't that what you wanted?"

Naias didn't want to risk upsetting her again, but it was impossible to create what she wanted in such a short amount of time. "We'll get some wine and sweets from Clement," she said, looking to appease her with a compromise.

"You told me he's going to want something in return," Khall grumbled.

"That's how bargaining works."

"No, there's no *bargaining*," Khall said, her temper flaring. "Clement needs to remember that he works for *me*. I feed him, bathe him, clothe him, listen to all his ridiculous demands, and all I get in return is a pitiful power that allows him to heal—not resurrect, not cleanse, because that's just too good for us—to heal, one person a day, and I have to tiptoe around his literally god-given schedule in the hopes that I am not fatally wounded twice in the same day, or worse, poisoned."

Naias's retorts rose like a cresting wave. Khallan's death

still haunted the queen, and the Iskanti raid had intensified it. She had no idea how lucky she was to have Strixahava—however weak—on their side, or a battalion of Faceless that was unceasingly loyal to her, or even *Naias*, the person who'd helped her take Haksa. She received no gratitude or thanks. Instead, she'd been relegated to fetching jewelry and food like a common servant.

She bit down. She would not lose control again.

"I'll get the sweets," Naias said, stalking out of the room.

CLEMENT HAD DEMANDED the highest room in the fortress, overlooking the sea. He'd somehow managed to delegate some Faceless into moving his chests and belongings into the room. A waste of their time. They had more important tasks to do.

"Get the stables in order," she said, dismissing them. "The horses need watering. Godchild, I need a flask of wine and your ginseng sweets. Khall's orders. I suppose her jewelry box is stashed somewhere here as well."

Clement pulled his lips into a smile, a gesture born more out of deference than true joy. "And what will Khall give me in return?"

Her gaze trailed to the bloodstained carpets that covered his floor. "What did Hammer give you for bleeding all over your silks?"

"Oh, many things."

Naias drew in an audible, frustrated breath. If she had to keep pressing him for answers, this was going to be a painful conversation. "Which are?"

"That's between me and her."

"I outrank you. I demand to know."

Clement chuckled. "That line may work on the page boys, but it won't work on me. Besides, you're Khall's right hand. What you offer exceeds anything a Faceless can give me."

I'm a Faceless too. Everyone won't stop reminding me. The Tevurian envoy was going to arrive any minute. Naias would keep running in circles if she argued. She threw her hands up. "Fine, when we're settled, I'll send someone to find a Lakhesterian diamond. You've talked about that for months."

Clement cocked an eyebrow. "Tempting, but no. Expending all that effort sneaking through Tevurian lands to get to Lakhest, all because you wanted some wine and sweets? I'm not a monster. We'll save the diamonds for another, fairer deal."

"Then stop wasting my time," she spat. "What do you want?"

He shook his foot. The chains that bound him slapped against the floor. "My leg hurts dragging this around."

She burst out laughing. The audacity. "No. That's not good enough."

"What's 'good enough'? Nearly dying during that Iskanti attack because I couldn't run? All of you scattered. You left me with Khall, and she hid behind *me*."

"That scattering protected you," Naias said. "Neither you nor Khall were hurt."

"And what happens when none of you are around? When things go to ruin, I want to die on my own terms, and not with a chain around my leg. I've not given you any reason to doubt me. After all, I've kept my word to *you*."

She darted to smother his mouth. Black lipstick smeared on her palm. "We're not talking about that right now. I've paid that debt a thousand times over."

"Now it's a thousand and one." He pulled her wrist away. "I've never had cause to ask you for this. I thought Khall was happy in Xinquha. *I* was happy in Xinquha. But if the child queen insists on repeating the mistakes of her father, then I want a way out."

Everyone tried to push her around, playing their stupid little games, all oblivious to the end goal. She shoved him against the wall, her face pressed dangerously close to his. "It's in your best interest to keep this regime alive," she hissed. "If Khall's dead, Tevu will reclaim this land. I'll remind you that they have a godchild of their own, whose powers are far superior than those of a man who can only heal one person a day. All the batik you wear, the wine you drink, the carpets that decorate your room, you think Tevu's going to provide that? You're *nothing* compared to Engale."

The polite serenity in Clement's face disappeared for a fraction of a second, but the mask returned as quickly as it left.

"I agree," he said breezily. "So that's why giving me the key to my chains shouldn't be a problem."

This request was worse than crossing Tevurian lands. A diamond was a solid, material thing, one that she could hand over and call her deal complete. A promise that he wouldn't leave, fulfilled on his whim? "If you flee—"

"Which I won't, as you've so kindly put it to me—"

"I will personally hunt you down and break both your legs. You'll never walk again."

"A fair punishment. I like my legs very much." He retrieved a small woven bag and a flask with a leather strap. A small box lay in his other hand, white pearl flowers inlaid in the teakwood cover. Khall's jewelry box.

He dangled the items in front of her. "Do we have a deal?"

A key for his silence. She'd made one mistake, and it cost her for the rest of her life.

She tossed the key onto the carpet, snatched the items, and marched away.

She draped the necklace around Khall. It was an unassuming trinket, a chain holding a single small Lakhesterian diamond, the gem settling in the dip between her collarbones. A gift from her father, back when the kingdom of Ashvi had encompassed more than one city. Naias had told her not to bother with luxury, as speed was of the utmost importance. Clearly she had not been listened to.

Khall practiced sitting. A hand on a knee, crossing and

uncrossing her legs. Feeble attempts at intimidation, the equivalent of a small dog yapping at a much larger enemy.

A Faceless entered the room. "Our Earthly Sovereign," he said, "Sahru Mohyri-Tevu, son of Emperor Tevu Rusari-Tevu, supreme prince of the Tevurian Empire, heir to the Tevurian throne and the northern kingdoms."

Naias stiffened. They'd expected an envoy, not one of royal blood. In the years during Khallan's war, she'd only seen the crown prince once, when he'd attempted—and failed—to negotiate his mother's release back to Tevu. She'd pitied what little she'd seen of him at the time: a jovial man whose goodwill was rapidly sapped by Khallan's hostility, eventually turning hostile himself. He'd been so earnest in getting his mother back that he'd suffered the humiliation of waiting in Khallan's court for three hours before the sovereign had deigned to show up.

"Now, now, Sahru is just fine." The prince swanned into the room, his unadorned blue cotton robes trailing behind him. Freckles and moles dotted his round face, bearing all the sun of Quctra and none of the horrors of war. A trail of gemstones glittered along his brow, his graying hair swept behind him. He looked about forty. Two Reborn stood behind him, in crunching heavy armor, holding a formidable chest between them.

"How are you both?" he asked, his arms open wide. "Khall, how you've grown. When was the last time I saw you . . . maybe eight, nine years ago, when we had that terrible business in Quctra? You were so quiet and shy back then, and look at you now. A queen."

Khall refused to stand, another lesson she'd learned from her father. She'd passively insulted Sahru by withholding a normal show of respect, but the prince didn't seem to notice. He picked up an overturned wooden chair and sat on it.

"And you, Faceless—"

Her lip curled. "Naias."

"I'm sorry?"

"My name is Naias."

He broke into a practiced smile. "Of course. I do not mean to offend. Naias. Once a Faceless, now an adviser. Congratulations."

Naias didn't like that he'd called her Faceless on sight, without bothering to ask for her name. She'd respond with an insult of her own.

"It's good to see you well. How is your mother?" She didn't care about Mohyri's well-being, but she wanted to remind Sahru of his broken family, particularly his mother's infidelity.

Sahru wasn't fazed by the implication. His persistent smile gave nothing away. "She is as well as can be, since the news of Khallan's death. I'm sorry to hear of his passing."

He'd given her no information. Was his mother happy, angry, grieving? Her true feelings stayed ambiguous. Sahru had won this little contest of words, and she didn't like it.

"You arrived quicker than I expected," Sahru continued. "My Reborn rowed themselves exhausted to get here. I suppose your Faceless wouldn't have flagged."

Naias stole a glance out the window. If the prince had surged ahead, he was alone.

"Yes, Faceless," Sahru said. "I have no military escort. I'm here to negotiate terms. Our second attempt in four months."

She clenched her jaw. *My name is Naias.*

"A second attempt?" Khall masked her nervousness with a sneer. "There wasn't even a first."

Naias wasn't sure if she liked this version of Khall. She'd advised her to behave more confidently since their meeting with Engale; instead Khall was drawing on her father's cruelty, using intimidation and condescension as a petty show of power.

He sighed heavily. "I agree our parley with Engale went poorly. My mistake. She didn't come back to report. I had to find out through the Reborn. Apparently she's off in Iskantupu somewhere, for reasons known only to her."

"A poor show of your influence, then," Khall said, "if you can't even summon your servant back."

Sahru chuckled, taking the slight in good humor. "You have a godchild of your own. You know how hard it is to corral them. We can't make them do anything they don't want to do, otherwise we get no use out of them at all. So we let her have her fun. Eventually she'll come back. They all do."

They come back. They all do. A phrase Naias had used countless times, to Hammer, to the Faceless, to herself when she gave up. Khall's kingdom was no better than Tevu's, but that was the way of the world. If she wasn't the one stepping on others, she was the one being stepped on. Who ruled didn't matter. At least she could advance in Khall's kingdom. She'd have to withstand the hypocrisy until she could make change.

"Apparently you have problems leashing your godchildren," Khall said with a smirk. "Unlike you, Strixahava is happy to stay with us."

"Ah, but does the same apply to the Maetherian girl?" He leaned out of his chair, looking around the throne room. "Does she know how the Ashvians treat those who aren't like them, that they tattoo children across the forehead and lash them for the slightest error—"

"What do you want," Khall snapped, her charade of intimidation quickly falling away.

He settled back into his seat, intertwining his fingers. "Better terms. Haksa is yours, and so is Xinquha. The lands that connect the two cities are yours as well. We'll recognize your kingdom of Ashvi."

"And in return?"

"In return, you give the godchild back."

"No," Naias said immediately. "I'm not returning a child to an empire that chained and beat her."

"Not to me. To Maetheria."

Khall was the first to balk. "But you took her from Maetheria in the first place."

The prince heaved a sigh. "My father made a mistake taking the godchild, doubly so by spilling blood in the hallowed glass halls of their university. Now Maetheria's resentment has escalated into open rebellion. I want to return her."

Ah. Naias steeled her face into neutrality. Tevu couldn't afford another uprising within their empire. The northern part of Tevu was fragmenting, buoyed by Lakhest's claim to independence a decade ago. The mountains of Iskantupu bordered the west and southwest, while Maetheria and Ashvi encompassed Tevu's southeastern border. They couldn't fight multiple fronts at once.

She leaned against the throne. *Let's see how the prince spins this in his favor.*

Sahru stood up, gesturing to the fortress. "Queen Khall, you know very well the burden of carrying your father's legacy. You took Haksa because of a memory of a kingdom. I, too, am encumbered by the weight of history. I will be frank: I'm trying to hold my father's empire together while he tears apart his life's work with his bare hands. My mother deeply regrets naming the godchild, and I mean to correct that."

There was trouble in paradise after all. Naias thought Mohyri had ended her six-year silence because she'd reconciled with her husband, but Sahru implied her naming was involuntary. Maybe the prophet queen still harbored a flame for Khallan. Gods, Tevu *and* Khallan, two cruel and terrible men. She had exceedingly poor taste.

Sahru continued to speak. "If peace means placating Maetheria and giving up Haksa, I'm happy to do it. We have no use for this port. The docks of Pakaala suit our needs just fine, and the seas are large enough for the both of us. Return the godchild to us and Maetheria will never know of your involvement . . . and your reluctance to return her."

Naias caught the bargain. He'd given them worse terms than Engale. This was blackmail. If Maetheria learned that Khall had abducted the godchild, their friendship would shatter. They might even ally themselves with Tevu and turn on her. She only hoped Soridian was already on his way, so that the news wouldn't reach him.

Regardless, Viridian was too precious to give up. Haksa and Xinquha held a fraction of her value. The histories mentioned an ancient time when Ashvi was the empire, not Tevu. If Khall wished, she could reestablish her control over the continent, one that her father only dreamed of and never achieved.

Her queen was naive, but the godchild's potential was so nakedly apparent that everyone could see it. Khall's answer came as no surprise.

"No. Why should I give you anything? You came to *me*. Truthfully, I'm surprised that this is not an unconditional surrender. We've taken Haksa from your disintegrating empire, and you think you're in a position to take Diavijra from us?"

Naias clamped down on Khall's shoulder, but it was too late. *Shit. Now they know her name.*

"I see," the prince said quietly. "Is that what she is?"

Belatedly Khall realized her slip. She covered her mouth with her hands.

Sahru turned to open the chest behind him. "I suppose we are at an impasse. Since you don't wish to negotiate, I'll convey to you my father's message."

He pulled out his gift, throwing it at Khall's feet. An unnamed head rolled from side to side, his short black hair caked in blood and dirt.

Khall yelped in surprise, and Naias put herself between them. "How dare you threaten us with this filth."

Sahru wiped his hands on his robes. "I don't want this either. The Ashvians living in the empire are my people too. But that's my father's message. We'll retake Haksa and we'll destroy you doing it. Maetheria will know about what you've done. I'd hoped that we could avoid all this, but I suppose if I were in your shoes, I, too, would not dream of giving up Diavijra."

For all his regret and sympathy, the Tevurian prince was still carrying out the wishes of his tyrant father. His remorse meant nothing.

"This isn't a negotiation," Naias said. "It's a threat, and yet another example of why no one wants to be part of your empire any longer. Khallan fought long and hard for our freedom. I do not intend to see us fall back into the arms of our gaoler."

He only shrugged. "I tried."

The chest closed with a bang, and Sahru left the room. The wine and sweets lay untouched. Naias picked up the head and threw it out the window.

Khall's voice barely made an echo. "Take him and bleed him slowly," she hissed through clenched teeth. "Separate his body into a thousand pieces. Send them back to his father, one at a time. Put his head on a spike in front of the bay, and then burn his ship down. That's what my father would've done."

Naias ignored the order. Khall was lashing out in fear, ignorant of the consequences. "He has a right to safe passage—"

"I do not care about rights. Tevu slaughters innocent Ashvians—*my people*—to get me to leave Haksa. Kill him."

Naias's temper flared. The Faceless were Khall's people too, but she never showed this much rage when they died for her. She'd taken the city only to withstand Khall's casual condescension, and she'd signed herself to Clement for wine and sweets that hadn't been touched, on orders that she knew were useless. Khall was acting like a petulant child again.

She would not lose control.

"Forget the prince," she said evenly. "We need to salvage our relationship with Maetheria."

"I am queen—"

Those three cursed words.

Naias lunged forward, gripping Khall by her wrists. "You are upset and irrational," she said, baring her teeth. "I'm angry that he's killed one of us as well, but there is nothing we can do about it. We need to focus. Do you understand?"

Khall trembled as Naias loomed over her. The remnants of the Iskanti attack still lingered, and the prisoner had implicated Naias in their foiled assassination plot. Until she found Jayal and Maka, Khall would never fully trust her again.

She let go. The imprints she left on Khall's wrists splotched red. "We need to sow confusion. Send a letter to Maetheria and tell them what Tevu says is false. When Soridian arrives, we'll pretend nothing's changed and hope the news hasn't reached him. Can you manage that without crying?"

Khall curled into a fetal position, massaging her wrists. She mutely nodded.

"Good." Naias stalked out of the room. Now that Haksa was theirs, she needed to clear her name once and for all.

26

Naias

A SMALL CHAMBER lay adjacent to the throne room. She could fit a table and chair in it, leaving just enough space to squeeze through the door. Naias knew this waiting room all too well. During the war she'd stood in this very spot, half deaf from gunfire, her caked hands smearing the walls with coppersalt, until Khallan had barked at her to report.

She hated the small, cramped space, but she had to stay here. Its proximity to the throne meant that she could overhear any judgments Khall would make in her absence. She couldn't sit on the throne itself, but she'd sit as close as she was allowed to.

An initiate entered the room and bowed. "Reporting on Jayal and Maka."

"Speak."

"They're missing. From the state of their homes, they've been gone awhile."

It had to be them. Jayal and Maka had attempted to assassinate Khall and stage a coup. Now that they'd failed, they'd fled before Naias could retaliate.

No matter. She smiled to herself. Part of the thrill came from the chase. Finally she could justify shooting them in the heads for all the groveling they'd put her through.

"Thank you," she said. "Bring the godchild's guardians to me. Black square, red diamond, and blue lotus, green circle."

The Faceless had looted the dead Reborn that guarded the fortress, and from the pile of goods Naias had picked out a small box of shells and conchs. She took them out, arranging them in various configurations on the desk, already cluttered with thick, dusty tomes. Nothing looked good. She gathered the shells back up. When Khall calmed down, perhaps she could ask her to arrange them.

The queen was very good at that, finding beauty in found things and transforming them into a piece of sculpture. She'd dry out flowers and thread them through vines, hanging them around her quarters. Naias didn't have her elegance. That was why she liked her so much. Her queen was everything she wasn't, and everything she wanted to be.

She directed her attention to the tomes. Immediately after moving in, Naias had called for all the accounts in Haksa, detailing every single piece of silver that entered and left the city. A cursory glance at the recent records showed they had some money left in the treasury, along with the taxes the Tevurians had levied on the Haksanis. She'd promised Basaa and Ayashara that nothing would change; the taxes certainly wouldn't.

Those two wanted money to flow in their direction. They could fix the tattered port, construct fresh rigs and docks, pay the dockworkers—and themselves—but a port wasn't going to protect them against Tevu. Merchants were a greedy lot. She'd have to caution Khall against their influence.

Tevu hadn't treated Haksa well. Most of the population were poor Iskanti dockworkers and fishermen who'd chosen to settle here rather than continue the nomadic life. Working for the Ashvian and Tevurian merchant class was a better prospect than surviving in the wasteland. Their stilt houses were woven from wood and attap, in tatters after battling decades of ocean winds. Even the stone-built fortress needed help; according to the reports, the dungeons leaked water.

She shut the book. Renovation was the least of her problems. Rebuilding the western city walls was crucial to defend against Tevu, as well as finding new Faceless recruits. Khall had promised to stop the blood tithe, and Naias was more than eager to find another way to bolster their numbers. But she could only give suggestions; Khall would be the ultimate arbiter of the silver.

Footsteps sounded by the threshold of her door. "You summoned me, Commander," Crescent said, bowing quickly.

"I asked for both of you. Where's Hammer?"

He shrugged.

Naias picked at the mark on her forehead. Years of scratching had left her skin scarred and calloused, drawing more attention to the very thing she wanted vanished. She knew she shouldn't, but picking made her feel better.

"Fine." She didn't have time to deal with Hammer's insolence. Her free hand pulled out the armband and coin she'd taken from the Iskanti prisoner. "Tomorrow, you and Hammer are to travel into Iskanti lands. Find the clan this armband belongs to and who paid them with this coin to assassinate Khall. I'm sure it's Jayal or Maka. Most likely both. They're missing from Xinquha. Find them, kill the clan, but bring the Ashvians to me alive. I will personally escort you both out the gates."

By sending Crescent and Hammer away, she achieved two aims at once. Not only would she find the men who'd plotted against her, but she'd sever that bond between Viridian and her unofficial guardians. They'd grown too close in the last four months, and when the child volunteered her power to save Crescent—*a Faceless, of all people*—Naias had a problem on her hands.

By cutting them off, Viridian would eventually cease to use Hammer and Crescent as a bargaining tool. It was easier to coax her with shiny objects than human lives.

"You and Hammer are no longer in charge of protecting Viridian." She tossed the coin and armband at him. "She's my responsibility now."

Crescent passed the coin through his fingers. His smiling mask betrayed nothing of his true emotions. "So this is how it ends? Viri's useful now, so you pay attention."

Naias glared at him. "Yes, Faceless," she said, emphasizing his rank, "this is how it ends."

"Let us say goodbye, at least, before we go."

Everyone wanted something, and she was so, so tired of bargaining. "I gave you an order. Go do it."

He tucked the armband into his belt. "Your tactical mind may have made you Khall's adviser, but remember the Faceless gave you Haksa. Khall protects you for now, but when our queen can't forget that mark on your head, you won't find solace with us."

She wasn't looking for comfort. She didn't need the Faceless or Crescent's condescending lectures. They weren't going to end the blood tithe. The Ashvians were the ones in power, and only they could do it. Naias had already made that first step. Khall had seen its brutality and given her word. All Crescent had done was take care of a child, a task anyone could've done.

"I've created more change than you ever will in your lifetime," she snarled.

He leaned against the doorway and scoffed. "Change doesn't benefit those already in power, Naias. They want to preserve the way of things. I don't see you changing anything; in fact, I don't think you intend on changing it either. Your survival depends on Khall's kingdom existing as it is. You bluffed your way into a relationship and got rid of everything that made you, *you*."

Without waiting for an answer, Crescent bowed. "Treat Viri well," he said, and left the room.

Hated by both Ashvian and Iskanti, now Naias was neither. Finding her identity was akin to being adrift at sea, belonging to no one, only herself. She'd anchored herself to Khall, hoping that the Ashvians would accept her eventually, but that Iskanti stench followed her like a dog to its master.

She harbored no illusions that it was an easy road. It'd taken invading a city to get a promise out of Khall. Now began the work of signing her freedom—and the end of the blood tithe—into law.

She was making change. Soon the Ashvians would see she was just like one of them.

27
Viri

THE FACELESS SURROUNDED me as we climbed up twisting stairs and curved corridors. I couldn't tell if any of them were Hammer or Rafaeis.

It was hard to find them in the sea of black anymore. Hammer rarely took off her mask since we left Xinquha, and I could only identify Rafaeis by his voice and hands. I tried to guess by their weapons and the way they walked, but I was wrong more often than not.

I missed them. In Xinquha, Hammer would come back every night, while Rafaeis would visit during the day. Things were different now. I didn't blame them for that. It was my fault too, for not listening to her.

She'd promised she'd come back. I believed her.

We reached the topmost level of the fortress. Only the lighthouse sat above us. One of the Faceless opened an iron door. The hinges groaned as it swung open, and they pushed me inside.

Light bled through narrow windows in the wall. My new room was sparse. A pile of furs in the corner, a bucket in the other. Everything was stone-built, the floors damp from the sea. Melted candles sat on a small wooden table. The door swung shut.

"At least it's bigger than my hut," a voice said behind me.

Hammer. She unmasked herself. Another Faceless stood beside her, tall and lean. It had to be Rafaeis.

They were here. I wasn't alone anymore.

I slammed into their bodies, leaving me breathless. My hands dug into their clothes, memorizing their muscles, how Rafaeis's back relaxed when he stood straight, while Hammer tensed as she caught my weight. Hammer enveloped me with her big arms, hugging me firmly. She'd missed me too.

Rafaeis bent down, burying his face in my shoulder. "We're here to say goodbye," he said. "Khall's sent us on a mission to Iskantupu. We won't be back for a while."

I'd barely seen them, and now they had to leave?

"No," I blurted. "Don't go."

"We don't have a choice, Viri," Hammer said. "Things have changed. They know what your powers are now. Your guard has doubled. Khall and Naias will want you by their side at all times."

Forced to stand next to Naias, who scared me, and Khall, who didn't see me as anything more than Diavijra. I shivered. "I don't want to be with them."

I'd chosen this, but it still hurt. To save Rafaeis I'd given them my power, only to be taken away from the very people I cared about. Papa died protecting me, Dada didn't recognize me, and Hammer and Rafaeis were leaving. It wasn't fair.

"Dada . . . Soridian, I met him, in Xinquha," I said. I wanted to tell them. They had a right to know. "He didn't know who I was. I hadn't seen him for a long time."

Rafaeis let go. His brown eyes regarded me with concern. "Did you tell him anything?"

"I tried, but he didn't know. Naias was there. I didn't want to say the wrong thing."

"Do you want to go back?" Hammer asked hesitantly. She didn't want to know the answer.

I didn't either.

Would I be happier back in Maetheria?

Dada's home wasn't my home, wherever he was. He didn't recognize me in Xinquha, much less take me back if I showed up on his doorstep and claimed I was his daughter. I'd lived in the university, in Papa's office, surrounded by books that I didn't read. But I'd never truly liked it there. It was too big, with too many wings and names and strangers, it was *cold and pallid, just like his dead body, his lips turned blue so quickly*

It was only important to me because he was there. When he died, the university died with him.

Home was now a small hut and a warm bed-stove, Hammer dangling off the edge of the bed while I squeezed against the wall. Home was by the river's edge, two masked Faceless laughing at each other while they combed my hair.

If I went back to Maetheria, I wouldn't see Hammer and Rafaeis again.

The thought made me angry.

"No," I said. "I want you."

Hammer knelt down. Her calloused palms scratched my hands. "I promise we'll come back," she said, her expression hard. "Someday we'll leave this place. The three of us, together. I don't know how, but we'll find a way."

I squeezed her close, and Rafaeis wrapped his arms around us all. "You'll have more lonely nights ahead," he whispered, "and more death and suffering that will hurt you. Survive it all, until we come back. Rise out of it unchanged."

survive

I gazed at both of them. Masked and maskless, named and unnamed.

"Show me your face and tell me your name," I said. "So I can remember your words and who you are to me."

Rafaeis lifted his mask.

Hammer whispered in my ear.

28

Elera

THEIR YAKS LUMBERED northwest, climbing the gentler hills. They headed past the fog and mist, until all that was left were the snowy peaks of Mount Iska, a mountain range that had fought the wind since its formation. Perfectly horizontal icicles swept across its face.

Sharpened rocks dotted the dunes. Their whittled faces bore the long, deep wounds inflicted by the howling wind. No life grew here, no spiny shrub or hard grass. Even the scorpions had scattered.

"We're looking for cairns," Rafaeis said. "The Iskantis use them to navigate. Sometimes they drape cloths on them for better visibility, but not always. We might find a few trade caravans there."

Elera couldn't tell the difference between a cairn and a regular stone. Everything blended in with the landscape, gray on gray. Iskantupu was so unfamiliar that she might as well have been dropped in the middle of the ocean.

"Should we be disguising ourselves?" she asked. They'd left Haksa wearing their masks and uniforms, with a few horsehair furs to keep them warm.

He shook his head. "The faster we attract attention, the better. Besides, I know who we're looking for." He flipped the armband over in his hands. "Red and yellow. It's Kujilun Gurabal's clan, but I've never heard of them raiding or fighting. Her clan has always consisted of tradespeople. A few of them came down to Xinquha a few years ago, and she mostly roams around the bay. She was very old when I last saw her, and I think that's why she doesn't travel deeper into Iskantupu. The land's too rough for her there."

Elera pulled her yak to a stop. "What the fuck, Crescent."

"What?"

"You already knew who attacked us?"

Rafaeis hadn't spoken of the men who'd nearly killed him, and he'd emerged from the experience as cheery as one who hadn't been stabbed with a dozen knives. He'd known all along, and yet he'd not expressed a hint of vengeance.

He mistook her outrage for not telling her sooner. "I didn't want this whispered back to Naias. She expects us to be gone for months, searching for this armband's owner. She doesn't know anything about the Iskantis and assumed I suffered the same ignorance as her. If we're lucky, we'll find Jayal and Maka in no time. I don't want to implicate any of the clans. We'll make one up when we return and tell Naias they're all dead. She won't know the difference."

"These clans you're protecting nearly *killed* you," Elera said, astonished that he still hadn't grasped the severity of the situation.

He shrugged. "I had my mask on. I was a Faceless, like everyone else. They have leaders to answer to, no different than us. I don't begrudge them their duty."

She could only gawk at his nonchalance. "I don't know how you're still so positive about all this," she said. "If someone tried to kill me, I'd destroy them and everything with it."

"Then it's a good thing they went for me instead," Rafaeis said lightly, urging his yak up a pass. "We have a few options. One, we come back sooner than Naias anticipates and watch her take credit for our hard work, or two, the same thing happens, but we savor our second date."

She laughed. The brazenness of this man. "We never had one to begin with."

"Ah, so this is our first proper date then," he said. "If you insist. What better way than whispering declarations of love in the snowy mountains of Iskantupu?"

She hadn't been back since she was taken as a child. Iskantupu had seemed livable then. She didn't remember the dry air causing her skin to crack and flake, or how she panted for every breath, or how the naked sun burned the back of her neck.

"It's a terrible place," she said. She missed Viri already. "The longer we spend wandering in it, the higher likelihood of us dying."

"Remember what I told you before, Elera? About seeing the world for what it is, and not its hidden threats?"

Rafaeis speaking her name into existence sent a jolt through her. "Fine," she huffed. "A date. I promise to enjoy it, in whatever's left of my cold, shrunken heart. I assume you already know how to find these people."

"You don't find them. They find you."

They rode across the steppes, a plain that never ended. It all looked the same. If Elera weren't watching her yak plod along, she could've sworn she hadn't moved at all.

"There," Rafaeis said, pointing to a pile of rocks. Ripped red flags draped around the cairn, flapping in the wind. Two hawks circled above them. "Remember, when they come, don't resist. We're here to find one of their people, not kill them."

He dismounted and took off his mask, tucking his crescent blades away into the sash of his belt. "Shout with me." He cupped his mouth and whooped into the air.

The hawks began to gather. Two, three, and then a dozen flew overhead, the cairn eclipsed in a dread of black feathers.

Elera shouted as loud as her lungs allowed.

All at once, the hawks swooped away. Shadows crept over the ridge of both hills. The hawks perched on the Iskantis' outstretched arms, a row of shadows silhouetted against the bright blue sky.

She lifted her hands, giving herself to surrender.

HER BONDS WERE practically made of string and twigs.

Perhaps they would've kept a normal person bound, but if she did so much as stretch, the rope would probably snap. She'd send the Iskantis into a panic. Out of respect for Rafaeis's plan, she kept the pretense up, but she itched to break away. Her confiscated hammer sat heavy on the back of her Iskanti escort, his body bent twice over, unused to the weight, while she swayed too easily on her yak. She didn't like this sensation, being without her weapon. She'd never lost a fight to warrant capture in the first place. The only time she'd been restrained was in preparation for the lash. Naias had been all too happy to do it the last time.

She didn't want to spend more effort thinking about that turncoat. Her focus turned to memorizing the Iskantis' armbands. They weren't all the same color. Red and yellow dominated most of the clan, followed by a scattering of green and white, purple and black, and many more. Near a dozen different clans, and yet they all worked as one.

They arrived in a large clearing on top of a hill. A river flowed downward, radiating gold from the setting sun. A few hundred gers had been erected along the river, fires dotting the spaces between them.

While Khall's and Clement's tents were put up with a few sticks, the Iskantis constructed their gers with a round wooden lattice foundation, covering it up with felt. They had sturdier, warmer dwellings, while Khall had given the Faceless no tents at all. The Iskantis treated their warriors better than Khall did her own guard.

They led her to the largest ger. She braced for a fall. She'd be shoved to the ground in some fashion, forced to kneel and feign respect to their clan leader.

They opened the tent flap for her, extended a hand to invite her in, and *bowed*.

A small furnace sat in the center of the room, white smoke trailing out of the crown roof above. Banners of different colors papered the walls. A bed of furs lay on her left, half-eaten bowls of mutton stew sitting on a short table on her right. Two guards stood on each half of the ger, their hands resting on their sword hilts. She felt as if she'd wandered into someone's home rather than a ruler's hall.

The chieftain stood with his back facing them, thick pauldrons of fine foxfur hiding most of his head, while the colors of all the clans trailed his belt. Behind him lay the largest horn that Elera had ever seen. Twice as big as an ibex's, in a startling shade of white ivory, it curled twice into itself, flaring into a large wide oval at the end. Golden tassels of white horsehair hung on its notches, alternating with strips of yellow and red cloth. Iskanti script had been carved on its surface. A precious family heirloom of some kind.

He turned around. A thick black beard hid his round cheeks, but he reminded Elera of the young Iskanti initiates, fresh children who hadn't yet been beaten down by the Faceless.

The man jerked his head back, an amused frown on his face. "Rafaeis?"

Rafaeis barked out a laugh. "Kujivhan? What are you doing here?"

"Loose their bonds," Kujivhan said in Iskanti. He crossed the ger in two steps, and just as Elera's hands came free, Kujivhan embraced the unmarked Faceless, lifting him into the air. *"Be glad I still recognize you. I was nearly going to ransom you off to Tevu. You've eaten well?"*

Rafaeis thumped Kujivhan's back. *"I have,"* he said, matching the chieftain's language of choice. *"Much has changed. You have to tell me what's happened."*

"Well, first of all, your Iskanti's gotten worse."

"Has it?"

"We have nine intonations, little brother, not one."

"*I haven't had you to practice with, that's why.*"

"*Ha, if this is an invitation back to Sin'kuua, I refuse.*"

Rafaeis and Kujivhan spoke as if they were brothers. Elera stared open mouthed at the two, dumbfounded. Not only did Rafaeis know the clan of his attackers, he was *friends* with their leader. "You know each other?"

Rafaeis shared a glance with her. *Play along*, he seemed to say, before the solemnity vanished into a big smile. "Kujivhan came to Xinquha a few times, didn't you?"

The chieftain put him down, gesturing for them to sit on the wool carpets. "*Terrible weather each time we went. Once the caravan got stuck in the mud. Took us half a day to dig it out. You lot have delicious sweetened rice cakes, but it's not worth the journey. If you stopped selling them next to roasted lizards and rats, I might consider coming more often.*"

"Yes, I remember that," Rafaeis said with a laugh. "*I ran myself exhausted digging you out of the mud.*"

"*All for a good cause. The silver from selling Quctran weedflowers to the Ashvian queen didn't go to waste.*"

Rafaeis looked around the ger, as if searching for something. "*I have good memories of your mother whenever you visited. She was kind to me when I was younger, ruder. I'd love to speak to Gurabal-mother again, see if she remembers me.*"

Kujivhan sighed. "*We have much to catch up on. Mother has returned to the sky.*"

"May Iskandraza mourn well," Rafaeis muttered.

Kujivhan cursed in rapid Iskanti. "*The pigfucking Tevurians have taken Oumujin. We had to perform her sky burial here. Two weeks—two weeks!—it took for her body to be taken by the wildlife. We had to coax the condors to come down this low. One day, with Iskandraza's blessing, we'll retake our home and brittle their steel with fire.*"

"I wish you success," Rafaeis said, "but truthfully, I'm confused. I see you've inherited Gurabal-mother's ger. From my understanding—a foreigner's, of course, who'd love to learn—I thought the title would pass to one of your sisters."

Kujivhan grabbed a teapot from the table, pouring out a milky, pungent wine. One cup for Rafaeis, another for himself. Elera didn't exist here.

She didn't fight. Rafaeis knew more about her own people than she did. He spoke with a carefulness that she'd never seen before, padding his words with how different he was and blaming himself for not fully understanding how Iskanti succession worked, when there was clearly no misunderstanding of any kind. A man was now in charge of multiple matriarchal clans. She didn't want to risk upsetting the game Rafaeis played.

"Things have changed, little brother." Kujivhan raised a cup, gesturing to Elera's uniform. *"Blame those who keep taking our children away. Tevurian or Ashvian, they all think us weak and press us into slavery. We had to fight back. We can't just be traders and herders anymore."*

"Your sisters didn't mind?"

"When wolves face starvation, they do not select the weakest hunter to lead them. I had the most fighting experience amongst all of us. If we are to commit to righting this wrong, change is necessary. My sisters, our matriarchs, the other clans, they all understood this. With any luck, more will join our cause, and we'll have an army large enough to rival Tevu."

Elera didn't believe a word of it. If his sisters had voluntarily relinquished their titles, they'd still be here, as warriors or counsel, sitting in his ger. She hadn't met a single woman since her capture. Only men surrounded them.

He hadn't been elected as chieftain. He'd taken power for himself. As to the fate of the matriarchs, she could hazard a guess.

Kujivhan drained his cup, slamming it on the table. *"I've shared my story. Now it's your turn to explain why you're wearing a Faceless uniform, wandering in my territory."*

The practiced smile didn't leave Rafaeis's face. *"Ah, yes, a strange tale, Gurabal-brother. I was traveling, as I am wont to do, and came across Khall's caravan, headed towards the bay. I thought to follow so I'd be safe on the road, and what happened? An Iskanti clan ambushed us at night. I was caught in it."*

He'd omitted some of the events, of Viri's and Clement's roles, but she sensed its purposefulness. No need to complicate a story when his intent was to guilt the Iskanti into offering up information.

Kujivhan gasped—too loudly, for her taste—and placed a hand on his chest. *"An unfortunate encounter. But you were unharmed, I hope?"*

Rafaeis shook his head. *"The Iskantis didn't distinguish friend from foe. I was injured. And you know who saved me from death? Her."* He pointed to Elera. *"I owe her my life. My clothes were completely ruined. This uniform was all they had."*

Kujivhan scoffed. *"How unlucky you are, little brother, to have fallen in with a group of Faceless. You know they're a bunch of blood traitors who side with the Ashvians. They kill us and kidnap our children."*

"If we're speaking of traitors..." Rafaeis pulled out Khallan's coin, letting the silver reflect the firelight before handing it over. *"The other Iskanti clans will be very disappointed to know that you're working for the Ashvians. The young queen captured one of your men and fished this out of him."*

Kujivhan drew away, as if the coin would curse him upon touching it. *"This must be a mistake,"* he said. *"You said it was dark? Your eyes have deceived one clan for another."*

"So this doesn't belong to you?" Rafaeis showed him the armband. *"If you weren't part of the attack, then you must have lost this to one of the other clans. But as you've told me, you're all fighters and raiders now. Did an Iskanti tradesperson fell you? You must've not been very prepared."*

The silence fell so harshly that Elera tensed her arms in readiness. If the talk went poorly, she could fight her way out.

Kujivhan waved a hand, dismissing his guards. He plastered a smile on his face. *"I've misunderstood your intent, Rafaeis. I thought your arrival was to turn this Faceless over to me.*

Instead, you've come to ask who paid us to assassinate the Ashvian queen. You're not as innocent as I presumed."

Did he suspect Rafaeis was a Faceless? His unmarked head had let him spin his tale as a traveler, and if he was exposed, all his secrets came with him, along with the godchild he was searching for. Based on how poorly Kujivhan treated her, she didn't trust him with a godchild either. She didn't want another to suffer the same fate as Viri. The truth behind Rafaeis's unmarked face was more valuable than unearthing Khall's assassins.

Elera chose to speak. "He is my hostage," she said in Common. "He understands the Iskanti ways. I don't. I wouldn't have found you if not for him."

Kujivhan barked a laugh, a mocking, bitter one. *"An Iskanti who doesn't speak our language, and based on the mess on your face, one who can't even escape properly. The Faceless teach you nothing."*

"No, they haven't," she said, brushing the insult aside. She had no room to be angry. Rafaeis's identity was at stake. "But if we go back with nothing, we die. Khall's orders. And since you nearly killed him, I think you owe him something."

The chieftain said nothing.

"Silver is silver," she said. "You accepted Ashvian coin to help them eat each other. I would've done the same. We only want to know who paid you, and we'll take them off your hands."

Kujivhan opened his palms in a gesture of apology. *"I regret Rafaeis was caught in the attack, but what you're asking me to give up is worth more than his life."*

"Then what do you want?" Elera asked.

He rose from his seat. "You, Faceless," he said, speaking Common for the first time. "Prove it. Free Oumujin. North ride, four days. *Eradicate the Tevurians from my home. Let me commit my mother to the land from where she was born, and I will give you what you want."*

29

Naias

SHE NOW UNDERSTOOD why Haksa's ancient kings kept the throne room on the upper floors. Its windows offered a complete view of the village, from land to shore. Columns of supply wagons rolled in from the road to Xinquha, laden with sacks of rice, the only foodstuff they had in excess. Ashvians followed the wagons, a mix of priests and attendants, hoping to find employment with the queen.

Khall shifted on her rocky throne, reading the book of accounts that Naias had given her. A woolen cushion pressed against her hip, where the sharpest seashells resided. The court lay empty; after Basaa and Ayashara's unwelcome intrusion, Naias had posted initiates by the throne room. No one sought an audience with Khall unless Naias allowed it.

Khall's gaze darted down the page. "I think we should fix the port first."

Of course she had to make it difficult. The arguments Naias had suffered since the march wore on her, and she didn't want to fight anymore. She'd been too direct the last time. It'd only reminded Khall of her true power.

She needed a gentler approach. "Don't you think the city walls are a bit too run down?" she asked. Defense had to be their first priority. Rebuilding the walls was the way to keep

Haksa from falling into Tevurian hands again.

"Yes," Khall said, "but we took this place because of the trade it'll bring. We don't have a lot of money, but if we use that to fix the port first, we can sell more grain. The docks are still made of timber and twine. We need to rebuild them with stone. We don't have to buy it either, if that's what worries you. We can use the stone from the wall—"

By Ashvalra. She wanted to reduce Haksa's defenses even further to make the port prettier. "Darling," Naias said, mustering as sweet a voice as she could, "do you remember what your father said about Xinquha? He successfully defended it because . . . ?"

Impatience seeped out of Khall, in her pursed lips, before a brittle smile took over. She didn't want to argue either. "I know, I know. It's surrounded by mountains. One way in and one way out."

"That's right. Haksa doesn't have mountains, they have walls. There's no point in fixing the port right now. The docks still receive ships."

"Not that well, there's only two, and one of them is falling apart—"

"But it's working. The wall isn't. Tevu could attack at any moment. The Faceless can only do so much if you don't have the infrastructure to protect them."

"Half, then," Khall bargained. "Half the money for the wall, and half for the port."

Did she not listen to the words that came out of her mouth? "The port is fine," Naias said through clenched teeth. "The merchants don't need the money, and they can't hold a sword to defend us. We can fulfill their requests later. They need us more than we need them. Right now, we need to protect ourselves against Tevu."

Khall bit her lip, as if swallowing the thoughts she truly wanted to voice. "I understand you used to be a Faceless." Every word came out slow and careful. "Battle is all you know, and I'm grateful to you for that. We wouldn't have taken

Haksa without your expertise, but we're here now. We need to govern. We need to make this a better place to rival Pakaala. If we spend it all on rebuilding the wall, we won't have anything left for fixing Haksa."

Only good for battle. Naias had never felt more stupid, being lumped in with the likes of Hammer, who didn't know anything else besides clobbering people to death. Naias's lack of knowledge wasn't her fault. It was Khallan's, and by extension, Khall's. He'd made the Faceless this way, on purpose.

Still, she couldn't see why they needed to fix the port when it still worked, albeit inefficiently. "There's nothing left to fix if Tevu comes and ruins it all again," she said. She'd fought too many of Khallan's wars to count, taking and retaking Quctra, Haksa, and when it all failed, their final retreat to Xinquha. "You don't remember when Khallan fought here. He couldn't finish the wall in time. Then the Tevurians came. All our hard work was for nothing."

Khall drew in a long, deep breath. "I don't want to fight," she said quietly. "If you feel strongly about this, then I trust you. Do what you think is best."

It took some persuading, but she finally yielded. Thank the gods Naias didn't lose her temper this time.

"You won't regret it," she said.

"We can move on to other matters, then?" Khall asked with a hesitant smile. "I would like to reappoint my advisers. One for production, another for labor, another for taxes, and the like. We can have an Ashvian court here."

An open invitation for another version of Jayal and Maka to swan in, when Naias had worked so hard to keep them out? Absolutely not.

"Let's save that for another time," Naias said diplomatically. "You wanted to secure your heir, didn't you?"

"Yes, but—"

"We need pages, maids, and attendants for you," Naias pressed on. "You need to look the part, now that you're a true and proper queen. I'll send for Ashvian boys and girls from good, documented families, and it'll help you with selecting your next heir. Once they're settled, I'll look over the Ashvians to serve you as advisers, and you can have your pick. Is that fair?"

Of course, she had no intention of calling in any Ashvian as an adviser. The Ashvian court would contain one person, and one person only. The ability to influence Khall's decisions would start and end with Naias. The queen's new attendants had to be young and loyal, unable to present any opinion on matters of state.

The Ashvians ought to count themselves lucky. Dispensing tea and dressing monarchs for a chance at the throne, all work done in comfort under a stone roof with a warm bed, while they whipped the Faceless for giving them that privilege.

This illusion of choice softened Khall, who quietly accepted this without a fuss. After all, Naias had been firm on rebuilding the wall, and by relenting to having an Ashvian court, albeit fulfilled at a later date, she'd given the impression that her queen had gotten what she wanted, when she'd gotten nothing at all.

This persuasion filled her with triumph. She liked Khall best when she was easy. Meek and small, eagerly accepting any scrap of affection. After the many slights from Sahru, she needed this win.

"One last thing. I need your seal." Naias had chosen to leave this until the very end, when Khall was fully worn down.

"What for?"

Naias knelt before her, kissing Khall's knees. Her hands slowly trailed up her thighs.

Khall hummed with relief. "I missed this."

Naias's blood didn't run hot enough for her own satisfaction, but Khall had wanted this since the march. Now was the best time to give it to her.

"We still need initiates for our fight against Tevu," Naias murmured, pushing up Khall's barkcloth dress, "but I want it to be voluntary. I'm sending a decree to the Ashvians to join the Faceless, if they so wish."

She'd rehearsed this near a dozen times, repeating the words to herself before she walked into court. Not a question, or a request. A simple, straightforward task to complete, no different than the routine maintenance of a pistol, and Khall would have no choice but to execute it.

Naias didn't wait for an answer. She gently spread Khall's legs open, revealing her wet cunt, dark and swollen, desperate for release.

"Wait," Khall squeaked. "This is the throne room, we shouldn't—*ah!*"

She bucked against Naias's tongue.

Naias loved this feeling, the ability to play Khall like a puppet, getting her to dance when she wanted, how she wanted, by pulling the right strings and withholding her release until she squealed and begged. It filled her with a control she'd never had, and would never have, beyond her love for this woman.

Naias rose up, her smile coming easier than she expected. Despite herself, she'd missed this too. She reached for Khall's clit, rolling it between thumb and forefinger, right at the spot that she knew she liked.

"Your seal, yes?"

Khall's head lolled back, her eyes half open.

"Yes."

30
Elera

Iskanti winter houses dotted the oasis, shacks built from stone and wood. They weren't much different from her hut in Xinquha, except the Iskantis were fortunate enough to forage their building materials from the steppes, rather than being forced into trading for it with currency that only Ashvi recognized. Elera and Rafaeis took watch, settling on a hill sparsely populated with twisting, hardy trees.

Furnace smoke trailed through iron pipes that jutted from the roofs. All the streets led to a thin river, which cut through the center of the hamlet. Flat rocks lay stacked on the river's edge, a makeshift bench that Iskanti women would've sat on while they washed their clothes. The steel-clad Reborn occupied the place now, splashing water to cool their sunburned heads.

A handful of farmers tilled the hard soil, no doubt forcibly brought in from the empire. Their clothes did not suit the mountainous climate—sweat soaked through their sleeveless cotton tunics, leaving their heads and limbs bare to the glaring sun, all the while shivering in the cold. They'd erroneously thought the summer would bring them respite, but Iskantupu only had two seasons: cold and downright uninhabitable. Wood fences lined the newly sprouted fields, a clear sign of Tevu's claim over this land. They'd been in Oumujin for a while.

"I'm not in the mood to kill civilians today," Elera muttered.

"Neither am I," Rafaeis said. "I'm thinking fire."

"Fire? Won't Kujivhan mind that the houses get burned down?"

"They're going to put all this farmland to the torch anyway. They want their grazing pastures back. Besides"—his cheeky voice returned—"I think Kujivhan needs to work a little in return for the injury he caused me."

She chuckled, snapping off two branches from a tree. Perhaps he wasn't completely devoid of vengeance after all. "Fire it is."

She sneaked to the southernmost fields, running a lit torch over the fences and sprouting wheat. On the western end, Rafaeis did the same. They started a line of fire, coming to meet at the southwestern point. The flames encroached on the hamlet.

They waited for the farmers to flee. The Reborn would assert control and attempt to extinguish the fire. Elera and Rafaeis would take advantage of the chaos, killing as many of them as they could until they, too, decided that Oumujin was not worth occupying.

It was too easy. She'd only known Kujivhan for a few moments, but it felt unlikely that he would've sent them to set fire to a field and drive out a hamlet surrounded by fences. His clan of Iskanti warriors would've been able to overcome a few Reborn by shooting them from afar.

"You know this man," Elera said to Rafaeis. "Does he seem like the type to send other people to fight his battles for him, however small?"

He shrugged. "I don't know. His clan is so new and different from the Iskanti way of things. Even so, I'm not surprised. Expending a Faceless and a wanderer instead of his own men? It sounds like an excellent bargain to me. Kujivhan doesn't have to deal with the logistics of feeding his army and corralling them to fire in one direction. You remember the last time Tevu hired the Iskantis as mercenaries. What a catastrophe. Sending us was the easier option. If we die, he can absolve himself of all responsibility."

The smoke turned into a thick haze. Someone shouted, and the Reborn by the river stirred into action, scooping up buckets of water. Farmers swung their sickles in the fields, cutting down a row of wheat to create a break, but the flames spread too large and fast. Tevurian faces swelled red as they jogged down the riverbank, spilling water all over their armor.

But the wind changed. Flame, wheat, and grass instantly whipped in a single direction.

Elera looked up. *It can't be.*

Clouds swirled above, a tendril snaking from the skies as it reached the earth.

"Run," Elera shouted, sprinting for the trees. Her hand had barely caught hold of some bark when a whirlwind struck the center of the hamlet.

In a flash, the stone walls blew out. The force launched Tevurians into the air, farmer and Reborn alike, their screams muffled by the screeching wind. The fire swirled into a bigger frenzy, sending the winter houses into flame.

Elera crouched down, hiding as much of her body as she could behind the tree. Rafaeis pressed himself against her, reinforcing her grip on the trunk with his own hands. Stone and debris slammed against their only anchor. It groaned under the force, a maze of roots emerging from the earth.

What the fuck was Engale doing here? It made no sense. A godchild of her power was not expected to look after a hamlet deep in Iskanti territory, overseeing fields that barely supported it.

But it didn't matter. She was here. Elera broke into a wide grin. There was no Viri to protect, no overriding orders, no excuses to be made. Engale had killed all the men who were supposed to protect her. No one would get in their way.

She'd take Oumujin from the most powerful godchild on earth and kill her while doing it.

Godkiller. The word sat on her tongue again, and she could taste its glory. She'd missed her chance once. She would not pass this up another time.

She stood up, grounding her feet in the earth, and pushed forward, one slow step after another.

Rafaeis grabbed her hand. "Wait." His voice was barely a whisper against the roar of the air.

Elera shook him off and walked into the center of the eye. "Don't interfere. She's mine."

31
Elera

SHE TRUDGED AHEAD, letting the hammer on her back weigh her down. Her body bent at an angle nearly parallel to the ground, a counterweight against the wind that threatened to sweep her away.

Engale wasn't visible in the swirling debris, but Elera knew her patterns. Tevu had sent her into every single battle since she'd come of age. Engale was the fulcrum from which her powers emanated. If she wanted to continue channeling the hurricane, she had to sit in the center of the eye.

The godchild's death was within reach. She took her mask off, flinging it into the wind. She wouldn't make the same mistake again. Pravaja hadn't known the face of her killer. She would make Engale remember. The world would finally recognize her.

Step by step, she pushed forward, until she crossed an invisible threshold and the howling stopped.

There.

A solitary figure sat on the remains of the riverside bench, swaddled in lambswool. She'd kicked her boots off and dipped her feet into the river, letting the last rivulets of water trickle through her toes, her attention unusually focused, as if she were seeing flowing water for the first time. A short mop of gray hair fluttered about her tired face.

Elera's boots crunched against gravel. "Engale."

Like all the others, the godchild's gaze came to rest on Elera's forehead. She smiled. "You're very brave, Faceless, to have walked through my hurricane." Her voice touched velvet and honey, her toneless Tevurian accent clear. "Were you looking for me?"

Elera reached for her weapon.

"Always more fighting," Engale said, with the weariness of a person twice her age. "Let me savor this silence for a moment."

"No." Elera stalked over, one hand loosening the cloth that bound her hammer.

"Sit down."

An invisible force pressed on Elera's shoulders. She fell like a clumsy duck, her legs flung haphazardly about the bench.

"You'll have your fight." Engale heaved a long, heavy sigh. "But sit with me for now."

Elera blinked, shifting awkwardly. She didn't want to obey, and yet Engale seemed so tired of it all. Sympathy flickered within her. She, too, was sick of the whole affair, running errands for an Iskanti in this dry and cold weather. It didn't suit her. She just wanted to go home to Viridian.

This was not how their fight was supposed to go.

A long silence passed between them. The whirlwind extinguished the last flames that consumed the hamlet.

"Are you done sitting?" Elera asked.

"Don't be so impatient," Engale said. "Give me a while longer."

Debris lay scattered around them, a mix of armor and household items—rakes, buckets, bits of wooden fence. A steel leg plate lay discarded on the ground, its Tevurian owner long tossed into the sky.

"I got tired of them hounding me," Engale said, following Elera's gaze.

"A wasted effort," Elera said. "You're Tevu's jewel. More will come."

Engale barely lifted a hand, gesturing to the whirlwind

surrounding them. "Until then, I have some time for myself. I'm surprised you're here, Faceless. Oumujin is a far ways from Xinquha. What brings you to this place?"

Elera stared incredulously. The godchild was *chatting* with her.

"I came here to kill you," she said.

Engale raised her hands in mock surrender. "So you've found me. What do you think?"

She could've declared herself and swung her hammer, but the conversational air that the godchild struck left her stunned. She blurted the first thing that came to mind.

"You were a lot balder."

Engale tossed her locks theatrically. "Ah, so we've met before. You like it? Hair's quite annoying when you control the wind. I have to spend my entire life shaven because I can't help whipping my hair into my own eyes. Everyone else has such pretty hairstyles. Lakhesterians braid theirs in such intricate patterns. I'd like to try it someday."

When Pravaja died, Engale's fury was unmatched. Elera had steeled herself for a godchild that despised caution and sought power, and yet here she sat, asking if her hair looked good.

"Was killing your own guard intentional with this whirlwind?" Elera asked, pointing to the sky. "You should've kept them. They'd protect you from me."

"Well, consider it a mercy. At least they have a fantastic view up there before they die."

Ashvalra help her. Killing Engale was going to be much harder than she'd thought. The godchild of wind and hurricanes, joking with a Faceless in the ruins of an Iskanti hamlet? No one would believe her.

"I'm just surprised that the godchild working for Tevu would rather help in its destruction than save it," Elera said.

"When you defend and destroy enough places, they all start to look the same."

"Then why Oumujin?" she pressed. "This place isn't important enough for a godchild to defend."

"They sent me to Xinquha. I lost interest on the journey back and stopped here instead." Engale leaned back with a smile, the scattered sunrays bathing her face in light. "I like sitting in the eye. It's quiet. No kings or princes to order me around, telling me I have to go attack this village or defend that fort, sending me to endless battles that I don't care for. In the eye, there aren't any voices. You Faceless were trained to obey. You must feel the same."

Elera cracked a smile. "Very much. I hate Khall and the lackey who stands by her side. I make their lives as difficult as possible."

Engale laughed. "It's fun to annoy powerful people, isn't it? They get so angry when you twist their arm even a little bit. And, oh, how comical it was to see your new queen try to assert her power. It's like watching a baby learn how to walk. But truthfully, she did look dreadful in that dress. Maetheria has the most gorgeous batik. She should send you there once in a while."

"You hate Khall as much as I do, but you haven't insulted me once. I'm a Faceless. I work for your enemy."

"You want one?" Engale studied her. "I suppose I expected you to be a lot uglier."

Was Engale implying she was pretty? Elera scrunched her face in confusion, then burst out laughing. "That's the blandest insult I've ever heard."

Engale shrugged. "It's easier to make fun of powerful people than powerless ones. If a king shits himself to death, that's a joke. If a farmer shits himself to death, that's dysentery."

Elera's cackle came out warmer than expected. "I thought you were going to be some bloodthirsty, arrogant god."

"Bloodthirsty, arrogant god*child*."

"Oh, please. You've adopted the god's name as your own, don't pretend to humble yourself."

Engale shook her head, a sad smile on her face. "You think I had a choice in my name? My circumstances are not so different from the one that stripped you of yours, and yet here we both are, fighting each other in a war that we don't care about. Honestly, Faceless, I quite tire of it. Don't you?"

Elera leaned back, gazing into the sky. The eye swirled above, an artificial silence surrounding them. Time ceased to matter. No orders to follow, no people to bother her. Little wonder Engale enjoyed sitting in the eye so much.

"But I have no choice," Elera said. "I can't summon a hurricane into a city. Tevu can't stop you if you really want to leave."

"But Khall has a godchild too, right? Why do they stay?"

"That's different. Clement isn't as powerful as you, and he's plied with drink and gems and smoke. Every want is satisfied, and all that vanishes if he decides to leave." It was her turn to study Engale. "But you don't seem hopelessly addicted to opium."

Engale let out a small laugh, her cheeks turning dusky pink. "I . . . I forget things." She wrung her hands. "When I went to Xinquha, I brought gloves with me. Dark brown leather, lined with wool. I know I brought them, I put them on my hands. But I lost them somewhere along the journey. I asked the Reborn for some new ones, but they told me I never brought gloves, or even liked wearing them.

"I had a favorite dress. Maetherian-made. It was gray, with patterns of storks and pigeons, and I liked how it fluttered with the little breezes I made. I kept it under lock and key, in a chest that only I knew. One day it went missing. There was no chest. No lock. It kept happening. Things simply disappeared.

"I thought I was going insane. But there was another who helped me. She gave me proof. The tufts of wool that stuck between my fingers. The gray fibers that snagged on my nails after I'd worn the dress. Then she died. I know she died. I saw it, right in front of me. I wanted to retrieve her body, but they pushed me away. Now they say that there was no other godchild besides me. They say I imagined her, I dreamed a battle where she died. I can't find anything that belongs to her."

She drew in a shaky breath. "Maybe I did dream up my gloves. Maybe I thought I owned that dress. Sometimes it frightens me that Pravaja might've never existed at all. The love I felt was so real, so true, and to be told that it was all a hallucination . . . I can't tell what is and isn't real anymore."

Engale turned to her, silent tears trailing down her face. "Please speak the truth to me, Faceless," she whispered. "Are you real? Or have I invented someone to take my cruelties out on?"

This was Viri's future. Naias could—no, *would*—attempt something as depraved as Tevu had, altering Viri's reality so she'd readily believe Elera and Rafaeis were all a dream.

She would not be relegated to a fantasy.

"As real as I can be," Elera said, holding Engale's hands. Her calloused skin ground like sand against the godchild's delicate palms.

Engale squeezed back, every breath a sob. "Help me leave," she said. "You know more about the world than I do. If I left, I'd die in a day. I'd hallucinate making a fire and freeze to death in the mountains because of it."

Oh.

Elera couldn't stop the bitter disappointment that rose up inside her. So this was what it led up to. Engale wanted help, not friendship. She'd been burned by this before.

She let go. "You want me to be your servant. The very thing Khallan made the Faceless for."

"Not a servant," Engale said, "and it won't be forever. Just until I can help myself. Your training teaches you to make fire, build tents, and live on soured milk. I don't know how to do that. I can provide protection with my power, and . . . and silver, if that isn't enough."

"There is no escape," Elera said with a bitter laugh. "You, a godchild with the strongest power this continent has seen in over a millennium, trying to hide? You'd be found within the day. No wealth in the world can change that." She took her hammer in her hands and untied the cloth that bound it, slowly revealing the engraved patterns on its metal face. "The only way out for us is to die, and hope we've left enough behind to be remembered."

Engale's face, once all flushed and smiling, went cold. "*You.*"

"I'll make it quick."

"Not if I make yours quicker."

A sharp wind flew out of the godchild. Elera dodged, and the force cut through the stone house behind her, slicing it in two.

Engale hopped back. The hurricane moved with her. Elera caught the edge of the storm, the winds nipping at her heels, lifting her into the sky.

Elera unhooked her rapier and flung it at her.

With a gasp, Engale put her hand out, summoning the wind to swipe it aside. The hurricane weakened for a moment, and Elera found her footing again, racing to close the gap between them.

"Too slow," she whispered in Engale's ear. Her hammer crushed against the godchild's ribs.

She fell backwards, spitting blood. Elera slammed her into the ground, pressing her foot on her chest.

Godkiller, she thought, the finiteness of the word filling her empty heart. She'd be remembered. Not as one of five hundred Faceless, but as Elera, Godkiller—

Her foot stepped on air.

Engale appeared beside her.

"Too slow," she whispered back, her hand pressed against Elera's chest.

A thousand needles pierced her body. Every part of her shook and screamed, her heart pounded faster and faster and it seized and she wanted to explode—

A force knocked her to the side. Engale stumbled back, gripping her neck. A Faceless stood between them.

Rafaeis.

He'd picked up the rapier that she'd flung at Engale and

stuck the tip of it through her throat. Blood seeped through her fingers.

"You better get that looked at," Rafaeis's voice murmured from behind his mask. "You'll bleed out in about three minutes."

Her eyes filled with fear, Engale disappeared in a gust of wind.

Elera's clothes had torn apart when Engale laid a hand on her, and a gash ran across her breast. A minor injury that didn't seem proportional to the near death she'd suffered. Nothing dire. Their missed opportunity hurt more.

She scrambled to her feet. "What the fuck was that?" she snapped. "You had a chance to kill her and you threw it away—"

He snatched off his mask. "Engale likes fighting from a distance," he said. "The heavier the foe, the better. She redirects your weapon's momentum against you, but she doesn't know what to do with shorter blades. When you get up close, she panics and tries to run away. I would've told you all this, if you'd stopped to listen."

He gripped her close, pressing their heads together. "Don't run off on your own ever again," he ground out. "I know you can take care of yourself, but you don't have to do everything alone anymore. I am with you, always."

His words unlocked something in her. No one helped her unless there was a bargain to be made. She'd been cynical for so long, rationalizing and protecting herself with quips and sarcasm, and only now was she forced to acknowledge the truth that she'd been so afraid to face.

Rafaeis had saved her because he loved her.

It was as simple as that.

Elera crushed her lips against his, wishing Engale hadn't left so she could savor this moment for as long as she could: a kiss, in the embers of a dying hurricane.

32
Elera

SHE PULLED AGAINST the opening of her uniform, glancing down her chest. Red veins spread like a spiderweb, creating a pattern no different from the mark on her face.

"Are you all right?" Rafaeis asked, tucking his mask away into his boot. They were returning to Kujivhan, and he had to play the nonplussed wanderer again.

Recovery was slow on the journey back. The air had dried out her skin, causing the wound to stay open. Her prolonged stay in the mountains had begun to affect her as well—she panted more, even while riding. Her hammer felt heavier. *She* felt heavier.

Altitude sickness and dry skin. She'd had worse. Her wound wasn't corrupted and it hadn't turned black. Only then would she worry.

"I'm fine," she said.

Kujivhan stood on the edge of his encampment, the thick furs on his hat and shoulders fluttering in the wind. A long line of men in multicolored armbands flanked him.

He held a small wooden box to his chest, wrapped in yellow paper, Iskanti script and red wax seals stamped on every face.

"His mother's bones," Rafaeis whispered in her ear.

Kujivhan had been waiting. Eagerly.

She dismounted before him, barely getting out "Oumujin is freed" before the clan erupted in a tumultuous roar, drowning out her next words. "It's ruined now. Your winter homes are no more."

Kujivhan handed the box to another, ran up, and wrapped her in the same bone-crushing hug he'd given Rafaeis. He easily lifted her off the ground.

Her chest hurt, pressed against his body. Abnormally strong, for one living on such thin air.

"It doesn't matter," Kujivhan said. *"The homes were due for some repair work. The walls didn't keep the winds out at all."*

Rafaeis walked up. *"No, apparently it attracts them, because the godchild of wind and hurricanes herself decided to move in."*

Kujivhan put Elera down, breaking into a wide grin. *"Found her, did you?"*

"She's gone, but not dead."

"Good enough. I wouldn't have asked if I hadn't tried myself. With enough time, we'll become a great army." He winked at them. *"What a shame that your Iskanti is terrible. You and a Faceless would've been a great addition to our clan."*

She'd been away from Viri long enough. Every day apart meant another day for Naias to corrupt her, just as the Tevurians had manipulated Engale's sense of reality. Khall was but seventeen when Naias wormed her way into her bed, parasite that she was, and seduced her in an instant. Not that the queen was some foolish waif either; Elera had fallen in love with Naias too, once upon a time.

Viri stood no chance. She was alone and afraid. She'd seek companionship, and Naias would be all too eager to give it. Eventually she would break. Viri would become another mindless pawn, believing that Elera and Rafaeis were all a dream.

It scared her.

"We came for the men who paid you," she said. "We had a deal."

Kujivhan smiled. *"You understand the language of your people, but you choose not to speak it. Give it a try."*

Elera's lips thinned. He knew why. He'd made fun of the way Rafaeis spoke. Despite looking every bit like an Iskanti, Elera was never going to be one of them. She was a Faceless and a blood traitor. Kujivhan dared to break from Iskanti tradition by uprooting his clan's matriarchy, yet Elera was still an easy target. They wanted a joke, and she was it.

When a farmer shits himself to death, that's dysentery. Even Engale, her enemy, had more sympathy than this man.

Instinctively, her hand closed into a fist, but Rafaeis swiftly held her arm down.

"Spare her your barbs," he said. *"Let's finish our business."*

Fuck, his grip hurt. It had to be the thinner air here, making her tired.

Kujivhan nodded to his men. The crowd parted as two warriors brought out a wicker chest, setting it before them. He kicked the basket open and pulled out two mud-caked heads.

Jayal and Maka had been dead awhile. The dry air had sucked out all moisture, leaving a pale blue membrane that wrapped around their skulls. Mud crusted over the crevices in their eye sockets. Maka's lower jaw was missing, with a multitude of deep cuts from his ear through his forehead. The executioner had missed a few times, perhaps on purpose.

Elera grimaced. They'd asked for men and been given two heads. "This was not what we agreed on."

Kujivhan shrugged. *"We agreed that I'd turn the men over to you, and I have. There was nothing in our deal about them being alive."* He stuffed both heads in a sack and handed it over. *"Besides, they were dead long before you came. We followed their plans in good faith, down to telling all our men a person named Naias was the mastermind. Since we were new and untested, I welcomed their guidance. They said the Ashvian queen was an easy kill and she was a coward who let her prisoners go. They were wrong on all counts. It was laughably easy to track them down after they fled Sin'kuua.*

Men who are used to sedentary life want to carry everything with them, and I mean everything."

Two heads were better than nothing. Elera took the bag, fastening it to her yak. The sooner they left, the sooner she could see Viri again.

Kujivhan turned away, retrieving his mother's bones with exquisite care. *"Well, our business is finished. Travel well—"*

"Wait." Rafaeis bowed before him. *"I have a favor to ask. I'm looking for someone."*

The chieftain grinned. *"Ah, finally. A simple, uncomplicated request. What are their banner colors?"*

"I don't remember. It's been fifteen years. The clan's matriarch was named Nasusorama, and she had a girl in her twenties with her."

"You've just described all the clans west of Mount Iska, little brother. Every mother and their daughter are named Nasu there."

Rafaeis's shoulders sank. *"I supposed as much. Thank you for your help."*

Kujivhan's sunburned brow frowned in disappointment, worried that he hadn't been helpful enough. What an odd man. He'd sent the both of them to recapture his village from a godchild without remorse, and yet this small request caused him so much more discomfort.

"Wait," he said. He retreated into his ger, and reemerged holding the enormous ivory-colored horn, the same one she'd seen him gaze upon.

"When the Destruction happened," Kujivhan said, *"Iskandraza gave each clan their own horn. It's a call for help. Supposedly it's incredibly loud, and it shatters the moment you blow on it. My grandmothers never had cause to use it, and neither did I. It's become more of a family heirloom than anything else."* He handed the horn to Rafaeis. *"It's yours."*

Rafaeis stepped back in alarm, slipping into Common. "No, I can't possibly—"

Kujivhan forced it into his hands. *"You gave Oumujin*

back, and you gave my mother rest. That means more to an Iskanti than you can imagine. You need this horn more than I do. Remember, Nasu is a westerly name. Circle south past Mount Iska, then keep it to your right. Don't bother climbing the mountain range as a shortcut. Many have tried and died. Follow the cairns, and eventually you'll see a dead tree covered in black cloth. That's where the clans meet to trade. Blow the horn there. I don't know if it'll even work, but maybe you'll find the person you're looking for."

Rafaeis wrapped his arms around Kujivhan's body, embracing him—as Elera had come to learn—the Iskanti way. *"This is more than I deserve. Thank you. May Gurabal-mother find peace in Oumujin."*

The Iskantis hugged far too much for her liking. Kujivhan himself was an infuriating person who barely noticed her and laughed when he did, yet he had a generous heart to those whom he considered friends. Rafaeis was a step closer to finding his godchild with his help. She couldn't fault that. Rafaeis was happy.

Her chest hurt when she smiled. She looked down. Pus seeped through her clothes.

Kujivhan thumped Rafaeis on the back. *"Travel safely, and may Iskandraza mourn well on your journey home."*

THEY LEFT KUJIVHAN'S camp, spending four days riding south, tracing their path back to Haksa. Every breath was difficult. Her entire body ached, and if she turned her head too quickly, she knew she'd fall off her yak.

She hated feeling weak. She'd grown up on these mountains, and yet Iskantupu seemed intent on driving her away. Her hammer could hit others, but it couldn't beat the shame out of her.

Rafaeis drew to a stop. The high altitude affected him too, his face slightly swollen and his cheeks reddened from the sun. The horn bounced against his chest. A cairn lay before them, and

Mount Iska loomed behind. If they headed left, they returned to Haksa. Right lay the wide reach, to the dead tree and his godchild.

"Give me a few more days," he said. "We'll go to the spot Kujivhan mentioned and use the horn there. We'll find Nasu and the godchild."

Her head hurt to move, but she shook it anyway. "We have to go back. For Viri."

Rafaeis urged his yak forward, turning right. "It's harder to break Viri out than to search for a few Iskantis. Let's find Nasu's clan first and see if they're still alive. If they are, we'll have a place to stay when we get her out. We cannot survive out here alone."

Elera steered her yak towards Haksa. "Getting her out is easy. Kill the guards before they know what's happening. Smash the door open. Take her. Leave."

Rafaeis's brow narrowed. "And then what? Have Khall and the entire Faceless army nipping at our heels? When they find her missing, their search will outrun even the fastest horse."

"That's the best solution I have," she snapped back. "The further we stray from her, the longer we allow Naias to seep poison into her ear. If this goes on, she'll forget about us and become Khall's pawn forever. We're going back."

"Too many people will come looking. We need to wait for the best opportunity. We need to find out who guards Viri's door, the patrol routes the Faceless take in that fortress, to go in undetected—"

"Sneaking. Scouting. Planning. Things we don't have time for."

His jaw tensed for the briefest moment. "We can't brute force our way in."

"Brute force has always worked out well for me," Elera retorted. She was running out of breath for this argument. "I've lived my whole life by it."

"It didn't with Engale."

Her cheeks flushed hot, but she shivered in the cold. "I would've killed her if you didn't stop me."

"Strange, given how *she* was about to kill *you* before I came.

What if she had reinforcements? Did you think about that? You went for Engale without a care in the world. Just endlessly running towards death, hoping to leave a memory bigger than who you are. Even Viri saw it."

She couldn't keep up. The air she took in didn't seem to be enough. Whenever her chest heaved, pain stabbed her body.

The world spun. She gripped the reins harder. She couldn't breathe.

"No," she said. What were they arguing about? Viri? "No, we—"

Her back slammed against the earth.

"Elera? What's happened?" Rafaeis's voice raised in panic. He dismounted, kneeling before her.

Days of pus and blood had left a dark stain on her uniform. Rafaeis ripped open her clothes, revealing the wound. The gash had grown longer, cutting across to her other breast. It smelled of death. Blackened veins spread across her chest.

"No, no, no," Rafaeis whispered.

Necrosis had set in. She tried to lift a hand to console him. It flopped uselessly at her side. "I've had worse," she panted. "I'll be fine. Just get me . . . get me back to Haksa."

"Haksa has no cure for the corruption," he said shakily. "Clement can't save you. Let me take you to Nasu. Please."

Fuck's sake, he'd saved her once already. She wasn't going to make this a habit. "I'm all right," she said, pulling herself up into a sitting position, and promptly collapsed. "I just need to rest awhile—"

"Shut up, shut up." His eyes brimmed with tears. "My godchild can save you. They're Chatrasaya. That's how they removed the mark on my head. They'll remove this infection too."

She couldn't stay awake anymore. Every other word passed by her.

He gripped her shoulders, shaking her.

"Say yes," he screamed.

"Yes," she said, and she remembered no more.

33
Viri

MORE FACELESS AND Ashvians moved into the fortress. The instructor who'd whipped me had come to Haksa as well. He stood in the courtyard, yelling at the other children.

I didn't have to tolerate them for long. Khall summoned a Haksani blacksmith, a big burly man, who came in with a pair of calipers, measuring the entrance to my room. I didn't know what he was doing, poking these twin needles into stone, twirling them up and down the walls, counting under his breath. When our eyes did meet, he regarded me with pity.

He came back a little after two weeks, a dozen Iskanti-Haksani laborers supporting him, hauling a thick iron slab into the fortress, numerous intricate locks on its face. Springs and levers flowed into one another, giant bolts jutted out its side. It was too big to carry up the winding staircase, so he and the Iskantis created a makeshift pulley, a system of wheels and axles lashed together with rope, heaving it up to my quarters. They tore my wooden door off its hinges and put this iron contraption in its place.

I was oblivious to it all. I was busy *hoping*, looking out the last window they hadn't bricked up. I squinted to watch every yak and horse pass through the fortress gates, making out the figures that sat on them. If they didn't have a hammer strapped to their backs, I moved on to the next one.

Hope.

Such a soft word. The Maetherian accent encompasses it completely. You have to open your throat to get the sound right, which means you can't yell or shout it. 'Hope' is whispered in a single breath, for it is too scared of the wretchedness of this world, and once spoken, it's gone forever. Suitable, I think, for the fleetingness that it brings.

Hope. Hope.

An exhalation, a puttering out at the end.

34
Elera

SHE RODE TOO fast to be on a yak.

The ibex's muscles ground against her thighs. Every bump and trot hurt. Her heart raced, and yet all her strength had left her. She was too tired to breathe.

Where did her yak go?

Her swollen hands fumbled for the reins, but someone pushed her down. A weight pressed against her back.

"Sit still," Rafaeis said.

"Where's my yak?" she repeated. The words slurred out her mouth.

"I sent it back."

"No, the heads . . ." She couldn't lose them, otherwise Naias would hit her again.

Rafaeis shushed her. "We're nearly there."

In the haze of her vision, a single black tree stood alone in the sand dunes, its spidery branches spreading its veins wide into the sky. Strips of cloth were its leaves, strands ripping apart in the howling winds.

They came to a stop. Rafaeis dismounted, and without a counterweight, Elera lost her balance. She slumped to the ground.

Her chest burned. Someone had cut her. She couldn't

muster up any more energy to remember who. Rafaeis looked so worried. *It's just a flesh wound*. All she needed was to lie down for a while.

He loosed a large, curved horn that was strapped across his back. He'd gotten that from . . . somewhere. She couldn't think. The ivory and gold gleamed bright against the tree, a halo against the darkness. He put the horn to his lips and blew.

A guttural, baneful scream split the air.

Her hands moved on their own, pressing against her ears to blot it out. How could something so pretty create such a terrible noise? It seemed to come from within the ground, like an earthquake, its vibrations defying the limit of human hearing. The ground rippled under her, drowning out all.

This is the sound of Iskandraza's lament.

A pair of hands shook her. Rafaeis shouted at her, seemingly unaffected by the sound. Shards of ivory lay embedded in his hands and uniform, pieces of it stuck in his long hair. The horn had shattered.

"It didn't work." His voice cracked. "Elera, stay with me."

What do you mean 'It didn't work,' I'm nearly deaf from it, she said, but no sound passed her lips.

She tried to get up. She thought she'd climbed onto her hands and knees, but for some reason all she could see was the sky, and a bump in the earth lolled her gaze in the direction of the spider tree.

The last thing she saw, before her weakness consumed her, was a flurry of wings, hawks perched on the shoulders of four people on ibexes, their silhouettes barely visible in the rapidly darkening shadow that swarmed her vision.

35

Elera

A GIANT SLEPT *under a gray sky.*

Elera couldn't see who he was. Heavy clouds drifted by her vision, colliding against one another. Flashes of lightning illuminated the world in purple and blue. No thunder rumbled in the aftershock.

But she felt him, a cresting melancholy that ran deep in his soul, and he didn't know why. He'd held this feeling for as long as he could remember, and he vaguely knew it was linked to someone who'd meant a lot to him.

He couldn't remember her name.

Why couldn't he? If he'd lost someone, why was this sadness so weak? Why didn't he cry, wail, beat his chest? This feeling trickled like a thin river, unceasing and irritating. He licked his lips, tasting it, but it gave him no sustenance, leaving him as unfulfilled as all the ages he existed before.

The earth rumbled: a mother rocking her infant to sleep. A tired, languishing rhythm, like all the songs that came before.

Sleep, *the earth whispered,* so you don't have to feel this pain anymore.

No. *He dug his fingers into the ground.*

The song came more urgent. Sleep, child, and dull your mind—

No. *His hands pulled up blue root and gray bone. Why couldn't he remember?*

It doesn't matter, *the voice said*. Dull your mind—

No.

He screamed, and the air ruptured with a long, terrible sound. Elera fell onto the quaking desert, coarse sand and glass rasping against her body. She covered her ears, screaming with him.

The sorrow struck him like a firebolt, his belly coiled in pain. He craved that noise, that wail when he'd lost everything.

I remember now.

He drank it in like a man parched, gasping as the memories flooded into his veins, of her and the way she curled her ankle around his leg, a finger tracing the hole in his chest, her swollen lips parted, open and drenched.

Yes. That's why he cried.

She's gone.

He'd forgotten she'd died. Hatred welled up within him. How dare he. Sleep had atrophied his memories, shrinking his love into a shadow of its former self.

Elera knelt alone on the apocalyptic wasteland, her chest black with corruption. His grief poured into her like a monsoon, and out flowed all the rage that made her.

More.

papa mama dead on the frozen wasteland, killed by khallan, he promised to spare them, he promised, *he promised*, crying, kicking, screaming as the black gloves took her away

More, *he groaned.*

holding hands with naias in unceasing darkness, whose lying lips whispered *i'm with you, forever*, only she wasn't here anymore, she'd gone and spread her legs for someone else

More.

viridian corrupted, the hope burned out of her blood, while rafaeis lay dead, his blades shattered, engale standing over her, triumphant, and she couldn't do anything, breaking all the bones in her useless body.

Yes.

His back bowed with a gasp, filling him up with a bitter pleasure long unremembered. The volcanoes erupted around him, red-hot lava spewing into the air. The gray wasteland of Iskantupu turned red, fire lighting the trees and bushes that lay in its path, melting the sand that covered the land, setting the world aflame.

And in the center of the carnage, Iskandraza shuddered with a final moan, turning to look down upon Elera. The stars of the universe glittered in his half-lidded eyes.

The Destroyer's smile was a terrible countenance to behold.
I've been waiting for you, Ragebringer.

36

Naias

THE HEADS OF Jayal and Maka sat on her table, the warm candlelight barely concealing the blue in their faces. Morning encroached, but no sun shone this day; lightning arced across the horizon, illuminating the roiling clouds in shades of pink and purple.

Hammer's yak had found its way back to Haksa, holding two heads and no bodies. Naias marched to the shore and screamed into the sky. Her orders had gone ignored. Hammer had heard the word 'alive' and willfully done the opposite, then absconded with Crescent to avoid punishment.

Those two were certainly missing, not dead. It was hard to imagine that Hammer *could* die. She'd survived every battle they'd gone into together, and it'd be ironic if she met her death in the freezing wasteland of Iskantupu. No, Hammer would never deign to put herself in such a state. She'd claw her way back to Haksa and maybe stab Naias before dying, because Hammer was Hammer and destroyed everything in her path for a laugh. How awfully convenient that Crescent hadn't returned either. They couldn't have both perished. One would've returned with news.

No, they weren't dead. They'd left.

A hundred lashes hadn't deterred Hammer from being a

thorn in her side, so she'd have to punish her through other means. Using Viri was a good start. She'd kept her locked in her room, ordering no one to speak to her. When her faith in Hammer and Crescent was fully broken and she was driven mad by isolation, Naias would be the one she'd turn to. The godchild would be so starved for affection that she wouldn't care who did the consoling.

Hammer wouldn't last long in the wastelands. She'd return half starved and dehydrated, begging to rejoin the Faceless. Barring that, the Iskantis would happily turn them over for some silver. They all came back eventually, and Hammer came back many, many times.

She pressed her fingers to her head, massaged her throbbing temples. She hadn't slept much since arriving. Staying in Haksa dredged up long-forgotten memories. Blood built these walls, and the echoes in the fortress sounded too much like screams. She wanted her anchor, the one who held her hand through the thunder and the noise—

Naias squeezed her eyes shut. The loneliness made her crave companionship, that was all. She held no love for Hammer anymore, especially when she flouted orders like this. The truth of her innocence had died with Jayal and Maka. No godchild on the continent could resurrect these men. Ashvalra died a millennia ago.

She arranged the hair on Maka's face to hide the worst of the cuts that underlined his jaw, but nothing could hide their drooping jowls and pallid skin. She dabbed a damp cloth around their faces, wiping the filth off as best she could.

Truthfully, Naias found some glee in seeing that Maka had died painfully. They'd gone through all this trouble to pin an assassination attempt on her because they couldn't bear to see their precious queen consorting with an Iskanti. They'd deserved to die like this.

She gently opened the door to Khall's bedroom.

The queen was still asleep. She'd moved her bed next to the windows, overlooking the sea. A gauze net surrounded her bed, protecting her from the gnats and mosquitoes that came with living in a waterlogged place such as this. The ruffles of her cotton gown fluttered in the breeze.

Naias didn't like the idea of her sleeping so close to the windows, but she couldn't bear to say no. After seeing her wilt in the damp and dreary monsoons of Xinquha, the least she could do was allow her a bit of sun. She bent down, arranging Jayal's and Maka's heads on the bedside table.

Khall stirred, breaking into a hazy smile. "Changed your mind?" she asked, tugging Naias's arm towards the bed.

She brushed her off. "I've dealt with the traitors."

"Wait, what?"

Naias gestured to the heads on the table. It wasn't the moment of triumph she'd imagined, but justice would have to do.

The smile quickly faded. "You killed them?"

"Not on my orders," Naias said. "I told the Faceless to bring them back alive, but it seems like the situation got complicated. Besides, they tried to assassinate you. The verdict was simply executed ahead of time."

Khall shook her head. "I didn't think they were the assassins. You came to that conclusion. Not me."

"Yes, because they were the ones behind it," Naias said, holding in her exasperation.

"I don't think there was any proof—"

"The coin belonged to them!"

"—and now, thanks to you, we'll never know the truth." *How convenient,* her face seemed to say.

A Faceless entered the room. "Commander—"

"Not now," Naias said.

"—the Maetherian army approaches. First Scholar Soridian wishes to enter the fortress."

Naias waved a hand away, as if dismissing an irritating fly. "Fine, fine. Let them through."

About time. Soridian had dragged his feet bringing his men here, letting Naias scramble to shore up Haksa's defenses in his absence. She'd summoned as many of the Faceless and initiates from Xinquha as she dared. The Faceless' footsteps beat against stone, echoing through the fortress.

Khall propped herself up on the bed. "I banished Jayal and Maka out of mercy, and you killed them without my permission."

"I didn't kill them," she snapped. "I *wanted* them alive. Their confession would've proved my innocence."

"The Faceless are under your charge. Their mistakes are your mistakes. You've proved nothing, except that two of my father's closest men are dead." Khall shook her head in disappointment. "Bury them in the royal way. Pack their tombs with earth, get the chrysanthemum seedlings in. Bring in the priests from Xinquha. I want to be there during the ceremony."

No, Naias wanted to scream. She didn't do all this only for Jayal and Maka to humiliate her from beyond the grave. She would've never gotten a royal burial. The Faceless weren't allowed that privilege.

Why was she still hearing footsteps? These hollow halls amplified every little sound. Whispers turned into shouts; a walk turned into a parade. It grated on her. She needed to think.

The shouts grew louder. Metal clanged against metal.

What's going on? Naias stalked out of the room.

An arrow whistled past her face, lodging in the wall beside her.

Men in green-and-yellow tabards swarmed the corridors, their swords and short crossbows out. The Faceless that guarded Khall's quarters pushed back, parrying every thrust.

Khall wandered towards the door, a blanket wrapped around her. "What's happening—"

The Maetherians took aim in the doorway and fired.

Naias pushed her down, narrowly avoiding a hail of crossbow bolts. She shoved Khall back into the bedroom and slammed the door shut. Wood screeched against the floor.

The Faceless bought her time, but a handful of guards wouldn't last long against an army. She grabbed the bedside table and pressed it against the entrance. Jayal's and Maka's heads tumbled to the floor. Chairs, wardrobes, and soon the bed joined the barricade.

Soridian hadn't come to help. The Maetherians had deceived their way into the fortress, and they had turned on her.

37
Naias

Tevu must've sent word to them.

She could think of no other reason. Soridian knew she'd kept the godchild, and so he'd attacked her to get Viridian back.

She gritted her teeth. What was a near decade of friendship with the Maetherian envoy for, if he chose to believe their oppressor rather than her? Even if Tevu convinced him, she'd expected a cordial talk, maybe over some spicy noodle soup. Maetheria was known for its scholars, not its battle prowess. Storming the fortress was a move that Naias could not have predicted.

She had to get to Viridian before them.

The Maetherians had blocked off the only entrance and exit. Only the window stayed empty.

Naias pulled Khall into the corner furthest from the door, hiding her behind a pillar encrusted with starfish and crustaceans. "Don't move from this spot. You'll be safe here."

She grabbed Naias's arm, trembling violently. "Are they coming to kill me again?"

"We'll find out when it's over."

"Don't leave me, Naias, please—"

Naias shook her off, leaning out the window. The waves

crashed below. She had no hook and rope, and she hadn't scaled walls since she'd become Khall's adviser.

Nautical filigree protruded from the walls, shapes of leaping fish and fictional sea monsters. She gripped the nose of a shark, testing her weight. Sturdy enough. She hooked her feet to the decorative elements below, pushing herself up, finding one handhold after another. Climbing came easier than she expected. She thought she'd forgotten most of this, but memory worked in strange ways during times of crisis.

Perhaps the Faceless stench would never leave her.

She reached the top level of the fortress, hopping through a window that led into its corridors. Below her, Faceless Swords clashed against Maetherian spears, who were slowly moving their way up, attempting to clear the high ground for their archers.

Naias's men were lucky to have learned the fortress's winding paths in the short time they'd known peace. The Maetherians made the same mistakes they had when they first took over Haksa—climbing up the first staircase they found only to have it lead to a dead end. They split their army when they came to the courtyard, believing the flanks could eventually meet in the center.

She threw open the door to Viridian's room. The godchild was curled on the floor, hands over her ears.

"The sound," she screamed, "it hurts, it hurts, stop it—"

Pretending she was in pain wasn't going to get her out of this. Naias hoisted Viridian to her feet and shoved her towards the open cloisters. The Maetherians had flooded the second floor of the fortress, and if Naias didn't act quickly, Khall would die.

"The howling, Naias, can't you hear it?" Viridian gripped her own hair, as if trying to dislodge something from within her mind, but her distress suddenly melted away. She blinked back to the present, utterly confused.

"It's gone, I—"

Naias didn't have time for this. She pushed the godchild out onto the arched walkway, overseeing the melee.

"Kill them," she said.

Viridian gaped at the sea of green-and-yellow tabards. She was old enough to know what those colors signified. Her people had come for her.

"No," she said.

Naias's grip tightened around her arm. "You will do as I say."

She winced. "Please, you're hurting me—"

"You did it with the Tevurians."

"That was different."

"Kill them now."

"No," Viri screamed, twisting away from her grasp. "No."

Everyone said the same shit. Bodies were bodies, and death did not discriminate. The gods didn't care if she was Tevurian or Ashvian or Iskanti. Iskandraza came for them all. If the godchild wasn't going to cooperate, then she had no other choice.

Naias pulled out her gun and pointed it at Viridian's head.

The godchild froze immediately. Good, she wasn't a struggler. This would go better.

"If you want her to live," Naias shouted to the Maetherians, "then you'll put down your weapons."

The soldiers closest to her ceased fighting. "Hold," they said, and a wave of the word rang through the fortress. "Hold, hold, hold."

The noise dimmed, leaving the crashing waves echoing through the halls.

"The girl is what you want, right?" Naias shouted into the silence. "Keep fighting and she dies." A show of confidence would discourage them. She cocked a smile.

In the open courtyard below, the sea of green parted for an unarmored man in flowing robes. His eyeglasses glinted as lightning flashed through the sky.

Naias bared her teeth in the falsest of smiles. "Soridian," she said, her voice dripping with sarcasm. "My old friend."

"You're not going to kill her," he said.

"I won't?" Naias scoffed. "You've lectured me endlessly that we're a barbaric people that send our godchildren out to die. Maybe I should just kill her. That's what you want, right? To confirm what you've always thought about me."

How much did Tevu tell Soridian? Did he know about Diavijra's power? If he didn't, she could lie and say her power was found wanting. She could pretend the godchild meant nothing to them and pull this bluff off.

Soridian raised his hands, in an attempt to calm her down. "That bloodthirst hasn't reached you, Naias. Those are Ashvian practices. Not yours."

There he went again. His insistence that she wasn't Ashvian only made her angrier. "I am just as Ashvian as the rest of them," Naias shouted. "You keep talking about how different I am, so you can sow distrust between me and Khall. It doesn't work, it'll never work, and I am fed up listening to your condescension. So it's your turn to listen. *Leave.*"

Viridian hadn't moved since Naias took her hostage. Her legs had given out, and Naias resorted to propping her up against the stone parapet. Her entire body trembled, seemingly oblivious to the talk around her.

This was all Soridian's fault. He'd forced all of them into this situation. The bitterness spilled out readily, faster than she anticipated. "You know what, I'll give you something else as well. My forgiveness. I'll excuse you for believing Tevu over me. Nine years of friendship, Soridian, *nine*, and you chose to ally with the enemy. You didn't even give us time to explain ourselves. They invaded your lands. We didn't."

Soridian's face stayed curiously blank, neither confirming nor denying the accusation. But there was simply no other reason.

"Are we really playing this game?" Naias pressed her gun harder into Viridian's head. The Maetherian army inched forward. "Come on now. You lot are cowards. You wouldn't have attacked unless you knew the godchild was here. Tevu told you. Don't pretend."

Viridian shifted in her grasp. "It was . . . it was me," she said quietly. "I told him."

Soridian's careful facade fell away. He stepped forward in alarm. "Viri, don't—"

Naias bent down. "When?" This child was more devious than she'd thought. Smarter than Khall, and younger by half. "How?"

"The feast. I told him about the river shining like a prism. Papa used to say it when we visited. Don't kill them. I'll stay."

She'd learned she could get her way after saving Rafaeis, and was trying to replicate it here. Naias smiled. "Good. I'm proud that you owned up to your mistakes."

The walls scraped behind her. Faceless had scaled the walls, assembling themselves in a line, their guns trained on the courtyard below them. Swords and Axes poured into the fortress, a perimeter of black uniforms surrounding the sea of green.

"Don't kill them," Viridian repeated. "Let them go. Please."

Maybe Naias ought to teach the godchild about the careful wording of bargains. 'Don't kill them' was a request so vague that anyone could skirt it. Naias could order their capture. Not dead. She could torture them until they were unconscious. Not dead. She could leave them in the dungeons and provide no food or water. She didn't kill them; the starvation did. Clement had learned after a week or two of demands. Viridian would learn too, once she'd made enough deals. There was a small window to take advantage of her naivete before she broke.

No, this was not the time. Without the element of surprise, Maetheria was no longer a threat. They'd come so far only through deception. Naias wasn't going to trust them ever again. Viridian's childish honesty meant she wouldn't leave, even if Soridian forcibly took her away. Let her play with her deals, for now.

"Fine," Naias said. "Let the Maetherians go."

"I revoke that order," a shaky voice said below her.

Khall.

Naias peered over the open arches of the cloister. Khall stood on the floor below her, still in her nightdress. She'd unbarred the door to the throne room and walked out, her head kept high, her expression hardened. No hunched shoulders, no scared looks.

"I revoke it," Khall repeated, her voice bearing more power and authority than Naias had ever heard her speak. "Capture Soridian. Kill the rest."

Between accusing her of assassination and the Faceless gaining the advantage, Khall had managed to dredge up her confidence at the worst possible time. If she killed all the Maetherian soldiers, it would make Viridian more difficult to handle. Her trust would be broken, and Naias did not want to start her relationship on such damaged grounds.

"Khall," she said, "I urge you to take some time to reconsider—"

"I *have* reconsidered. I'm done with these attempts on my life. There must be consequences." She raised her hand and the Guns cocked, a singular metallic sound.

Viridian went rigid in her arms. Naias rushed to capitalize on her fear, covering the godchild's eyes with her hands.

The pistols exploded, cerulean sparks lighting the air. Maetherian soldiers screamed in the wake of the white haze, rearing back, and the singing clash of steel rang in her ears.

The Faceless enveloped them. Naias reeled at Khall's stubborn defiance. She'd never behaved like that before. Naias used to be able to alter her decisions with a bit of cajoling, and if that didn't work, she applied a bit more pressure. No longer.

At least her tactics bought her time. Khall was alive and they had the godchild. Maetheria was doomed either way.

Naias drew back, her grip on Viridian tight, and dissolved into the group of smiling faces.

38
Elera

A BABBLE OF voices woke her up.

"*Have you eaten well?*" someone asked in Iskanti, their words quick and sharp.

"*I have, Angkrasa-mother. The cooler winds bring ships along the strait of Paka Ala.*"

"*Flags?*"

"*Tevurian. Thirty ships, at least.*"

"*Sailing north?*"

"*No, south. To Hahg'sva. An attack, or trade, who knows.*"

"*Thank you, sister. Be careful by the coast. May Iskandraza mourn well.*"

"*Always. May Iskandraza mourn well.*"

The ground crunched under her. She'd been placed on a makeshift sled of woven branches. A yak pulled her along.

She blinked. Black larch branches trailed overhead. Tiny leaves broke away with the slightest breeze, shriveled and withered. One landed on her face.

Where was she? Her hand groped for her hammer, but a heavy fur had been wrapped around her body, while ropes lashed her to the sled.

Rafaeis's chiseled face materialized in her blurred vision. "You're all right," he said, plucking the leaf off her cheek.

"My hammer," she blurted.

He pointed to his back, her weapon wrapped in thick cloth. "I have it, don't worry. But fuck Ashvalra, do you carry this weight around all the time? I feel like a slug strapped to a boulder."

She breathed a laugh, only for her lungs to catch, turning her amusement into a coughing fit.

"She's awake," Rafaeis said in Iskanti, and the sled ground to a stop.

More people appeared, four in all. They wore layers of yak fur coats and hawk feathers woven into cloaks, all in shades of black and brown. Elera guessed the eldest woman was the clan's matriarch. Sunspots and wrinkles lined her sun-beaten face. Silver fibers wove through her coat, hawks and ibexes embroidered on its hem.

One of the younger men looked exactly like her, sharing the same nose, eyes, and tall forehead. His face was all anger and disdain. The third man had long gray hair, rings threaded through his Lakhesterian-styled braids, while the last person reminded her of Rafaeis's mixed heritage—masculine and beautiful, freckles dotted their light brown skin, and lavender-colored eyes peeked out from the hood they swaddled themselves in. A kettle of hawks perched on every part of their body.

Rafaeis gestured to the woman in silver. "Nasusorama Angkrasa, the matriarch of the Angkrasa clan. Her son, Nasyuk. The rest of their clan, Caush and Iavahl."

"Are you still in pain?" Iavahl asked, their slow, enunciated accent indicative of the northern Tevurian kingdoms. They unwrapped the furs around Elera, then slowly pulled apart the cloth bandages to reveal her wound.

The spiderweb of blackened veins had shrunk to half its size, leaving an imprint of blue and green. The cut gaped, oozing pus and blood, still deeply imbued with corruption.

Iavahl shrugged the hawks off. "Let me?" they asked, and pressed a finger on the open wound.

A brief warmth spread through Elera's chest, and when Iavahl released, a tarry substance beaded on their fingertip.

"Chatrasaya," Elera breathed. "You're the godchild we've been looking for."

"I prefer Iavahl," they said with a gentle smile. "Chatrasaya purges poisons and excises tumors. But today, for me, it is a drop at a time. I have kept the corruption at bay for now, but the air is bad here. Iskandraza does not want your wound to close. It will get worse, even with my help."

Elera grabbed Iavahl's hand, scooping up the drop. It smeared on her fingers, grainy and thick. "This is how you took away Rafaeis's mark?"

They nodded. "Two years, it took. We lost him when Khallan's war happened. We went back to Quctra many times, but we never found him."

"Mark bad," Nasu said in broken Common. "Soul lives, forehead. Bad to"—she mimicked the needle and hammer tattooing into Elera's forehead—"Iskanti believe."

Elera wasn't surprised. Khallan had always thought the Iskantis were beneath him. This desecration had to have been done on purpose.

"Are we done?" Nasyuk tapped his foot impatiently. *"The chill comes. We need to keep moving if we want to make time."*

Nasu nodded to Elera. *"The air will be better where we're going. You'll recover faster there."*

They moved through the forest, spiny larch trees extending to the sky, shielding Mount Iska from view. Rafaeis rode beside her on a yak.

"How did you find them?" Elera muttered.

"The horn," he said. "When I blew it, nothing happened, then it shattered in my hands. I thought it was defective. Nasu's clan arrived not long after. Iavahl said it was the most terrible sound they'd ever heard. I think the horn can only be perceived by godchildren."

She shook her head. "I heard it too. Then I dreamed of Iskandraza."

"You're not a godchild, are you?" he asked, frowning.

She pointed her finger at a tree, willing it to burst into flame. It stayed whole. She'd expected as much.

"The gods like them young. I would've known by now. Besides, Iskandraza's been dead forever." She scratched her head. "Maybe I thought I heard it. I was hallucinating a lot."

"The winds are strong on the wasteland. How are you feeling now?"

Her chest hurt less with every breath. She was actually hungry. If the place they were traveling to was better, as they said, then her wound would close and she'd be able to move freely again.

In the forest, no cairns guided them. The sun was their only compass, and they moved in the direction of its arc: westward. A herd of long-haired yaks and ibexes trailed behind, harnessed into a line, one behind the other. Brass bells dangled from their horns, a dull symphony as they marched. Furniture, rolled-up felts, and wooden lattices swayed on their backs.

Nasyuk rounded out the caravan, sitting backwards on the last yak. He held out a lashed-twig broom against the forest floor, sweeping it back and forth. Hoof prints and sled depressions disappeared under a fresh pile of leaves. He was covering their tracks.

If she was lucky, a few weeks of rest would close the wound, but now her chest hurt with a new pain altogether. Viri was still in Haksa, and yet here she was, heading west, straying further and further from the coast.

When she recovered, she had to go back. She may have only just learned about cairns, and now they moved in a part of Iskantupu where there were none to be found, but she had to risk crossing the wasteland again. She'd nearly died getting here, but she couldn't leave Viri alone.

And yet Rafaeis watched her, wearing a smile that could light up the darkest night. He'd found his godchild and his adopted clan.

If she left, he would follow. She'd thwarted his previous efforts to escape by simply existing. Love kept him here, but he must've been thinking of Viri too. Their bond was so strong that it was impossible not to, and yet she passed between them unspoken.

She'd have to leave in secret, whenever that was. His freedom had come hard won. A free Faceless, the first ever to do so, and to survive despite it all. She couldn't let him give that up.

She played along. "Better. Much more enjoyable than a lashing, that's for sure."

He laughed. "If a lashing is your baseline for an enjoyable experience, then everything in life should be filling you with happiness. Cynical, sarcastic Elera, skipping through the fields? Perhaps I might even hear you sing a song."

"You can try, and then you'd wish you were dead. I'll sound like that dreadful horn."

The land tilted downhill, leading into a tunnel hollowed under a mountain. Nasu released Elera from the sled and handed her a walking stick. She hobbled into the cave, chest aching with fresh exertion.

A gentle trickle of water echoed past the dull clang of the cowbells. The earth under them felt softer, wetter—the yaks' hooves sank in—every step gentle on her stiffened knees. The further they trod, the more the entrance shrank, until she failed to see it at all.

But light spilled through the other end of the tunnel. The trickling grew louder. Water droplets flashed as they fell.

When Elera emerged, she gasped.

Red flowers grew up to her knees. Moss padded every stone, creating a thick carpet of deep, viridian green. Tall, lush mountains and trickling waterfalls surrounded them. The mountains' peaks disappeared into the low-hanging clouds, traces of snow dusting their slopes. The humid air wet her face, but unlike Xinquha, it tasted crisper, cleaner.

"Hidden," Nasu said, putting a finger to her lips. *"Iskandraza made this."*

"The Destroyer?" Elera asked in disbelief. "Hard to imagine he'd create anything, much less this."

Nasu smiled. *"Ah yes, the Ashvians taught you that Iskandraza killed Ashvalra and destroyed the world, didn't they? But we believe differently. When the Destruction happened, Iskandraza found it in himself to save some of us. He trapped his voice in the horns that brought us to you, and created these hidden valleys for us to find refuge. The Iskantis are the descendants of those chosen few.* See? Iskandraza destroys. Also saves. Special place. Safe."

Elera glanced back to the tunnel. They'd walked through an empty riverbed. The water had dried out from the heat of summer, but the autumn monsoon season approached. With cooler weather and rains, the riverbed would fill up again, closing off both entrance and exit to this place.

Safe, or trapped.

She couldn't tell.

39
Viri

Naias told me my people put up a fight after Khall ordered them to die. They tried, but the Faceless fought better. I didn't know if she was lying. All I knew was that the fortress was quiet again, the crashing waves roaring in my ears.

I asked about Dada. He was locked up in the dungeons below the fortress, she said. At least he was alive. She'd kept her promise.

Dada came back for me. He came back. I thought he'd forgotten about us, me and Papa, but he didn't. He recognized me in Xinquha, in that grazing pasture, and he brought an army to get me back.

He loved me still, just as much as Papa, and Elera, and Rafaeis. My body trembled with the strength of it. All of them meant so much to me, yet I'd never been more alone.

I dreaded sleep. It was the little death, where I didn't remember when I lost consciousness. It was so cruel that your body reminded you every night that this was how you died. You wouldn't know it. You'd just decide not to wake up one day.

A day turned into a week, then a month, and then two. Every night I died.

And the world still turned.

Time didn't stop when Papa died, or when Elera and Rafaeis saved me, or when my powers came. There was a whole world that moved on with their lives, oblivious to mine. On and on and on, and still the grief stayed with me. They never let me see Dada, and I thought Elera and Rafaeis must have died on their mission. It was the only explanation as to why they never came back.

Oh, how I hated Naias for sending them away. I should've killed her then. I should've killed them all. Death was the kinder path. None of us would've suffered so much afterwards.

I thought I understood war. I thought it was about people fighting and losing. But it was much more than that.

When I put Papa's death next to the rise and fall of empires, he was just a speck in time. How awful it was that his death shook me so deeply, yet when the world turned enough times, no one would remember what happened to him, or what happened to me.

I could handle grief within the framework of my short life. How my powers blessed and cursed me in the same breath. The people I met, horrific in their brutality and tender in their love. The promises I kept to them, and the promises they broke to me.

But my life, measured in the infinite timeline of the universe? It is a grief without walls; one that defies any word.

40
Elera

With her limited strength she helped Caush water the ibexes and yaks and, with Rafaeis, dug the trench that marked the privy. These practices came naturally to her, the Faceless having taught her these skills. The rest of the clan pitched their gers, one by one, unfurling wooden lattices in a circular pattern. Iavahl climbed atop, carefully slotting wooden poles into a hollow dome. Caush and Nasu guided the ends of the poles onto the edges of the lattice, creating a sloped roof. Together, they draped heavy felt over the whole structure and lashed it together with thick cords. By the second ger, Elera couldn't do more than hold the rope while the others worked.

At the end, she lay splayed on the meadow, grateful it was over, but Nasyuk gruffly tossed her a long sash.

"*Follow me,*" he said. "*We're going hunting.*"

Elera wheezed, pointing to her chest. "I'm not going to be of much use."

"*Kch, the exercise will do you good, Faceless. You've slept enough on the sled already.*"

He hiked to the edges of the mountain range, picking out a goat that grazed not far from camp. A natural goatherd, he corralled the animal, encircling it, but the goat found an opening, bolting in the other direction. Elera tried to tackle it, but missed as it deftly swerved to one side. She fell on her ass.

Nasyuk laughed at her and chased after the goat, penning it in until exhaustion set in and it could walk no more. He grabbed its horns and straddled its body.

"The sash," he said.

She was a novice again, gasping for breath after running a few steps. She handed the felt strip over and lay on the grass again.

"We don't waste blood here," he said, blindfolding the goat. Nasyuk muscled his hands around its neck and, in one swift move, snapped it in two.

He carried the carcass back to camp, mounting it on a wooden tripod. Elera slowly followed, finding a thick branch that served as a makeshift walking stick. She arrived out of breath and in time to see Nasyuk making a small slit in the goat's neck, draining the blood into a large bowl. He dipped a small cup into the blood, mixed it with a splash of yak's milk, and drank it raw.

He offered a cup to her, grinning. *"It's good for your health,"* he said. *"You'll recover quicker."*

She tried not to look disgusted. Blood wasn't the problem; she'd eaten blood sausages before, but they were solid and cooked, mixed with rice if she had the scrips that day. But raw?

Nasyuk scoffed. *"You Ashvians eat lizards. They have no blood and their tails drop off. Such unnatural creatures."*

"I'm not Ashvian," Elera snapped in poorly intonated Iskanti, a feeble attempt to distance herself from the people she served.

He shook the cup at her. *"Prove it."*

She snatched it from his hands. Milky red bubbles frothed on the surface. She took in a deep breath.

"Are you bullying our guests again, Nasyuk?" Iavahl's voice floated on the wind. Two enormous hawks perched on their shoulders.

Thank Ashvalra. She approached Iavahl, grateful for a

distraction, but the largest hawk spread its wings and *shrieked* at her.

Elera shrieked too, the valley echoing with the screeches of bird and terrified woman.

"Do not mind him," Iavahl said with a laugh. They reached into their belt, feeding the bird a bit of meat. "This is Dapo, the oldest hawk amongst us. Nine years and five months. His time with us is almost up."

"Can't catch a goat with birds," Nasyuk muttered behind them. He pulled out a skinning knife, making a long cut along the carcass's flank.

"Nasyuk prefers to hunt with his hands and feet," Iavahl said, taking the cup from Elera's hand. They downed it in one and smacked their lips. "An unfamiliar taste and texture to those who first come here. I took my time too."

"You grew up here? But I thought the Iskanti clans never accept outsiders." Kujivhan may have broken from tradition, but being Iskanti triumphed over all. Even he did not dare to breach that code.

"Mostly. I was Tevurian. Well, Tevurian in the most technical sense. That squabble is no longer my business. Mohyri named me when I was . . . five, six, and they raised me to be a godchild. But they judged my powers pitiful. I could not face the truth. Nasu talked me down from taking my life. At the time it was just her and Nasyuk. Caush was a Lakhesterian orphan who wandered into Tevu. He was about to be pressed into the Reborn, but Nasu took him away. The four of us became a clan. A strange one, comprised of found children. It is ours."

Nasu's little clan was far more radical than she'd realized.

"I'm sorry," Elera said.

They smiled. "I am not. I am grateful to have found Nasu. She was the one who taught me how to raise these hawks." They raised the arm Dapo sat on, resting it on Elera's shoulder. The hawk hopped off readily and stared at her.

She stood very still, her shoulders tensed. *Don't peck out my eyes.*

"You like them," Iavahl said. "When we traveled here, I always saw you looking."

Dapo stretched his wings. Feathers beat against her head, sending her hair astray. "I do like them," she said. "I wish they liked me back."

"These are bonded, that is why you have such trouble with them. They see you as a stranger."

"Taken as a young fledgling," Elera muttered, "to train and serve a single master."

"And yet when we let them free, after their ten years of service, they continue to live and flourish."

"Don't the hawks miss you?" Every time she wanted to stop thinking of Viri, she thought of Viri. Love wouldn't let her forget. Like the old hawks the Iskantis left behind, she'd abandoned her. They would've bleached her hair by this point. A white-haired godchild, perfectly groomed, instead of the unwashed mess she'd first met in the wagon. A Maetherian godchild, fighting for Ashvian freedom.

"Some of them do come back," Iavahl said. "They follow. We have to travel far to set them free, and then hide in the forest until they cannot see us anymore. You hear them cry for days afterwards. But yearning for the familiar is a natural part of life, even when that same familiarity only brings them pain. Rafaeis likes the birds too, perhaps for the same reasons as you. So I will say what I said to him: You were once bound to a master, bred and beaten to forget your instincts. But a hawk is still a hawk. Now that you are free, you can choose how you want to live."

The birds took flight as Iavahl pressed a finger to Elera's chest. A drop of black tar beaded in the space between them. "Tevu told me that godchildren were special. I wasted my childhood training for something I could never be. When you are brought up to believe that you were destined for greatness, only to realize you never had it to begin with . . . it is a bitterness and rage that words cannot express."

They let go, wiping their fingers on their tunic. "I am still a godchild. But I chose to be a hawk-hunter. I have become more than what destiny gave me. That path was always there for you. One day, you will find the courage to walk it too."

41
Viri

Two maids brought me into a small bathing room. We were right next to the ocean, but they soaked me in a wooden tub filled with water. They brought the lye out to bleach my hair. In Xinquha, the black leeches smelled terrible, but this one was worse. It burned the inside of my nose when I breathed.

They didn't have Rafaeis's carefulness or Elera's speed. They complained their hands stung and went to wash it off, leaving me alone in the bath.

I kept asking for Dada. They told me he was still alive. I thought that saving him would make me feel better, but it didn't. I couldn't save everyone. All the Maetherian soldiers had died. I didn't know their names, or the lives they'd lived, but they'd traveled all this way and fought for me, and death was their reward.

This was my fault. It was all because of this cursed power, and I didn't want it. I dragged my nails down my arms. I couldn't think as much when my body hurt. Maybe that was why I hadn't cried in the wagon. It was simpler to focus on the physical pain and survive than to think about the grief without walls.

My hair soaked in the lye longer than it should have. My scalp felt like it was being stabbed by a million needles. The maids didn't come back, so I slid down the tub and washed the burn away. Clumps of hair fell out.

Another attendant entered my room, placing a barkcloth tunic on the table. "The queen wants to see you," he said. "Get dressed."

I cleaned myself off and hurried into the throne room. Khall sat by the window, wearing cotton robes she'd pilfered from the Tevurian garrison. Her legs curled up on the chair, one hand absently picking the spots below her chin, while the other held a long scroll. She stared plaintively at the ocean beyond the throne room, ignoring the row of children that knelt before her.

"I don't know any of you," she said. "None of you have seen battle. I nearly died, twice. My heir needs to be fearless. When the knife comes for you, I need to know that you'll stand your ground and fight back. You can't be a coward, soiling your bed and letting the poison kill you. You need to be strong, and brave—when you're trapped in the dirt and an Iskanti raises his sword above your head, you'll tear *his* head off and spit on his corpse."

If Naias were here, she would've said something comforting, but the throne room stayed quiet.

She waved a hand, dismissing them all. "Get a sparring circle erected here," she said to the Faceless guard. "I want to see them fight. That'll help my choice."

As the girls and boys shuffled past me, Khall returned to looking out the window. She wore no crown or jewelry or furs. Summerbell flowers were braided through her hair. She looked like a girl who didn't want to grow up. She looked like me.

If she weren't sitting on the throne, or wearing those Tevurian robes, she could've passed as any other child. Maybe another godchild that Elera and Rafaeis had to take care of. We'd play by the river together, scrubbing each other's hair. It wouldn't hurt as much when Elera and Rafaeis had to leave. I'd have her. I wouldn't be alone.

"Do you like being a godchild, Diavijra?" Khall asked, jolting me from my thoughts.

I didn't know if she wanted my honesty. The smile on her face back when she ordered me to kill the fox told me everything. She liked my powers. I didn't.

She didn't wait for an answer. "I don't like being queen. I have a fate foisted on me that I never wanted. I would've been happy in Quctra, lying in the fields, happily married to the one person my father didn't want me to love. Godchildren must feel the same too. Gods gave you power and you had no choice but to receive it. But you can make change for the better. I can't. Naias wants me to kill people. It's part of being a queen, she says. And so I do."

"You don't have to," I dared to say. She wanted the same thing I did. A normal life. Going home. A family.

She turned to me and the wistfulness died. The throne scraped against her dress as she got out to take my hand. "Let's go into the city. I have something to show you."

We left the fortress, past the moldy stairs and salt-encrusted corridors, past the repaired fortress gates, and came to the town square. I fidgeted in her grasp. The Haksanis had crowded to look at something, murmuring under their breath. The Faceless escorted us, pushing the townsfolk away.

"I thought like you once," Khall said to me. "And then I grew up."

Our guards parted, and I saw a platform built of wood. A lone man knelt on it, tied to a stake.

Dada.

His body kept shifting between his knees and feet. When he saw me, his lips twitched into a sad smile.

No. She couldn't have brought me out here to watch him die. I shook my head, as if my denial could change what I saw around me. "No, I told Naias not to kill him."

"You're right," she said. "Naias isn't killing him. You are."

Inexplicably, my hand tightened around Khall's, when I should've pushed her away. The crowd faded. I was in the university again, focusing on the brains that slid down the glass. I wanted to vomit.

I dug my nails into my arm, bringing me back to the present. "No. I want him alive."

Her face settled into a practiced calmness, devoid of the daydreaming girl I'd seen in the throne room. "That wasn't the way you worded your demand, Diavijra," she said evenly. "You asked Naias not to kill him, and she isn't. Consider this a lesson, if you want to continue bargaining with me in the future."

Why did I ever think that she would've been my friend? She blamed Naias for making her this way, but Naias wasn't the one that took advantage of my honesty. Khall was far more cruel.

I wasn't going to keep my promise to a monster like her.

"I won't kill him," I said.

Her lips twisted into something ugly when she bent down to whisper in my ear.

"If you want to see Hammer and Crescent again, you will do as I say."

Fear sharpened in my heart, the worst I'd felt in months. They were alive?

"I've kept them in the dungeons. If you refuse to kill Soridian, I'll order their execution. Kill me, and all of us die. Save two lives, one, or none. Your choice." She held up three fingers. "In three . . ."

Was she telling the truth? No one guided me. Naias wasn't here. Elera and Rafaeis weren't here. Papa wasn't here. It was just me and Khall, and I had to choose if I believed her in this split second of a moment.

I didn't want to go back to Maetheria. I wanted Elera and Rafaeis, and despite all the lonely nights, I still clung to the belief that they'd come back for me. Khall gave me that, however cruel it may have been.

"Two."

But Dada had come back for me too.

So many people loved me, and I couldn't save them all. My body bent with rage, my anger directed at no one but myself.

All I knew then was that I wanted them more than Dada. I was wholly, incredibly selfish.

"One."

I stepped forward.

Khall nodded and rose up, her body straight, chest open, all that befitted a queen, and addressed the crowd. "Let this be a warning to all that resist my claim to the kingdom of Ashvi . . ."

Her words turned into a jumble. All I could know and see was him.

Tears ran down Dada's face. "I'm sorry for not being home. I'm sorry that I couldn't save you."

"No, it's my fault," I choked out. "It's mine, it's mine."

"Don't blame yourself, Viri," he said. If he weren't bound, he would've hugged me, I knew he would've. "Don't ever think this was your fault. You did the best you could. I love you. Survive for me, for Papa. *Survive*."

It never occurred to me to kill Khall in that moment. I froze, like I always did, and thought the only way forward to seeing Elera and Rafaeis again was to kill my own dada.

If I knew what I know now, I would've sunk Xinquha, Haksa, Tevu, and all of its people into oblivion. But I didn't. I trusted the word of a queen because I didn't know any better. How would I know better? How would I have thought differently? You read the timeline of my life and laugh at all the mistakes I made, because that's what you are, aren't you? A judge of others, confident that this would've never happened to you, while forgetting all the errors that comprise *your* life.

I don't want to describe to you how he died. You consume my story for entertainment, to savor every spurt of blood, every gruesome detail, until your primal thirst is sated. His death didn't happen to you. You could've been one of the many people in the square that day who gathered to groan and grimace and laugh, and then went about the rest of their lives when it was done.

Grief is such a personal thing. It slams into you like a

hurricane while leaving everyone else intact. But they suffer their own storms too. We try to share in it, find solace that we're not the only ones, yet when all the condolences are done and the tears and laughter end, you are alone once more.

You know how *it* feels. It is impossible for you to know how *I* feel.

But fine. I will give you an image. Imagine a girl who watched her dada die. Her eyes are wide, and her tears dried on her face. Yes, she's cried after all, but she doesn't know it.

She doesn't know it because she is not here; she's searching her memory over the last months, scrutinizing every little action that led to this point. When she told Soridian about the river shimmering in a prism of light. She shouldn't have said that. When her powers manifested. She shouldn't have told Khall that. When she listened to everyone who told her: *survive*, and her path ended with taking her father's life.

She thinks, *If I had done this differently*, as if her regret could change the present around her. As if she could will all her decisions away and manifest a new reality.

It doesn't happen.

She doesn't want to be here anymore.

Her mind closes, and she is no longer Viri.

42
Diavijra

The twisting corridors gaped, an endless mouth, swallowing her whole. The Faceless surrounded her, oblivious to the hollowness of it all.

"I want to go to the dungeons," Viridian said, but no one listened. No one ever did. Her chains dragged along the stone floor.

Smoke wafted through the hall. Clement's head peeked out from the damp pillars of the fortress. He'd come out to watch and done nothing to help. He could've stopped Khall by talking to her, or threatening her, or something that leveraged his experience as the only godchild who knew how to survive in this world, and yet he had not lifted a finger.

"I want to talk to Khall," she said, louder. "I've done as she said. I want to see Hammer and Crescent."

Clement's languid voice snaked into her unwilling ears. "A word of advice, little godchild—"

"I'm not talking to you," she hissed. "Leave me alone."

Viridian hated him. The night he saved Rafaeis seemed like an illusion. He'd moved with such urgency and concern then. There was a part of Clement that desperately cared, but like a wisp, it vanished as quickly as it came.

His face contorted into something resembling pity. "When

the Maetherians attacked, did you hear a howling too?"

She stopped. No one knew anything about the sound, and she'd dismissed it as a hallucination.

"Leave her with me," he said to the Faceless.

Her guard shook their heads. "Our queen's orders—"

Clement didn't let them finish. He placed a hand on Viridian's back and pulled her into his room. The door shut behind him.

Candelabras stood on every surface, melted wax leaking all over the tables. He'd boarded up the windows, keeping the smoke in. Sheer silk in riotous colors hung from the ceiling in waves: an artificial cloudscape to replicate the sky he'd shut out. A chime made of earrings and necklaces dangled in the center of the room, lazily swirling in the haze.

"That howl you heard was a summoning," he said, brushing past her, jewelry clinking with every step. He sank into a green-and-gold embroidered couch, picking his pipe up from the rich angsana table beside it. He tipped out the burned tar and packed the pipe bowl with more opium. "Some king's gotten their hands on a horn, and some of us will be foolish enough to answer. Put it out of your head. You may hold the power of gods in your hand, little godchild, but there are empires and kingdoms that play a game larger than you. Khall has changed since Xinquha. She's just understood what being a queen is. I've seen it in new monarchs. They throw their power around for a while, making and breaking promises on impulse. She'll grow out of this phase. Don't be surprised if you can't see Crescent or Hammer at all."

Viridian had killed her father because Khall hadn't grown up. People lived and died by Khall's judgments, yet she wielded power like it was a toy.

She couldn't stop her hands from shaking. She didn't want to. "Then I'll kill her."

"All right," Clement said patiently. "Say you do, then what?"

"Then I'll find Hammer and Crescent," she snapped. "And we'll leave this place and never come back."

He shook his head. "You think too small. Let's say you kill Khall. She has no heir—"

He was making excuses for his inaction, and she didn't want to hear any of it. "I don't care, she—"

"Shut up, child, and let me teach you. Khall has no heir, and she's dismissed all her father's advisers. Naias is an Iskanti, and a former Faceless at that. The Xinquhans will never accept her as the new Earthly Sovereign. The throne lies empty. Tevu will take this opportunity to attack and restore their old borders. The kingdom of Ashvi will lose everything they've gained. They'll lose Haksa, they'll lose Xinquha. All Ashvians—including the Faceless—will be reabsorbed into the Tevurian Empire. That is, if Tevu allows them."

He took a long draw from his pipe. He was kind enough not to blow the smoke in her face, but he didn't stop it from reaching her either. "Did you know the blood tithe was a Tevurian practice first? Khallan borrowed it when he sought to reestablish his kingdom. The people who make up the Reborn have little in common besides the heavy armor they wear, because the empire is so large. They're allowed to speak their own dialects, practice their own faith, have families and children . . . Maybe that's why they keep losing to the Faceless. Tevu sees Khallan's blood tithe as unnecessarily cruel, and yet they are cruel themselves. When Tevu is crossed, he crushes all resistance. Priests, peasants, the Faceless—yes, including your beloved Hammer and Crescent—will be annihilated."

Viridian did not have that kind of clairvoyance. She was twelve, only a child, and had suffered one devastating loss after another. Now Clement expected her to play politics. She had to learn all these unspoken rules so quickly to survive.

"I used to think like you," Clement said, reclining on his couch. "I thought that if I somehow killed my gaoler, I'd be free. That moment came to me a little less than a year ago, when Khallan drank that poisoned ricewine.

"We'd planned this for years. Nine, in fact. It took a long time to gain each other's trust. Khallan was a tyrant. I thought we'd be better off if his daughter ascended the throne. When Khallan summoned me as he shat himself to death, I smiled and told him, 'Chatrasaya's who you're looking for, not me.' Oh, what glee I felt! When he died, I was promised that Khall would be taught differently."

The brief happiness disappeared into a long sigh. "But look where we are now. My struggle is a little harder than yours—my powers do not cause harm, only heal the people who hold my chain—but it's not Khall you want. It's the blood tithe. It's monarchy. It's Tevu's insatiable greed in conquering every part of this continent. It's Khallan's want to reclaim a memory of a home, a desire that he passed down to his daughter, who does not understand why, but does it anyway. And all that cannot be erased with the death of a single person."

"And this is how it is?" she asked in despair. "I have no power, and I cannot change anything. But I can't go on like this. I just killed . . . I killed—"

Clement smiled softly and put his pipe down. He walked over to a shelf that burgeoned with boxes of jewelry and glass figurines, but from within the clutter he withdrew a tiny wooden box, no bigger than his palm. He carefully pulled out the three trinkets Viridian had seen in his tent during the march to Haksa: a tiny hourglass, a blue gem, and a glass pendant.

"You'll find a way out of your grief," he said, cradling the little ornaments in his hand. "I did."

The world turned, her life a speck in its unfurling threads. Both her fathers' deaths would cease to matter one day.

Impossible. She hurt so much. It was unfair how it could be so easily forgotten. She dragged her nails down her arm. Long red welts formed on top of her scarred skin.

"I don't know what else to do," she cried.

Clement handed her the pipe. "Sometimes the best thing to do . . . is to forget."

43
Naias

THE AUTUMN SOLSTICE was a sacred affair to the Ashvians. When the weather cooled and the harvests ended, they celebrated Ashvalra's bounty, praying for the remnants of her magic to return next year. Khall had ordered Naias to oversee it, overriding her protests. This was a job for someone who didn't have to worry about Tevurian invasions and rebuilding walls. She had so much to do.

Three months ago, she'd sent out the call for royal servants and Faceless initiates together. Since then, she'd received almost a hundred children to serve Khall, and the attendants to train them, so much so the fortress resembled more nursery than court.

She quickly ushered the newest batch into the throne room, entering without a summons. Khall was dragging her feet on picking an heir, her one responsibility, and Naias had moved on to overwhelming her with untrained children. Not only did it mean less time spent with the queen, but she hoped the incessant noise would force her to make a decision.

Naias read off a scroll. "The twenty priests from Xinquha have arrived, and another ten Ashvian children are here as your attendants. We've enough fish from the Haksanis, and the shipments of rice are coming in as we speak—*what is going on?*"

She'd nearly tripped into the sharp end of a dagger. A sparring circle had been erected in the throne room, and two boys no older than twelve hurled themselves at each other. They swung wildly and without finesse, daggers firmly grasped in their hands.

Khall watched the fight like a man possessed, tracing every swing and every parry.

"I'm choosing my heir," she said. "A show of strength will help."

"With real blades?"

"If they can take a life now, it means they aren't scared. The next sovereign should be fearless." She leaned forward on her chair. "Go on."

One child kicked the other to the floor, dagger raised above his head.

Out of instinct Naias stepped in, snatching up both weapons. "Go back to your instructors," she said to the children. "Don't ever fight like this again."

"I'm not picking an heir today, it seems," came Khall's sarcastic response.

Naias tossed the weapons aside. "A fight to the death is not the way. What happened to the other Ashvians? I've sent you dozens of eligible children in the last few months."

"None of them were strong enough."

"For now," Naias said, trying to keep her voice patient. "Pick a few and spend time with them. Sift through and we'll find the brighter one amongst them. You might even become friends. They're all from good Ashvian families, but you have to take them on first."

"And let another potential assassin into my circle."

Naias threw her hands up. "Once again, no one's trying to kill you."

"Why are you always pestering me about heirs?" Khall snapped. "Do you want to see me die so badly?"

A Faceless initiate entered the room. "Basaa and Ayashara seek an audience with the queen, Commander."

Naias normally despised these interruptions. The long periods of intimacy they'd shared in the leaking palace were now a thing of the past. The work never stopped since they'd arrived in Haksa. Naias still refused to admit advisers into Khall's court. She'd delegated the lesser jobs to Ashvian loyalists and the Faceless, but everything still went through her. Any interruption meant less time with Khall, one less kiss, one less night spent together. A worthwhile trade, to keep her close.

"Let them in," she said.

The couple seemed little worse for wear since the Maetherian attack. They held two large jars between them: mustard vegetables pickled in brine and chili.

Khall spoke first. "Basaa, you have children. Why don't you put them up as heir?"

Basaa shifted uneasily. His prosthetic foot creaked under his weight. "Our children, ah, don't qualify."

"What, because Ayashara is Iskanti?" She shrugged. "If they're not cowards, I don't see why that's a problem."

Naias jerked her head back in surprise. Khall had overthrown centuries of Iskanti prejudice so casually by saying she wasn't opposed to naming an Iskanti as heir. She should've been encouraged by that, but Khall's fear of assassination had grown so large that it superseded her father's decree that only an Ashvian could rule an Ashvian kingdom. For the queen, strength was the only important quality.

Naias chose to say nothing. It was a hopeful change, even if it was driven by terror.

Basaa plastered a large smile on his face. "Even so, I think our children enjoy the freedom of the sea. They'll get bored very quickly in this stuffy fortress. I promise you they'll be terrible servants. I thank you for considering them, but to the point of our visit today."

He stepped forward, handing the jars over to Khall with both hands. "We only wanted to reiterate our gratitude for protecting Haksa. These pickled vegetables are our thanks. A classic Haksani dish. Our dockworkers inhale these whenever Aya makes a batch. I guarantee it won't disappoint."

More flattery. Naias saw it for what it was: a plea that an attack of this magnitude wouldn't happen again, but Ayashara knew very well that this had to be spelled out to the queen.

"I cannot emphasize enough how much the Haksanis seek normality," she said.

"I know, I know," Khall said dismissively. "It won't happen again. Thank you for the offering. You're dismissed."

The door closed behind the merchant couple, leaving Naias and Khall in the throne room. The rush of the ocean waves lingered between them. It had been a long time since they'd been alone like this.

Naias eyed the jars. "You need to eat. You haven't had a proper meal since we left Xinquha."

"I'm not hungry," Khall said, putting them on the floor.

Both of them knew it wasn't true. Nine months had passed since Khallan's death, and she'd made no progress on assuaging Khall's paranoia. Even with a taster, Khall still believed someone was going to poison her. Naias couldn't convince her otherwise.

"You can go too," Khall said, quick and curt.

They hadn't spoken—really spoken—since the Maetherian attack. Soridian's death sat uncomfortably with her. Now that Maetheria wasn't allied with them, she had to defend Haksa on both sides. She had a Tevurian attack to prepare for.

She'd overheard the pages gossiping in the corridors, and that was how she found out Soridian had died. It bit her deep that she'd discovered a friend's death like this. Killed not by the godchild, but by the hand who controlled her.

Her accomplice, gone, in the blink of an eye. He'd procured Khallan's poison for her, hoping for a better world. And her repayment for his help? Doing absolutely nothing as he knelt on the execution floor.

It wasn't completely her fault. He'd overestimated Naias's power over Khall. When the queen was frightened, nothing

Naias said could dissuade her, and Soridian had paid for it. In a way, it was *his* fault for attacking them. Had he waited outside and negotiated terms, like Sahru, this would've all gone differently.

She'd spent nine years gaining Soridian's trust. For as long as she'd known him, he'd always dragged his feet, and yet he'd chosen recklessness at the end.

His death caused a new problem. Khall had taken matters into her own hands and killed a Maetherian envoy. Not only was Tevu looking to retake Haksa, but now Maetheria would seek revenge as well. Khall needed to know she'd made a terribly stupid decision.

"I wasn't told about your plans for the godchild," Naias said. "Bringing her out to kill Soridian."

Khall drew her shoulders up. "You didn't need to know."

"As your adviser—"

"Yes, yes—"

"—I'm here to help you protect your kingdom. We've angered Maetheria. I'll send someone to speak with them. We can't fight both them and Tevu. We have to prevent total war."

"I'm done talking," Khall said. "That display in the square will spread through the entire continent. Everyone will know we have Diavijra, one of the three progenitors from which all other gods descend. No more sending out Faceless to kill in the shadows. We hold the power. They should be coming to *us*."

"And what happens when the godchild discovers that we have neither Hammer nor Crescent in the dungeons?"

Khall waved a hand. "You'll find something. We found it in Clement."

I'm not here to clean up your mess. Of course it would fall to her to scramble for a solution when Khall had none. How quickly things fell apart. She wanted this to be a happy partnership, where she would make the decisions and Khall would be her public, acceptable, un-Faceless face. They'd oversee the little village of Xinquha, finding the best way to make it flourish. She would've been happy with that, but Khall chased her father's legacy, and since then all Naias could do was pick up the pieces after her.

Fight after fight after fight. It was all for her freedom and ending the blood tithe, but even that didn't stop the toil that wore on her.

"There's a chasm widening between us," Naias said quietly. "I see you running ahead, and I don't know if I can ever catch up. Not being there with you . . . It scares me, Khall. I feel like I'm being left behind, like I'm a Faceless all over again, and no matter how hard I try, I'll never be worthy enough."

Khall blinked in surprise. "Naias, I—"

She didn't wait for her to finish. Naias bowed, leaving her queen to sit on her brittle throne.

SHE WALKED OUT to meet a dozen sun-beaten, skinny Iskanti-Haksani boys waiting in her office. In their hands lay a piece of dirtied paper, folded up multiple times, the Faceless mask printed on it.

While nearly all the Ashvians had sent their children to serve Khall, not one had volunteered for the Faceless. In her desperation, she'd put out the call in Haksa as well. The boys held out the paper, pointing at it, and spoke in rapid Iskanti dialect. She couldn't understand a word.

Naias frowned, gesturing to the paper, and spoke in broken Iskanti. *"You . . . uh, Faceless, want join?"*

They nodded. They spoke no Common.

"What do you do now?" she asked. She mimed a variety of jobs. Building, hauling, fishing—

They cupped their hands.

Begging.

The poorest of the poor, in Haksa. These boys had no future here and believed enslavement would bring them a better life. The Faceless had scrips and rations. If they worked hard enough, they could even build their own huts in Xinquha.

She'd be saving them from poverty.

Her nails bit into her palms. This was no different from the blood tithe, except now the Iskantis freely proffered their necks to the slaughter.

This wasn't what she wanted at all. She wanted an end to it, and for the Ashvians to fight their own war against Tevu. Her mind raced. If asking the Ashvians to volunteer didn't work, then she'd have to do it by force. She had Khall's seal, and conscripting them was but a decree away. They'd have no choice but to join the Faceless.

But if they refused? What then? Would she have the Faceless forcibly take them away, the same way they did with the Iskantis? Naias would've savored the poetic justice, but it was no way to keep the peace between a queen and her subjects. They'd lost Maetheria as an ally and now fought Tevu on their own. She couldn't risk a civil war as well.

"Commander." Two priests and a committee of Ashvians crowded behind the threshold of her door.

She groaned, rubbing her forehead. "What is it now?"

"The solstice preparations are nearly done, but we're short on the sweetened offerings, and we need a few more goats. We also need your approval for Ashvalra's avatar, the godchild is waiting in her room—"

So much work and so little time.

They desperately needed initiates, but she screamed against this injustice. It was the blood tithe with a smile, and she could not be a part of it.

No, she had time, she had time. Change came in tiny, excruciating steps. She wasn't Hammer. She'd have to persuade the Ashvians the same way she did Khall. Tevu moved slowly, and they had the northern rebellions to quell. Construction resumed on Haksa's walls; the village would survive without a few Faceless initiates.

She had time.

"Go home," she said to the boys, and left for Diavijra's chambers.

* * *

"We should paint half her face gold," one priest said, his paintbrush hovering over Diavijra's cheek.

"No, paint her whole face," another priest said. "The festival honors Ashvalra, not her."

"Is it not better to show that two of the progenitor gods have chosen to be with our queen?"

They turned to Naias.

She sighed. This bickering was a waste of her time. "Paint her whole face," she said, arbitrarily picking a side. She didn't care for the specifics.

She tried not to look at Diavijra herself. There was a blankness there that she'd seen in the children of the blood tithe. The embroidered silks and jewelry the priests smothered her in couldn't hide it.

"I want to see them," Diavijra said quietly.

"After the festival is done," she said, blurting out the first thought that came to mind. "It'll put Khall in a good mood. She'll be more likely to let you see them if she's happy."

Diavijra said nothing else. Naias didn't press. She didn't want to. She'd put a gun to her head, threatened her, and forced her to kill her own people. It was a miracle that neither Khall nor she was already dead. Their lives hinged on the lie that Hammer and Crescent were in the dungeons somewhere and Khall had the key.

She couldn't tell Diavijra that her two favorite people were missing. Hammer's return was taking longer than expected, but she was certain at least one of them would come back. She just needed to buy time.

Naias picked at her mark. All her plans had been thrown into disarray. She'd hoped to weaken the bond between Diavijra and them by now, but Soridian's execution had only served to reinforce it. Now the godchild asked for nothing else except them. She couldn't keep this lie up for long.

Leading tired her more than she expected. All this whispering, scheming, planning, rehearsing. It wasn't her. Soridian had known who Viridian was the moment he met her in that horse pasture. He'd played Naias. She'd never been able to control any political conversation when he was involved.

At heart, she was still a fighter. A Faceless. An Iskanti.

Only good for war.

She dug a fingernail into the center of her forehead. Maybe she wasn't cut out for power. If she left, she wouldn't need to whisper in Khall's ear anymore, or constantly need to prove that she was as worthy as any Ashvian. She'd happily move back to Xinquha, living out the rest of her life hunting wild game. She missed shooting; adrenaline sparking from her emptied lungs as she steadied her aim, waiting for the best moment to pull the trigger. A simpler life. Here, she treaded water in a rising tide, and every wrong move threatened to drown her.

The priests posed Diavijra's arm, smearing gold everywhere, and thrust a sheaf of rice into her hands. They spun her around, looking to Naias for approval.

"Fine, fine," she said, barely looking at the girl.

Priests and attendants lined up before Diavijra, wearing barkcloth robes of red and gold, swinging smoking jars of incense. As they walked out the fortress, they chanted prayers in the Ashvian dialect.

> *O Ashvalra, who sleeps beneath:*
> *Hear our cry and let us reave*
> *the one who killed you*
> *and brought us grief*
> *O Ashvalra, reborn again:*
> *Grant us men the hope you bring*
> *upon the corpse of destruction*
> *the dawn of spring*

Cooped up in the fortress and intent on rebuilding the walls surrounding the city, Naias hadn't properly seen Haksa.

Iskanti script lined their signs, their books and accounts. The occasional Lakhesterian limb flashed out from robed men, while the Iskanti fishermen shouted across the street in a blend of Iskanti dialect and Haksani. She tried to listen, but in the end it all blurred into a jumble of noises.

The procession brought them to the Haksani temple of Ashvalra, not far from the square where Soridian had been executed. This temple had seen better days. The old foundations of the original temple extended all the way out to the shore, and now only a shell of it remained. The wooden columns bulged from decades of exposure to the rain, while attap leaves patched the gaping holes in the roof. The fabric that decorated the pillars and ceilings of the temple was coated in a layer of gray dust. Curtains draped in place of doors, concealing the small quarters of the local priests.

Even the statue of Ashvalra was well worn, her features smoothed and rounded from years of weathering. In this version she sat cross-legged, her palms turned out. The Haksani priests draped her in bright yellow fabric, the only clean item of clothing in the dust-ridden temple. Incense papers scattered in her lap.

The Xinquhan priests had repurposed the execution platform, moving it before the statue of Ashvalra. They guided Diavijra to stand on it, blocking the statue from view.

The prayer crescendoed as the Xinquhan priests knelt before Diavijra. In the wings of the temple, the Haksani priests gathered, their hands hidden behind their off-yellow robes. They did not kneel, a silent defiance against their conquerors, a refusal to bow to the different practices they'd brought to Haksa.

Naias ignored it. Unhappy priests were not on the list of problems that needed solving right now.

"The blood moon will rise in a few minutes," Naias said to Diavijra. "People will come by and lay their offerings in front of you. You need to stand here until the ceremony is over, all right?"

The godchild said nothing.

Naias returned to the fortress alone, rummaging its cellars for something the Tevurians left behind. Within the damp crates she found a porcelain bottle of wheat beer from Quctra. Good enough.

She made her way to the ramparts, sitting on the parapet that oversaw the square. The fireworks and songs would make her forget for a while. She uncorked the beer, raising it to the sky.

I'm sorry it came to this, Soridian. Sleep peacefully.

Khall's voice drifted along the breeze. "May I join you?"

Naias almost tipped her bottle over in shock. She hurried to her feet. "Of course," she said, even though she wanted to be alone tonight. "I'll send for a chair."

Khall shook her head. "It's all right, I'll stand." The wind pulled against her batik silks, leaving an imprint of the bones protruding from her fleshless body. She'd weakened since coming to Haksa. She glanced at Naias's bottle.

Naias passed her beer over, but Khall didn't take it, eyeing her with expectation. She sighed, pressed the bottle to her lips, and drank.

Khall took it.

Haksanis with weathered faces and rolled-up breeches gathered in the square, holding fiddles, cymbals, and trumpets. Fishermen. Naias liked listening to them, even if she didn't understand the Iskanti songs they sang. Every morning they chanted as they pushed their boats out to sea, plucking on two-stringed fiddles as they waited for their bait to catch. In another life, she could've been one of them.

"I've had some time to think," Khall said. "You were right. It made no sense for you to plan the Iskanti assassination. You protected me with your life when Maetheria attacked. You wouldn't have done that if you wanted to kill me. I'm sorry it took me so long to notice. The fear . . . It, it overwhelms sometimes. I become my father when I'm scared, and I don't like it."

It didn't bring her any relief. All it'd taken to clear her name was an ambush, the death of her friend, and breaking the godchild.

She'd sacrificed so much, and all Khall could talk about was her precious feelings. 'Overwhelmed by fear'? Naias breathed in terror every hour of every day, that one day she'd lose all she'd gained, relegated back to being no one, with the incorporeal weight of power disappearing from her grasp.

This child queen didn't know fear, but Naias tried to comfort nonetheless. "The attack surprised everyone. It was my fault for not seeing it sooner."

Khall's face scrunched from the bitter aftertaste of beer. "I heard you take control, when you used Diavijra as leverage. I remember feeling jealous while hiding in the throne room." Her voice cracked. "Jealous that you can make decisions in the heat of battle like that, while I fall apart because all I can think about is that I'm going to die. What I wanted to say was that you've shown an incredible courage that I never had. You bought the Faceless time to protect the fortress. You protected me from Maetheria. You got Diavijra to do what we needed her to do. I want to be you, Naias, and when you took control with the godchild, it all came clear to me. You were risking your life out there while I cried inside a room. I don't want to do that anymore. I need to behave like a queen, like you've always asked me to." Khall leaned forward and squeezed her hand. "And I'm doing that now."

But not like this. All her urgings had resulted in a girl snatching power for herself without fully understanding how to wield it.

Soridian had died so she could regain Khall's trust. Maetheria was no longer their ally. Diavijra hated her. They were alone fighting against Tevu. She'd burned countless bridges to get here. Jayal and Maka had wreaked more havoc with that single Iskanti attack than they could've ever dreamed of.

The Xinquhan priests continued their prayer, Common words praising Ashvalra soaring over the din.

The Haksani priests ignored the godchild, their yellow cotton robes congregating to face the worn statue of Ashvalra behind her. They began to chant in dialect.

"What are they doing?" Khall asked. "Don't they see the godchild in front of them?"

Haksani priests walked past Diavijra, planting their incense sticks and bowls of attap fruit before the smoothed statue of Ashvalra.

"Ignore it," she said. "Haksa has its own practices of worship."

"They're not speaking Common."

"It's Haksani, an Iskanti dialect. They've always spoken it."

Khall shook her head. "Get rid of all this Iskanti speech. They'll speak and write in Common. They'll lay the offerings before Diavijra, not that statue."

Please, please, don't make this into a problem. "Darling," Naias said, the word like rust on her tongue, "it's a small difference. They worship the same god as us. We have our way of honoring her, and they have theirs."

"Haksa is part of our kingdom," Khall said. "They'll follow the way we do it. My ancestors were the first of Ashvalra's children. We know the rituals better than anyone." Khall gestured to the celebration before her. "Whatever this is changed in our absence. We're going to set it right. If they resist, burn the temple down."

Naias's mouth dropped open. "What?"

"I need to stop being weak," Khall said, oblivious to her shock. "My father died and they thought they could take advantage of me. Maetheria, Iskantupu, Tevu. All of them. I won't let that happen again. They need to know who has power, and like a trapped beast, I will retaliate when prodded."

"That has nothing to do with Haksa," Naias said, trying to pull her from the edge. "These people didn't ask to be involved in the restoration of your kingdom. You have their land, now let them live their lives as they wish."

Khall shrugged, nonchalant to her exhortation. "You're

right, they didn't ask for it. But they don't bear the weight of history like I do. The legacy of Haksa surpasses their short lives, and they don't understand the importance of unifying these disparate cities into a singular kingdom. In the eyes of history, they are children, and they'll resist when we spoon them medicine they do not want. We do this for the greater good."

"Burning down Ashvalra's temple is not medicine," Naias protested. "You will turn the wrath of the priesthood against you. The whole city, even."

"Better to burn down a building than kill living men with Diavijra," she said. "They've seen what we do to our prisoners. This is a kindness. A warning. And if they continue with their petty resistance . . . then it'll be more than just a building and a statue."

The musicians plucked their fiddles. Cymbals and gongs clashed with the beat. An explosion of sound, to proclaim the end of the harvests.

Her queen was too far gone. Naias shook her head. "I won't do it. Find someone else."

Khall's pretty face twisted into a grimace. "I'm doing this for us, Naias. We need to keep our kingdom safe and whole. You've seen how lazily Tevu has ruled its empire, allowing the kingdoms it swallows to continue to govern and pray as they've always done. It is precisely that loose hand that has caused its disintegration. I won't have that for my kingdom . . . our kingdom, together."

Together? Another slip of the tongue. Naias held her breath. She couldn't possibly be implying—

"Marry me," Khall said, cupping her cheek. "I'll name you as heir. You're the only one I trust. You're fearless, and all a sovereign ought to be."

Naias blinked in shock. Her Faceless past would all be forgotten. Khall was marrying *her*, an Iskanti, and she would inherit the Ashvian throne.

This was an act that could reverberate for generations. The

Iskantis wouldn't be reviled by the Ashvians anymore. With time, they could mingle in society together; soon they'd see that they were all the same and they didn't need the blood tithe to protect themselves from Tevu. Iskanti children needn't fear being torn away from their families any longer. Naias could create real, lasting change.

But her position as heir was secure only as long as Khall was in love with her. Naias would have to keep this charade up for the rest of her life.

Forever. She'd have to do this forever, feasting people she didn't like, deciding which one of her friends would die, sending a child to massacre the soldiers of an empire. The road to freedom was paved with the deaths of others.

Is this a sacrifice I'm willing to make?

Khall mistook her stunned silence for joy. She pulled Naias forward, drawing her into a long kiss.

"Now you'll never fall behind," Khall murmured against her lips. "Burn the temple, and you'll be with me, always."

44
Elera

THE ISKANTIS CELEBRATED the autumn solstice in a smaller way. When evening fell, Elera helped clear a spot for a wood fire and, at Nasyuk's direction, scattered a few pebbles and small rocks into the flames. While the stones heated up, they prepared the feast.

Nasu cut out and cleaned the stomach of a goat to make tripe. She stuffed chunks of mutton, water, and yak butter into the cavity.

Donning a pair of thick rawhide gloves, Nasyuk grabbed the stones, hot from the fire, and quickly dropped them into the tripe. They tied off the cavity with rope. The meat sizzled inside, while steam swelled the tripe into a balloon. It expanded so much that Elera hid behind Iavahl and their numerous hawks, fearing the whole thing might burst.

They waited until the blood moon rose past the mountains before cutting open the tripe. Steaming, juicy meat spilled out, and Nasu spooned the thick stew into bowls, topping it with a layer of yak's yogurt. Caush hauled out jars of Iskanti milkwine.

In the weeks after her rescue, Elera's wound had closed, leaving a red gash where the gaping infection used to be. A black spot the size of her thumb remained imprinted on her chest, and it still ached if she ran too fast. Nothing she couldn't handle on her own.

And when the corruption fully disappeared . . . this valley, too, would become a distant memory.

She liked the quiet air here. Xinquha celebrated with too much fanfare and noise. They'd probably gotten Viri to play dress-up this time. Usually the task fell to one of the Ashvian girls who auditioned for the honor, but it wouldn't surprise her if Khall wanted a godchild to play a god. Viri would probably stand for hours, a sheaf of rice in one hand and a flask of water in the other, and then later be punished if she moved too much.

She didn't deserve any of it. Elera should have been there, joking with her about vain queens pleasing dead gods, to take her mind off her aching feet. Maybe she'd even take her horseback riding after the whole ceremony was done. Viri always liked horses.

Iavahl ladled the wine into six wood-and-silver bowls. The blood moon shimmered on the liquor's white surface.

Nasu's clan raised their bowls to the sky. *"Mourn peacefully,"* they murmured in unison.

Elera quaffed hers in one. It was far too sour for her taste—she preferred the sweeter ricewines—but it was the only alcohol they had, and she wanted to stop thinking.

As they drank, Nasu spoke. These words came practiced to her, a story that she'd told many times before.

"Rageful Iskandraza was born with a hole in his heart. He scoured the earth to fill this hole. He gathered ice from the mountains and stuffed it in his heart, but the ice melted away. He gathered lava from the volcanoes and stuffed it in his heart, but it burned his chest. He gathered ash from the earth and stuffed it in his heart, but it crumbled in his hands.

"He grew angry that he could not fix the hole in his heart. He stamped his feet, breaking apart the earth. He slammed his hands on the water, creating tsunamis that flooded the lands. He shouted into the volcanoes, spewing more lava into the air.

"Ashvalra saw this and asked Iskandraza: 'What upsets you so?'

"'There is a hole in my heart,' Iskandraza said, 'and I cannot fill it.'

"So Ashvalra kissed the hole in his heart, planting earth and seed within him. When it bloomed with flowers and trees, Iskandraza rejoiced, for he no longer wanted. The earth sprang and grew, the rivers flowed eternally, covering the mountains with grass. They fell in love. Together, they gave birth to gods, and man.

"Man grew up and ate what Ashvalra sowed. They cut down her trees to build their houses, then planted more seeds to grow more trees. Iskandraza was pleased, for it showed them that destruction and creation were both of the same cycle.

"But man wanted more. They ate and feasted, warred and razed, and they took and took until Ashvalra could not give any more. The god of rebirth crumbled into dust, her ashes scattered to the wind.

"When she died, the earth in Iskandraza's heart died as well. His rage filled the rivers and erupted the volcanoes. He tore himself apart, and his blood filled the earth and stained the moon.

"Time diminished his rage, yet when the blood moon rises, it reminds him of what he lost. Every twelve years he wakes and makes the earth die, searching for his lover to fill that hole in his heart, the hole that empties him of compassion and keeps him in sadness and in want."

Nasu filled her bowl again. "May Iskandraza mourn peacefully."

This was the first time Elera had heard this version of the story. In Xinquha, the legend went that Iskandraza killed Ashvalra. Man honored Ashvalra's legacy by rebuilding from the ashes, in defiance of the Destroyer. The two gods were opposing forces, eternal enemies clashing through the eons.

But Iskandraza had appeared in her dreams, the echoes of his meek sorrow still lingering in her memory. He'd drunk from her anger to remember his own, shaming himself for forgetting his lover's name.

The Iskanti version of the story felt familiar, somehow. Perhaps her parents had told her and she half remembered it. Maybe it was her proximity to Mount Iska, and the remnants of the Destroyer's spirit still haunted this land.

Iskandraza had killed for love. She liked this narrative better. That was what she'd do for Rafaeis. For . . .

Fuck's sake. Not Viri again. It was such a nice night too. Elera downed more wine. She hadn't recovered enough to leave, and unease swam deep in her mended heart. It was only a matter of time before the godchild succumbed to a corruption of her own.

Viri was a wounded bird, *her* wounded bird, whom she saw herself in and wanted to save. But Elera had abandoned her, no different from the people who'd looked away when she was whipped, and the numerous times she'd begged for help after she escaped only to be turned over for a bag of silver.

Nasyuk brought out a woven wood drum, lined with colorful beads on the side, the hollow top stretched over with sheepskin. The beat started soft and slow, and the clan rose to dance. Nasu was slow in her movements, deliberate and practiced as she gracefully moved from one foot to the other. Iavahl danced wildly, every move different from the last, unafraid and new. Caush held Iavahl's hand, following their energy.

Elera didn't join them. She stared into the fire. Iskandraza was born with a hole in his heart, and now she'd created a hole in Viri's. She'd left her to her fate as a butcher of men, a path she'd never wanted.

Viri would break eventually. Once she gave up, she would die like Elera had: a death of the mind. No one survived. Elera didn't. Every waking moment in the Faceless was a fight, where she lashed out and was lashed in return, a solitary person raging against a construct that Khallan had created, reinforced by Ashvians and Faceless alike.

The retaliation never ended. She was just one person, fighting wave after wave of people who didn't care and thoughtlessly obeyed. They could rest and she couldn't. Eventually she would falter.

It wasn't right that she could savor mutton stew and watch people dance, hidden away in a place that no Ashvian could find, and Viri wasn't here.

Something cupped her cheek, drawing her gaze away from the fire. She blinked as Rafaeis's hazel eyes and unmarked head bled into view, his expression fixed in a moment of concern.

She loved him too, this strange, overwhelming euphoria that consumed her every thought. A protective determination simmered beneath her love for Viri, but this one was simple, unconditional, and it terrified her to surrender it.

Any choice meant losing one of them.

Viri or Rafaeis.

"I'm tired," she said, and left for Iavahl's ger.

A furnace sat in the center of the room, smoke piped out into the open hole above. Instead of the coarser yak skins, Iavahl had draped their bed with foxfur and wool. Wooden stools and tables had little hawks painted on their legs, flying up into a bright blue sky.

Being the youngest of the group, Iavahl had invited them both to sleep here. Elera curled up with the leftover wool. These were much softer than the horsehair furs she'd had in her Xinquhan hut, and yet she fidgeted, unable to find a comfortable position. In a huff, she tossed the furs aside and lay on the felt-carpeted floor.

A lean shadow hovered by the entrance.

He'd followed her.

Between them stood a table stacked with gloves. Iavahl had so many to handle their beloved birds: big ones, thick ones, ones with massive holes in them that they couldn't bear to throw away. They were both a godchild and something else. Why couldn't she have that? Instead, her life comprised of wearing a smiling mask and being forced to fight for another kingdom's freedom.

She barked out a laugh, sinking under the absurd reality that they lived in. "I want everything," she said, her first true words to Rafaeis in weeks. "I forced myself into thinking that glory was enough, but it's not. I want you, and Viri, and Nasu, and Iavahl, and this valley, and the hawks who hate me, and this little clan that tolerates me. I want it all. It's not fair that Khall gets to have it. She has Viri and Naias, she has power and love and a home. Her father stole my life from me. She comes from a line of murderers, kidnappers, abusers, and still she gets rewarded for her cruelty. She doesn't deserve happiness, so why am I the one who has to choose?"

"Choose what?"

She shut her mouth. Fuck. The wine had made her stupid.

"Choose what, Elera?"

She said nothing.

"You're still recovering. You can't save Viri if you're dead."

"I'm fine," she blurted, dropping all pretenses. "It's healing on its own. Iavahl doesn't have to do much anymore."

"Elera."

"I abandoned her," she burst out. "Naias will slither her way in and turn her against me. Viri will kill and kill and eventually she'll become dead to it all. I can't let that happen. I have to go back."

"*We* have to go back."

She knew this would happen. "No. You have nothing to do with this. Viri's my responsibility. You've found your freedom. You can't give it up. I told you, I've lost my chance. Viri can't leave. The world won't stop coming for her. The Faceless is where I belong, and I'll be with her until I die."

He pushed her down and kissed her, fiercely, trying to capture all they felt and never said. He pulled the sash off her waist.

She broke away. "What—"

"Shut up," he said, pulling off her trousers.

Everything coalesced into a singular point, from the grief of her murdered family to the terrible life she was forced into, her hate of Khall and how she took after every little feature of her father, her fury when Naias left her, her hurt when they hammered the mark into her head, and how she loved this man so much, like a steady heat that flowed through her all this time, and she'd never known it.

But she couldn't have everything. It was him or Viri, and she made her choice.

"Rafaeis, I—"

"Shut up." He rolled her to the side, his hard cock pressed against her back.

She wanted it, desperately. She wanted them together, closer than they would ever be again, for one last time.

He hooked her thigh across his arm, his fingers pressing against her clit in steady rhythm. His thrusts came strong and slick, savoring every motion between them.

The dance continued outside, drumbeats and laughter drowning out their gasps. Her chest still burned, but she pushed it aside, focusing on the heat sharpening within her. He groaned too, his breath shaking and hot in her ear.

She came hard, sweet pulsing between her legs while he surged against her back, shuddering with his own release.

Let this last forever. I don't want this to end. She squeezed as hard as she could, drawing out every throb and twitch between them, until the heaviness flooded her body and she could do no more.

He released her, panting, and they stared up at the open crown of the ger. A scattering of stars dusted the night sky.

All was quiet. The celebration outside had ended. In the silence, Viri's presence still lingered.

She couldn't escape. A wasteland separated them, and yet she clung to the godchild every waking moment.

She blinked the tears away. "I have to go back."

Rafaeis's breath came steady and low. "I know."

"The autumn rains will block off the valley. I won't make it back here."

"I know."

"You have to stay. You're free now. This is what you always wanted."

His fingers brushed against hers. "I know," he said for the third time. "But I am with you, always."

45
Diavijra

ASHVIAN PRIESTS ENTERED the Haksani temple, opening every drawer and scouring every shelf, gathering all the scrolls and scriptures they could find. Faceless Hammers took their weapons to the statue of seated Ashvalra, each successive blow sending a cloud of pulverized stone into the air.

A handful of Khall's attendants held buckets of pitch, smearing them along the temple pillars, tables, and walls. The Haksani priests had barricaded themselves in their small quarters with broken furniture. They clashed their gongs and cymbals in protest, yelling at anyone who came near.

The Faceless smashed a battering ram—a fallen log retrieved from the forest—into the temple's crumbling walls. It didn't take long. They entered the gap, seizing the Haksani priests, who kicked and punched back, having no weapons of their own.

"No killing," Naias had expressly said to the Faceless, when she'd given the order to tear the temple down. "Not a single death, or I'll personally see you lashed."

That hadn't stopped Khall from insisting that Viridian accompany the Faceless. She was brought out as a bluff, her presence made to scare the Haksanis into submission. Naias had argued with her, but the queen had ultimately won, as she so often did nowadays.

Books, paper, and shop signs littered the streets. Any item that had Iskanti script written on it was tossed to the ground, destined for the bonfire in the square. The burning had already started before Viridian left the fortress; the smoke plumed acrid and black, casting the seaside city in a gray haze.

The Faceless bound the hands of the priests, dragging them out into the street. Haksani folk stood outside their ransacked homes. Steel Lakhesterian prosthetics flashed amongst the wealthier men, while others sat in wheeled chairs or propped themselves up with wood crutches. They'd all suffered during Khallan's war, and they all glared at Viridian.

She hadn't asked anyone to do this. Since the execution, she'd become the face of Khall's new kingdom and borne the brunt of the public's anger. She sucked on the pipe she'd borrowed from Clement. The smoke settled her, muting the prickling under her skin. She didn't have the authority to stop the temple burning, but still she wanted to try.

"Stop." Her voice barely broached a whisper in the crackle of the bonfire behind her. The priests ignored her.

"Stop," she said, louder now, trying to suppress the tremble in her voice. "Dia—Diavijra commands you." The name twisted awkwardly around her tongue, the stresses placed in all the wrong places.

One of the priests briefly glanced in her direction, amusement on his face. He ignored her and went back to work.

"Please." That was not what a god would've said, but despite all her well-intentioned efforts, she wasn't Diavijra. She was someone else.

The same condescending priest gave her a strained smile. "Leave the work to us, little one."

She couldn't take it anymore, being ignored and called by a name not her own. An empty fire flared within her. It burned red-hot and black, smoldered in nothing and emanated no heat, a chasm of uncontrollable anger. She pulled the fury from her belly and pushed it right into the face of the smug priest.

Him. Just him.

In an instant his face swelled to twice its size, bulging bright purple. He gagged, holding his hands to his neck.

But her anger did not dissipate. All that she'd suppressed since the execution erupted within her, unstoppable, pouring into a scream that grew louder and louder until all the priests surrounding her fell to their knees.

Her previous massacres had been done at night. It'd granted her a mercy, preventing her from seeing the worst of the deaths. Not so in the misty afternoon sun. Eyes bulged in shock as they tried to suck in air. They clawed at nothing as they collapsed, blinded by the void. The smug Ashvian priest, through sheer luck, managed to grasp her foot. He choked out the word "godchild" before she stepped on his hand, screaming

"MY NAME IS VIRIDIAN!"

Upon her cry, the square descended into chaos. Haksanis, Iskantis, and attendants fled, ash and charred paper flitting into the air. Only the Faceless ran towards her, in an attempt to restrain her from using her power.

It was easier now. She'd justified her previous killings as protecting the ones she loved, but she had no reason here. She was simply angry and hollow. She directed her power at the Faceless, then the Haksanis, the tradesmen, the backbiters, the fishermen and gossipmongers, and anyone who was unfortunate enough to be caught in her gaze.

The priest that groveled by her feet went limp. For a man who blathered so much, his lungs didn't keep a lot of air.

Suddenly, hands clamped down on her eyes. She couldn't see anymore. The string of power snapped away from the people she was trying to kill.

She spun around, shoving her attacker away.

A scarred cerulean sun filled her vision.

"Stop," Naias said, her face pale with fear.

Talk. That was all she could do. Naias couldn't kill her, because she was too valuable, but Viridian didn't think the same about her. If she couldn't touch Khall, then she'd kill the person she loved most.

In this moment, Viridian understood *power*.

i can do anything i want, she thought, seized by this sudden enlightenment. *anything.*

She threw the rock and string again.

Naias's face turned blue. Her hands clawed against Viridian's face as she fell to her knees, her breath shallow against her ear.

Death was a toy to her, in the same way it was to Khall. Lives were plentiful and cheap, disconnected from the people that lived them, because she didn't have the capacity for empathy anymore. No one cared about her dead father, so she, too, stopped caring about them.

Viridian stepped away, letting her collapse to the ground. "GIVE ME HAMMER. NOW."

Naias gripped her chest, retching. She couldn't speak.

Viridian wasn't going to get any answers if she died. Clement used his power as leverage to buy all his jewelry and batik, and if he could do it, she could learn to do it too.

She tugged at the string, pulling the rock back with only the gentlest of motions. "Give them to me."

"I can't," Naias gasped between words. "They're . . . they're not here."

"Where."

"I don't know." She looked up with bloodshot eyes. "I sent them to Iskantupu, and they haven't come back."

Viridian's hands trembled with anger. Khall had lied. She'd never kept Elera or Rafaeis in the dungeons. That deceitful, heartless, thieving rat, who'd used a false pretense to make her kill her father—

"They'll come back soon," Naias hurriedly said, knowing that her answer didn't satisfy. "Hammer always does. I know her. When they return, you'll be the first to see them, I promise you."

Pretty words did not lessen the pain of Khall's betrayal. All that made Viridian died in the void, leaving only the cold vacuum of rage.

"Your promises mean nothing," she screamed. "Khall lied to me. Dada died for a *lie*, she lied, she lied, she lied—"

"But I haven't," Naias said. "I told you I'd spare Soridian. Khall overruled me. I fought with her about it. I knew it was wrong, I knew it would hurt you. She ignored me."

Viridian didn't believe any of it. Naias had frightened her and put a gun to her head. She trusted this woman as much as she trusted Khall. Both were cut from the same cloth, eager to deceive and flatter their way to getting what they wanted.

Naias continued to babble. "I'll send the Faceless to search for them at first light tomorrow. I won't hide them from you, or stop you from seeing them, but Iskantupu is a large place. It'll take time. I know you don't trust me, but I care about seeing my deals through. Khall doesn't. We'll do this together, godchild. I'll help you find them. I *will* find them."

She didn't want to hear more empty promises, but she listened anyway. There was nothing else she could do. She couldn't change the past, or bring her father back to life, or will Elera and Rafaeis to appear before her.

Naias gave her a way out. She promised hope. Tomorrow the search party would ride to Iskantupu. The day after that, they might find Elera's tracks. The day after *that*, they might even run into the both of them, and they'd all be reunited again.

Hope was all Viridian had, and she had to make one more deal to get it. Honesty and truth meant little in this world. Everyone wanted something, and human lives were currency.

"Fine," she spat.

The embers of her anger entertained the thought of killing everyone in Haksa. If they were all dead, she'd be free. No more deals and agreements and promises that people couldn't keep. No more games with unspoken consequences, no more kings and queens to make those rules.

But her quick mind fluttered like the wings of a butterfly. She didn't know where Haksa was on a map, or how she could find Elera and Rafaeis on her own. Her power granted death to others, not survival.

It was the wrong choice to kill Soridian. She should've killed Khall instead and let her estranged father bring her home to

Maetheria. All she'd wanted was someone to keep her safe. She'd chosen to save Elera and Rafaeis, only to find out she'd been lied to all along.

She was twelve. That kind of choice should never have been foisted on her.

Viridian stumbled to the shore, pulling at her white hair, thin and weak from the lye. It fell apart in her hands.

Love and remember. Elera and Rafaeis taught her that. But what could she remember, other than the ones who'd died for her? Who could she love, now that there was no one left?

Nothing changed if she killed one Haksani or a thousand. She could destroy life and air, but she couldn't make bread or fire. Her hands held the power of gods, and yet she was still acutely, painfully human, trapped in the life I made for her, chained to Khall by necessity.

Viridian fell to her knees, her blood-caked nails tearing at her broken skin, and raged into the sea.

46
Elera

THE MORNING MIST obscured the peaks of the mountains surrounding them, a beautiful, hazy dream. Birds trilled, their melodious song dampened by the roar of the waterfalls.

Elera wrapped up her hammer in cloth, fastening it to her back. She would miss this place.

Rafaeis gathered skins of mare's milk and small parcels of cheese, loading them into saddlebags. He approached Elera, reins in hand. "Are you ready?"

"Ready for what?" a Lakhesterian accent asked, every word a drawl. Caush stood by the mouth of his ger, his gray hair immaculately braided, arms folded across his chest.

He wasn't supposed to be awake. During the solstice, Elera saw him down at least three large jars of wine on his own, enough to kill an ox. They were returning on a suicide mission to get a godchild, with no plan on how to fully escape Khall, Tevu, or Maetheria. He didn't need to know.

"We changed our minds," Elera said, finding the easiest of excuses. "It's too wet here."

Caush shook his head. "No, no, no. You traveled through the wasteland to find us, and shattered Iskandraza's last horn to summon our Iavahl. Now you're leaving? I don't believe it. Tell me the real reason, or I'll get the hawks to attack you, and you don't want that."

"Fine. Nasyuk doesn't like me."

"Nasyuk doesn't like anyone. Try again."

"You lot sing too loud."

Caush chuckled and did not deign this insult with a response.

She sighed. The truth, then. Maybe he'd realize how ludicrous their plan was and leave them to their fate. "There's a godchild we need to save. We're heading back to Haksa to get her. We won't be back in time before the valley closes."

He stared at her incredulously. "That's it? You have another that you want to rescue from Ashvi?" He burst out laughing. "Draza fuck me, I thought you two were planning something serious, like climbing Mount Iska or something."

He marched over and snatched the reins from Rafaeis's hand. "You're part of our clan now," he said. "We don't split up and go our separate ways. We talk and make a decision together. This is a rule as ancient as Iskandraza himself. You two are new, so I will forgive you this grievance."

She barely registered that he'd taken offense. She and Rafaeis were part of the clan. He'd said it so casually, buried under the lecture that they were planning to leave without saying goodbye.

She belonged. She finally belonged, in this ragtag group of a found family, and she was going to give it all up for Viri.

Time and again the gods granted her that cursed word, 'hope,' except she didn't dread it anymore.

Caush placed a hand on each of their backs, ushering them in the direction of Nasu's ger, the patchwork tent pitched next to a field of brilliant red passionflowers.

"I request a council meeting of the Angkrasa clan," Caush said in Iskanti, patting against the mouth of the tent. *"Time to wake up, Nasu-mother."*

ELERA'S HEART BEAT fast as the clan entered Nasu's ger, one by one. In contrast to the blue sky and brown hawks painted on the furniture in Iavahl's tent, Nasu decorated her own ger in red, filigreed with silver thread. The repeating patterns of woven animals, trees, and Iskanti script created a kaleidoscope of dizzying shapes. Everything looked busy, and that made her more nervous.

As matriarch, Nasu sat at the opposite end of the ger's entrance, on her bed of fur and feathers. She groaned, holding her head in one hand, while the other held a cup of warm water flavored with ginseng. Caush and Iavahl took up the space to her left. Nasyuk knelt on her right, his back straight and arms resting on his thighs. They hadn't suffered the wine's aftereffects as badly as Nasu, but their eyes were bloodshot, and Iavahl's head lolled about the cushions. Elera and Rafaeis sat near the entrance, behind the furnace.

"Caush has called this council on behalf of Elera and Rafaeis," Nasyuk said in Iskanti, his frown already signaling his distaste. *"They will state the reason for this meeting first, followed by a discussion and vote. However, my mother holds the final decision. Should she disagree with the majority, it is within her right to do so."*

Elera swallowed hard, the lump in her throat larger than she'd ever experienced. How odd that for someone so unafraid in battle, her voice shook when speaking to four other people.

"We want to save a godchild," she said. "Her name's Viridian, a child of twelve, and she has the powers of Diavijra."

Caush's smile vanished. He'd known they were going back for a godchild, but the fact that Viri was one of the progenitor gods made it much more complicated.

Her fingers twisted into a knot. If they said no, she was fine with that. They were willing to listen to her. That small comfort meant so much. "She was abducted from Maethcria. Khall wants to restore her old kingdom of Ashvi. She's already used Viri's power to take over Haksa. I know that's just the first of many battles."

"You took us in," Rafaeis said, *"and we want to save one more. I know it's a lot to ask."*

"*It is,*" Nasu said, her mouth grim. "*Why not return the girl to Maetheria?*"

"*If she wants it,*" Rafaeis said, "*but I doubt Maetheria will allow her to live peacefully. They have their own struggles with Tevu.*"

Iavahl leaned forward, clearing their throat. Without the hawks smothering them, they looked so much smaller. "Viridian is under heavy guard, yes?"

Elera nodded. "Khall has the Faceless. I'm one of them, but I don't know if I can fight off a hundred who received the same training as me. When word spreads, the other kingdoms and empires might start a search of their own."

"*It'll not be safe for us anywhere,*" Nasyuk said. "*Every empire will want her for their own gain, the Iskanti clans included. Kujivhan's assembling his unnatural army in the east; Diavijra will be godsent to him. Not to mention this will harm our trade. The cities tolerate us enough, but not with two ex-Faceless and a godchild.*" He stroked the rich fabric draped around the walls of Nasu's ger. "*You won't have this silver anymore, Mother.*"

"*It'll harm us only if we bring Elera and Viridian along,*" said Caush, his smile returning. "*Rafaeis has no mark. Viridian can hide at a distance. Elera can take care of her while we're gone. They don't have to enter the cities with us. I can't see why our trade would be any different. When Elera's mark is erased, Viridian will have grown up, and things might have changed by then.*"

Nasyuk rubbed his face in his hands. "*What's the point of having Faceless when they can't accompany us to the markets? What's the point of having Diavijra if she's going to be hidden away in the mountains?*"

"*The point is she's not Diavijra,*" Iavahl said gently. "*She's Viridian.*"

Yes, yes, she's Viridian, Elera thought eagerly. *Not a godchild, but a human, like us, free to determine her own life.*

But Iavahl's cool, unsmiling gaze pierced her. "I sympathize with her plight, but it is not wise for us to rescue her."

Elera fought down a rush of anger. Iavahl was a hypocrite, killing with kindness and refusing to do anything that resembled action. "You're a godchild too. You were rescued."

"No, my circumstances were different. I was a useless one in the eyes of Tevu. They did not care if I lived or died. I could vanish without notice. Diavijra could help control the very continent. I know all too well the fate laid out for unloved godchildren, and she is not one of us. Taking her in puts us in even more danger." They turned away from Elera, addressing Nasu. *"You've founded a clan that only we understand. No Iskanti would've rescued us. You have. I want to keep it intact. Help those that can be saved, but only within our power. We've no way to stop these empires from coming after her. Saving Viridian will mean our destruction."*

Nasu frowned. *"Elera, what will you do if we decide not to help?"*

She sat up straight. Iavahl's refusal had only made her more determined. "We'll go after her ourselves. After that, I don't know. We'll learn by necessity."

"Learning on the run, while in the wasteland?" Caush asked incredulously.

"I know how dangerous it is to harbor someone like Viri," Rafaeis said. "It's why we wanted to do this alone. It puts you in danger, and that's the last thing I want for the people who helped me."

Nasu rested her head on one hand, the other arm propped on a raised knee. Her brow was still furrowed in contemplation. *"But you'll go, regardless of our decision?"*

"Yes," they said together.

"Then we'll vote. Nasyuk?"

"No."

"Caush?"

"Yes."

"Iavahl?"

"No. I'm sorry."

Nasu leaned back, running her fingers across her lips and chin.

Three and two. No overwhelming consensus that swayed one way or the other. Nasu still held the final decision.

She abruptly stood, signaling the rest of them to leave the ger with her. They emerged back into the cold air. The valley's morning mist had begun to dissipate, snowy mountain peaks blending into a gray sky. The matriarch stood there for a long time, surveying all they had.

Elera's breath echoed in her ears, every beat of her heart rushing blood to her head. She desperately wanted to take the ibexes and ride for Haksa immediately, but this was not her decision to make. Going back for Viri benefited no one, except her.

Finally, Nasu beckoned her over.

"Your request risks our safety for very little gain," she said. *"I don't expect the godchild to protect us. She wants to escape from her own power, and she shouldn't come to us only to be asked to use it again."*

She pointed to the valley's mountain range. "Iskandraza, he make this. Long, large. Easy to hide. Ashvians, they don't know how to live here. They cannot take mountains." Nasu turned to her with a wide smile. "So we take Viridian."

She must have heard wrong. Nasu couldn't have said what she said. Like how Iavahl had deceived her into thinking they were going to agree, Nasu was stalling until she eventually said no as well.

But Nasu didn't waver. *"We're nomads. We've survived the winter without these valleys before. What's one more?"*

She was truly going to help.

Elera wrapped her in a hug, lifting her off the ground. Now she understood why the Iskantis chose this as their form of greeting. She could've squeezed all the air out of Nasu from the strength of her gratitude.

"Thank you," she muffled into the matriarch's hawk-feather cloak. "Thank you, thank you."

Nasu groaned, patting her on the back. *"Put me down. I'm going to throw up."*

She'd never experienced this type of kindness before. Elera swallowed, trying to cover the hollowness in her throat. "We're putting you through enormous, terrible risk," she said in disbelief.

"It's a risk that we should take. It's the Iskanti way to give freely." Nasu's smile quickly faded. *"Well, it used to be. I fear that what defines us now is not who we are, but who we are not. I see the Iskanti clans reacting to the blood tithe. Our way of life is crumbling. The matriarchs are dying. Sons, warriors, and fighters take our place, crying for revenge. We answer cruelty with cruelty. That is what we've become. Vengeance in the guise of justice is not worth erasing all that we are."*

Elera said nothing. She didn't mind Kujivhan's cause: raising an army to wreak havoc on the empires that hurt them. The Iskantis' tradition of passivity was the reason her family had died. Khall and her kingdom needed to burn if they wanted anything to change.

But Kujivhan had rejected her from his clan.

Nasu didn't.

The matriarch's leathery face wrinkled into a smile. *"Go get the yaks ready,"* she said, shooing Elera away. *"Rafaeis, Iavahl—break down the gers. We need to move before the frost hits."*

With a full heart, Elera departed for the grazing pastures. As she busied herself reattaching brass bells to the yaks, a hand clamped down on her shoulder.

Nasyuk glared, seething anger and resentment. *"Unlike that heathen Kujivhan, I actually respect my mother's wishes,"* he said. *"But know this: If you put my family in any danger, I won't hesitate to kill you."*

Without waiting for a response, he shoved Elera's hammer into her arms.

"You'd better know how to use that."

47

Naias

THE FACELESS BOWED before Naias, unlocking the overwrought door to Viridian's room. White smoke billowed in her face, shafts of light filtering through the haze.

"Dia—Viridian?" she coughed out.

Bare feet shuffled against the floor. Viridian stumbled out of the fog, holding a pipe. Ankle irons dragged behind, shackling her within the confines of the room.

Naias pursed her lips. She plucked the pipe from the godchild's hands and doused the embers in it. If she ignored the girl's new habit, the opium they imported would double, now that both Viridian and Clement wanted it. They couldn't spend more money on frivolity. She needed to urge the godchild towards things fit for her age instead.

She'd brought a little wooden doll, setting it on the table. A bronze wire threaded through its blocky limbs, allowing it to be posed if the child so wished. A little smiling mask was attached to its head, while scraps of black cloth had been pinned together to resemble the Faceless' clothes.

She handed Viridian a scroll. "I'm sending out the search party today."

Viridian snatched it and squinted at the words. "It says here you're sending five Faceless."

"Five is sufficient."

"You have five hundred. Send them all."

Naias suppressed a sigh. Viridian was a child, prone to emotion and devoid of tactical thinking. She had to explain why, bracing herself that cold reason might not dissuade her. "We need the Faceless here to protect Haksa. We can't lose all of them."

"You have me," Viridian said. "I'll kill them for you."

"Against Tevu, maybe. But the Haksanis are growing angry. They didn't like it when we burned the temple."

"I can kill them too."

The ease with which Viridian uttered the sentence unnerved her. There was a deadness in the way she moved, the way she spoke. She'd stopped caring. She'd sold her soul to get Hammer and Crescent back, and now all her efforts focused on this one singular mission.

Naias shook her head. "We still need a garrison here. I'll send twenty."

"A hundred."

"Fifty."

"Fine."

Fifty Faceless to find two people. Naias scratched at her mark. This had better be worth it.

"And I want them alive," Viridian said. "Not to be killed by the Faceless, or you, or the Iskanti clans, or in some way that you could label their deaths as an accident. I want them in Haksa, alive and whole and conscious, where I can see them breathing with my own eyes."

The deal with Khall had shaken her. All these specifics weren't necessary for Naias, knowing what was at stake if both Hammer and Crescent were dead, but she nodded, sitting by the table and uncorking a small bottle of ink from her pouch. She scribbled the clause down on the scroll. The girl's trust had been broken completely, and Naias needed to restore it, step by excruciating step.

Still, she needed to temper Viridian's expectations. "We

won't find them overnight," Naias said. "Iskantupu is a large and cold place. It might take weeks, months."

Viridian's gaze stayed fixed on the table. She hadn't touched the doll at all. "Does Khall know you're helping me?"

Naias rolled up the scroll. She dreaded walking into the throne room now. Every report turned into an argument. Khall would listen briefly and then demand they do it her way. She'd kick up a fuss over the number of Faceless they were sending out, and then leave Naias to face the godchild's fury.

"No," she said.

"Congratulations," Viridian said flatly. "Heir to the kingdom, and nothing changes."

Naias picked up the toy and pulled its arms backwards. Crescent had said the same thing. She would've fought back, once, but her fights with Khall had left her too exhausted to be angry.

"I've done *some* things," she said in exasperation. She twisted the arms into a knot, tightening it as far as it could go. Its joints creaked under the weight. "I'm trying, I really am."

Since Maetheria stormed the fortress, Khall had asserted herself, relegating Naias to organizing harvest festivals and tearing down Iskanti signs. 'Heir' was a vanity title. She was a servant, doing what Khall didn't want to do. She'd wanted out of the Faceless for that very same reason. Surely sheer hard work would overcome her failings for being born different, but she found herself in that same position again.

Being heir hadn't changed anything.

She'd once thought that all this scheming and plotting and *friends dying* would lead to a happy conclusion, but that fabled day would never come. Tomorrow would bring more of the same shit, and the day after, and the day after that. The Ashvians tolerated her as consort, but they wouldn't accept her as queen. If Khall died, Naias would face an angry people chafing under the rule of a lesser being. It was all but certain that Ashvian loyalists would attempt to seize power for themselves and cast her out.

Her struggle never ended.

At least she'd stopped the blood tithe. Since turning away the beggars, she hadn't recruited a single Iskanti into the Faceless. She'd sacrificed her freedom for future Iskanti children to not know the pain of being separated from their families. They'd sleep in their gers under the full moon, blissfully unaware of the person that prevented their entire lives from changing.

It doesn't feel worth it, Naias thought in a burst of selfishness. *I don't want to be the one who suffers so others can stay happy.*

Soridian had warned her, pointing out the mark on her head every time they met. She'd hated him for reminding her of her difference, but now she understood.

Naias swallowed, speaking all she knew and never admitted. "I am powerful only because Khall allows me to be."

Viridian plucked the toy from her hands, unfolding the doll's knotted arms. "I like this version of you better."

Naias blinked. "What?"

"Where you don't pretend. When you're sincere. Underneath it all, you care, but you hide it by scaring other people. That nice part of you died, didn't it? Hammer tried to kill that part of herself too."

all girls, the three of them, and naias was the eldest, the most capable, the smartest, because father said so, and she smiled so much her skin cracked in the dry, freezing wind

"I don't *care*." Naias bristled and towered over Viridian. "You want sincerity? Fine. Hammer abandoned you. She left to escape punishment, and she'll come back because she can't survive out in the wasteland. Everyone's out for themselves, and Hammer is no different. Truth gets you nowhere, godchild. You learned that when you made that deal with Khall. Sincerity gets you killed."

A less battle-hardened child would've shrunk back at this show of intimidation, but Viridian sat hunched over in her chair, staring up at Naias, unblinking.

"What I can't tell is your feelings for Khall," she said. "You do all the things that love does. You hug her, kiss her. You're even marrying her. But you hide your feelings when they're real, and you're not hiding here. You're showing off. I don't think you love her."

"Of course I love her," Naias snapped. She wanted to go back to Quctra, where summerbell flowers grew abundant. Khall had kept bouquets of them in her room so the stench of sex didn't linger. Naias had loved playing with Khall's hair those nights, a curtain of velvet black, her skin shaded blue by moonlight. War raged still—her whole life was molded by it—but those early days with Khall had granted her a control she'd only dreamed of.

But buried underneath those memories was a love hidden further still. It wasn't as pretty as Khall's; there were no wheat fields to lie on and no hair to run her fingers through. It was in the fighting pits, hollowed out under the earth, hidden from Tevu. It was Hammer's steady breath and strong hands, helping her remember that she had a body, instead of a formless soul that floated in a pitch-black void. They'd found a way to survive together, and that meant more than all the summer days with a princess.

Do I love Khall?

The iron door to Viridian's quarters groaned open, a welcome interruption from a tedious conversation. Naias happily dashed her thoughts aside. She had a city to run.

A Faceless stepped in, saluting them. "The Earthly Sovereign has sent for Diavijra. The dockworkers are striking, and she wants the godchild to send a warning."

SHE RUSHED TO the shore, Viridian firmly in hand.

Barrels of goods lay stacked on the wooden piers. Some had fallen into the sea. Crates trapped in seaweed and fishing nets bobbed along the tide. Cranes lay abandoned, while wet, frayed ropes tangled around the jib.

The whole place stank of rotting fish. Naias tried not to slip on the layer of slime that coated the docks. Only the sampans stayed clean, the fishing boats neatly anchored in rows along the shore. Men didn't care for anything besides the property they owned.

The Iskanti dockworkers sat outside empty warehouses, in damp green-gray tunics, kept at bay by the Faceless. They all glared at Khall. The queen had chosen to meet them wearing—very unwisely—richly patterned batik silk. She'd swapped out her summerbell flowers for gilded angsana leaves, meticulously woven through her hair. The coffers she'd plundered from the Ashvian temple had gone on to fund a series of increasingly extravagant dresses, which Naias had tried to stop.

Khall had refused. "I need to look the part of a queen," she'd said. "That's what you taught me."

Naias could do nothing else. Khall had turned her words against her.

Basaa and Ayashara stood by the warehouses. They'd chosen not to wear the Ashvian colors this time, picking tailored gray tunics that resembled the ragged attire of the dockworkers.

This place wasn't like the execution square, where the Ashvians and Haksanis mingled together. As Haksa was a city that slipped in and out of the Tevurian Empire, the Iskantis were considered equal citizens under Tevurian law. But past the surface-level harmony, there still rested an unspoken hierarchy. The menial jobs still lay with them. The docks were an Iskanti enclave, and they did not like the Ashvians here.

Basaa hurried forward, as quick as his foot allowed, his hands twisted in anxiety. "I apologize for asking you to be here, my queen, but the Iskantis won't listen to me anymore. If our ships aren't loaded, we sell nothing. If we have no silver, we can't pay your taxes. A prosperous city benefits us all, and we ask you to mediate."

"Tell them the Earthly Sovereign orders them back to work," Khall simply said.

Basaa sputtered in confusion. He'd expected something else—a long impassioned speech on how the dockworkers were a valuable part of the city's industry, perhaps—but Khall had burned sympathy out of herself long ago. Raw authority was her weapon of choice now.

Khall raised an eyebrow. "Is there a problem?"

He quickly shook his head, turned to the striking dockworkers, and said something in the Haksani dialect.

One of the dockworkers stood up, gesturing wildly. Spit flew from his mouth. *"You're a foreigner,"* he shouted at the queen in Iskanti. *"You have no right to put these shit rules on us. Go home."*

"Go home, go home, go home," the crowd chanted.

"They're upset that our dialects have been banned from Haksa," Basaa politely translated for her.

Khall scowled. "Haksanis speak Common. It's about time the Iskantis spoke it too. Arrest everyone who refuses to work. Let Diavijra play with them."

Ayashara pressed a hand against her husband's chest, stopping him from translating Khall's words to the dockworkers. "You promised us nothing would change," she said through clenched teeth. "We came to you to fix this, but you're destroying our way of life."

"Watch your wife, Basaa," Khall said. "Or I'll have her arrested too."

"We only want what's best for the city," the merchant said quickly, bowing low. Jeers rose from the Iskantis. "These men work for us, and if you kill them—"

"I'm not going to kill them," Khall said with a condescending laugh, aware of the power she held. "Just enough to show what would happen if they continue to resist. They're willfully speaking another language that doesn't belong on our land."

Naias couldn't stay quiet anymore. "With all due respect, we are on *their* land."

Khall's lips sat in a thin line. She marched over, her jeweled sandals sliding on water and creaking wood. When she got within arm's reach, she yanked Naias close.

"This is why I didn't want you here," she hissed in her ear.

"I knew you were going to start a fight with me in front of everyone."

Naias twisted away. She had to fight. Viridian stood by her side like a motionless puppet, waiting to be fed instruction. No one wanted to help the Iskantis, even in a place like Haksa, and it fell to Naias to protect them, the same way she'd protected Hammer and the rest of the Faceless. It was Khall's foolish decree that had started the strike in the first place.

"I warned you against this," Naias said, "and now you're paying for it. You shouldn't be punishing others for the mistakes you made."

"We have argued about this at length, *Commander*," Khall snapped, "and your stubborn refusal to understand Haksa's Ashvian history borders on treason." She turned to the Faceless. "Arrest the dockworkers."

The air rippled with anger. The dockworkers rose to their feet, shouting in Iskanti and Haksani dialect. They yelled at Basaa, who kept his head down, his hands folded beneath his robes. The Faceless moved between them, shoving the Iskantis away.

Khall was going to start a riot, and she didn't know it.

"Why are you behaving like Tevu?" Naias asked in a burst of indignation. "They razed Xinquha to the ground, and you're doing the exact same thing here."

Khall bared her teeth in fury. "Do not compare me to our gaolers again, or I'll have you arrested as well."

Every other sentence from her mouth was a threat. Her way of asserting her newfound power was through endless punishment. It was almost like her vow to be a merciful queen had never happened.

"Khall, these are your people," Naias said. "They are not your enemy."

"'My queen.'"

"What?"

"You will address me as 'my queen' in public, Commander, as a person of your rank should."

Naias wanted to tear off Khall's overextravagant dress and scream. *We're fighting over the lives of men, and you want to lecture me about titles?* "You turn the city against you," she said, "and soon there won't be a city left to rule."

Khall drew herself up, steel-straight, and her face went still. "I'll call off the wedding."

No. Naias froze. She would not take this away from her, not when she was so close to having it. "This has nothing to do with my love for you."

"It absolutely does," she seethed. "You openly pick a fight with me in public and question my decisions. I won't be lectured to by someone of inferior birth with no connection to Ashvian history. You've overstepped your boundaries, Commander, now fall in line, and we'll both get what we want."

The dismissive way she brought up Naias's Iskanti blood hurt her more than she'd expected. She'd thought this wound had healed. After all this effort, time, and work, she'd hoped that Khall had seen beyond the mark on her head, and that she was like the rest of them.

A slip of the tongue. Everyone was angry, and Khall always said awful things in the heat of the moment.

Viridian was no help. Her blank gaze wandered around the docks, as if she had no idea how she'd gotten here or why.

Naias swallowed. She'd burned the Haksani temple and threatened a child, and a friend had died. Now, the Iskantis had to be tortured to save her marriage to Khall.

She'd come so far. She couldn't fall now.

Naias sank into a deep bow. "As you wish, my queen."

48
Elera

SHE HATED THE wasteland. Fucking despised it. She didn't care if it made her less of an Iskanti. The gods should have never made this place.

When she'd first ridden here to find Kujivhan, she'd had nothing but her Faceless uniform and a few horsehair furs, and now was woefully unprepared for the oncoming Iskanti winter. She had to borrow one of Nasyuk's coats, a thick burly garment made with yak wool and felt. His clothes were the only ones that fit. Despite it, her hands and feet stayed permanently cold. Nasyuk, of course, never passed up an opportunity to laugh in her face, and called her a 'soft little lamb.'

But he'd also manhandled her into wearing a thick fur cap, also his, one that wrapped around her head and buttoned below her chin. He roughly tucked a cotton kerchief into the corners of her cap, creating a mask that shielded her peeling nose and lips from the elements.

"Thank you," she mumbled.

"Can't hear you."

"Fuck off."

She missed the valley and its mild weather, a life surrounded by abundance. She didn't freeze in the mornings or sweat herself into a giant walking blister. She'd almost learned how to corral a wild goat properly.

But she'd have plenty of time in the valley, with Rafaeis and Viri, if this all came to pass.

The sparse autumnal rains had created patches of green in the wasteland, blooming with peashrubs and thick needlegrass. Nasu navigated the desert with these oases as her landmarks, for the yaks needed to graze, and the clan in turn needed their milk for sustenance and their manure for heat. Every time the yaks shat, Elera scooped their droppings up into a large wooden bucket, letting it dry in the sun.

This meandering journey meant a month stretched into two. Every day she had to suppress her instinct to tear away and cut through the desert on her own. Her basal self didn't care about Nasu's kindness, but her basal self didn't care about perishing alone in the wasteland either.

They camped once again on a small patch of needlegrass and sagebrush, already frosted over with the setting sun. Nasyuk, Rafaeis, and Elera unloaded the wagon, swiftly pitching a single small ger with a furnace in the center. Putting up any more was a waste of energy. If they needed to reach the temperate coast before winter, they had to keep moving.

Nasu entered the ger first, as the matriarch of her family, followed by Nasyuk, Caush, Iavahl, and finally Elera and Rafaeis. They sat in a circle around the stove, a small pillow each, pressed shoulder to shoulder. Elera tossed a bit of dried yak shit into the furnace, lighting it with some grass as tinder. Glorious heat filled the tent. Everyone raised their hands to the fire. Elera didn't care about the musty smell; she could finally move her fingers again.

"We're about a month away from Haksa," Nasu said. *"Perhaps you may tell us your plan to retrieve little Viridian. The other matriarchs tell me that Tevu's ships sail down south, presumably to attack the Ashvian queen. If we continue traveling at this speed, we may arrive a few days before they do."*

Iavahl put up four fingers. *"As far as I can see, we have four problems: Ashvi, Tevu, Maetheria, and Kujivhan. We must deal with them all."*

Elera had thought long and hard about this since her recovery, to find some way that her hammer could realistically triumph against a garrison of Faceless. She was proud of her fighting skills, but not too proud to admit a losing battle when she saw one. Rafaeis had the right way of it.

"We need to sneak her out before Tevu attacks." That was as far as she could think. She was no commander. Naias would've crafted a plan twice as sophisticated in half the time.

Nasyuk shook his head. *"Take her during the attack. Use Tevu as a distraction to leave."*

"There is no distraction," Rafaeis cut in. "If Tevu attacks, Viri will be close to Khall at all times, guarded by the Faceless. She did that with Clement."

"Pretend to be another Hammer and Crescent, then," Nasyuk said in a huff. *"Infiltrate the Faceless that surround her. Take Viridian, and kill the queen. Ashvi is dead, the Faceless are leaderless, and you don't have to fight them anymore."*

"No," Rafaeis said. "You ask too much. The Faceless will overwhelm us. If Khall is killed, her heir will resume power quickly. Nothing will change. The Faceless will stay loyal to Ashvi. They don't have . . . what we have."

Nasyuk shrugged, the strength of his indifference nudging his mother and Caush aside.

"We need time to understand what's changed in the five months we've been away," Rafaeis continued. "Viri could be locked in Quctra for all we know. When we return, we need to find out who protects her, how we can sneak her out, and when we can leave. We must do this before Tevu attacks. War brings chaos, and we cannot linger."

Iavahl retracted a finger, leaving three. "Let us say you have rescued Viridian. Once they know she is missing, Tevu and Ashvi will both give chase."

"Tevu is strong only because of Engaleveya," said Caush.

"If she dies, Tevu is toothless. They'll lose their fight in the north, and the Faceless will overwhelm them in the south."

"When and how?" Elera asked. "We fought and injured her in Oumujin. I don't see her riding off into the mountains again. She'll be surrounded by Reborn. We'll never catch her alone."

"If she has Reborn with her, then fighting with the Faceless gives us better odds," Rafaeis said. "You were so close to dying then."

"Don't remind me," she grumbled.

"More Faceless means more targets," Caush said with a nod. "If Engaleveya is surrounded by others, she can't focus on you all the time. Your chances of success will increase that way."

"Then I'll say what I said before," Nasyuk said, slamming his palm on the felt carpet. *"Tevu's attack on Haksa would be the opportune time to strike. Wherever the godchild's locked up doesn't matter. Khall will bring her out to fight. You kill Engaleveya. Some Faceless will die. We weaken both. Take the godchild away."* He dusted his hands. *"Done."*

The plan sounded right to her, but she felt strange knowing Engale wasn't long for this world. She'd liked it when they sat together in the eye of the hurricane, sharing that quiet moment when neither of them had to fight anymore. Engale had seemed almost human then.

Almost.

The godchild of tornadoes had a tenuous grasp on reality, and truth be told, it was better to put her out of her misery than let her live this half-crazed life. If Engale had to die to ensure Viri's survival, Elera would make that trade a hundred times over.

Live or die. Nothing else.

"Maetheria, then," Iavahl said, ticking off their third finger. "I would ask what you would do about them, but I know Nasu-mother has her answer."

"With diplomacy," Nasu said. *"The remaining matriarchs*

have no quarrel with them. We've been met with respect and peace in the few times we've traded there. However, we don't know if Viridian wishes to return to her homeland. I suggest you prepare for that eventuality."

She'd been warned about this multiple times, but it made Elera mad every time she thought about it. She'd come all this way to rescue Viri, only to be told she wanted to go somewhere else? No. Maetheria was a sleeping tiger, no better than any other kingdom. They ransomed escaped Faceless back to Khallan for coin; the dozen red lines across her cheeks were proof of that. Viri would only be used for their own fight against Tevu.

She loved Viri so much that she would have her, or none at all.

It was spiteful, she knew, and this journey across the wasteland had been an . . . *experience* in suppressing the worst parts of herself. But this was her nature. Live or die, with no in-between. She would've killed that corrupted lizard if Viri hadn't pleaded with her to let it go.

All her life, she'd done the opposite of what everyone told her to do. If someone told her she couldn't have it, she'd walk through fire to get it. And if they wanted to take it away, then she'd rather burn it all.

Thoughts fueled by bitterness and resentment. She was working on it.

"And finally, Kujivhan," Iavahl said, one finger pointed to the sky. "I think he is the greatest danger. His army grows every day."

Elera shook her head. Grand strategy wore her head out, but she knew plenty about hand-to-hand combat. "He's no threat. Numbers do not make strength. It's quality. He needs another decade of training, and when he can actually fight me, we'll be long gone by then."

Iavahl tilted their head from side to side. "I do not agree," they said. "Many have tried to unite the Iskanti clans and failed. I thought his attempt insignificant too, but he has come a long way in ten years."

"Regardless," Caush said, "his danger is contingent on escaping Tevu and Ashvi first. He is not attacking Haksa nor does he have Viridian. We have time to deal with him later."

"Then here is the plan," Rafaeis said. "We will return to Haksa and find out where Viri's intentions lie. When Tevu strikes, we will use that opportunity to kill Engale. Once she is dead, we must have Viridian by then. With her on our side and Engale dead, neither Tevu nor Ashvi will be able to stop us from leaving."

"And what will you do if it all goes awry?" Iavahl asked.

Rafaeis grabbed Elera's outstretched arms, still warming by the fire. It seemed like yesterday that she'd been caught in the embers of the dying whirlwind, when Rafaeis had promised her she was no longer alone. That moment had torn out the bitterness she'd nursed from Naias's betrayal. She'd found a new love, a new family, one that she was still trying to patch together.

"Two things must happen." Rafaeis's eyes met hers, fierce in their sincerity. "Engale must die, and Viri must leave. If one of us is killed—"

Her breath caught in her throat. "Don't fucking say that."

"If one of us is killed, our aims won't change. Engale must die, and Viri must leave. Promise me."

A life for a life. She could manage that.

His death, however—

"I promise," she said.

49
Naias

HAKSA'S MERCHANTS HAD come in bigger numbers, filling up her court, begging her to stop taking their workers away. There was anger in the streets now, they said.

Khall stood firm, resembling more of her father each passing day. "You wanted me to fix this problem for you," she spat, "and now you want me to stop. I'm finished listening. Leave my court, or it'll be you next."

More people filled the dungeons. Khall wanted the dockworkers alive but shaken, and it fell to Naias to escort Viridian down to the hold. During one of the sessions, Naias had come up with the brilliant idea of putting a blindfold over the godchild's eyes after it was done. She couldn't attack anyone else, especially if her arms were bound, and she ceased to be a threat until she was escorted to her room. Naias was proud of that. Khall could have shown a bit more joy when she told her, but the queen only nodded, followed by a curt dismissal.

It'd been an exhausting day, but Naias didn't have time for sleep. She sat in her office, focusing on the thick book splayed open on her desk. *Compendium of Ashvian Practices: Customs, Marriage, and Laws*, flipped to the section on marriage.

She couldn't control Khall any longer, but she could control her own wedding. She had a month to plan it, and she was determined for it to go on without a problem. Naias didn't care for the dress or the banquet, but the ceremony needed to be precisely executed. She wanted it legal, in Haksa and Xinquha, and every step of this ritual had to be followed to the letter. The exact number of priests, the exact material of the bowl (the Ashvians always liked their angsana), the exact age of the goat, and the exact amount of blood they needed from it. She wasn't going to get her marriage annulled because she knelt too early or smeared the libation on her lips at the wrong time. She'd been staring at the same page for an hour, the candle reduced to a fat liquid stump.

A light clinking alerted her to someone at the door. Candlelight burned her vision into white and red spots, and she squinted to make out the shadowy figure in the dark.

Clement.

Since the incident with the dockworkers, he'd swapped out his colorful batik robes for plain brown barkcloth. He hadn't changed out of it either, judging from the dark stains that seeped through his armpits. In his hand clinked the three trinkets that never left his side: the little hourglass, the aquamarine, and the glass pendant.

"I remember them, you know," he said softly. "I thought I didn't care anymore. But I still do."

His sunken eyes bore heavy bags, his eyelids pulled so far down that he resembled an old man. Naias had never seen him more exhausted. Strixahava's godchild slept for most of the day, and smoked himself to a stupor when he was awake. He didn't have a reason to be tired. *She* did.

"I don't have time," she said, waving a hand to dismiss him. "Talk to someone else."

Clement bent down and placed each trinket on her table.

"Little Sajavera," he said, pointing to the sand-filled hourglass, "who spent her powers building sandcastles. But she could never produce enough to make a dam. Seven years old. We left her on the wasteland."

The aquamarine glimmered purple in the candlelight, the

butterfly trapped within blackened into a shadow. "Ciera, taken from Lakhest. She liked bees and ladybugs so much. Always asked me how cocoons worked. She was convinced the caterpillar and butterfly were two separate insects, because she could only control one and never the other. Aged eleven. She disappeared when we were in Quctra. I think the Faceless killed her in the wheat fields."

"I'm sure all this is painful—"

"Risha here had the worst curse of all," he said, tapping the glass pendant. "The god of the streams manifested in him through copious sweating. His palms, arms, back, always a waterfall. He went through so many clothes, and in the end he decided to walk in the nude. It was easier. He liked playing in the water. I think he would've been a great swimmer. Aged nine, the last godchild that Mohyri publicly named, until Viridian came along. He died here, in Haksa, drowned in the sea."

Naias glared at him, saying nothing. If he wasn't going to obey her dismissal, then she'd give him complete silence.

He fiddled with his trinkets, twirling the aquamarine around, casting bright cerulean shadows on her book.

"Why are you still here?" he asked, every word a heavy sigh.

Stupid man, asking her this question when it was he who'd barged in unannounced. "If you haven't noticed, I have a lot of work to do. I have to take care of Diavijra, make sure our supplies from Xinquha are coming in, I have to oversee the Faceless, and I have to plan the wedding—"

"No. Why are you still here, watching this farce? You left the love of your life to seduce this young, malleable princess, and you've turned her into a monster. Khall has burned the Haksani temple down, and she's moved on to torture. This is only going to get worse."

This was the reason he'd come. Suffering through his sad stories just to be rebuked. Naias shook her head. "Khall's scared and she's throwing a tantrum. Every protest is a personal attack. Let her ride her fear out, and eventually she'll realize there are easier ways to make people listen. It won't get worse, I promise you."

But her words further inflamed his hostility. Clement's tired face twisted into a sneer. "*You promise?* You promised me we'd be free from the tyrant, but now tyranny is all I see. I cannot stand by and watch this happen any longer. I don't know how you can. You poisoned Khallan for a better world, and *this* is the world you deliver."

She caught the implication in his words. He was going to leave. She'd given him the key to his chains, fantasizing that his partial freedom fulfilled hers by extension. She didn't think he'd actually do it. He loved his silks and sweets too much to put it all behind.

She was wrong.

"Are you leaving now?" she asked.

"Soon."

If he left, she'd be the last of Khallan's conspirators. She'd created an uneasy alliance with Clement and Soridian, one formed from shared purpose and belief. But Soridian was dead, and Clement didn't want to be here anymore. All their work, vanished, in the blink of an eye.

The looming isolation struck her heart.

Clement, she now realized, was a friend.

"I don't want to be alone," she blurted. "Don't go."

Clement's gaze hardened. "I *will* go, Naias. The question is, will you stop me?"

Two exhausted souls stared at each other.

50
Diavijra

I'M SORRY, YOU thought this part was slow? *It's the same,* you say, as you read the justifications that Naias repeated to herself, when the temple burned, when the priests died, when the Iskantis were tortured, when Clement left. All this could've been shorter if Naias acted sooner, if Viridian were smarter. You know, you understand, you say, in the warmth of your room, on your chair, in your bed, now move on.

No. Read it all.

Tyranny doesn't happen in the blink of an eye. It is a slow descent, helped by the complicity of those who think they have no power. Naias was here for a long time. She didn't change.

I would've acted differently, you say, thinking up all the different vectors that make you special. *I would've seen this for what it was. I would stand up against injustice.*

But you were there when Viridian killed her own father. What did you do then?

You are so resilient and yet so strange. You can sit with the worst atrocities, and then complain nothing is happening.

I know, I know. You can't possibly handle so much pain at once, and so the brain flattens, normalizes, until you cease to feel anything at all. People died, yes, we know, it's very sad. Now, what else?

I never understood why bā didn't run your lot to extinction. He saw something worth saving, even after you killed the only person he ever loved. The others believed in you too, sharing their powers because they trusted in your ability for change.

I was one of them.

Look where we are now.

Being functionally immortal meant I would inevitably forget the histories and people that made me who I am, but your memories are even shorter. You don't learn from suffering. You didn't learn the last time Viridian spoke with her voice, before she gave it up to me.

You read our lives because you want to be entertained. But it's the same story. Of death, and tyranny, and the banality of it all.

And you don't like it anymore.

But you won't do anything about it, will you?

Fine. The next part goes faster.

You don't get to complain.

51
Elera

NASU'S CLAN DECAMPED from the wasteland, the tall, icy peaks of Mount Iska firmly behind their backs. Every so often lightning arced across the gray sky, frightening the yaks and ibexes. They stamped their feet and brayed, while belated groans of thunder rolled across the cold desert.

Iavahl cheerfully dismantled their ger in the howling wind, humming a song, but Nasyuk scowled as he wrapped his hunting tools up. *"A storm's coming. An ill omen."*

Elera ignored him. Monsoons happened in Xinquha all the time, and no one ran in the streets screaming that it was the end of the world.

Caush undid the ropes that lashed the ger's lattice foundations together, folding up the wide pieces of felt that encompassed their tent. Their hawks soared overhead, catching the wind currents as they dove and ascended again.

Elera loaded the furnace onto a yak, strapping it down. *They're all doing so much for us.* To save one girl, she'd decamped an Iskanti clan, forced them away from their valley of abundance, and made them roam the rapidly freezing desert longer than they should have.

They had to get Viri out. Naias would've gotten there first, maybe convinced the godchild that she was better off in

Haksa. She might've even made Elera the enemy. If by some horrible fate Viri refused to leave, Elera might have to resort to taking her by force. They had to succeed, for all of Nasu's generosity to mean anything.

Nasu and Nasyuk stopped packing abruptly.

"Iskanti?" Nasyuk muttered. *"Kujivhan's clan?"*

Elera glanced around. Bare desert lay before her, the howl of the oncoming winter chill the only sound in her ears.

"Let's hope it is," Nasu said.

The ibexes flicked their ears forward.

It came as a tremor in her bones first, a weak evocation of Iskandraza's horn. The dunes pulsed under her feet, steadily growing louder, until a thousand hooves hammered against the earth. Their yaks pulled against their reins, brass bells clanging a dissonant melody.

In the distance, horses blotted out the horizon, a line of black uniforms and smiling masks.

Faceless. A lot of them.

They were at least three weeks away from Haksa. Either someone had escaped—*Viri? No, they would've sent more*—or they were on their way to attack someone. Perhaps Naias had found out about Kujivhan's army. Rafaeis had sent back Jayal's and Maka's heads; maybe something on them had provided a clue to their executioner.

"They're not coming for us," Rafaeis said, as if trying to convince himself. "Khall would never commit a group that large just to find two Faceless. Let them see through us."

"Speak for yourself," Elera muttered. Out of everyone in Nasu's clan, only she had a mark. They would spot her immediately.

Nasu hurried over, pushing Elera behind the largest yak. *"Hide,"* she said. *"I will do the talking."*

Nasyuk, Iavahl, Caush, and Rafaeis stood in front of the caravan, blocking her from view. Her instincts screamed to fight her way out, as she so often did, but she bit down. Let Nasu help her. *I'm not alone,* she repeated over and over.

A Faceless rode up to Nasu, his horse panting mist and spit. "Iskanti," he said. "We're looking for two people. One has a black square and red diamond on her forehead, wielding a hammer, and the other has a blue lotus and green circle, wielding a pair of crescent blades. Have you seen them pass this way?"

They were looking for her and Rafaeis. She didn't know why, but it put their plan in danger. They'd intended to enter Haksa quietly to find Viri, and being captured complicated their rescue. If the Faceless found out Nasu was harboring the two people they were looking for, they'd be captured, or worse, killed. None of her clan knew how to fight.

Nasu squinted. "Eh?"

"We're looking for—"

"Eh? What?"

"Faceless," the man said, his voice carrying the loudness and impatience of dealing with older, slower folk. "Have you seen them?"

She pointed behind the man, in the direction he'd come from. "*Hahg'sva*. Many Faceless."

"No help at all," the man said, not bothering to mutter. He pulled his horse away, and the rest of the Faceless parted before Nasu's caravan, flanking them as they passed. Elera crouched beside a yak, poles and felt strapped to its back, her face pressed up against its hide.

She didn't dare breathe. The herd might move.

Lightning arced the sky once again, brighter than ever, its jagged branches striking the tip of Mount Iska. The yaks and ibexes screamed and scattered, their bells echoing in the thunder.

Shit. She was exposed. Her hands grabbed her yak's long mane, mustering all her strength to still it. Through a gap between the beasts, a smiling black mask faced her direction.

She ducked immediately. The eyeholes of their mask were too narrow to make out where they were looking from that distance.

She held her breath.

Please let them miss me.
Please.

The rhythmic clop of the horse's hooves grew louder.

Nasu swore in an obscure Iskanti dialect. *"Don't you have more important shit to do than to harass an old woman migrating for the winter? Ungrateful, spoiled children. The Ashvians have taught you nothing."*

"Don't aggravate them, Nasu-mother," Iavahl said. *"We cannot fight against so many."*

It didn't deter the Faceless. They dismounted, drew their sword, and wove through the herd. Elera stood within an arm's length, blocked by her one yak.

She slowly reached behind her back, gripping the handle of her hammer. She would not let herself be captured without a fight.

They came closer. The air quietened to an eerie silence.

There was nowhere else to go.

The last yak was pushed aside.

Their eyes met.

"Don't make this difficult," they said.

"Fuck you," she responded, and swung.

The Faceless sprang into action as bones crunched under her hammer. Their horses encircled their clan, closing off all means of escape. A mounted Gun aimed their weapon at Nasu. Their orders came clear to her: Capture the Faceless, kill the rest.

She wasn't going to let that happen.

Elera dove forward, smashing her hammer against the horse's legs. The horse screamed, tumbling face-first into the ground. Elera pulled the Gun off and finished them with a blow to the head.

Nasu, Caush, and Iavahl froze in the center of the encirclement, while Nasyuk had pulled out his hunting knife, waving it erratically. They were nomads, not fighters. Elera had to get them out first. Their survival in Iskantupu hinged on their freedom.

Rafaeis knew this as well. He leaped up, his crescent blades drawn, and slit the neck of a Faceless on horseback. He pushed the body off. Nasyuk quickly mounted it and blindly grabbed for one of his clan. He found Iavahl, pulling them up behind him.

The Faceless moved closer, the perimeter tightening, a noose around their necks. Nasyuk turned his horse in circles, looking for an opening.

Fury sparked her body, fusing into her a new, impermanent strength. If they weren't going to give her an exit, then she'd make one.

She ran forward, swinging wildly, breaking the legs of all the horses that stood before her. They collapsed in a loud discordant scream, sand flying into the air, and their riders jumped off, lunging for her. She parried them with a single sweep, knocking their weapons aside. The encirclement broke, a momentary opening surrounded by fallen, kicking horses.

"Hurry," she screamed to Nasyuk.

He whipped his horse, steering himself and Iavahl through the gap.

Rafaeis had cut an opening of his own, riding a horse he'd stolen from the Faceless. He whistled, waving his blades in the air. Half of the Faceless company split away, giving chase. He'd provided a distraction, enough for her to help Nasu and Caush—

An enormous force slammed into her.

She fell to the ground, barely gasping for air, the blurry outline of a horse against a lightning-filled sky, and someone punched her in the face. Her vision went dark, morphing into a thousand red stars. She managed to climb to her knees, but someone yanked her tunic from behind, choking her. She clawed frantically, searching for their eyeballs, so she could scratch them out.

Killing them would have been easy if they were Tevurian. But these Faceless had gone through the same training as she had, and now she fought fifty versions of herself—some of them quicker, others calmer, with none of her weaknesses.

More Faceless dove on her. She buckled under the weight, but with an excruciating yell, she summoned more of that fleeting adrenaline-driven power, her muscles tearing against the force of more than a dozen men. She swung, her hammer smashing into anything and everything, but whenever one fell, more appeared in their place.

Her limbs soured with fatigue, her strength rapidly fading. This wasn't a fight. This was an endless punishment, no different from when she'd been lashed for every little rebellion. A fresh wave of Faceless converged to attack the same feeble corpse, beating her until she could no longer withstand the pain.

Her swings grew weaker, her hammer heavier. Someone tripped her and she fell, and the Faceless piled on her again. Knees pressed into her back, knocking all the air out of her lungs. They shoved her face into the sand.

There were too many.

They forced her arms apart. Finger by finger, they pried her hammer out of her grasp.

"No," she shouted.

She struggled as they bound her arms and legs. Next to her lay Nasu and Caush, injured and unconscious. Nasu's long hair obscured her face. Blood trickled down from Caush's temple.

Iavahl, Rafaeis, and Nasyuk were nowhere to be seen, but the victory lay half empty.

There was no returning to Haksa secretly. Nasu and Caush were captured, and Viri was still trapped with Khall.

All was wrong.

Elera screamed and screamed, flooding her rage into the bitter land that she'd once called home.

52

Naias

On the morning of her wedding, Basaa died.

His body lay outside the family's stone house, his night-robe shredded to pieces. His prosthetic foot was missing. The thief had violently torn it off; bruises and claw marks lined his leg. Blood defaced the walls, writing out sharp-cut lines of Iskanti script.

Naias folded her arms tightly across her chest. She'd warned Khall about this. Basaa had had no elite soldiers to protect him, no stone fortress to shield against a furious mob. In their anger, the Iskantis had found the easiest target to hurt.

A Faceless hurried over to her and bowed. "I've asked the locals about the words on the wall, as you've ordered."

"And?"

"'Haksani traitor.'"

The mark on her forehead burned with scabs, but she couldn't help picking it further. She didn't want to punish more people. If Khall caught wind of this, she'd seek revenge. The Iskantis were angry enough, and inflicting more violence on them would risk open rebellion.

She had no choice but to report this. Basaa's death was so public that the queen was going to find out one way or another, but she could buy time, at the very least. The wedding ceremony was happening in an hour. Maybe Naias could utilize the day's euphoria and hope the violence stopped with the Haksani merchant.

"Get a priest and commit him to the dead, quickly," she said. "A *Haksani* one. Bar any Xinquhan priests from touching his body. I don't want this to be even more of a spectacle than it is already."

The Faceless saluted. "One last thing, Commander. His wife is in the house."

Ayashara was still alive.

Naias grumbled. She didn't want to be the widow consoler. She barely knew the couple, and her sympathies started and ended with *I'm sorry he's dead*.

But she had to pretend. Once again, she was picking up the pieces of Khall's recklessness. The Iskantis already hated all she stood for. She didn't need an upset widow to turn the merchants against her as well.

The door dangled off its iron hinges. Cabinets lay in disarray, drawers emptied on the ground. The beds had been ripped apart, presumably in the hope of finding silver hidden in the feathers and straw. Only the family paintings remained, all slashed into pieces on the floor. The Iskantis had looted the place.

A large gash ran through the dining table, probably made by a cleaver. Ayashara sat by it, swathed in a bloody gray robe. Three children fiddled with the cracks in the tiled floor. It surprised her. Basaa had mentioned they had children, but not this many. Three—*three!*—to raise alone.

Naias rapped a knuckle at the door, stepping into the house.

Ayashara's head snapped up, her expression hard. She clutched a totem of Iskandraza in her hand—a slender black stone with a hole carved in the center.

"Faceless," she said in a heavy Iskanti accent, "do not burden me further."

There was no trace of the Ashvian barks that Ayashara had employed in court. She'd pretended she had an accent to curry favor, hiding her roots, so that their new queen would like her.

Naias didn't begrudge her that; after all, she did the same with Khall, ridding the sharp pronunciations in her speech to sound more like one of them.

That charade didn't matter here. Iskanti spoke to Iskanti, two women laboring under the Ashvian queen who lashed them both.

"I wanted to make sure you and your children were unharmed," Naias said, eyeing the three boys that crouched on the ground. "I'll find those responsible for this."

"I know who's responsible, and no, I won't tell you." Ayashara's fingers absently tugged at her tunic. A large purple bruise splotched around her neck.

Naias let out a tired sigh. Just her luck. Ayashara was as obstinate as Hammer. "If you won't tell me who, then I can't help you."

"What you're offering is not help," Ayashara said, her eyes narrowing. "What you're asking me is to give up the Iskantis who murdered my husband, and your queen will kill them in the square like she did the Maetherian envoy. Haksa will descend into civil war. I have no need of further bloodshed. So no, I won't tell you. For this peace, I will receive no justice, and I will suffer alone."

Naias lost her patience. "Don't play the noble victim," she said. "Had you truly wanted to protect your men, you'd have sided with them in the strike. But you wanted your money. You asked Khall to force them back to work."

Ayashara's chair screeched across the floor. "What else could we do? Since you took over, Tevu has stopped receiving our ships. You send rice to our docks, but there's no one to buy it. You haven't fixed the port, or shored up our trade, or given us anything to smooth over the disruptions of your invasion. Tevu was our biggest buyer, did you know that? We were forced to make the best out of a bad situation. If only you'd heard the conversations Basaa had with our men before he decided to go to Khall!"

Ayashara pressed an accusatory finger into Naias's chest.

"What have *you* done? You're an Iskanti, heir to a kingdom, and you've done nothing to protect us. You stood aside and watched our temple burn. Our books, our language, our people, everything."

Marriage, marriage, marriage. Everyone assumed Naias would become powerful through it, when she couldn't see anything but another lifetime of servitude. No one understood, everyone presumed. She was tired of being the sacrificial goat, the one who had to placate the angry masses. This wasn't her fault.

"I told Khall not to come here," Naias said through gritted teeth. "I told her not to burn down Ashvalra's temple. I told her not to torture the striking Iskantis. My marriage makes me a prisoner of this system, forced to serve a queen who doesn't listen to a single word I say."

The children stopped playing, their hands stilled. They hunched into themselves, as if wishing they could disappear into the floor. The sight of their fear only made Naias angrier.

the pastures didn't look that barren; goats tottered about, plump and full, she played catch with her sisters while mother stood against a blue sky, blocking out the cold afternoon sun, a bag clinking in her hand—

"I don't want to be here," she said, her voice rising. "I don't want to be standing next to you, trying to dredge up sympathy for a man I barely knew. I didn't want anyone to lose a father, or a husband, or to leave children to their own. The blood tithe stripped me of everything. I wouldn't wish that betrayal on anyone else, least of all a child!"

Ayashara's gaze made the characteristic flick to the center of her forehead. "You were taken," she said, her expression softening.

abandoned to a man wearing black who she didn't know, mother peeling fingers away from her arm, one by one, all the while naias screamed why? what did i do wrong? what do my sisters have that i don't? am i broken? i'll fix myself, i promise, don't leave me, please.

"I was *sold*. She had three to choose from. She chose me."

Ayashara gathered up her children, ushering them out of the hut. "Go outside and play. Stay where I can see you."

They ran out, all knobbly knees and matchstick limbs. Perhaps a little older than Viridian. A little older than *her*, when she was sold off to Khallan.

Ayashara paused by the door, watching as her tallest child fashioned a ball out of dried rattan, kicking it into the air with the flat side of his foot. The other two boys counted each kick, jostling each other aside as they waited for their brother to miss. Faceless surrounded the house, hands resting on their weapons, deterrent enough for anyone who dared to approach.

Ayashara's voice was barely above a whisper. "When the men burst through these doors, the thought crossed my mind that they might take my children away from me. In a flash, I knew who would survive and who would not. The tallest child there is Junaruya, my second born. He knows Haksa's streets better than I do, and he's only ten. It was him I whispered to, in that void where time stops, and the seconds feel like hours, when I thought my life was at an end. I told him to take care of the others." She reached for Naias's hand, tracing the calloused lines that formed along the crook of the commander's fingers. "I think your parents knew that out of the three of you, you'd survive."

Survive. She'd cut off so many parts to survive that she couldn't recognize the carcass of her old self anymore.

She'd let her old love go in a bid to gain her freedom. *A necessary sacrifice,* she'd told herself at the time. She'd killed the king for the same reason. He would've never let an Iskanti taint his daughter. She'd discarded the Faceless and her heritage so as to succeed in a land that hated her for being different, and yet the Ashvians never saw her as an equal.

What was left? Nothing.

She survived and became nothing.

A Xinquhan page ran up the cobblestone street, stopping in

front of the Faceless perimeter. He held out a scroll with a red seal on it. Naias couldn't hear him speak from this distance, but the Faceless nodded and turned to Ayashara's children. They let the ball drop to the ground, faces all smiles and teeth, and one of the shorter children raised his hand to greet them.

The Faceless wrenched his arms together.

This wasn't right. Naias had given no such order. She hurried out of the house.

"Faceless, unhand him and declare yourself. What crime has this child committed?"

The soldier saluted, handing over the scroll, its red wax seal swaying heavily at the bottom. "Earthly Sovereign Khall has enacted the blood tithe in Haksa, Commander. We're to collect the eldest child from every Iskanti family and deliver them to the fortress."

No. No, no, no. She snatched the scroll, reading it. The Faceless was right. She couldn't overrule this decree; the seal was in Khall's name.

The tallest of Ayashara's children ran up. His features resembled Ayashara's in every way, from the fire in his dark eyes to the jut of his chin, with little trace of his father's pleasant features.

"He's not the eldest," he lied, pulling his brother aside. "I am."

Junaruya.

"No," Ayashara screamed, rushing to drag her son back, but Naias grabbed her tunic. The fabric ripped under her fingers.

Her mind swam with panic. She no longer had control of the Faceless. Khall had resurrected the blood tithe, presumably in a fit of revenge against the Iskantis. She'd broken a promise—a personal promise—to Naias, and the hurt from this betrayal shouldn't have consumed the deluge of realizations that flooded her head, but it did.

Little by little her power was being stripped away. It frightened her to think of her place in this new hierarchy. Was she still second in command to the queen? Would she still remain one of her advisers? What did being heir mean now? Was she just a powerless consort: no control in kingdom politics, no control over the Faceless, no control over ending the blood tithe?

In the midst of her struggle, another Iskanti child was going to be separated from their mother. Naias wanted to scream at the injustice of it all. Basaa had sided with Khall during the strike, and that had protected him against nothing. His family still suffered the consequences of the queen's wrath.

As the Faceless led Junaruya away, trumpets and horns sounded in the distance, an atonal blare that resembled more noise than music. Khall would be making her way out of the fortress by now, veiled and beautifully dressed, a procession of pages and maidservants accompanying her. The wedding ceremony had begun.

"I'll handle this, I promise you," she said, her body trembling with the earnestness of her conviction.

Ayashara's tears streamed down her face. "Don't lie to me."

Naias planted a fierce kiss on her forehead and crushed her in an embrace. The kiss was devoid of affection, the embrace not meant to comfort. It was a shared anger in their blood that ran generations long, a collective mourning of the children that were taken away from them, and the determination that this, *this* would be the final time they'd ever suffer that loss.

"As one Iskanti to another, I swear to you I'll make this right."

53

Naias

She didn't have time to change. Her unworn dress would have to stay in her quarters. It was better to show up poorly dressed than be late for her own wedding.

The execution square had been refashioned into an altar. Viridian stood on the same platform Soridian had died on, once again dressed as Ashvalra. Her ankles bore the wounds of wearing leg-irons for too long, weeping pus and blood. A blindfold concealed her eyes. A tall wooden podium overseeing the square had been built for her. Behind them, half a dozen rows of Iskanti folk knelt at knifepoint. Faceless swarmed them all.

Three bowls had been laid on a table before the godchild: water, earth, and goat's blood. The ritual honored Ashvalra with earth, water, and blood, the three sacred elements required to make life. They were to exchange vows, cross their arms to drink the water, rub the earth on their foreheads, and smear blood on each other's lips.

Naias failed to see how it honored the god of rebirth, when they'd created this farce of an avatar by using Diavijra.

A Faceless pushed past the crowd, his tattered uniform caked in dirt. "The search party has returned," he whispered in Naias's ear. "We've captured Hammer and two Iskantis who aided her escape. Crescent is missing."

Naias clenched her teeth. Not now. Not when she needed to stop this blood tithe from happening. If Viridian knew that Hammer had returned, she'd murder everyone in the square to get to her. There were too many threads to pull. She needed control, and this was not the place.

"Where are they?" she asked.

The Faceless nodded past the rows of kneeling Iskantis. "Just beyond."

"Keep them where they are," she said. "Don't let the godchild see them. When the wedding is over, bring them to my quarters."

He hurried away just as Khall walked up to the altar, clad in layers of red batik silk. Patterns of trees, flowers, rivers, and hawks wove through her wedding dress, embroidered in a dazzling array of multicolored threads. She wore a headdress styled as a bouquet: bougainvillea flowers fashioned from gold and pink sapphires. A curtain of pearls partially obscured her face.

Naias would have been stunned by how beautiful she was, but behind her the Faceless moved towards the fortress with children in tow. Their struggle dug out trenches in the sand, while others kicked and screamed in their captors' arms, crying out for their parents. The Iskanti families that knelt behind Viridian shouted after them, their collective chorus drowned out by the blare of the wedding horns. Khall smiled, oblivious to everything around her.

"Do you even love me anymore?" Naias burst out.

Her surprise resembled a startled little bird. "Of course I do."

"Then why bring back the blood tithe?"

The delicate beauty immediately faded. "Circumstances have changed," she said slowly, as if Naias hadn't been executing her orders the moment they'd arrived at Haksa. "The Iskantis need to be taught a lesson."

Naias couldn't let her go ahead with this anymore. She had to be honest, to take away this power that blinded Khall to everything else. "Haksa's rebellion is your doing."

Khall flared with anger. "Because *you* have done nothing. I promised not to use the blood tithe, but our numbers have dwindled since Maetheria attacked. We haven't conscripted anyone since we arrived. I looked the other way, because I love you. Now I'm being accused of the opposite. Is this what my kindness has wrought? Look at what the Iskantis have done to my city. All the ships have stalled, goods rot on the docks. Haksa isn't a port anymore. They've killed Basaa. This crime will not go unanswered."

Khall pointed to the rows of Iskanti folk bound behind the altar. "Goat's blood is a pitiful offering to Ashvalra. We'll smear Iskanti blood on our lips instead. Diavijra will do us the honor, and fear will stop this rabble."

Naias wanted the horns to blow louder, so she could at least pretend that she'd misheard. But her denial ended here. She'd allowed the temple to burn, erased a language she didn't speak, and voluntarily allowed the dockworkers' torture. Now Khall had brought back the blood tithe and wanted to kill Iskantis for an insignificant ceremony.

It'd taken her a long time to understand what Soridian was trying to tell her, but she finally recognized it. He was right. He'd seen it in the short moments he'd stayed in Xinquha, in the ruined temple of Iskandraza, in the torn history of the Faceless.

This was a genocide.

Naias yanked off the curtain of pearls that obscured Khall's face. Beads scattered to the floor. The force of her strength pulled the headdress off. Khall gripped her head, squealing in pain as it tugged against her hair.

"What are you doi—"

She wanted to see every part of Khall's face, from her sunken cheeks to her doll-like eyes, when she spoke. "You are massacring an entire group of people just to show off. This isn't governance. It's tyranny. Remember when you started your reign in Xinquha? You didn't want unnecessary bloodshed. You wanted to rule with mercy."

"And look where that got me," Khall spat. She grabbed the bowl of blood, flinging its contents to the ground. "An assassination attempt and our ally dead. Mercy doesn't grant power, Naias. *Power* grants power. When everyone sees that we have Diavijra and the might of the Faceless, Haksa will bend, and we'll all get what we want."

She raised her hand, and a page scurried forward, taking the godchild's blindfold off.

"Diavijra, kill them. One row at a time. Let them watch."

Viridian dropped the sheaf of rice and ascended the podium, her shackles jingling against the platform.

She raised her hand, and it began.

54
Elera

SHE STRAINED AGAINST her bonds, her arms still tied behind her back with a thick coil of rope. If she put her mind to it, brute strength could tear the rope apart in time. A few fibers snapped, but it wasn't enough. She kept pulling. Skin sheared from her wrists, coarse straw stabbing into flesh. She'd refused to stay quiet, so the Faceless had shoved a spiked iron bit into her mouth, gagging her. Drool and blood stained her gray tunic.

Her chest hurt. The corruption had spread further during the weeks of her capture without Iavahl to keep it at bay.

Nasu and Caush lay beside her, heavily injured. Since the fight, Caush had never regained enough awareness to form a full sentence. His breathing was shallow, and the head wound he'd suffered hadn't healed. His matted, unbraided hair draped limply around his face. Nasu was bound and gagged with rope. A mixture of fresh and dried blood smothered her face and neck.

Rows of Iskanti-Haksani folk knelt before them, evident from their laborer's clothes and the dialect they wept in. The Faceless pushed the first row of prisoners to the fore.

Viri, painted in gold, emerged from the explosion of red confetti and silver tassels. Her once thick wheat-colored hair was now thin and gray. Bald spots dotted her scalp. That cursed chain was still shackled around her legs.

She used to have a smile, once, when she'd sat atop Elera's black mare, waving back at her in delight. Now she looked like she'd been wandering in a stupor. She stumbled to the top of the podium, every step a plod.

Elera cried out Viri's name, but pain pierced her tongue and the bit filled her mouth with blood.

Viri raised her hand, and the first row fell.

The crowd wailed and bellowed, shaking the ground beneath her. The Faceless surrounded their queen, their weapons pointed outwards, a disproportionate defense against the surge of Iskanti anger.

"If none of you shut up, I'll have all of you killed," Khall screamed. "I didn't want this, but you all wouldn't stop complaining. You wouldn't listen to me. *I have Diavijra!*"

Elera never stopped looking at Viri. The obedience came so quick, like she'd done it a hundred times before. She saw it in the slack jaw and dead stare, just like the other Faceless children when they finally broke under the lash. Elera had looked like this when she'd given up too, the moment she'd decided subservience was the path of least resistance.

She'd come too late.

Black uniforms hoisted the second row of Iskanti folk to their feet, pushing them to stand atop the bodies of the first. Some buckled, some wept, but all died under Diavijra's hand.

Her speed was no accident. She'd done this before.

No one could do anything besides watch. No one wanted to die, and no one cared enough to save lives that weren't their own. Viri simply continued. Nothing on her face seemed to indicate she cared.

The Faceless pulled Caush up to the platform.

Diavijra raised her hand.

"No," Elera said, but the bit muffled her cry. Her muscles strained, pulling against her bonds once again. Blood rushed to her head.

He twitched once, and his shallow breathing stopped.

Viri hadn't seen or heard her. Corpses piled high, a massacre enacted, an executioner indifferent to it all. The crowd's bellow quietened into silent horror.

The Faceless hoisted Nasu up.

The fibers around Elera's wrists snapped, one by one. She couldn't break them fast enough.

"No, Viri, wait, stop—"

Nasu said nothing. She didn't smile or frown, and when Elera met her gaze, she wasn't there. Flat, unaffected. Maybe it was a look of betrayal, the hurt that Elera couldn't save them. Maybe it was grief from Caush's death. Maybe she lamented that she hadn't listened to her son and left Elera and Rafaeis to save the godchild on their own. Maybe it was regret at taking in those that didn't belong, only to have death as their reward. Maybe it was the exhaustion, being bound and beaten, and knowing how it all was going to end, that their executioner didn't matter anymore. The matriarch did not dignify Elera with some noble, martyred final speech to help with closure.

Nasu gave her nothing as she drew her last breath and fell to a twitching heap on the ground.

Viridian was gone.

There was no coming back from this illness. Chatrasaya couldn't cleanse this poison. Strixahava couldn't heal this wound. All the hope in the world couldn't force this reality to change.

And she was next.

She couldn't die like this. She wanted a warrior's death, her trusted hammer in her hand and a laugh on her lips. She wasn't going to die bound and kneeling, suffocated by a godchild whom she'd failed to save, with neither weapon nor Rafaeis by her side.

The pain didn't register anymore. With a guttural roar she tore the bonds loose from her arms, climbed up the pile of corpses, and launched herself at the platform. She didn't have her hammer with her, but her thickened, bloodied fist was good enough.

Khall, Naias, and Diavijra stood astonished, frozen, as time expanded before her. She'd interrupted a wedding ceremony. Khall's wedding dress rivaled the attire of Tevurian royalty, while Naias wasn't wearing anything appropriate. How odd. She'd spent her entire life working towards this.

She didn't have time to kill everyone. Only one.

If she killed Khall or Naias, another noxious weed would sprout in their place, searching for the one pawn to turn the tide in their favor. Khall had an heir; Naias would've made sure of that. Their deaths changed nothing.

That left—

She couldn't kill Viri.

She couldn't do it. This massacre wasn't her fault. It was Khall's.

But she was gone. She'd killed Nasu.

She couldn't be gone. There had to be some way to stop her.

Viri had said that her power affected only what she could see. Those large, alarmed eyes that stared at her right now, tracing her path as she leaped into the air.

An easy thing to pluck them out.

It was awful, but Viri would be alive. Crippled, but alive, ruined by the person who loved her.

Would Viri even forgive her? Carrying this bitterness towards her savior and mutilator, for the rest of her life?

No, dead was better. Viri was gone, gone, gone. Blinded or not, no antidote would cure the corruption embedded in her. She had tasted power, and she knew how to use it. She'd find another way without her eyes, and then Elera would have to remove those parts of her as well.

Pulling arms off a toy doll.

Dead was better. If Viri died, no one would take advantage of her anymore.

Her heart constricted at the thought. It was too much, too much. She was still worth saving.

Even when she'd killed Caush. Even when she'd killed Nasu.

She was still worth saving.

But if Viri never existed, she wouldn't have to make this choice.

If Viri stopped existing, she'd never have to make this choice again.

Dead was better.

She couldn't have everything.

Her fist aimed for the godchild's head.

55
Elera

A FORCE YANKED on her foot.

Her jaw slammed against the ground, and the bit dug deep into her tongue. Blood sprayed on the hem of Khall's dress. Red stars filled her vision.

In the haze of regaining her bearings, Khall's voice shouted over all.

"Treasonous Faceless, looking to assassinate me in broad daylight—"

Something cold and thin pinned her neck to the ground.

A crescent moon blade.

"—Iskantis, all of them, conspiring with a Faceless to rob me of my throne, I knew there was a traitor in our ranks—"

Naias's hushed voice interrupted her. "Let's get you to a safe place, my queen."

"No, no, no," Khall said, pushing against the Faceless that looked to take her away. "Kill the Faceless. Kill her. Kill all the Iskantis, the Faceless, everyone that worked for her. KILL HER FOR PLOTTING AGAINST ME."

The blade disappeared, replaced by swords and axes. Elera looked for her betrayer, but a blur of black uniforms piled on top of her.

This is the end.

Viri gawked at Elera's swollen and bloodied face, tense with astonishment.

Some semblance of humanity remained in the godchild after all. Elera wanted to kiss and kill her in the same breath. Nasu and Caush had chosen to save her and died for it. If she had gone at it alone, none of them would have been affected. They would've stayed in the valley with the rest of her clan, waiting out the year to see the dawn of spring.

This was Rafaeis's fault. All his idealism, all that love, meant nothing when they were Faceless, forever second to the people they served. That cursed word—'hope'—had poisoned her mind, convincing her that the world was ultimately beautiful, when in the end it was just a meaningless series of events, steered by petty men with power.

The remnants of that poison still lingered as she looked at Viri. She wanted to say one last goodbye, to say *I did this for you, and look how much it took me*, to be granted some forgiveness and gratitude, so that Nasu's blank face wouldn't be her last memory before she died.

Khall bent down, a firm hand pressing down on Viri's shoulder, and leaned into her ear. She was too close, too possessive. Elera wanted to smash her head in.

"Diavijra," Khall said, "draw out her death. Prolong it, make her suffer."

Viri gave no response, still paralyzed with shock. It created a strange disappointment in her. She'd longed for Viri's voice, even if it was to hear her obey this tyrant's orders. She'd always known Viri froze in moments like these, and she'd mistakenly taught her to accept it. She should've taught her to kill everyone here, and then herself.

Naias stepped out between them. Lightning cracked across the sky. The roiling clouds from Iskantupu spread east, making their way to the sea.

"Let me do it," she said to Khall. "This Faceless is under my command. Let me deal with her."

No. She struggled, her protests muffled by her bit, but the

Faceless pressed down. Her shoulders bent, ligaments tearing under the weight. She wasn't going to let Naias have the satisfaction of killing her. Viri was bad enough, but not the woman who'd left her. Never her.

Khall narrowed her eyes. "Then do it."

"Let me handle it the way the Faceless have always done. Not here."

"Now."

Naias sank to her knees, gripping the hem of Khall's dress. "I promise to return with her head, or you can have mine. Please let me do this. As a . . . as a wedding gift."

Groveling, always groveling. Even when Naias's own inevitable death came at Khall's hands, she'd still be begging. This was a worse death than being killed by Diavijra.

Khall openly sneered. "You accused me of not loving you, and now you want a gift."

Naias bowed even lower, ever the sycophant. "I'm sorry, my queen. I was frightened. You know how it feels, the inability to control your own fear. Give me another chance. I shouldn't be ungrateful in the face of your generosity. I'll spend the rest of my life repaying your kindness."

This charade of flattery seemed to placate her. She walked to the bodies, drawing her finger across Elera's bloodied face. Her other hand gripped a fistful of red soil. Viri disappeared into the sea of Faceless bodies.

Khall reached over, dabbing Naias's head with earth and smearing blood across her lips.

"I want her head by sundown, wife," Khall said. "Not tomorrow, not someone else's head, not some message delivered down these treasonous Faceless who will betray me at a whim. You. Her head. Tonight. If I don't have it, it'll be yours next."

56
Elera

NAIAS PULLED ELERA to her feet. The Faceless bound her from shoulder to wrist, her entire upper body immobilized. Naias yanked at the end of the rope, leading her past the city walls of Haksa, to the gradual slopes that made up the base of the mountains. The sparse forest cast weak shadows under the midafternoon sun; most of the trees had been felled in the last decade of war, and they hadn't grown back.

Much had happened since she'd left. The stench of rotting and burned human flesh filled the air. Stakes stuck out from shallow graves, next to smoking pyres, but there were too many to bury. Piles of corpses lay out in the open, green Maetherian robes and blue Tevurian tabards all mixed together, their colors peeking from the creeping frost. Flies and maggots wriggled in open wounds, eagerly devouring what was left.

Naias kicked Elera behind her knees, forcing her down.

"I'm taking the gag out," she said, undoing the muzzle that wrapped around her head. "Don't cut your tongue."

Too late for that. Elera spat out the iron. Her mouth felt like it was on fire, but at least she could move her jaw again. A useless bit of kindness before she died.

She couldn't resist taking one last jab. "Aw, wanted to hear my voice before I die?" Her lacerated tongue slurred out the words.

"And I thought you didn't love me anymore."

"What did you think assassinating Khall would accomplish?" Naias asked sharply. "You take the godchild and run away into the mountains together?"

Elera scoffed. "Please, I wasn't going after your bride. She's not worthy enough to die by my hand."

"So you were going after me, then? I went out of my way to find you, and this is how you repay me."

Naias had sent the Faceless search party. She'd caused all this. All those deaths were on her hands, this spineless lackey who only wanted to impress the queen.

Her head pounded with blood and rage. "Just kill me," she said. "If dying means I don't have to talk to you anymore, I'll gladly take it."

"I am patching a sinking ship with my bare hands," Naias burst out. "I'm saving your life."

One life. Her life. Nasu and Caush didn't matter to her, or whatever she'd done to Viri, or the Iskantis who'd died just so their blood could seal her marriage to Khall. "Take me to the beach. The sun will help you see where you're aiming your gun."

"Shut up, shut up, *shut the fuck up.*" Naias gripped Elera by the shoulders. "Khall has unraveled because of you. She's been scared since the march from Xinquha. Your assassination attempt will destroy us. I don't know what she's going to do. Imprisonment? Torture? Mass executions? Every action I take, every little argument with her, will now be met with suspicion. I'm trapped. My work has been undone because of you."

Elera forced out a laugh. She was the one at death's door, and yet Naias still thought about herself. "Keep deluding yourself that Khall will end the blood tithe. I didn't undo any of your work, because there wasn't any to begin with. All you did was whore yourself out."

Naias punched her across the face.

Elera hit the forest floor, cheek throbbing in the aftershock.

Her teeth didn't get knocked out.

Naias had pulled back.

"Coward," Elera spat.

But Naias wasn't listening. Snow crunched under her boots as she headed towards the rotting corpses. She picked out a fresh female Iskanti body and pulled out her dagger, severing the tendons around her neck, hacking as quickly as she could. The flies buzzed angrily around her.

She tossed the head at Elera's feet, then ran her too-soft hands over Elera's bleeding face and mouth, smearing red on herself and the head.

"Ow," Elera said, even though it didn't hurt.

Naias said nothing, studying the dirtied and bloodied head between them. She then dropped to her knees, stabbing the head with as much force as she could muster. Slice by slice, the head lost her nose and part of her jaw, her eyelids half peeled off. With a final thrust, Naias ran her knife through the corpse's forehead, where the Faceless' mark would have been.

Naias stood up, panting, and cut Elera free. "Go," she said. "Be grateful for the love we once had. This is my final mercy to you."

Elera had had an inkling of Naias's plan the moment she severed the head from the body, but she'd refused to admit it. Staying alive meant thinking of a *future*, and the struggle to survive as an exile that belonged neither to the Faceless nor to the Iskanti. The oncoming winter would doom her.

Naias's mercy—if it could even be called that—forced her to consider it. All she could do was stare glumly. Was she grateful or angry? She couldn't tell anymore.

Naias raised her pistol and fired it into the air. The trees shook; frightened birds took flight, filling the sky with a shriek.

She stalked away with the severed head in her hand. "If you come back, I *will* kill you."

SHE WAITED UNTIL she could no longer hear Naias. In the silence, with blood still dripping down her chin, she spoke.

"You stopped me. You didn't stop Viri, but you stopped *me*."

With a whisper, Rafaeis dropped from the tree. His sunken, pale face bore the signs of sleepless nights, the ragged journey he'd taken to get here.

"I'd only just arrived. I saw your aim."

"She killed Caush and Nasu."

He clutched his chest in anguish. "She didn't know who they were," he said, going through the same excuses she'd experienced moments before. "She was just following orders from Khall, she had no idea who they were to us."

"Reason with it all you like, but her death was the only way."

"Both Nasu and Caush are dead, and you want Viri to be part of their number as well?"

She couldn't cry, not now. She pushed the grief away, steeling herself to convince Rafaeis. "She massacred all the Iskantis. There's no saving her. She's gone. I was next. You saw it."

"No." He walked past her. "You know so little about her. Viri wouldn't have followed through. She would've turned her power on Khall, and her death would've been our escape. We can't give up on her. Even if she killed . . ." His voice choked. "You still can't see any other way besides live or die. Perhaps for a corrupted lizard, or a lame horse. Not Viri. There's always another way. I'm going back."

The roots of denial sank deeper in his mind than hers. He was wrong. There was no other way. Nasyuk and Iavahl were long gone, and their matriarch dead. They couldn't survive the wasteland without them. They were trapped here, Viri most of all, and the next time they met her, they would not be so lucky. She'd spent just as much time with Viri as Rafaeis had—no, more—and he wasn't going to lecture her about how much she did and didn't know.

She clamped a hand on his shoulder, forcing him to turn around. "I do know," she said angrily. "I've been through it. When they beat me and I couldn't fight anymore, I obeyed. We're either going back to kill her, or we'll have nothing to do with her at all. She's beyond saving."

"Viri isn't *you*," Rafaeis shouted, pushing her away. "She

never was. You think she'll turn out the way you did. You think the Faceless broke you and made you this way. I went through it; we all did! *We're not you*. You think this world is a cruel and ugly place, that you need to kill or be killed to survive, and you've never once tried to change it. *You* inflict this pain on the rest of us."

It broke her heart to hear him speak it. Fine. If she hurt them, then she'd cut them off. They didn't have to tolerate her presence anymore. She didn't need him; she didn't need anyone. She'd been perfectly happy minding her own business before the both of them tore out everything she was and forced her to become someone else. She'd told him that she was beyond saving all that time ago, and he'd refused to accept it.

"Go, then," she said, giving him the bitterness he needed. "See for yourself what she has become. You're blinded by your own hope, Crescent, if you think this world will reward you for your kindness. It is a fantasy. The gods are indifferent to our lives, and they will happily kill us and everyone else. Look at what they did to her. You refuse to see that. And you blinded me too. You let me believe, for one moment, this terrible, beautiful lie, that we could run away from this life."

She stood tall, and her mind closed, pushing out the soft, useless parts of herself. *Sever the limbs to protect the heart*.

"I hate you for allowing me to dream," she said.

Her whispered breath led to an avalanche of fury. His beautiful face curled into a snarl.

"You hide behind sarcasm and insults because you're afraid that if you laid yourself bare, there would be nothing. You're so absorbed in protecting yourself that when you lash out, you don't care how you affect the people who love you. Gods, I loved you so much it hurt."

And there it was, tumbled out of him, the words she'd longed to say all that time ago.

He grabbed her into a furious kiss, love and hate all at the same time, his tongue shoved into her tattered mouth, tasting her blood, while her lips caught on his teeth.

Everyone close to her had died, except for this man, whom she desperately wanted to return to the valley with and pretend nothing had ever happened, and he didn't want to go with her anymore. He willingly walked to his death, in his furious, delusional belief that Viridian could still be saved.

She would not.

At the moment she thought her life was at an end, she became the coward, acting in the same way she always did—alone and recklessly. This was her path. It'd always been.

She broke off the kiss, shoving him away. Elera did not meet his eye as she walked past him into the mountains, to nowhere. She pressed her lips together, wanting to keep the taste of him in her mouth for as long as she could.

"I love you too," she said, "and we are done."

57
Diavijra

HALF A DOZEN Faceless shoved her into her quarters. With swift precision they fastened her leg-irons to the hooks embedded in the walls. She fumbled to take the blindfold off, and the door slammed shut behind her.

Darkness engulfed the room. They'd bricked up the last window. It wasn't much different than the wagon Tevu had used when they took her away.

Her bitter laugh rang through the room. The irony of it all. She'd always known that she'd traded one prison for another, but for all of Khall's and Naias's claims that they treated their godchildren better than Tevu, these walls showed her that they were all the same.

Her head spun with confusion. Elera's fist had been aimed for her. The muzzle had concealed nearly all her features, and her face was swollen from being hit, but the black square and red diamond on her head had told Viridian everything she needed to know, and it filled her with immense joy and fear all at once.

Why did she want to kill her? What had she done wrong? Where was Rafaeis, and why had Elera returned alone, so heavily injured? Was this part of some plan to deceive Khall? No one told her anything.

In the end, when Elera was dragged onto the platform, all her choices pointed to killing Khall.

Clement had warned her against regicide, but she couldn't let Elera die. Khall gave the orders. If there was no queen, then there were no orders, then they would be free.

But people had reacted far quicker than she. Viridian was still a child, after all, and had none of the training of warriors. Naias had whispered "Don't do anything" in her ear and stepped forward, parleying with Khall. Then she and Elera disappeared into the mountains, and that was the last Viridian saw of them.

With a cry, she slammed her fists against the wall. Every single time she faced danger, her mind and body refused to work. She hated that part of herself.

No longer. She was not going to wait for Naias to come solve her problems. After Soridian died, she'd waited for Khall to hand over the Faceless she loved, only to be told it was a lie. If Naias refused to meet her, then she was going to start killing her way out. She was still shackled to the room, but when enough people died, someone would have to make a deal with her. Haksa, Tevu, and Maetheria could burn for all she cared. She just wanted Elera and Rafaeis back.

Her hands shook. She wanted the pipe, to let smoke take the deaths away.

Something scraped within her door. Iron scratching against iron, as if the locks were being tried.

"Viri," a muffled voice said. "Are you there? Viri?"

Her name. Her true name. Not Diavijra, not godchild, not Viridian, but simply Viri, the name spoken by those who loved the bones and flesh that made her. She scrambled to the source.

"Who are you?" she whispered into the wall.

"Rafaeis."

All she had was a disembodied voice, from which there was no way to ascertain his identity. "Prove it."

He paused. "I came to you in the wagon, when we were marching on Haksa. You told me about your father and how he fought for you. I told you not to forget that love."

Viri bit back a cry. It was him. "How did you come back? When?"

"Only just," he said. The scraping continued. "I'm trying to get you out, but these aren't simple padlocks. They're linked to some mechanism, and there's a sequence to this, I think. My picks don't work. I don't know if I can break them."

"Are you with Elera? I saw her with Naias and they went into the mountains."

"We don't have much time," he said, sidestepping the question. "If I can't open this door, or if Khall comes back again, I need you to do something for me. Tevu is coming to invade Haksa again. Engale must die. I'll . . . I'll have to make a deal with Naias. She's a tactician, and her knowledge will help us defeat Engale and the Reborn protecting her."

"No," Viridian said. She didn't care for the person who'd taken everything dear away. "Naias is a liar. She took you away from me. I don't want anything to do with her."

"This is our only choice, Viri," he said, his voice so quiet that she strained to hear him through the wind and stone. "I didn't want this either. I had others with me, and we'd planned on taking you into Iskantupu, but . . ." He stopped himself. "Don't worry about that. Engale must die if we want to survive. Tevu and Khall will chase you when we leave, and we need all the help we can get. Whatever order Naias gives you, follow it. I'll be there in the melee. Win this battle for us. If you can kill Engale, do it."

"But there'll be so many people. I won't know where you are."

"I'll be where Engale is. I'll take Elera's hammer from Naias. Engale will be drawn to it. Do you remember how it looked? Gold plated with a steel tip, a latch at the end—"

"—to pull the rapier out," she finished. "Why does Naias have her hammer? Where is she?" He'd danced around the question over Elera's whereabouts, and she wasn't going to let him avoid it any longer.

He avoided it anyway.

"Did Naias kill her?" she asked, expecting the worst.

"No. Elera killed herself."

"Why? How?"

"She thought you were corrupted by Khall. She gave up hoping to save you, and the darkness turned in on itself."

"But I wasn't corrupted," she protested. "I wouldn't have killed her."

"I know. That's why I'm here to take you away. We planned this together, before she . . . she left."

She didn't want to believe it. "Tell me the truth, Rafaeis. Is Elera really dead?"

A long silence.

"She won't come back," he finally said.

Viridian collapsed against the wall. Another love relegated to a memory. Papa and his leaking brain, Dada and his twitching hands, and Elera, muzzled and bound, her bleeding fist inexplicably aimed for her.

Rafaeis wasn't going to be one of their number. She couldn't lose any more.

"I know staying to fight is a heavy thing for me to ask," Rafaeis said. "You've suffered since we left. But I promise this will be the last time. After this battle, you'll never have to use your powers on another person again."

She knew this to be a lie. Clement had taught her as much. "No. There will be more."

"It won't happen," he ground out, every word carrying the gravity of his conviction. "I swear it."

Her hands clawed across the rough stone, a poor substitute for his body. How cruel the gods were to keep him so close, and yet she couldn't see or touch him.

"I'll win Haksa for you," she said. "If you think this is the best way out, I'll do it. When it's done, we'll leave together."

"I'll be holding Elera's hammer," he repeated. "Look for me."

Almost a year had passed since she'd been rescued from the wagon. Her life had changed so much since then. "Why did the gods choose me?" she asked. "Why did they give me powers I didn't want?"

"I don't know," he said. "I'm sorry I don't have answers for you."

She stared at the bricked window, imagining yellow angsana trees against the tall, lush mountains, a misty sun hidden behind their peaks. "I'm tired of this life. If I had wings, like a butterfly, I could fly away from here."

"If you had wings, you'd no longer be human."

She breathed a laugh, casting mist on her steel chains. Maybe it was a sob. She didn't know.

"That sounds better," she said.

Footsteps shuffled against stone. I can tell you it was Khall and her child servants, because I know what happened. Viridian hated her for interrupting them, ruining the fragile reunion she'd waited so long to have.

"I have to go," Rafaeis said. "Remember what I told you."

i couldn't say goodbye

Her steel door groaned open, light blazing through her room. Viridian flinched, putting her hand up to shield herself. Rough hands wrapped around her shoulders. Khall pulled a blindfold over her eyes, extinguishing the light. A cold and heavy shackle settled on her collarbone.

"Move," Khall shouted, yanking the chain.

Unprepared, Viridian fell on all fours, her knees scraping against the floor.

"You're coming with me," she said. "The Faceless stand in the courtyard. None of them can be trusted. You will kill them all."

He must have left, then. If he'd known that Khall had ordered the Faceless' execution, he would've stayed and killed her and

i couldn't say goodbye

Viridian, it's all right, sleep, I can speak for you

i couldn't say goodbye

i couldn't say goodbye

i couldn't say goodbye

58
Naias

She pulled the iron bolt across the door to her quarters, leaning Hammer's confiscated weapon against the wall, and set the disfigured head on a table. So much of the woman's defining features had been chopped off that the head barely looked human, much less Hammer's. Only time would tell if it was enough.

Everything was falling apart. Of all the things she'd chosen to fight for, in that moment, she'd let Hammer go. Out of respect for their history, she'd said, a history that consisted of bickering and fighting. That stubborn Faceless had undermined everything Naias had worked for at every turn. This last assassination attempt was her chaotic swan song.

But Naias couldn't bring herself to stand by and watch Hammer die. That woman always ran headfirst into trouble and survived with the help of others who were stupid enough to care, and never once bothered to thank them. Falling in love with her was a mistake.

Because of her, Khall had become a tyrant, walking the path of her father.

No. She clawed her face. Everything that happened was always someone else's fault, and now there was no one left to blame. She couldn't lie to herself anymore. This wasn't Hammer's doing, or

Jayal and Maka's, or Soridian's. Khall hadn't turned into this on her own. Naias had lost her temper, isolated her, told her to be a queen, and then silently followed instruction when she lost her power. She was culpable in this too. Clement had said as much.

They should've never marched to Haksa. Khall was gone, and she couldn't change her anymore.

Naias kicked the hammer aside and paced the room.

The loud *clang* did not come. In the flicker of the candlelight, a long shadow stained the walls.

An intruder. She hadn't heard him enter. Naias swiftly drew her gun.

A tall, lean man in Faceless uniform stood by the window, holding Hammer's weapon in both hands, crescent blades strapped to his thigh.

She frowned. Crescent would only return for one reason, and meeting his commander wasn't it.

"She's not dead," she said. "I let her go."

"I know. I saw her before she left."

"Stupid of you to come back, then."

"Stupid of you to continue staying. Tevu looks to attack soon. Their ships sailed past Pakaala two weeks ago."

Crescent hadn't come all this way back to keep the kingdom of Ashvi intact. Knowing Tevu's movements was so valuable that he wouldn't give it away for free. "And what do you want for this information?"

"Viridian."

Naias burst into a hard laugh. "No."

"I'm not asking for your approval," he said, without a hint of amusement. "This is my bargain, Naias. I've faced Engale and lived. You, Viri, and I can bring her down together. Her death benefits us all. Without her, Tevu will never win against the Faceless. This will be our final battle. When it's over, I will take Viri and leave this place, and you'll not follow, no matter how much Khall pleads and begs you to find us."

Naias shook her head. "You won't survive. It won't just be us coming after you. Tevu and Maetheria—"

"I'll handle that. You deal with Khall."

"I don't have as much power over her as you think I do."

"You'll come up with an excuse. You always have." He nodded at the severed head. "You let Hammer go, and Khall isn't any wiser to your manipulation. Now that you're married, you can finally make everyone forget that you were Iskanti. That's what you wanted, right? You never cared about us. You just wanted to get out of being a second-rate servant."

Naias pulled the trigger, firing the bullet a fraction above his shoulder. To her glee, he flinched, but the eyes behind the mask glittered with fury.

"With Hammer gone, I'm your best chance against Engale. Kill me, and I promise you Viri will not use her powers for anything. Your dream to restore Khall's old kingdom will turn to ash. Regardless of your choice, I swear to you: Even if Iskandraza himself strikes the ground between us, Viri will leave Haksa with me."

Crescent strapped the hammer to his back and scaled the window's ledge.

"I will get you your false freedom," he said. "In return, you will give me mine."

59
Naias

SHE WAITED UNTIL she could no longer see the sun over the horizon. The darkness would conceal the head's features better.

Naias bowed as she entered the throne room. A blindfolded Viridian flanked the queen, the glint of iron links binding her hands and feet together. The chain Khall held ended in a shackle around the godchild's neck.

"I can't find Clement," Khall said without preamble. "Where is he?"

Her chest hollowed in despair. He'd left without saying goodbye, that heartless little shit. This secret they'd harbored together for nine years didn't mean anything to him at all.

Soridian dead, Hammer exiled, and Clement gone. She was truly and utterly alone.

She made up a lie. It didn't matter anymore. "He's probably drugged up on opium, passed out in a corner somewhere. I'll find him for you, but first, I've done as you said."

Naias tossed the head on the floor, letting it roll towards Khall's feet. A mass of black hair covered its features. She hadn't washed the blood off herself either, letting it crust on her arms and clothes.

Khall squinted at her body. "Are you hurt?"

"Bruises, small cuts," she lied again. "Hammer was a fighter."

"And that's her head?"

"I cut it off myself."

Khall prodded the head with her foot. The noseless visage flopped over to face her.

"She kept fighting, even though I'd cut out one of her eyes," Naias said. "She didn't falter when my blade lodged into her neck. She moved like she was possessed. She tackled me to the ground as I pulled out my gun; the bullet went straight into the air. But I pulled out my blade and rammed it into her skull."

Khall let out a long, aggravated sigh. "All right, I've heard enough. Get this thing out of my room and clean up the floor. I don't want to see a speck of blood, understand?"

Her deception worked. Despite it all, she found no relief, only a lingering bitterness. At least she'd done something in saving Hammer's life. A small consolation for making this monster of a queen.

"Thank you for your gift," Naias said, remembering she needed to flatter. "She threatened your life. I couldn't let that stand. I'll investigate the rest of the Faceless and make sure this hasn't poisoned our ranks."

"That's not needed anymore. I've taken matters into my own hands."

Dread pulled at her heart. Surely she wasn't too late to fix the mess Hammer had left behind. "What do you mean?"

"A Faceless betrayed me. They can't be trusted, so I had Diavijra kill them. We need a fresh start. You can begin by training the children we took in this morning. I want a detailed report of every single initiate and where their loyalties lie."

There were three living, breathing people in this room, and it was completely absurd that Naias was the only one in shock. Tevu was sailing to attack. Khall had no army. They might as well have opened their gates and invited them in.

"How are we supposed to defend—"

"Diavijra, obviously," Khall huffed.

Viridian swayed on her feet, the blindfold hiding all her emotions. She was not here. She hadn't been for a while.

Khall was so swept away by the godchild's power that she didn't see how this could only end in defeat. Diavijra was powerful only because there were people to protect her. Without the Faceless, no one could sink the Tevurian ships that would attack from the sea, or sabotage their supplies, or scout for their position, or stop the archers and gunners from taking aim at Viridian's head . . .

There was nothing to keep Khall in power anymore. When they lost Haksa, Tevu would come for Xinquha. They'd dismantle all that she and Khallan had built. This all ended with Khall dead by Tevurian hands, and she was dragging Naias down with her.

She ought to tell her about Tevu's attack. Naias could still salvage some form of defense with the newly recruited children. She knew Tevu's patterns. They always attacked during the day, and if Engale was in the mood, they sent her to wreak havoc first, followed by the Reborn in heavy armor.

If they placed Diavijra in the lighthouse, she could kill all the Tevurians before they even reached the gates. All the initiates needed to do was to defend the sea with cannonfire so the godchild's position wouldn't be hit by the ships. She'd have to train them, quickly.

There was also the option of retreating. There was still a garrison stationed in Xinquha. They could retreat and defend the single choke point in and out of the city, a far better defensive position than Haksa.

But regardless of her choice, children weren't trained Faceless. They were young, undisciplined, and scared. When their inexperience caused their inevitable death, she'd have to find more bodies. The blood tithe was the fastest and most efficient way. She'd tried to change it, asking for volunteers for the past seven months, and all it'd gotten her was more Iskantis.

Crescent had told her change didn't benefit those in power. She didn't believe him then.

She'd tried. By gods, she'd really tried. She'd put off the blood tithe as long as she could, but now Khall had taken control, and fear guided her hand. In the absence of a solution, she returned to the familiar.

The struggle never ended. In all the fighting, scheming, and loyalists returning, peace was but a dream. This was what she would do too, if she became queen. When problems mounted and became impossible to solve, she'd revert to what worked, changing nothing.

All roads led to this.

She'd become Khall.

Naias stole a glance at her. The queen's eyes bulged wide, darting to shadowed corners and flinching at the smallest breeze. She no longer shimmered with promises and youth. Gray in skin and gray in hair. She'd aged a millennium since they'd left Xinquha.

Khall impatiently played with the chain in her hands. "Anything else?"

Let it burn. She won't survive without you.

She was done. Let Khall drown in her own power. She'd destroyed herself for this woman and gained nothing as her reward.

Naias bowed for the last time.

"No," she said.

60

Naias

THE DARK CORRIDORS howled with the echo of ocean waves. The porous stone sheared her palm as she gripped it to stop herself from falling. Her breath hitched, unable to stop the racing of her heart.

For the first time, she didn't know what to do.

She couldn't turn back, but there was nowhere else to go. Xinquha was Khall's territory. If she left for Maetheria, they would turn her in immediately. She didn't speak Iskanti; the clans in Iskantupu would reject her utterly. Her only option was to walk the road to Pakaala, a port controlled by Tevu. Maybe she could hide her mark until she smuggled her way aboard a ship, and she could leave the continent forever.

If she survived that long.

And then what? She'd only heard stories of the lands beyond, where the people there ate each other and breathed fire to summon gods from the sky. It sounded terrifying.

She slapped herself. *Stop spiraling. Think.*

In the blurry fog of her fate, one thread stayed clear to her: The children of the blood tithe were kept in the dungeons below. When Tevu inevitably took Haksa, they would die. Nuance didn't matter in war. Naias could keep protesting that they were victims of Khall's tyranny, but Tevu would only see them as Faceless in training, if not Faceless themselves.

Her mother had put her future in the hands of another. Naias never forgave her for that. She didn't know how to engineer her own escape, but at least she knew how to help them.

An Ashvian youth sat by the entrance to the dungeon's narrow stair, sleeping against a polearm two sizes too large for him. In absence of the Faceless, Khall had relegated the royal attendants and Ashvian civil workers to become guards. Brass keys glinted conspicuously on his belt.

He jolted awake at the sound of her footsteps. "The queen says no one's allowed here," he said loudly, scrambling to his feet, but Naias pushed him back down, looming over him. She wasn't as quick as she used to be, but at least she was faster than an untrained youth.

Intimidation was the quickest language for obedience. "You'll refer to me as Commander, boy, or it'll be the lash that you'll receive next," she said sharply. "You forget that I outrank you. Give me the keys."

He snapped into action, the brass jangling as he handed them over.

"Good," Naias said. "Leave for Xinquha and give the Faceless this message: 'Haksa has fallen. Defend the gate.'"

The youth blinked. "Haksa has fallen? Commander—"

"You'll do as you're told. This is a matter of critical urgency. Take your fellow Ashvians with you. The attendants, the maids, as many as you can. Travel swiftly. Don't stop to rest until you reach the city, do you understand?"

He saluted in all the wrong ways, barely covering his face and his bow too hasty, but Naias didn't care for propriety anymore. He pattered down the corridor, and Naias entered the dungeons below.

She knew this path too well. The darkness crept in the further she went, her raw palms brushing against the stone for purchase. The ocean waves swamped out all other sound, and when she reached the bottom of the stairs, freezing water bit into her feet, the shock of the cold making her involuntarily gasp.

The encroaching storm had caused a tidal surge. After close to a year of being here, they still hadn't repaired the leaking dungeon. Naias had chosen to spend the money on the western wall instead. The threat of Tevu attacking had been so much more pressing at the time.

She waded through ankle-deep water, the silence punctuated with the rhythmic pounding of the waves against the walls.

"Junaruya?" she called.

"Here."

A dozen children crammed into a cage, sitting on top of black uniformed bodies. Dead Faceless. Khall hadn't bothered clearing out the corpses. Darkness and terror was the first step in breaking them. She, too, had been molded by this.

Junaruya stepped to the front, his body shivering and wet. Red welts lined his hands. Blisters, from being in the water too long.

"I need you to be very quiet," she whispered, unlocking the dungeon gates one by one. "All of you will do exactly as I say."

There were forty, fifty of them. She pulled out her dagger, handing it to Junaruya. "Take this, stay at the back. Make sure the others don't straggle."

She emerged on the ground floor. Servants milled about the courtyard, oblivious to the oncoming Tevurian attack. Most of the fortress lay unguarded, but the sound echoed louder in the emptiness. The smallest whisper could make its way to Khall, who saw death around every corner.

She pressed against the walls, keeping her footsteps soft and her body in darkness, ushering the children to do the same. Her path led to a small barnacle-encrusted gate and, beyond it, the wide sea. Naias had utilized this postern once, when she'd smuggled Viridian into the lighthouse.

She pushed the gate open. Roiling clouds obscured the full moon. Good. The rising tide would drown out the sound of their escape.

A small fleet of sampans lay anchored at the docks. Naias picked out the biggest children of the bunch, putting rowing poles into their hands.

"You're oarsmen. Row to shore. Keep your boats close to the fortress walls; they're not made for deep water. When you reach land, tell your families to stock up on food and bar their doors. Tevu will attack soon."

One by one, the sampans launched, taking a dozen children at a time. She was the last to leave. If the other boats fell behind or drifted to open sea, at least she could be there to help.

The waves calmed the further she rowed. Dead fish and black seaweed floated around her. As her boat approached the fishing docks, the sour odor of rot thickened the air. Junaruya waited for her by the pier, standing above a slimy layer of decomposing jellyfish and squid. Most of the children had gone. A handful lingered, squeezing water out of their clothes.

The tip of her boat had barely touched shore when she jumped out, shooing them away. "What are you doing? Go, go. I told you—"

The children hugged her.

That shut her up.

Her arms dangled helplessly, not knowing where to touch or how to touch them. They were all wet, stank of rotting fish, and their clothes slopped against each other. In all her years, this was the most uncomfortable hug she'd gotten.

This was the only hug she'd gotten.

She didn't want to be anywhere else.

"We don't have much time," she said, keeping her voice steady. "Go. Your families will want to see you."

One stayed. The mask of Ayashara looked up at her.

She dreaded seeing her again. Rescuing them was an act so instinctive that anyone with a conscience should've done it. She didn't want to be fawned over or bask in some undeserving glory. What was going to happen tonight was her doing, and this was her smallest of attempts at atonement.

"Junaruya, I don't think this is a good idea."

"Juna. And no, you're not leaving until you've met my mother again. You saved us. She'll be very angry if I let you go."

He pulled her away from the docks, weaving through the paths with the speed of one who'd lived here all his life. When they came to a stop, she barely recognized Ayashara's house, a green-gray shadow of misery, with not a light illuminating its windows.

Ayashara hadn't moved from the table. She'd lost both her husband and her son. In the throes of loss, time ceased to render meaning. Naias had seen this stare a thousand times, when the Faceless had returned from fighting Khallan's war.

Juna jumped into her arms. She barely seemed to register his presence, but she blinked, recognizing him, and life returned to her.

"Oh, Juna, you're back, you're back." Despite the wet, Ayashara held him tight, burying her face in his hair.

Against her better judgment, Naias allowed herself to smile. In her youth she'd fantasized about her own mother's reaction when she returned to Iskantupu. That dream had died a long time ago, but now that she'd made it happen for another, that proximal joy seemed to partially fill that hole.

At least she'd fulfilled one promise. She couldn't reunite Viridian with her guardians, but at least she'd managed this one, and fifty others whose names she'd never know.

Naias cleared her throat, ending her moment of vulnerability. "Tevu sails down the strait to take Haksa back," she said. "Bar your windows and doors. You can salvage some planks in the graves outside the city."

Ayashara looked up, anger in her tear-ridden gaze. "No. We're leaving. I am tired, so tired of war. I've lived in Haksa all my life. I remember when Khallan came and took the city, and then Tevu burned us to drive him away. Not even a decade has passed and his daughter has repeated his mistake again, swearing this time it'll be different. It's not. Before Khallan, kings came and went. They also said the same thing. 'It'll be different.' Yet here we are."

She put Juna down and reached for Naias's hand. "And you'll come with us. I didn't see it at first, but you've also suffered under Khall. You don't belong here. You saved my son. Now it's my turn."

Her breath caught. Ayashara's offer gave her the possibility of a life. A family, where she might finally be loved. She could have a mother again; she could have siblings to play with, to live the childhood she'd never had.

Yes. She wanted to leap into her arms and kiss her. *Yes, yes, yes. Take me with you, please.*

But where?

She'd avoided the uncertainty of her future, and now she faced the precipice once again. The cerulean sun marked her everywhere. It was impossible to escape. If she was caught, Ayashara would be implicated too. She had no way of knowing how Tevu would treat them. They simply could not outrun an army.

Clement, Soridian, and Hammer were gone. She wouldn't endanger anyone else. She was alone, utterly and completely.

Naias stepped away.

"I have unfinished business," she said. "I'm sorry."

A pained look passed Ayashara's face. She tugged on the totem around her neck, snapping the twine loose, and pressed the cold stone into Naias's hand.

"Remember me," she said, her voice hard. "We'll find each other again. I swear it on the gods."

ONLY ONE PATH was left to her.

No guard saluted her as she saddled Ayashara's horse and rode out the city gates. The ramparts lay dark and bare, as if the city had been long abandoned.

She rode north, following the coastline, until the silhouette of the fleet of Tevurian ships appeared, sharp against the lightning. The Reborn encampment flickered to life in the darkness, row after row of square tents and pointed tops, lit orange by the braziers. They'd cut down part of the forest to accommodate their numbers.

They were only a few hours from Haksa. Any patrol would've uncovered this immediately, but Khall had killed the Faceless and kept her remaining attendants in the fortress, protecting her and only her.

She will not survive this.

The Reborn spotted her. They lumbered over in their blue tabards, their swords out, focused on deciphering the mark on her scabbed forehead.

She dismounted, raising her empty hands. "I offer my surrender. Bring me to your prince."

She'd made Khall. Clement left her knowing it, and Soridian died for it. She couldn't control the queen anymore, but she could at least try and fix the mess she created.

Surrendering to Tevu would inevitably lead to her execution, but she was strangely calm about it all. There was no escape. She'd said so, to Hammer and anyone who'd listen. She wasn't the type of person to stow away on a ship and flee the continent. If she'd had that kind of courage, she wouldn't have seduced Khall all those years ago. She stayed because freedom—true freedom—was far too frightening.

This land was all she knew, and if she had to die here, then she'd do it on her own terms.

They walked her past the tents, endless rows of them, the ground stamped flat and bare. At the very end of the encampment lay the largest tent amongst all the others, propped up by a platform of wooden stairs. Blue Tevurian flags were planted on either side of the entrance. Despite the color, each flag looked different. Tevu had entwined their symbol of five golden crossed swords with the regional sigils of the lands they'd conquered. Haksa was there too: a gray lighthouse embroidered in front of the swords, its thin silhouette barely visible against the gold.

She entered the tent, and the Tevurians put out a wooden stool for her to sit on. One candle flickered in the darkness. Thunder groaned above.

A loud yawn came from the other side of the tent, obscured by curtains and lattices. "Who?" the prince murmured. More people whispered back.

One servant boy shuffled past the curtains, holding a teapot and cups on a tray. With delicate precision, he poured a strong amber-colored tea into the cups, presenting one to her with both hands.

She studied Tea Boy's face. A young man, his cheeks reddened with acne, his little button nose still highly placed on his features, and lips not yet thinned with age. The blue robes fit him well, the hem still free of dirt. Very young, and very new.

Maybe he'd been picked from the streets. Maybe his parents had pushed him to join the Reborn. There was no mark on his face, not even a hint of facial hair—the Reborn were all clean shaven.

If only her mother had sold her to Tevu instead. Perhaps she would've lived a happier life, dispensing tea for sons of kings.

The prince emerged past the partition, rubbing his eyes. Tea Boy handed him a cup.

"Good evening, Faceless," the prince yawned, wrapping his blue robe about him. "Do I need to look over my shoulder for an ambush, or have you come here in good faith?"

I'm not Faceless, I'm Naias. The label still stung, even when she'd given up on such a future. Marrying the Earthly Sovereign herself hadn't removed the identity she'd so desperately wanted to shed.

She swallowed the insult. The Faceless' tactics of attacking by night had embittered the Tevurian prince. Pitched battle was Tevu's preferred method of combat. Naias had never given them the opportunity. Let him slur.

"No ambush," she said, holding her hands up again. "Not tonight, at least."

He chuckled. "Then I must admit my surprise to see you here. My people are under the impression that you've come to surrender. Is this true?"

"Yes."

"You know my next question."

I want to die. "I don't want to fight anymore. Neither does Haksa. I'm in no position to request this, but from one commander to another: Stop this madness. Please. Khall won't surrender, so I ask you for this grace. We're held in the thrall of a child who doesn't know when to let go. Spare them."

He raised his pierced eyebrows, diamonds and sapphires glinting in the candlelight. "But that's not what she wants," he said. "That's what *you* want, and—forgive me for saying—that means little to the kings and queens we serve."

Naias worried her lip. "I see the bloodthirst and cruelty rising. Khall has slaughtered all my men. Haksa has no army. Walk in and take the city, but to what end? You'll force her back to Xinquha, and her bitterness will permanently latch her to the dream of empire, thinking she's like her father, the victim of taking what's rightfully hers. She'll plot revenge. In a decade she'll come for Haksa again. Is that not what happened with Khallan, when you drove him out of Pakaala? When he drove *you* from Quctra? We repeat history over and over again, making the same mistakes the old kings did. I beg you, give Khall Haksa. Break this cycle of endless war."

She drew in a deep, shaky breath. She'd revealed more than she'd expected, of Haksa's defenses and her worst fears in Khall, blurted to her enemy because she had no one else to tell. "You wanted peace when we took the city. I ask for it now."

The prince drained his tea, staring into his empty cup. "You bring distressing news. What about her two godchildren? Are they still with her?"

"Clement has fled. Viridian is untested. You have Engale."

"And she's killed all the Faceless?"

"A garrison remains in Xinquha," she said. "When she's pushed back there, I only hope she has enough sense to spare them, especially if she wants to defend the last city she holds."

His lips pressed into a straight line. "I'm sorry for the loss of your men. Such needless deaths."

A prince of Tevu, empathetic to the Faceless? Tevu himself would've celebrated with glee at this news. "Don't perpetuate what your father has done," she said, latching onto the tiny crack in his armor. "You have the power to change things. I can't. I'm . . ." She laughed helplessly. "I'm a Faceless."

Tea Boy swanned over with the teapot, extending his arm to Naias. *More?*

She stared glumly. Perhaps he'd kill another his age on the battlefield one day, carrying an oversized sword in his delicate hands.

The prince traced the rim of his cup. "You are right," he said quietly. "I don't like war. The whole theater of it is a bitter brew to me. But you're optimistic in thinking Khall's ambition will stop at another empire's surrender. My parents loved Khallan. They allowed him to play lord of Quctra for over a decade. But he wasn't content with that. He wanted more. If I let Khall have Haksa, she will do the same.

"We're doomed to fight. Like you, I partake reluctantly, but the difference between us, Faceless, is that I know why it's necessary. It is only through death and defeat that someone like Khall will understand the consequences of her ambition."

He lifted his hand, and two Reborn approached. They fastened iron chains around her wrists.

She didn't fight back. All her strength left her. This had been her last effort in righting her wrongs, and it had ended in complete failure. Now she would be taken to the king, put on a show trial, and executed. Tevu always liked to humiliate his enemies in public.

The prince accompanied her out of his tent. "I'm sorry it didn't turn out the way we'd hoped," he said. "You came to us in good faith, and so I will give you this in return."

Wind whipped her hair. The drizzle of the oncoming storm turned to shards, piercing her face with a million pinpricks. Countless Reborn assembled in neat rows, waiting for orders. These men didn't wear steel. Leather cuirasses took their place, fastened over cotton tunics of Tevurian royal blue.

Engale strode past her without a word, her furious gaze set upon Haksa. She ignored everyone, her mind coalesced into a singular focus. The Reborn shuffled aside, breaking their ranks for her. Those who didn't were sent into the air.

Sahru raised his hand. A trumpet sounded, and they began to march.

A Tevurian advance, at night, in the rain? They never used surprise.

"A change of tactics," Sahru said casually, as if remarking on the weather. "You wouldn't meet us in open battle by day, so one must adapt to their enemy's ways, wouldn't you agree?"

The Reborn led her into a reinforced wagon. Through the narrow space between the bars stood the flickering lighthouse of Haksa.

To keep her soul, to save Ayashara, she'd damned Khall and the Ashvian children who served her, and left Viridian to fight alone.

There was no clean choice that left everyone whole. She'd tried. At this late hour of her guilt, she gave her life over, the ultimate penance, but it was the smallest of dams, pushing against a seismic storm.

Naias slammed her fists against the iron walls. Everyone only looked out for themselves in this world; it was high time that she snatched this mercy for herself. She would die, and she welcomed it. No one sacrificed themselves for her, why should she constantly throw her body against the wave of queens and princes until she couldn't give any more?

But in the darkness of her gaol, when silence engulfed the cabin so loudly that her ears rang, all she saw was Viridian, blindfolded, her neck chained to Khall's delicate hands.

61

Diavijra

B̲a̲n̲g̲.
Bang.
Bang.

Cannonfire slammed against the fortress walls. Khall jumped from her throne, clutching Viridian's chain in terror.

"Where's Naias?" she shouted. "Where's Clement? Tevu is attacking. Where is she, that traitor?"

More cannonfire resounded. The floors trembled, and Viridian grasped the throne for support. Debris from the ceiling fell on her. Khall's remaining attendants rushed in, thirty, fifty, filling the room. They didn't know what to do and looked to their sovereign for guidance.

Khall didn't know either.

"Go and guard the fortress gates," she said. "Arm yourselves, quickly."

They obediently stumbled down the twisting corridors, slipping on rain puddles, but didn't know where to go. They'd never entered the Faceless quarters, nor had they held a sword in their lives. These were children of farmers and craftsmen. They'd come to dress queens and serve tea.

Khall pulled on Viridian's chain. "You're coming with me," she said, dragging her to the lighthouse. "I have to do everything myself. Everything. I sacrificed so much for her and she goes missing. Where are her scouts? Why didn't she know about this attack? I'm surrounded by incompetence. She's betrayed me, she's gone and defected to the clans, where's Clement? My Faceless, they—I need the Xinquhan garrison to come quickly, I need a messenger—*boy!*"

She stopped a young servant, still in his dressing gown. "Go to Xinquha. Tell them I need the Faceless to come to Haksa, now, now, now."

(The boy never made it. He died by the fortress gates.)

Khall entered the lighthouse, its wooden door an unassuming little thing, worn down from the salt-filled wind. She took the stairs too quickly for Viridian; with the blindfold on, she couldn't see where she was going. Her restraints tore at her skin as she fumbled her way up, her legs moving a small step at a time. The chain around her neck ran taut from the distance.

When they reached the top, cold rain splattered on Viridian's face. A weak, familiar heat burned on the brazier, the same flickering light that Rafaeis and Elera had used to kill the Tevurians when they first took this place.

Khall yanked the blindfold off, turning her head towards the coast.

"The ships, the ships," she said. "Sink the ships, kill them."

Viridian squinted, trying to find them through the cover of night and rain. Lightning struck the horizon, briefly lighting the sea white.

Rafaeis had told her to follow Naias's orders, but Naias wasn't here. He hadn't planned for Tevu to attack in the middle of a stormy night either. Sighting Elera's hammer was nearly impossible in the dark.

But the battle happened regardless. She had to follow through with his plan. If she lost, she would end up in Tevurian hands again, captured by the same people who'd beaten and starved her in the wagon. Engale had to die, and then she'd be with Rafaeis again.

She forced her eyes wide, overriding her instinct to blink, for wherever Engale or the hammer was, Rafaeis would follow. She just needed to find one or the other, and all three would never leave her sight.

The Reborn hauled a battering ram to the fortress gate. Khall's servants huddled behind, their torches nearly extinguished by the storm. Some figures streamed back into the fortress, towards the postern that overlooked the sea. Enormous waves slammed against the side of the lighthouse, but the children jumped in regardless, bodies sinking into the crashing tide, and never resurfacing.

"Traitors and deserters," Khall hissed. "Kill them, kill the Tevurians in the ships, kill them all."

More lightning revealed a fleet of ships by the coast. A silhouette, nothing more, much less the crew that manned them. She doubted her power would reach that far. She squinted and thought about the string and the rock.

Nothing happened. If they choked or writhed, the rain hid it from her. The ships continued to float along black waters.

"You're not doing anything," Khall shouted.

"I'm trying, I don't know—"

Khall pulled her chain, yanking her away from the coast. Viridian stumbled to the floor again, the iron collar constricting her throat. She gasped for air. All she needed to do was survive until Rafaeis came for her.

Khall hoisted her to her feet, forcing her to look in the direction of the city gates. "Kill them, the ones in front. Now."

A rhythmic *bang* shook the gates. The Reborn were ramming it down. Khall's untrained attendants crowded behind it, weaponless, looking for guidance.

No hammer.

Who did Khall want to kill? What did 'the ones in front' mean? Viridian saw more Ashvians than Reborn. Most of their enemy were hidden behind the gate.

"I don't understand," Viridian said.

"Stop lying. You've done this under Naias's orders. We're in the lighthouse, just like when we took over this place, and the enemy is right in front of us. You know what to do, stop pretending like you don't."

Killing the remnants of Khall's servants seemed a completely senseless move, but before she could say no, a distant *boom* sounded to her right, too mechanical and short to be thunder. They both flinched, and Khall dragged Viridian along the parapet. Her cheek scraped against coarse stone, prickling with pain. It was growing clear that Khall's strategy was to point her in whatever direction held the immediate threat. Naias would've had a better plan.

She must have left. Viridian didn't expect her to take her along, but against all odds, she'd hoped, even in this terrible, bitter world, where she was both a target and a liability. Rafaeis's lessons had blinded her to this truth, as he'd done to Elera. I pitied her for it. Viridian harbored a stubborn belief in your goodness, only for it to be extinguished when the worst parts of your humanity revealed themselves over and over again.

The cascading rains no longer tamped down the wind. Palm trees swayed in circles, bending in half, threatening to snap. The very air howled. The lighthouse flame whipped back and forth, weakening with each successive blow, until it was snuffed out altogether.

The clouds twisted, a black cone steeped in lightning swirled towards the fortress gates. With a loud *roar* it slammed to the ground, ripping the Haksani wooden houses into the air. The Reborn cried in panic.

She was here.

"Are you hiding, Godkiller?" Engale shouted through the storm, her voice amplified by her own power. "I have given you your title, murderer of Pravaja. Come out and face me."

Viridian pushed Khall away, searching for the godchild. Lightning now provided her only source of illumination. The fight unfolded before her in flashes, like a series of starkly drawn paintings.

Engale stood just beyond the fortress, every swing of her hand releasing a gust of wind that smashed against the gate.

Reborn flew into the air.

The gate broke in two.

The Ashvian children tried to run away.

Then nothing.

Darkness engulfed her sight for a long, long time. Sleet and rain pierced her shivering body.

Lightning flashed again.

Corpses littered the ground, Engale's wet robes clung to her, bright blue against a sea of red. She fought with someone on the front lines, an overconfident servant of Khall's who'd decided fighting her was a better death than fleeing.

"Who the fuck are you," Engale screamed, holding him up.

Tevu's cannons sounded again, ignorant to Engale's vengeance. Iron shells smashed against the lighthouse, a hundred battering rams, throwing Viridian and Khall off their feet. A chunk of the wall blew out, hitting her face, bricks exploding into gray mist. Bright red spots flooded her vision.

She tried to blink it away. The weaknesses of her mortal body would not stop her from finding Elera's hammer. Her legs swayed as she pushed herself to stand, and she leaned over the parapet once more.

Something glinted. She thought it was the rain at first, but it shone like a comet, heading towards Engale.

It's him.

She'd finally sighted the hammer. No more surveying the battlefield, wholly reliant on lightning to see, gingerly raising her hands and hoping Rafaeis wasn't caught in it. He was here. She homed in on the glinting hammer, determined not to lose him to the darkness.

Engale must die.

Viridian was in a perfect position. With Engale distracted fighting the page, she could end this before Rafaeis ever reached her.

She drew black fury to her fingertips.

The two buckled instantly, no different from the people

she was forced to kill. Engale wasn't special. Godchildren or mortals, death came for them all the same.

Viridian kept channeling my power, her body glowing with the void, focused singularly on Engale and the shattered gate before her. Even as the lightning disappeared and plunged her into darkness, Viridian pushed on, imprinting onto the shadows where Engale stood, hoping that memory itself could serve where her eyes could not.

Another flash of light.

Now Engale stared directly at her.

The godchild's eyes leaked blood, a mixture of rage and hurt on her face. Viridian had expected the rage, but not the hurt, the way her brow furrowed, mouth downturned, as if to ask, *Why?* Viridian didn't care. They'd never met, and Rafaeis had ordered her death. Engale was a bad person, like the Iskantis and the Tevurians.

But I don't know about that. Perhaps Engale couldn't imagine one godchild hurting another. She'd only known Pravaja, after all, and they'd been lovers. Maybe she saw this as a betrayal. Children wielding the power of gods, turned against each other, for you to squabble over kingdoms and empires.

Viridian pointed at Engale and drew further into my power. She had to die, now.

Engale screamed.

Her siren's cry pierced our mind, a needle spiked into flesh. The shock wave turned the rain into frozen bullets, flinging in all directions. One cut across Viridian's cheek, but the sting of it was but a whisper against the cacophony. The very earth exploded where Engale stood, uprooting rattan palms and the remaining foundations of Haksa's last stone buildings.

Engale did not stop screaming. Viridian couldn't stay on her feet. The pain was too much. She fell behind the broken parapet, pressing her palms to her ears. The wind whipped into a hurricane, roaring under the cry, and it grew louder and louder, radiating into her, tearing apart the cells that made up her body, and her eardrums pounded in tandem, threatening to burst—

And all at once, it stopped.

She pulled against her chains, gasping for air. The world swirled around her. To her side, Khall knelt on all fours, vomiting up a pale yellow bile.

She stumbled to her feet, peeking over the parapet. Rafaeis. She needed to find him.

Engale had disappeared. Only a shallow crater remained. The corpses of children and Reborn alike splayed along the fortress walls.

The cloud of dirt slowly dissipated, and through the haze emerged the silhouettes of hundreds of Reborn soldiers, some on foot and some on horses, marching towards the gate.

Haksa had fallen.

This was her chance. Engale hadn't died, but she wasn't here, and surely she'd injured her enough to buy some time for their escape. Rafaeis waited for her outside, and they could finally be free.

Rafaeis. Rafaeis.

Viridian snatched her chain from Khall's loosened grip. She tumbled down the stairs in her leg-irons. The siren scream still rattled her, and going down in circles made her dizzy. But her bruises didn't matter. Rafaeis was here. Her ankles bled freely, leaving a set of red footprints behind her. She tripped and fell on the last step, her knees and palms scraped raw.

The Reborn were waiting for her. They packed the lighthouse entrance, with no room for escape.

"Diavijra," one of them yelled. "Diavijra is—"

She turned my power on them.

The gates were close. So close. The lighthouse exited into the courtyard, and once she crossed it, she'd be free. She held one hand out, stepping around the bodies and into the open square. The Reborn backed away. Cowards, all of them. They weren't Elera.

"You will let me go," she said, "unless you want to die."

"Viri."

Her name. No one used her name.

The guards parted to reveal a man in the most ornate suit of armor she'd ever seen. Five crossed swords were etched into his mountain-patterned armor, and a jewel-encrusted blade hung from his belt. A soldier followed behind, holding a parasol, shielding the man from the rain.

A Tevurian. He did not deserve to address her like that.

He took his helmet off. A middle-aged man—a little older than her dead fathers—with curled salt-and-pepper locks, his brows pierced with a dazzling line of gemstones.

"You don't know me," he said hurriedly. "I'm Sahru, prince of Tevu. I've come to take you home."

She pressed forward, one hand out. She'd stop for no one but Rafaeis. "I'm not getting taken by Tevu again."

"No, there's no more 'taking.'" He shook his head. "We're not abducting you. I've arranged for your passage to Maetheria. First Scholar Arvadian waits anxiously for your return."

"Liar," she said, holding her chain close to her chest. She'd been promised so many things by so many people. She wasn't going to trust another Tevurian again.

Sahru sank to his knees and pressed his head to the rain-slicked floor.

"I'm sorry," he said. "I'm sorry for my mother naming you, and the pain my father caused you. I'm so sorry, for all of it."

The gesture rippled through the Tevurians like a wave. One by one, the soldiers knelt before her, until the entire fortress bent in regret.

An apology. Only Elera and Rafaeis ever said it, blaming themselves for not being able to yoke the world, but now the world bent to her. All her suffering, finally, *finally* acknowledged, and even though she didn't want this act of contrition to affect her, it did. A silent, delayed justice.

Against her better judgment, she stopped.

Sahru lifted his head slightly, daring to look at her. "You were violently taken from your parents and forced to watch them die. This I never wanted. We shouldn't have taken you at all. My father was doing so well, and when Pravaja died ... Well, never mind him. Here, let my Reborn take these chains off you, if you'll allow me."

Khall's wails echoed through the castle walls.

The chain sat heavy around her bruised neck, its weight a constant reminder of the mad queen and all she'd taken from her. A man with a pair of bolt cutters appeared, wedging its prongs between her manacles. Her teeth rattled as he pried off the collar. The leg-irons followed, shaking loose from her ankles.

"No more chains," Sahru said. "If you wish to ride on a horse or on a palatial bed, I'll personally see to those arrangements. You can go home, Viri. Isn't that what you wanted?"

Home. The blood on the glass walls had haunted her until one day it didn't. All the deaths since then had blended into one. Her fathers, the Iskantis and Haksanis, Faceless and Reborn, any who dared to cross Khall. Her journey from Maetheria to Tevu, then to Xinquha, then Haksa. The mountains, the sky, the earth, it all looked the same.

She hadn't thought about home for a long time.

In that emptiness burned Rafaeis and Elera: Her calloused hands running through Viridian's hair as they sat by the river, bickering over nothing. The way he'd soothed her when she finally came to admit her father's death. When she'd taught her to remember, and he, to love.

And only one of them was left.

"I'm not going back," Viridian said.

Sahru shook his head and smiled, filled with the condescension of an adult talking to an ignorant child. "You're free. You don't have to stay here."

"I'm not staying. But I'm not going with you either."

The smile disappeared. He said "you don't understand,"

and that was when Viridian knew his offer of freedom was a lie. Like Khall and Naias and all the rest, he'd made a deal with someone else she didn't know, playing with her like a little wooden toy. The rest of his plea fell into a babble of meaningless words.

She walked past him. "If you stop me, I'll kill all of you."

She crossed the courtyard, all the way to where she'd last seen Engale. Her siren shock wave had left a crater. Uprooted trees, stone ruins, and uncountable corpses lay scattered all around Haksa. She ignored it all.

The hammer shone clear against Rafaeis's back as he knelt in the center of the crater, holding another body.

He was here.

She laughed and cried, in joy and in relief, running towards him, past the broken gates and over the blue and red uniforms, pulling against the mud sticking to her feet.

"Rafaeis," she said. "Let's go. Let's go, right now."

But the person looked up.

It was not him.

Viridian slowed to a stop, her mouth agape. Elera's face bore all fury, her teeth clenched with rage.

And the body she cradled—

i couldn't say goodbye

—was his.

62

Elera

SHE CAME BACK because of him.

His final kiss seared into her memory, the metallic taste of their anger and the fury of their love. In her mind she kissed him a hundred thousand times, reliving this singular memory over and over again, to remember how he felt against her lips, his hand pressed firm and proprietary on her back.

But the more she remembered, the more the memory changed. He grabbed her with his left hand; no, his right. He had his crescent blades with him; no, he didn't. She couldn't recall the tree he'd jumped from; it became an angsana. Even the words he'd said to her shifted, phantom phrases that floated in and out of unfinished sentences.

Eventually he'd become a ghost too. An imprint of how she remembered him, and not who he actually was. A blurry mess of colors and evoked emotions.

She couldn't forget him. She wouldn't.

When night fell, she couldn't light the smallest flame for fear it would signal her position. Without her hammer, she might as well have strolled into battle naked. She missed her clan, deeply. She wanted to go back to the valley when she'd first emerged from the cave, breathless and awed by its quiet beauty.

The night of the autumn solstice had devolved into a haze of pictures and feelings, Nasu reciting Iskandraza's pain, and how much Elera loved that story over the one she was taught, and how Iavahl and Caush danced by the fire, free from the burdens of empires and the people who controlled them. For that brief, brilliant moment, she wasn't alone.

She'd convinced them to leave it all behind because she'd wanted to save Viri . . . and then she didn't.

She was so sure she'd done the right thing, until she saw the Tevurians march. An attack by night? That wasn't a Tevurian thing to do. Rafaeis was going to be there, and he'd probably fight Engale to get Viri out. He'd kill himself, the stupid fuck.

He believed Viri wasn't gone. That infuriating hope carried him on, no matter how awful the decision.

It was both his biggest strength and weakness, but she'd loved that about him, the ability to see beauty in a world where there was none. She'd tried to push him away, walling herself off, but love had wriggled into her hardened heart despite it all. She dreamed once again of the soft, lush grass that filled the valley, Rafaeis's body atop hers, their gasps pained and sweet.

It wasn't hard to love, when she had nothing left.

He'd saved her twice, and in return she'd abandoned him for what, saving this child they both cared about? She had to come back. She'd help him defeat Engale. Maybe he'd even been right that there was still a chance of saving Viri, bringing her back from the ruthless killer they'd trained her to be. When it was done and Rafaeis still hated her, she'd let him go. If Viri chose him over her, she was fine with that too.

But fuck the gods if she wasn't going to try and reunite the family she'd torn apart. She returned to Haksa to find forgiveness in the ones that were still able to give it to her.

The rain stung her eyes. She shielded her face with her hand, slipping on muddy paths, trying to keep her balance as she pressed against the waves of Haksanis fleeing the city. They paid no attention to her mark. They fought for their survival and had no business crossing the path of a Faceless.

It wasn't the wind, but the commotion that placed Engale. The crashing force against the fortress walls echoed through the city. She ran towards the source.

The Reborn infantry had retreated amidst Engale's crazed advance, limiting casualties inflicted by their own godchild, choosing to attack at range with cannonfire instead. They boomed in unison, iron shells whistling through the air, exploding as they hit Haksa's lighthouse.

She'd arrived mid-battle. Rafaeis stood against Engale, in his black uniform and mask, her hammer firmly in his hands. It clearly weighed him down; his movements were slower, his swings weaker. That fool's strength was always his speed; why was he using her weapon?

He parried Engale's swipes, her hands encircled with blades of concentrated wind. With an overhead strike, Engale lodged the edge of her magical blades into his hammer, cutting into the steel.

She grinned, yanking the hammer out of his grasp, but as the hilt flew away, Rafaeis unlatched the rapier within. He slashed at her, and Engale threw up a gust of wind as a barrier. Debris swept up around them.

Elera's hammer landed in the decimated remains of the executioner's square. She picked it up and sprinted towards the both of them.

The rapier fit him better. He closed the distance, sidestepping the blasts of wind that she threw up between them. His limbs moved in a blur, not looking to inflict a heavy, fatal blow, but to kill her with a thousand cuts. She wouldn't be able to avoid them all.

This was Engale's weakness. He'd said so, when he kissed Elera in the hurricane all that time ago.

But the godchild held up her arm, blocking his next swing. The rapier slashed deep. Blood rapidly stained her blue robes.

"You're real," she screamed, tearing off his mask. "You're real, and I'm not scared of you anymore."

Rafaeis winced against her grip.

Engale's frightened countenance fell to fury. "Who the fuck are you?"

This distraction was her moment. Elera sprinted forward, hammer in hand. Heavy footsteps slapped against the mud.

Engale's focus snapped in her direction. Rafaeis pulled out his crescent blades, cutting into the arm that held him. She screamed, releasing her hold, and Rafaeis dropped to the ground. His blades flashed, aimed for her knees.

She kept running. *Good. We'll end her together, just like we did before.*

The blood on her fingertips bubbled.

Her body stopped on pure instinct. Barely out of the boundaries of Diavijra's power, Elera's breath had already left her, and as much as she tried to suck in air, nothing existed in the void.

Engale and Rafaeis both collapsed.

"No," she gasped out loud, not knowing where Viri was. "You're killing him."

Engale's furious face turned towards the fortress, and Elera glimpsed her bloodshot eyes before it all disappeared into a screeching, ruinous whirlwind.

The force of Engale's scream threw her off her feet. Corpses and rocks and rattan palms flew into the air, smashing against the blackened ruins of the city. Elera's back hit something solid. Her ribs shifted, and then broke. Pain shot through her body, her screams inaudible against the whirlwind, but only a single thought consumed her mind, pulsing with every heartbeat.

Rafaeis. I have to get to Rafaeis.

The siren cry ended. Elera fell to the ground and doubled over, squeezing out all the pain in her back. She didn't have time to recover. Engale had vanished. The monsoon returned in a sudden downpour, turning the ground to mud.

With a great effort she stumbled to the gate, stepping over the bodies of Reborn and Xinquhan attendants, abandoned weapons rattling under her feet. Rafaeis must have escaped in time. The moment when Engale looked to the fortress, he must have known, surely.

But a body lay close, too close, where the scream had struck a deep crater, crescent blades still firmly gripped in his hands.

His mouth dripped red foam. Blood slid from his closed eyes. Maybe if she forced them open, he'd wake up. Maybe this was a ruse, to let Engale think he'd died, and he was just sleeping.

He stayed still.

The earth below her trembled. Behind her, the Tevurian cavalry approached, their thousand horses clad in steel plate, escorting their prince, trampling over the bodies of their fellow infantrymen.

She gathered Rafaeis in her arms, wiping the blood off his face with her sleeve as the Tevurians passed her. The hollow in her throat expanded as her denial compressed, seeking some tangible expression, someone to blame, someone to hurt.

A voice rang through the rain. "Rafaeis, let's go. Let's go, right now."

She looked up into the wide, confused gaze of Viri.

Her gray tunic slopped at her ankles, her wrists and neck free. Khall didn't even need to chain her down anymore. That was how obedient she was now: The child had become the butcher. Elera understood this, as she, too, had become one, a long time ago. A machine that belonged nowhere, bred only to follow orders.

"You killed him," Elera said, her voice seething in whisper.

Viri buckled before his body. "He told me—the hammer—I thought—I thought you were dead."

"You thought wrong."

Here she faced singular, undeniable proof, and Rafaeis had to die for it. Viri was gone. In killing Engale, she'd sacrificed her own. Just like Nasu, just like Caush. People who'd loved her, dead by her hand. Unthinking obedience to a pitiful defense, all ending in failure.

This is a mercy, she thought as she saw the end. There was no wheel-breaking, no end to the blood tithe, no escape from Khall or Tevu or the Iskantis and their petty little squabbles that threw all their lives into chaos. Rafaeis was dead. The hope that he carried was gone. The godchild was caught in everyone else's schemes, no different than Pravaja, or Engale, or any of the godchildren that came before her. She was no longer Viri. She was Diavijra, corrupted, her true name and identity forgotten, even to herself.

She'd caused so much anguish. All that Elera loved had died because of her.

It ended now.

And so Elera wrenched the crescent blade from Rafaeis's hands and slit Diavijra's throat with it.

63

Naias

THEY'D TRAVELED FOR weeks. She hadn't been allowed out of the wagon except to relieve herself, and the fetters stayed tight around her wrists. Bruises formed along her bottom, every bump in the road eliciting a groan from her.

Winter had arrived. Light flecks of ice drifted down the coast. The steep mountains of Iskantupu loomed to the south, and the road they traveled on provided more surf than gravel.

Brittle obsidian statues of the gods lined the path. As soon as one disappeared from her sight, the next one appeared in the distance. Travelers had used them as road markers, back when Haksa and Pakaala were both under Tevurian rule. Their shapes were unlike the humanoid statues that the Ashvians preferred; abstracted, formless pieces, unconcerned with mimicking reality. One had long wavy lines running down the side of a soft square, another looked like a fist had squeezed a lump of wet clay. No one knew which gods they symbolized. That information had died with the people that built them.

All but one. The totem Aya had pressed into her hand.

She passed another statue, one of a misshapen sphere half sunk into the ground. Huts cropped up the further she traveled. They were near.

Instead of wooden piers, Pakaala's docks were stone-built,

stretching far out in the ocean. The Tevurian fleet anchored here, hundreds of galleys loitered on the open seas, forming a perimeter around the city. Blue banners flapped from the balconies of stocked warehouses. Crates and barrels overflowed on pallets. Despite the piles of wet snow, the place didn't stink of rot.

They passed a market, merchants hawking baskets packed with fish, eel, and small crabs. They shouted in a mix of Common and Iskanti dialect, often swearing in the latter. They didn't seem to mind Tevurian rule. The Tevurians didn't seem to mind *them*.

She gawked at the bustle of the port. This was what they could've had, if she'd listened to Khall and repaired the docks. She'd been so fixated on defending Haksa that governance had become an afterthought.

A mere Faceless, only good for war.

Khall was right about her.

The wagon creaked to a stop. The center of power in Pakaala was located in the heart of the city, taking the form of a beautiful villa built from blue-gray seastone. Barnacles still grew around its foundations, while the pillars were carved in delicate relief, hinting at nets, anchors, and fish. White and blue daisies sprang on carefully manicured grass. The combined flag of Tevu and Pakaala—a blue trout against five crossed swords—hung on standards, their hilts buried firmly in the ground. As the Reborn led her into the villa, her feet shuffled on plush carpet.

Breezy corridors and high ceilings. Every wall was adorned with paintings of the three progenitor gods. Bulbous chrysanthemums bloomed in vases, their earthy fragrance suddenly subsumed by the unmistakable smell of opium.

One of the many ornate doors opened, and Clement swanned out, clad in multicolored robes and jewels. He spotted Naias, raising his eyebrows in mild surprise.

"Commander."

Naias gritted her teeth. "I gave you the key to your chains, and you've only gone and shackled yourself to another."

He smiled, drawing a breath on his pipe. "I do not look to beat the tide, only to swim with it."

She bristled at his indifference. He'd had the privilege of a freedom she didn't have, and he'd completely squandered the opportunity. "You had the chance to carve your own life. You don't have a mark on your head. You could've gone back to Lakhest and been a free man, or used your powers to actually do good. You could've been anything, and you chose *this*."

Clement's placid smile disappeared. Naias thought she'd gotten to him, but he looked past her, above them, watching for something. His eyes bulged wide.

She followed his gaze to a corner of the villa. Nothing sat there, except a mural of Iskandraza depicted as a titan, a fireball in his hand, striking the earth beneath him.

He dropped his pipe and scurried past her. "I'm sorry, I have to go."

All the better. She would've happily stuffed that opium down his throat. Sniveling little coward.

The corridors shrank the further they walked, as if she'd been shoved to the back of an alleyway. Naias frowned. Show trials were loud, public events, inviting the audience to boo and jeer like they would at a play. This part of the villa didn't suit such a display.

They came to a stop at the end of the hallway. They opened the last door, and beyond it, in a small, cramped room, sat the prince of Tevu.

The chill of the ocean breezed through an open window. Intricate patterns of diamonds and interlocking swords were woven into his robes, glimmering as he looked up from his desk.

"I like conducting business in a smaller setting," he said. "There's less weight to my words when I'm not shouting it into a hundred ears. It helps me think better."

The beauty of this place didn't suit her, one who was born in the wasteland. She glanced down. The mud under her boots had caught on the plush carpet. A trail of black footprints followed her.

"Never mind about that. The servants will clean it. Leave us," he said, waving a hand. "I thought you might want to know what happened in Haksa. What a massacre. I don't blame you for deserting. The dungeons were full of Faceless bodies. We found Khall in the lighthouse, crying for you."

At the ultimate moment when Khall had truly needed her, she'd left. She'd ranted and raved about traitors, and it'd come true. Naias did betray her in the end. "Is she . . ."

"Captured, alive, and imprisoned. Father will want to render judgment personally, but we all know where this leads."

Khall, dead. The phrase tasted strange to her. "And you agree with him?" she asked.

"I do not," he said immediately. "But my counsel was soundly refused. I'm loath to make her a martyr, but I'm afraid I have no choice. At least people forget the dead faster than the ones we keep alive."

"The kingdom of Ashvi is truly finished, then," Naias muttered. She'd staked her survival on Khall's establishment of her kingdom as her only chance at freedom. Now she was alive in a world where that kingdom didn't exist.

"And yet I cannot savor this victory," Sahru said. "The godchild is dead. We found her body next to a man in Faceless uniform, but he had no mark on his head. The godchild killed him, and yet her throat was slit by his blade."

An unmarked man, disguising himself as a Faceless. Only a fool would do that. "He's no Faceless, then. All of us have the mark. Maybe Engale was the instigator, and her power caused the blade to hit the godchild."

"Engale has given us no answers. I've never seen her like this before. We've used every method we could think of. We've even returned Pravaja's belongings to her, but she's stayed quiet. I don't think it was her. If she killed Diavijra, she'd have reason to celebrate, not withdraw like this."

The Voidbringer was dead, because Naias had chosen to leave. She could still see the glint of the girl's chains by twilight, held by the shaking, emaciated hands of the woman she'd once loved.

No matter. Naias wasn't long for this world. When Tevu executed her, these feelings would all go away.

"What will you do with her body?" she asked.

"We've sent her back to Maetheria with the promise we'll bring her murderer to justice, but I doubt that will placate them." He pinched the bridge of his nose, sighing deeply. "You don't understand how much trouble this child has given me. The love between my parents is well and truly finished. My father spent the last six years of their reconciliation proving himself to her, and he threw it all away because Pravaja died and he needed a new godchild. Now that Viridian is dead, I have to contend that Maetheria will not give us peace. My father is bent on quelling them, but escalating their anger with violence is the surest way to make them turn on us faster. It is the way it is. I do not decide on these outcomes. Maetheria will fight, and unfortunately I must respond. This is why I wanted to speak to you. Faceless, I would have no better honor than to have you as my general."

"I—what?" She was here to stand for a sham trial and be tortured. Not for a promotion.

"You defended Xinquha for your sovereign, and you killed Pravaja. You then took Haksa and drove away the Maetherians. Any king would be lucky to listen to your counsel."

She shook her head. "Prince. I didn't kill Pravaja, another of my Faceless did. I took the credit to give them anonymity, so you wouldn't assassinate our best. Trial me, let your Tevurians hurl their insults, and kill me. I'm not interested in fighting anymore."

"You say that as if to discourage me. Your tactics took Haksa, and you're loyal to your soldiers. Battle suits you."

Only good for war. She didn't want to be part of it anymore. "I counseled Khall not to march. I knew what it would cost. I'm not getting dragged into Tevu's endless fights."

Sahru leaned back in his chair. "If you become my general, you become Tevurian. We provide for our men, like any standing army. You're free to love and marry, to raise your children should you choose to have them. This is a standard offering to any who join the Reborn. Of course, living to reap its rewards is a different matter, but as my general, you'll have much better arrangements befitting your rank."

"I assume your father won't like that you're recruiting a Faceless into the Tevurian army," she said.

"My father likes winning, and the 'how' is my responsibility. He doesn't need to know every little recruitment drive we undertake." He pulled a key from his belt and approached her, fiddling with her manacles.

"I never thought to congratulate you on your wedding," he said. "You're heir to Ashvi. When the Earthly Sovereign dies, we'll need someone to rule Xinquha in Tevu's name."

With a clang, her bonds dropped to the floor. Sahru's outstretched hand opened with earnestness. "You'll do well here, Naias."

Not 'Faceless.' Naias.

There was no future for her in kingdoms where her kind were hated, and the prince offered her a way out. A new life. Not only that, but a comfortable life. He'd given her hope when her only path had led to death.

But that promise was a brittle one. The mark would never leave her. Jayal and Maka had sneered at having to work with an Iskanti. Khall had claimed to love her and yet called her inferior. It would be no different in Tevu.

"You need time to think," the prince said, the indecision clear on her face. "I'll see to it that you're settled here, but I'll need an answer soon. Maetheria riots, and I need to know if you will help guide our efforts to victory."

Sahru and his escort led her up the stairs, ending in an ornately carved door of nautical filigree and dolphins, painted in white and blue. A pair of Reborn stood watch, saluting the prince as he approached.

"One more thing," he said, laying his hand on the door handle. "Khall hasn't stopped asking for you since we got here."

Naias stepped back in alarm. She'd cut off all ties the moment she left Haksa. Sahru had brought her here, ostensibly out of courtesy for the queen, but he might as well have ordered her to admit her desertion.

"I don't want to see her," she said.

Sahru's brow wrinkled into a sympathetic smile. "Regretfully, even if she is disgraced royalty, she is royalty. It's respect."

"And what about respecting *me*?" she snapped. "What about my wishes? Every time I go back, she hates and loves me in the same breath, twisting promises and claiming she keeps them. She pulls me in, like some invisible force, and I fall for her all over again." She clasped her hands together, trying to stop them from shaking.

Sahru placed his steady, unwavering hand on her shoulder, presumably to reassure her. She pushed him away. His abuser wasn't waiting on the other side of the door. Sahru was a prince. He knew nothing of the hate she'd suffered.

"I know," he said. "I told her it's better to let the love die than seek closure. My parents loved Khallan. They were together, the three of them, until he broke their hearts. I told them the same thing all those years ago. But we are not architects of these decisions, Naias. She is queen, you are not, and we must obey."

He opened the door.

64

Elera

Caves dotted along Mount Iska provided temporary respite from the wind, but Elera still shivered from the cold. Hollowed out by folk who'd made this summer pilgrimage centuries ago, faded red prayer flags draped over the entrances, welcoming anyone who needed refuge. She'd entered one, the flags long ripped to shreds, half of it buried in snow.

The horse she'd stolen from Haksa had died six days ago, having been ridden to exhaustion, and she made the rest of the journey on foot. The deep winter frost bit through her leather shoes, her fingers and toes tinged a shade of blue and black. Her ribs hadn't healed, and she'd broken something in her back when Engale's scream flung her away.

Every part of her body burned. The corruption flared once again, the black spiderweb reemerging across her chest.

Her hammer weighed ten times more than it was supposed to, but she kept it strapped to her body. The pain was temporary. She was nothing without her weapon, and she would die with it.

Caush had said no one climbed Mount Iska anymore. Too dangerous, he'd said.

She wasn't looking to live.

All she had left was a churning anger within. That was what

Iskandraza drank from her. Rage instead of water. Well, here she was, filled with it. She'd spit on his temple and then die on its peaks. It all ended up the same. Fuck this god, and fuck the world he'd made.

A herd of ibexes galloped past the cave, unperturbed by the cold. Her ears strained for lingering sounds. The crunch of snow, the shuffling of prey animals fleeing. Sounds that Rafaeis had taught her, to move quietly and unseen, things she'd never thought of, as a Faceless who charged directly into battle.

Only the howling wind remained. She wiped frozen snot away from her nose and reemerged from the cave, climbing further up the mountain.

Every breath took effort. Elera still wasn't used to these high altitudes. She'd nearly died here from a small cut, surely she'd die from frostbite, broken ribs, and sunstroke. No cloud cover helped shield the rays that beat down on her. That would be too merciful.

Her limbs soured with fatigue, every step dragging. Near the top of the mountain, her left leg buckled. She leaned against the mountain wall, creeping against it for support. She couldn't blink the black spots away anymore. They stuck in her vision, holes that she couldn't see through, while her mind drifted in and out of consciousness.

The string of disintegrating prayer flags ended in front of a large cave obscured by snow and icicles. The mountain's peak curved in like a crescent moon, as if a large hand had broken a chunk of rock away. She shuddered through her sweat-soaked clothes. This was the highest she could go.

Her purple frostbitten hands dislodged the snow from the entrance, digging a hole large enough for her to squeeze through.

Xinquha built temples to Ashvalra, erecting statues of her in various poses with her sheaf of rice. This temple to Iskandraza had nothing but a gray square plinth, smoothed to a shine. Empty offering cups sat frozen, the food they'd once housed crumbled into dust. Iskandraza had been dead a long time, and the Iskantis no longer came to pray.

Death was too good for him. The Destroyer would hear her beyond the grave.

Elera drew her hammer and struck the plinth.

Boom. The blow reverberated through the cavern. Rocks dislodged from the ceiling, scattering to the floor. The plinth cracked in the center.

It wasn't fair that Rafaeis had died by the hand of the very child they'd come to love, and she'd killed that child fearing what she would become. The gods and this terrible, indifferent world had cursed her with despair, and she would return it a hundredfold.

Boom.

Why did she have to suffer? She never cared for the fate of the continent, never involved herself in its politics and squabbles, and yet in this battle without stakes, it was she who'd lost the most.

No one else was punished. Why didn't any of these cruel kings and tyrannical queens have this? *Why her?*

Boom.

She'd saved a godchild, and that kindness had become a crime. Her anger had carried her to the peak of the mountain, to return the pain they'd inflicted on her, and now there was nowhere else to go.

With the last of her strength, she smashed the plinth to pieces. "Destroy this earth, kill me," she shouted as the mountain shook around her. "I don't care anymore."

The cave roared in response.

WHY WOULD I WANT YOUR LIFE, WHEN YOU DO NOT?

A GREAT FORCE pressed on Elera's shoulders. She buckled before the broken stones. Her knees crunched, then shattered.

The voice spoke at a level beyond physical comprehension, vibrating into the very particles that made up her body.

HUMANS OFFERING THEIR SOULS, he scoffed, ***THINKING IT THE ULTIMATE SACRIFICE.***

She writhed on the ground, hands blocking her ears, curled into a fetal position, screaming.

GET UP.

The invisible force gripped her waist, pulling her to her feet. As soon as it released, she fell again, unable to hear anything else besides the ringing of her own pain. Her hands grasped frantically for support, fingernails snagging on the broken plinth.

In the darkest part of the cave, a giant masked face emerged, leaning towards her. It looked to be made of candlewax, stars and galaxies floating through its black canvas. The mask had cracked at the bottom, and beneath the universe Elera saw flesh.

Iskandraza.

"I thought you were dead," she panted. "I thought you all were."

Dead, asleep, it is all the same to us. The voice lowered in timbre, taking the form of a man's. *I've seen the way your people use our powers. You sap my children in every incarnation until they lie comatose. Some never wake. Those who do remember all you did to them, and swear never to grant such power to you again.*

From the darkness, a large naked man of middling age appeared, his sunburned skin a deep, dark brown. His eyes and hair glittered with the universe. A black mass protruded from the spot where his heart would have been, rotted veins webbed over his chest.

Iskandraza glided over to Elera, unperturbed by the cold. He gently pressed his finger into her temple, and fire seared through her mind—

the blood of the gods looked exactly the same, her crescent blade drawn through diavıjra's neck, the cerulean sun snarling at her, nasu's empty stare and open mouth, gasping for air, wheezing, a thousand blank faces judging nothing and everything, rafaeis's bright and beautiful body sinking into the rain and mud, stolen by the lady of the earth

"I felt your rage," Iskandraza said, releasing his hold. "All the blood you've spilled, the deaths you've caused. You want to annihilate this earth. You want my power."

She gasped in what little air she could. The blood in her veins seemed to have been replaced by pure poison. Every part of her body wanted to kill, and every part of her body wanted to die.

"Others used to come up here asking for petty things," he said. "Land, power, the death of their enemies. The usual requests, the boring ones. But not many wish for destruction like you. The spider does not bite the hand it sits on. If the earth sustains you, why destroy it?"

She pointed a shaking finger at his chest. "You destroyed the earth for that."

He chuckled. "And you want to do the same? To be a mournful fool like me?"

"I don't care how you do it," she said. "Kill me if you have to. All of it needs to die."

"Again with the human sacrifice. That's no use to me."

"Then name your price."

"I want the sound of your lament."

She'd expected material demands—gold or oils or food, escalating into hearts and flesh and burning men on pyres.

"I don't understand," she said.

Iskandraza walked behind her, lifting her hammer as if it were a leaf. "I want the sound when you've lost everything. You used my horn. You've heard my cry. I want yours."

"You *have* everything," she snarled. "You've taken Rafaeis, you've taken Viri."

"There's one more," he said, tossing the hammer in his hands. "This. Your ability to fight. Your eyes and ears."

She shook her head. "Without those, I can't be your godchild. I won't know where I'm going, or what I'm doing."

He scoffed. "'Gods' is a poor name that you've given us. We're souls in this realm, and our power comes from our very lifeforce itself. We're untethered by the gravity of time, space, or physics. Whatever the soul imagines becomes true, because nothing is tangible to a soul except itself. All is possible. Your eyes and ears, even your strength, will cease to matter when your body is linked to me. I will manifest your reality for you." His gaze flicked up and down her ravaged body. "Starting with your broken ribs."

She'd be wholly dependent on him for the rest of her life. Without sight or sound, she would no longer be a warrior. She'd be a godchild and nothing else. Iskandraza would strip her of her greatest pride.

"Why did you say you were waiting for me?" she whispered. "You called me Ragebringer."

A glimmer of sadness passed his face. His hand raised for the slightest moment, as if to touch his blackened heart, but he stopped.

"I forgot what that wrath felt like," he said. "Every night I replayed her death in my mind. I'd pull the memory out of my head, reliving every second, every action, every cry. I lived it from every angle, even as it hurt me to see her die over and over again. I thought that if I didn't, the memory would wither away. Only through grief could I be reminded of how ardently I loved her. I knew I would forget. I knew."

He turned away. "And I did. One day, I no longer wept. I forgot my grief. It terrified me."

Rafaeis. Viri. Nasu. Caush. Their names seared in her memory. She wouldn't let them go. She'd lost everything else. Only anger was left, and if she gave that up too, then she was nothing.

An empty shell was worse than death.

"Then let us never forget," she said. She took his hands and placed them on the sides of her head. "Take it. Use me."

His thumbs dug into her eye sockets. "Mourn for me, godchild, and the world will know the pain they've put upon us."

Her body instinctively clawed against the force that pressed into her eyeballs, while the wind howled again, screeching through her ears, ringing, piercing her brain, no different than that ungodly voice Iskandraza used, her mind split apart as her body reknit itself, her knees reforming, her ribs resetting, a distant relief that meant so little in the wake of this pain and she should've just died on that plinth instead—

He let go.

She crumpled to the ground. The broken ribs she'd suffered were but a shadow of how useless she felt now. She couldn't lift herself up anymore.

Something wet dripped down her cheek.

All was dark and quiet.

65

Naias

Royal garments draped everywhere in the room. Cotton robes, tunics, coats, embroidered in gold and silver, all dyed in Tevu's colors, provided by the empire.

Khall had ignored it all. She sat in an ornate chair, wearing the remains of her wedding dress, a desperate bid to keep Ashvian red in a completely blue room. She shivered in it, its scraps unable to keep her warm. Her matted hair twisted about her face, leaves and branches stuck in its tangles. Combs and a tub of clear water sat in the corner, untouched. Despite Tevu's politeness, she'd refused to groom herself.

The Reborn bowed. "Queen Khall, I present Naias of the Faceless."

Naias wanted to quit the room, but she had no choice. The doors would be locked until Khall—or Sahru—deemed it time. After all this, she was still a servant, beholden to the whims of those in power.

Khall knocked over her chair as she ran over, cupping Naias's face with her dirt-caked hands. "Oh, you've come," she said, and kissed her.

A time ago she would've wanted this: the submission and the love. Everything was different now. She'd abandoned Khall and dared to consider Sahru's offer. She didn't know what to feel anymore.

Khall sensed it on her lips. She drew back and slapped Naias across the face.

"I see," she said, her voice trembling. "You made a deal with Tevu. What was it? Your loyalty in exchange for my capture?"

Naias's cheek throbbed, but she swallowed the pain, saying nothing. Let her release her anger. That was the least she could give her.

Khall hit her again. "You betrayed me, you abandoned me when I needed you the most. I was so scared when the Iskantis attacked us on the road, and then when Maetheria came, Naias, you—you *left* me, in my bedroom, alone. I was so scared. I just wanted someone to talk to, to tell me my fear wasn't irrational, and all I heard from you was 'Be a queen.' I wanted to be kind. I wanted to spare the Iskanti raider, but you forced me to kill him. You made me a murderer. You never loved me. You only pretended to."

"No," she blurted. Khall could question everything she'd done, but not that. "I loved you more than anything in this world."

"'Loved.'"

"You changed."

"And I wasn't who you wanted me to be." She pressed her palms to her face, holding back a sob. "I tried to get away from you. I tried to make new friends, and you killed them. You killed Jayal and Maka. You killed Basaa. You saw the power I was gaining, and you didn't want me to have it. 'Be a queen, be a queen.' You didn't want me to be a queen, you wanted me to be your pawn. Losing Haksa made me realize how utterly dependent I was on you. I didn't know war, I didn't know how to fight, and I had no one to teach me, because *you* killed them and drove them all away. This was all your doing, and I fell for it like the fool I was, believing that someone in this world had the audacity to love a timid little girl like me."

This soft and vulnerable show would've made Naias fall to her knees and beg for forgiveness once, but there was no love there anymore. There was no need to wheedle and tease to get her to say yes. She didn't need control over another anymore; she'd lost it the moment she'd surrendered to Tevu. All that she'd loved about Khall had disappeared the moment when there was no more kingdom to liberate.

But something deep within—the remnants of true love, perhaps—made her pull Khall into a tight embrace. "I'm sorry," she whispered, her final confession to the monster she'd made.

"I don't want to die," Khall sobbed, collapsing against her. "Don't leave me, please. Save me."

And then she heard it.

The sound struck like lightning, sudden and terrible, a mournful wail that permeated every living being and constructed edifice. Naias's veins swelled, her blood vibrating at the same frequency with the walls, the leaves, the earth and sky.

The land responded in kind, as if the cry had awakened it. Explosions rumbled beneath them, growing louder and louder, one after the other.

The door burst open. Reborn hurried in, taking Khall by the arm.

Shouts and screams pulsed through the walls. Tevurian officials streamed out of the villa with them, baffled looks on their faces. One carried a bag that clinked within; a Reborn snatched it from his hands and threw it aside.

"We need to leave this place," the Reborn said. "Now."

The wail resurfaced again, piercing her skull. She clapped her hands over her ears, trying to stave off the cry.

What is this horror? This can't be Engale's doing.

The ground juddered, knocking everyone down. The villa's ceiling—an ornate mural depicting the story of Ashvalra's murder—cracked and smashed to the floor. Rays of light smoked through the dust and debris above them.

"The pier," one of the Reborn said, roughly hoisting Khall to her feet. "Get them to the boats, hurry. Leave the rest."

Between the steel bodies that separated them, Khall kept her grip tight around Naias. "I don't want to die," she said.

They emerged from the villa. A red sky engulfed them. Plumes of smoke bloomed from Iskantupu, blotting out the sun. An avalanche of lava cascaded down the mountains, engulfing the obsidian statues, spreading to the port.

She gaped. This wasn't Engale. It was—

"Iskandraza," Khall whispered.

The Destroyer had come to end the world again.

The very air burned, earth disintegrating under her feet. Volcanic vents erupted in a line, jets of superheated steam bursting through, vaporizing anyone that stood above them. Houses collapsed into clouds of dust and thunder. Charcoal seared her tongue.

Fleeing folk swamped the remaining boats, looking to escape to the ocean. Sampans capsized from the weight, sinking their passengers into rapidly heating water. A larger rowboat stayed docked, housing half a dozen men, most of them Reborn. Their swords beat away anyone else that tried to climb in. Sahru and Clement sat in the middle, alarm on their faces.

It was Naias's turn to grip Khall tight. No one survived Iskandraza's wrath.

But Khall glanced back. Her tears had disappeared.

Naias knew that look. It was an ugliness so casual that she doubted Khall was aware of it at all. The same ugliness when Khall had wanted Viridian's hair dyed white instead of black, when she'd wanted everyone to speak Common, when she'd so offhandedly said that Naias was of inferior birth.

Naias was Iskanti, and she wasn't worth saving.

Khall twisted her arm away.

"No—"

The Reborn shoved Naias aside. She fell into shallow water. More folk fled to the sea, splashing as they fought over floating logs and overturned boats. Clement rose to his feet, shouting, but she couldn't hear him through the roar of the pumice that had begun to hail around them.

Khall climbed onto the boat. The men pulled their oars. The Tevurian galleys waited in the open sea.

Left to pick up the pieces once again.

In the face of the apocalypse, a defeated queen was still more valuable than her. *Her*, who'd captured Xinquha and Haksa, who'd fended off the Iskanti and Maetherian ambushes, who'd killed a king and seduced his daughter, who'd stopped Viridian from killing everyone, whose absence had caused Haksa to fall.

And still, she was worth nothing.

She wasn't going to be left behind anymore.

Naias dove into the water.

Steam vents erupted under the seabed. Magma spilled into the ocean, a fog of steam obscuring the horizon as water mixed with fire. Her skin blistered and burned, but rage suffused her with strength, numbing her to everything else.

Her fingers gripped the edge of the fleeing boat. It was enough. With a drowned yell she arose from the foam, yanked Khall's gray hair, and pulled her off. A jet of boiling water erupted before her, pushing the boat away.

Naias hooked an elbow around the queen's neck and pushed her down. Sahru and Clement shouted at her, meaningless words beneath the roar of pumice hail.

Water bubbled around Khall's pale face. She clawed against Naias's hands, but it was like fending off a rat. Her emaciated body had left her with no strength to fight. Naias's skin scalded red from heat. Her body screamed to flee, but there was nowhere to go.

She burst out laughing as she held her lover down. What else could she do when faced with the microcosm of her existence? She'd played politics to survive, human games where they squabbled for a piece of memory, a sliver of land, a moment of power. She'd spent her entire life with this woman, and when she'd caught a glimmer of a future without her in it, the world told her that it was impossible. Nothing mattered when Iskandraza rose again.

Khall jerked underwater. Her nails tore open Naias's skin.

"Shh, it's all right," Naias said, mimicking how Ayashara comforted her children. Her tears dripped into the blood, breaking apart the long, lazy rivulets that drifted out of her wounds. Why was she crying? She didn't love Khall anymore, there was no reason for this sadness.

Ah, it ruined the sight. Blood looked so pretty when it pulsed in water.

She could let go. She'd pleaded for Khall to be merciful. Why shouldn't she try to embody the trait that she'd preached?

But she was petty.

This was her moment of liberation. There were no politics, no promises, no Faceless or Iskanti. She was *Naias*, a human burning in the gurgling sea, like the rest of the poor souls around her.

Khall stopped moving. Her hands and arms dangled listlessly like a jellyfish, red ripped silks blooming like algae.

She was free.

Naias let out a long exhale. She leaned back, floating on the water's surface, barely registering the pain of her scalded skin, and closed her eyes. Dead bodies and red clouds disappeared into black, allowing her to force her own reality into existence.

In her last moments of consciousness, of all the people she could think about, it was Elera she settled on, Naias lying in her firm lap and wrapped in her arms, their lips meeting in the quiet darkness that frightened them both.

The white sun dissolved behind a blurry cloud of ash.

66

Naias

Blue Tevurian sails unfurled before a red sky, stretched to bursting.

Hot, acrid air whipped past her face. It felt as if water had filled her head, sloshing back and forth with every lurch of her body. Her tongue, swollen with salt, lolled in her mouth.

"She's alive," a voice said.

Naias turned to her side, throwing up bile on a wooden deck.

"I hope she's worth it, Clement," said another.

Too many hands grabbed her, propping her up. In the blur of her vision, her skin bore no burns or blisters, as if the boiling water hadn't touched her. She flexed her fingers. It didn't hurt.

"I healed you," Clement said. "We took you from the water."

Her head bumped against a rail, forcing her to meet his concerned gaze. A long bloody gash ran across his eyebrow and down his cheek. His piercings were gone, and his hands clean of silver and gold.

It was odd to see Clement not wearing any jewelry. He looked plain, naked even. Without his shimmering chains, Clement was an ordinary man, and not the grandiose godchild she'd come to know.

She didn't want to see him. Death was supposed to release

her suffering, and yet she suffered still. She wanted Hammer, Ayashara, her mother, even Khall—

Her heart stilled in realization.

That's right. She'd killed her.

Sahru's face sharpened into view.

She groaned, holding her head in her hands. "Not you too."

"Iskandraza has returned," the prince said grimly. "You've caused a great trouble for me in killing Khall, but Clement pleaded for your life."

They'd saved her. She couldn't even die on her own terms. They'd crushed her last protest, her refusal to follow the fate they'd chosen for her. That momentary feeling of peace was all the happiness she'd ever needed, and they wouldn't let her keep it.

She swung a fist at Clement's face. Her arm was shaky, her balance uneven. He caught it easily, holding her at bay. Black ash pelted around them.

"You should've left me to die," she said.

"Your death means nothing in the face of the apocalypse," said Clement. "Iskandraza has returned. Ashvalra and Diavijra are gone. All the gods we have left are their children, the minor ones. We're not enough."

Naias shoved him away. "If Iskandraza is alive, then so are the others. Diavijra will infect someone else. There are countless temples to Ashvalra. Go summon her."

"It's not that simple. Hammer—Elera—is his chosen."

She blinked. "What? How do you know her name?"

Clement raised an unadorned hand to his chest. "Something changed in Strixahava when the Destroyer awoke. Like a weight had been lifted off her. I feel pockets of her memories as if they're mine. I can recall the cave that Iskandraza awoke in, even though I've never stepped foot on Mount Iska. Hammer was lying in front of him. Her name just"—he raised his hands helplessly—"appeared in my head, like I've known it all along. There's a terrible dread within Strix. I think this all happened before, and I—she doesn't want it to happen again."

Sahru nodded. "That's why we need you," he said. "Clement said you have a history with this Elera. You could—"

"No," Naias laughed. "No, no, no. Whatever we had died a long time ago. You have the wrong person. You need—"

"Viridian," Clement finished for her. "But she's dead, and the gods saw fit to keep you alive."

"Gods have nothing to do with it," she snapped. "*You* drew me from the water. Don't make me fight Hammer. She hates me more than you."

Clement pointed at the volcanic eruption over Iskantupu. "Do you know what's going to happen if we don't stop this? The volcanoes will burn for a hundred thousand years. The magma they spew will blot out the sky. The sulfur that follows will turn to acid, and its rains will poison the lakes, rivers, and oceans. The fish, the plants, the very earth will die. We die. Everything dies."

She didn't want to hear any more talk of lands and gods and people she had to save. "I'm free of Khall, and you don't need me as Tevu's general. Not even the biggest army on the continent is going to stop Iskandraza's wrath. I made peace with my death the moment I surrendered myself to Tevu. Maybe you should too."

"You sound so much like Hammer," Clement said, his voice soft.

"You took my death from me," she spat.

"The other gods will help. You won't be alone. Strixahava, Chatrasaya, Arjuneira, Engaleveya—"

Naias laughed harder. "Other *godchildren*? No. You were hard enough to deal with, Clement, much less corralling more like you. You want me to work with Engale, who Tevu can barely control? Then I have to ingratiate myself into Tevu's ranks with this mark on my head, to deal with men who hate me simply because I am Iskanti, and somehow get all of us to work together to fight Iskandraza's chosen? *Fuck* no."

"You have my support," Sahru said. "I am Tevu's prince. The Reborn will listen to you, on pain of death."

Power in the hands of men all sounded the same. Forcing others to yield, giving them no choice. Obedience didn't erase the hate they had for the Faceless or the Iskantis. "I'm not a godchild," Naias said. "I can't heal anyone or summon the wind. I don't know what you want me to do."

"You know Hammer," Clement said. "You know how she thinks, and where she'll be next. We can't stop the Destroyer, but we can stop her."

"And when she dies, Iskandraza isn't going to give his power to another?"

Clement frowned. "I don't—Strix doesn't remember the last time Iskandraza granted his soul to another. When he destroyed the world, he did it on his own. He never used us."

Naias gripped the rail, wanting to hurl herself off the ship. They'd brought her back purely on a guess. "So you don't know. We're mortals battling a god, and we won't even know if it'll end."

Sahru knelt before her. "I don't want to do this, but if you refuse to help us, you become our prisoner. You know the ways of my father, the techniques he uses to break people into submission. Don't force my hand. Please. You were a commander once. I beg you to become it again. We saved you because we need every chance to stop Iskandraza. You know battle. The Reborn will need you. My father will need you. Help us end this destruction."

Naias burned with hatred for this man, who only pretended to be sorry for the threats he made. The chain came for her again, the cold iron of duty wrapped around her neck, leashing her to a cause she did not want.

She had no choice. Tevu wouldn't let her die. They'd keep her here, tearing her apart until she broke and said yes. Even Iskandraza's apocalypse could not set her free. In her future, all she saw was more war. More fighting, more dying, more corpses consumed in fire. All in the name of saving people.

Khall had fought for the same thing. She'd thought she was saving the continent from Tevurian rule by restoring a memory of a kingdom that only she and her father desired. That ambitious dream had ended in a whisper of ash and smoke.

No different. Naias ran in circles, her life forever unchanged. She buried her face in the wooden planks and cried.

67

?

Oh, you're awake. Are you all right?
let me speak.
Are you sure? You don't have to.
you don't have to protect me anymore. i want to.

68

Viri

THE ISKANTIS DO not bury their dead. They ride to the tallest mountain that they can find and commit the body to the condors. The soul is released to the sky, so that Iskandraza may see them on his snowy summit.

The Ashvians dig graves. Flesh and bone nourish new life, and the soul is embraced by the lady of the earth.

The Tevurians build pyres. An ancient practice, this one, now repurposed. Endless war grants them little time to follow the rituals of those they conquered.

They burned *his* body. I felt it, the ashes of all that made him scattered into the soil. They left none for me. The men muttered vague prayers, wishing the immolated returned to whichever god they worshipped. They practice these rituals with little care.

I thought the release of my soul meant that I would become omnipresent. I expected to see the entire world in my mind, like a prisoner in a towering castle, watching people carry on with their lives.

It wasn't that.

The sensation was like being kept in a dark room, no different than the wagon Tevu locked me in, or the stone walls that surrounded me in Haksa. My eyes—or at least I thought

I had them—were wide open, and yet I couldn't see or hear anything. I wriggled my toes and fingers, but without eyes to see them, they were just thoughts, an illusion that I gave myself that I still had a body.

Everything before me was a realm of infinite possibility. All that I could construct in my mind could become true, but only to me. When I stopped thinking, the world I constructed also stopped existing.

When I slept, my emotions stopped too. Rage, sorrow, grief—what are they, but neurons firing in your brain?

Diavijra thought the same.

Long ago, her father wandered the world with the hole in his heart. He was always searching for the woman who mended him, and he never shared that ardent love with anyone else. Diavijra didn't know the depths of his pain then. He never told her.

She was the first of his children. He left her on the once-rich lands the men call Iskantupu today, and she would wait and wait and wait for him to return.

He never came back. Diavijra sat on the lush grasses for centuries. She cried, because her heartbreak mattered more than his. He ought to have loved her better, taught her better. Ashvalra? Who was she, and why was she more important than her?

He destroyed the world for someone who'd died eons ago, while Diavijra, still alive and desperate for his love, wasn't enough.

Every child believes they are the center of the universe. She was the center of her own for a long time.

In her bitterness she birthed the void, the ten-thousand-year lull where nothing grew after her father left it. She sucked out all that was good and great from the earth, and didn't care who she hurt, because *she* was hurt, and that was all that mattered.

But still the sadness filled her chest, overfilling it, uncontainable.

Neurons. That's all it was. She closed her eyes and forced herself to sleep, dulling the connections that made up her soul, so she wouldn't feel the pain again.

And then she grew up.

She couldn't pinpoint the exact moment she learned empathy. Only when enough time had passed that she had a life to reflect upon did she realize how difficult she must've been. Her outbursts had left vacuums in men, inflicting suffering worse than those who'd died in the angry eruptions and bubbling seas. These deaths came for no reason, and those who loved them wailed against the temper of a child, who only sought love from her father.

I didn't see these memories. I knew them, like the instinctive blink of an eye. It was a knowledge so natural and unconscious that it felt strange that I'd lived without it at all.

If she had a body in this void, I would've shaken her. *How could you be so stupid?* I asked. *Didn't you see how much suffering you caused?*

Signals pulsed through our consciousness, polychromatic frequencies and wavelengths that coalesced into a single emotion: guilt. As acute as my own. She knew now that others lived rich, full lives, and they weren't things to be used and thrown away.

But you used me, I said.

I'm sorry. I didn't know what else to do.

A memory surfaced between us. Mountains rumbled on the blood moon, twelve years ago. Molten sorrow churned below, confused by its own weakness, waiting for someone to incite it into rage. Diavijra heard his restless slumber, mourning for a lover that he couldn't bring back.

A time ago, she might have continued to sleep too. *Let the world suffer his wrath,* she would've said. *This is what you get for having his attention.*

But she was no longer a child. She woke, putting her soul into another for the first time. Into me.

A harrowing experience. She was trapped in another's body,

a puppet master imprisoned within her puppet, unable to move a finger or shout a word. All she could manifest were the things I hadn't made for myself: the void. Her power. She existed in a dissociated stupor, her body not her own.

And when Iskandraza fully woke, using Elera as his vessel, it was too late. His rage bled into his children—they originated from the same cells, after all—jolting them from half-remembered sleeps, their pasts imprinting into their chosen humans like a thunderclap. That was how Diavijra came to me.

My memories swam in the same stream as hers, overlapping each other. The life that came before me felt one and the same, and yet we were two separate souls, linked by a web of electric signals.

I can't rest, Diavijra said desperately. *I must stop bā. I have to find Ashvalra. I'll scoop up her ashes and resurrect her if I have to.*

Are you going to give your soul to another again? I asked.

A million, billion neurons fired **NO**, lighting the darkness in red. ***No,*** she said. *No. I destroyed your life. I won't do that to another again. I need to find Ashvalra another way.*

I didn't want to help. She felt it too, in the nerves and chemical reactions that connected us. Tevu took me, Khall abused me, and Elera killed me.

My short life had been defined by suffering, and yet I was supposed to save the very people who'd hurt me. Now my fate was inextricably linked to a god's, something I'd never wanted in the first place. Returning to a life before Diavijra sounded better, back to being that frightened lamb when Tevu first took me, dazed and oblivious, so that I didn't need to think or feel anything. I could sleep.

But I wasn't a child anymore.

Electric impulses fired again, creating a blurry image of a river. Flowering angsana trees sprouted from the steep Xinquhan cliffs. Above them, white, fluffy clouds.

Hands tugged at my hair, one rough and one slow, my scalp

tingling with their touch. Elera started from the left, and seconds later, Rafaeis's hands followed, rubbing each strand of my hair with dye, scooped up from that foul-smelling bucket of fermented leeches.

They made me so happy. I loved them and the family we accidentally made together. The world ripped us apart: Khall, Naias, Diavijra, all.

But we were complicit too. We destroyed ourselves. Rafaeis shouldn't have come back. I should've watched for him better. Elera should've trusted me to fight.

That's the nature of family, isn't it? We're never truly of one mind. We quarrel and bicker, argue and shun, and yet we experience the greatest joy when we're together. We don't forget the careless cruelty done to each other, but we grow with it. Survive it. All of it—good and bad—becomes part of us.

Leaving Elera meant betraying all that Rafaeis stood for. He embodied hope and love, and all the good that bloomed even in the bitterest of winters. He couldn't disappear.

Ashvalra is the god of life and rebirth, I said. *If we find her, can she bring Rafaeis back?*

Stopping bā has to be our only concern, Diavijra said. *We can't waste time on resurrection.*

Then we want the same thing. You hope finding Ashvalra will stop Iskandraza. But I know Elera will end the apocalypse if Rafaeis comes back. I promise you. If you want my help, this is my one condition.

Synapses hummed with displeasure, but for a reason that surprised me entirely.

We are agreed, Diavijra said, *but you don't have to bargain with me ever again. I'm not your gaoler. We do this together.*

My imagined lips curled into a sad smile.

Stopping the apocalypse was only a half truth, for both of us. It didn't need to be spoken. What we really wanted, selfishly, was to reunite our broken families. Her with her parents, and me with mine.

Gods, I wanted us together again. I'm so sorry for killing him. I grieved his death. Surely Elera did too. Why were we mourning separately, with this vast distance between us? I wanted to hug her and feel her rough hands covering mine, rather than existing in this nothingness.

Am I a fool for wanting this? I asked. *She killed me, and I love her still.*

The void exhaled with a quiet laugh. *I wish I didn't want bā as much as I did. If you're a fool, then I'm one too.*

Manifesting myself back into the world was easy. It was simply our consciousness, like all the gods that existed. A soul that floated amongst the wind and sand.

Imagining myself was a different matter. I didn't want to roam the world as nothing. So many times I'd suffered instances where my body was not my own. Diavijra didn't like it too. I wanted feet and hands to control, to roll my eyes and smile with my mouth, to hear the laugh that emanated from my throat. To be me.

Atoms and cells coalesced, locking themselves together. The body is a construction almost machinelike, and yet has all its little biological flaws. Moles appeared on my face. My sandy Maetherian hair returned.

I chose to keep the slit in my throat. I left a small mark, like the scratch of a fingernail. She taught me to remember. Well, I'll remember what she did to me.

I looked the same, but I was fundamentally transformed, neither alive nor dead, a soul that existed only because Diavijra chose to stay awake.

She was going to change too.

How do you want to look? I asked.

Pulsing waves dimmed to a flutter as she crafted her answer.

I've never had a body, she finally said. *Picture me as your friend.*

She couldn't be Elera or Rafaeis. Their lives intertwined too closely with mine. It wasn't Naias, who frightened me, or Khall, who used me.

Khall.

Despite all the suffering she'd caused, I couldn't shake the image of her looking wistfully out the window, in the moments before she made me kill Dada. Crouched on her seashell throne, hair loose from the ocean breeze, picking at her chin. She'd looked like me when I'd stared out the glass of the university, dreaming of shimmering rivers and batik dresses.

What did she say? Ah, yes. She didn't like being queen. She wished for a life free of burden and choices. A life where she and I could have been friends.

I think I'll grant her this wish, although she will not know it.

Diavijra appeared before me, black hair combed to a shine, wearing a crown of her favorite summerbell flowers. Her red dress flapped in the cold desert wind.

I grasped her hand.

"Let's go find Ashvalra, together."

ACKNOWLEDGMENTS

It's a common refrain that every novel retains some part of the author in it. Hammer's anger stems from my own, and I see the bruised innocence of my younger self in Viridian, who had to learn—like I did—that people aren't kind.

But what surprised me was how this became a book about loneliness, and for one brief, beautiful moment, you didn't have to be alone in the world anymore. When I first started writing, I had every intention of doing it myself. After all, my artistic life has hinged on doing everything on my own. I'll be fine.

But by chance I read a guide on getting published. Why not? Let's send out some queries and see if someone writes back.

Someone did. Jennifer Azantian became my agent.

Thank you, Jen, for being the first person to believe in my work, and for your relentless drive in getting this book made. Few are lucky enough to have someone so steadfastly supportive in every aspect of production, and I'm grateful to count myself as one of them.

And then more people wrote back.

I'm beyond fortunate that Michael LaBorn and Amanda Raybould acquired this book. Thank you, Michael, for being so firmly in my corner, for being this book's staunchest champion, and for seeing its promise when my own belief was flagging. I could not have asked for a better advocate and friend. Thank you, Amanda, for your thoroughness, expertise, and gentle hand in making this book a better one. You've provided one of the best collaborative experiences I've ever had, and my favorite moments in this book would not have happened if not for your guidance.

Thank you to Girl Friday's copyediting and proofreading team: Alyssa, Erica, Janice, Nicole, and Valerie, for your thoughtfulness and Herculean attention to detail. To Abi, for corralling us all in one direction. Thank you to the Bindery team: to Meghan, Matt, Shira, and those who were instrumental in building the infrastructure for this book's publication journey. To Charlotte Strick and the design team, whose excellence created the novel of my dreams. To Charis Loke and her brilliant mapmaking process that makes me want to be a better artist. To CJ, Brittani, and Lavender Public Relations for their tireless efforts in pushing this book in ways I could've never imagined.

Thank you to the Solaris UK team: Chiara, for your editorial support, Jess and Natalie for marketing and PR, Sam, for your beautiful cover work, Dagna for production, and Owen for sales. This book is all the richer with your help.

Thank you to Aqsa, Arnout, Ben, Dana Floberg, David Markiwsky, and Kelsea, for beta reading and your feedback. To Mom, Dad, and Julia, for all your support and joy.

What started out as a story written by a stubborn lone wolf has become a tapestry woven by many people. I never thought I'd be part of a collective effort such as this. Thank you all for this incredible experience.

And finally, to my husband: Your unconditional love is the reason why this book exists. Who knew meeting in a video game would lead to this!

ABOUT THE AUTHOR

Elaine Ho is an award-winning Asian American illustrator and author. Ho received a degree in psychology before pivoting into art full-time, working as a concept artist in theme parks and virtual reality before becoming a freelance illustrator. She is the former art director for *khōréō*, a speculative fiction magazine focused on the diaspora experience. Having bounced between the US and Singapore for most of her life, she belongs to both and neither. *Cry, Voidbringer* is her first novel.

FIND US ONLINE!

www.rebellionpublishing.com

/solarisbooks /solarisbks

/solarisbooks /solarisbooks.bsky.social

SIGN UP TO OUR NEWSLETTER!

rebellionpublishing.com/newsletter

YOUR REVIEWS MATTER!

Enjoy this book? Got something to say?

Leave a review on Amazon, GoodReads or with your favourite bookseller and let the world know!